Dear Reader,

This month I am delighted to bring you the second longer novel by best-selling author Patricia Wilson, who is, we know, very popular with romance readers. And we're sure that Julie Garratt's second book for *Scarlet* will greatly please her existing fans, and capture the interest of many new readers. In addition, we are glad to offer you the chance to enjoy the talents of two authors new to the *Scarlet* list: Jean Walton, who lives in the USA, and Michelle Reynolds from the UK.

One of the many joys for me when I select each month's books for you, is that I am able to look forward to hearing *your* reaction to my selection. Of course, as *Scarlet* grows, the task of choosing new stories to offer you is becoming ever more interesting as so many talented authors are keen to join our list. Naturally, this means that it is also more of a challenge for me to get the balance of the four books right for you. As always, I invite comments from readers, as such feedback is vital in helping me do my job properly – so I look forward to hearing from *you*.

Till next month,
Best wishes,

Sally Cooper

SALLY COOPER,
Editor-in-Chief – *Scarlet*

About the Author

Patricia Wilson was born in Yorkshire and is married to her childhood sweetheart. Her husband's work took them to live in Singapore and Africa and Patricia now lives most of the time in the South of France or Spain. She gave up her career as a teacher in order to write and has become so popular that over eighteen million copies of her books have been sold throughout the worl.

Patricia first started writing when she was in her teens. She tried writing children's stories, detective novels and historical romances, before realizing that she should focus her efforts on becoming a romantic fiction writer. Her books always reflect Patricia's deep interest in people and her sensitive understanding of personal relationships.

Scarlet is delighted to bring readers the second longer novel by this best-selling author of over forty romances.

Other *Scarlet* titles available this month:
CHANGE OF HEART – Julie Garratt
CAROUSEL – Michelle Reynolds
A CIRCLE IN TIME – Jean Walton

PROLOGUE

The houses were three storeys high, facing each other down each side of the long street. There was a comfortable uniformity about them, the privet hedges giving them an illusion of privacy, the tiny front gardens with low wooden gates protecting them from the road. The gates and front doors varied in colour of paint but it was too dark to see that clearly, except where the gates were painted white.

It had been raining earlier, and the light from the street lamps gave a glistening distinction to the road that separated the rows of houses. It ran like a shining ribbon between the lights and disappeared into darkness where the street ended and deserted wasteland stretched shadowy and silent towards the next inhabited area.

The last house in the street was in total darkness except for one front window at the very top, and even this light was dimmed by curtains drawn against the night. In every other house in the street the front rooms were glowing with light, the flicker

1

of televisions showing where the curtains were not closed. People came into the rooms, stopped to talk or sat to join their families gathered around the set. This was a street of warmth, normality and safety.

But the end house stood aloof, silent and dark, attached to its companions but certainly not one of them. The hedge separating it from the next house had been allowed to grow high and wild, shielding it from intrusion. The tiny front garden was paved in concrete slabs where weeds forced their way up to the air, surviving there until the winter frosts killed them.

In the lighted room at the top of the house there was little furniture, and what was there was old, left over from another time. There was a wardrobe that contained few clothes, a shabby dressing table with a huge mirror and one straight-backed chair placed before it.

The light in the ceiling had no shade but the angle-poise lamp on the dressing table was new and flooded stark illumination across the face of the woman who looked into the mirror. She stared back at her own reflection as she coated her lips with colour, bright red, glistening like the street outside. The colour was startling against her pale skin, but she was beautiful, and would have been more so had it not been for the total lack of expression on her face.

The make-up deliberately emphasized her pallor, draining away any normal colour. Her eyebrows were drawn on with the same deliberation, deeply black, incongruous, debasing the natural beauty, cheapening her face. She closed the lipstick methodically and placed it on the scarred top of the dressing table, never glancing at it. She smoothed her hair and then fastened a wide Alice band in place. It held the heavy fringe down on her white forehead and was as black as her hair, although it gave off none of the shine. The wide band was black velvet and matched the short dress she wore.

She stood and reached for her coat, a short black raincoat, shining like plastic and hanging no lower than the dress. The ensemble left a long length of slender leg visible and she watched herself for a second, turning to view the effect, neither pleased nor displeased.

At the last minute she opened a drawer in the front of the old dressing table and took out a thin, deadly-looking knife. She lifted her skirt and slid the knife into a wide elasticated band near the top of her leg. It was black like the sheer tights and the knife fitted snugly, sliding into position with a one smooth movement, sword into scabbard, gun into holster, a weapon in position, ready.

Letting the short dress fall back into place, she smoothed her hands down her thighs. Nothing showed. She was slender, beautiful though slightly bizarre. She looked vulnerable and defenceless, she knew that, and the red lips turned down in a slight sign of amusement as she put on dark glasses that hid her eyes. She flicked off the lights and left the room.

Ignoring the darkness of the two flights of un-carpeted stairs, she went down, her high heels sounding loud on the wood and louder still on the tiled floor of the hall by the front door. The whole house echoed with the unmistakable impression of emptiness, the hollow sound reverberating as she snapped the outside door shut behind her.

She closed the low front gate with the same methodical action she had used to replace the lip-stick and then she walked away from the houses, away from the street, and headed for the lights of the city that glowed brilliantly not too far away across the gloom of the wasteland.

Her hands were in the pockets of the shiny raincoat, her black hair as smooth as silk, the long legs moving with a slow, measured pace that showed no fear of darkness. Vulnerable and completely alone, she melted into the shadows and disappeared.

CHAPTER 1

The plane flew on through the night and Dan Forrest didn't need the sound of the captain's voice to tell him what to expect.

'Twelve degrees Celsius, intermittent rain . . .'

He stopped listening. His head was pounding, threatening to leave his shoulders and he didn't want to hear about temperatures; he had a pretty good idea what his own was. The lights were not particularly bright but they hurt his eyes all the same. He was in trouble and he knew it.

'How do you feel now, Mr Forrest?'

The stewardess leaned over him, looking concerned. She was a pretty girl and normally he would have been interested, but at the moment he wasn't capable of working up the enthusiasm necessary to flirt. The outstanding thing about her was that she cared whether he lived or died. That was really important to him right now. She had been fussing over him for the last couple of hours and she knew how bad he felt.

'I'm still alive – just about,' he grunted. 'When do

we land? I missed what he said, apart from the bit about the cold and rain.'

'It's cold because it's evening in London, and the weather hasn't been too good these past few days but it's going to pick up during the week. The seat-belt signs will be going on in about five minutes.' She gave him a worried glance. 'I could get you another brandy if you like; there's just about time and it might help.'

'Kill or cure, you mean?' Dan muttered. 'Can't feel any worse than I do now. Make it a double again.'

He looked out of the window into the darkness. What the hell was he doing here? He could have stayed in New York and started the lecture tour instead of putting it off. He had cancelled appointments to come here, messed up his tight schedule. He didn't need any sort of aggro, particularly this sort. He didn't take kindly to illness, but he would have to take it this time whether he liked it or not.

It had hit him right out of the blue. The flight hadn't even got halfway before he knew he was in big trouble. He should still be in New York, tucked up in bed with Mary Lou fussing round him like a little black hen. Instead he was going to land in the cold and the rain, feeling like death and uncertain how he was going to manage. Why the hell was he here?

He muttered under his breath. He knew exactly why he was coming to London. He loved the place and he expected it to rain on him, expected it to feel cold even at this time of year. He didn't need to help promote his latest book, but it had been an excuse to come to England and wander around his favourite city, pick up old threads.

Besides, he always looked forward to a tussle with Martin Newman. Since his books had been first published over here, he and Martin had become firm friends, and young Jenny was a constant source of amusement, even though she was as unpredictable as a skittish colt and often a source of embarrassment.

He tried to grin but pain shot straight through his head and he reached for the brandy with shaking hands when the stewardess came back. He rarely felt that he actually needed a drink but right now he grasped it with a forlorn hope that it would help him to cope with the pounding head and rubbery limbs.

'Do you think we should call ahead for an ambulance?' She hovered over him anxiously and Dan shot her a pained look of utter disbelief.

'It's flu, honey, not the plague.' She looked downcast and he relented, softening his voice with difficulty. 'Thanks, but I'm being met. One good night in bed and I'll be back to normal.'

She nodded dubiously and left, and the seat-belt lights came on almost at once. He fastened himself in with the ease of long practice. He hadn't exactly intended to have a good night in bed – well, not by himself at any rate. He had rung Antonia before he left New York. She hadn't forgotten him, even though it was over a year, but she would not

7

appreciate a germ-bearing visitor. Nothing about Antonia suggested Florence Nightingale.

It didn't matter much. Martin would be meeting him and taking him to his hotel, then he could get his head down and sleep, providing he could get his head out of the plane without falling over. Sitting comfortably was a painful procedure as it was, and walking would be worse. Maybe he should have asked to be met with a wheelchair. His Aunt Luce always did that, even though she could walk with the best of them. She said it saved hassle, and she was cunning enough to be right most of the time.

He couldn't take any hassle. Any problems, however minor, and he would keel over. There would be no roaming around London tonight and no champagne in his suite with Antonia. When Martin met him he would be safely taken care of. At the moment he felt anything but safe, in need of help for the first time in his entire life. He had never looked forward to seeing Martin more than he did now.

'I'm sorry to drop this on you, Helen,' Martin told her worriedly as he packed his briefcase. 'I'm always there to meet Dan myself when he comes over but it's impossible tonight. Jenny will be arriving at the station at just about the time that Dan's plane lands.'

'It's all right.' She smiled across at him and gathered her bag, ready to leave. 'I'm not doing anything particular and it's actually a good idea.

After all, I'm the one expected to work with him. I may as well face him now as later.'

Martin made a wry face at the slight edge of reprimand in her voice.

'Don't believe everything you hear about Dan Forrest, Helen. I've known him for years. Most of his reputation was made up by the Press and Dan just shrugs it off. He says it helps to sell books and he's not likely to go down under it. He can handle just about anything – and even that has to be an understatement. He can handle everything.'

So why can't he handle a taxi and get himself to his hotel? Helen thought irritably. Why do I have to be landed with him?

'I always understood it was good writing that sold books,' she murmured drily, and Martin cast a sceptical glance in her direction.

'Come on, now. A little publicity never did any harm, and Dan gets plenty of that.'

'So why is he coming over here for more?'

'Actually, he's doing it for me,' Martin said seriously. 'With Dan here the sales will go up and I never turn down cash. This isn't an easy business to be in at the moment. Dan likes London in any case. He used to live here a long time ago and he's still got plenty of friends in England. I think this is just an excuse to come over and visit them again. But try to keep in mind that he does have a new book out and that, apart from anything else, like my friendship with him, he's important. Go easy on him.' He glanced at his watch after this muted warning. 'Look, I'll have to go. Mo will be getting into a panic; she thinks Jenny is still a little girl.'

'On your way, then. Don't worry about a thing. I'll be on time to meet Mr Forrest if I leave now. I'll take him to his hotel and leave the rest to you. You can visit him later and catch up on the gossip.'

'No way,' Martin laughed. 'If I know Dan, he'll not want any visitors until late tomorrow. He'll have his day planned – and his night.'

Helen tried not to tighten her lips disapprovingly, since Martin was a friend of this important personage. What Dan Forrest did with his days and nights had nothing to do with her, until Wednesday. Then she was supposed to take him under her wing and deal with him. She collected her coat and made her way to the foyer, stopping to put it on when she saw it was still raining. She made a run for her car, her long legs covering the distance quickly. Being wet and in a hurry just added to her irritation at this trip. Dan Forrest was absolutely nothing to do with her at all.

There was plenty of time to get to the airport but Martin would have to really move to meet the train and Margaret would be fussing. Helen relaxed and grinned to herself. Why Margaret permitted Martin to call her Mo was a mystery that only love could explain, but Margaret and Jenny were the reason for Martin's existence. It was something she couldn't understand. Nothing mattered to Helen but her work. She set tight barriers around herself and kept them in place at all times.

She frowned as she backed her car out of the parking space and slid into the traffic. Meeting Dan Forrest was not part of her work, and shepherding him around from one cocktail party or book-signing to another was not part of her work either, but that was what she was landed with even though her own desk was piled high with untouched manuscripts. While she was pandering to this playboy author, her real work was sitting there waiting, her real authors kept in suspense. To say that it was irritating was putting it mildly.

Still, Martin was more than her boss, he was a good friend, and his wife Margaret was a good friend too. As for Jenny, she might be a child no longer but she was scatterbrained enough to get into trouble if Mummy and Daddy were not there to grasp her firmly by the arm as the rain came in. In any case, if she had to deal with Dan Forrest she might as well meet him now as later; at least she would then know what to expect on Wednesday.

Helen stopped at yet another set of traffic lights and glanced at her watch. Things were moving slowly. There were queues where she had never expected to find queues. If she couldn't get through the traffic faster than this, then the mighty author would be waiting for her, no doubt picking up girls to pass the time.

She suddenly frowned, realizing that she only vaguely knew his face. She knew his reputation better. At this rate, though, he would be the only one left from the flight and would take no finding at

all. She wondered how he would react to being kept
waiting. She didn't particularly care how he reacted.
Martin had only just dropped this extra job in her
lap, as he had intended to meet Dan Forrest himself.
The mighty could fume for all she cared. Her excuse
was watertight. In actual fact, she was doing Martin
a favour. This was beyond the call of duty – way
beyond.

Dan came through Customs and looked around for
Martin, not too surprised when he couldn't immediately see him. By now his head was so bad that he
had difficulty seeing anything at all. Everything was
spinning slowly. His eyes were half closed with pain
and he was shivering with cold in spite of the heat in
the airport building. He felt so ill that he was almost
ready to lean on Martin's shoulder and refuse to lift
his head. It was the first time in his life that he had
felt vulnerable and it came as a really shocking
surprise.

   But Martin wasn't there. The reality of it
dawned on Dan bit by bit when nobody came
forward to claim him and take matters in hand.
He was left standing alone and he couldn't believe
this was happening to him. Life was smooth. He
made very sure it was smooth: no cracks, no
hassle, no commitments. He needed all his mental strength for his job, It occupied his life to the
exclusion of almost everything else. Other things
were merely on the outside edge of his life,
peripheral.

He leaned against the wall, too shaken to consider what to do next. Get a taxi? Make it to the hotel and hope that the reservations were in place and that Martin hadn't disappeared off the face of the earth before he could make them? It was too much effort to think with what seemed to be roadworks going on in his head. It was too much effort to walk another step; his legs were like rubber bands. He couldn't even summon up the energy to collect his luggage. If he tried to do that he knew perfectly well that he wouldn't make it. He didn't really seem to have a lot of choice about things. He would die here, right by this wall. It was the only decision he was capable of making.

'*Mr Forrest*?' The voice came over the speaker in a curiously disembodied way and Dan tried to work up some interest in the name because it had to be him. He used to be called that before he stepped out of the plane into this pain-filled world where nobody helped if you were dying in front of their eyes. '*Will Mr Forrest please proceed to the main exit?*'

'How?' Dan asked aloud, drawing curious glances in his direction. He had been here plenty of times and he knew how to get out of this place. The exit would be about fifty miles away as he felt right now. It was completely beyond his capabilities. He stayed put, well aware of his own limitations, but the voice came again and again, nagging him, ringing round in his head, prodding him into action.

He pushed himself upright and went forward, keeping close to the wall in case he needed it. If he could stay vertical until he reached the door he would summon up the last strength he possessed and kill Martin for this. He would choke him and have the satisfaction of knowing that they would die together, friends to the last.

Martin wasn't there. The voice stopped nagging and while Dan stood there, dazed, swaying on his feet, unable to make his eyes face any sort of light, another voice began.

'Mr Forrest?'

This new voice was sharper. It also sounded vaguely reprimanding and Dan felt extremely surprised by that. He couldn't remember having done one single thing wrong. All the bad things had happened to him, and he was most definitely the injured party. He managed to place the sound and slowly turned towards the source of it, taking a good deal of care with his head movements in case his head came off, rolled away and caused unseemly embarrassment.

It was a woman, and normally that would have interested him immediately, but right at this moment he couldn't care less. He could hardly see her anyway. She was just a hazy outline in some sort of coat.

'I'm Helen Stewart, Mr Forrest. I came to meet you because Mr Newman was not able to come himself. He sends his apologies. I have my car outside. I'll take you to your hotel and Mr Newman will contact you later.'

She held out her hand in a vigorous, efficient manner but Dan didn't take it. He would have

14

missed it if he had tried. She sounded cold and brisk, totally uninterested in his failing condition. He was fading away, dying as he stood and she ignored it all.

She seemed to be swimming before his eyes and he wished she would make some goddamned effort to keep still. He wished her voice were a little more sympathetic – but she had a car; he had heard that. It had stayed in his brain like a light. If he could make it as far as her car he could sit down. If he was going to die he could do it in comfort.

'Fine,' he managed in a slurred voice. 'Collect my luggage, will you, honey?'

Helen sat beside him, negotiating the traffic, staring straight ahead, seething. She had shown him where the car was and he had simply fallen into the passenger seat and left everything else to her. He hadn't said another word. She had been forced to collect his luggage like a porter, stow it into the boot of her car and gently but firmly push him over so that she could get into the driving seat, because he was slumped down with his eyes closed and his body half over towards her.

She did not feel at all gentle, and she would have liked to give him a vigorous push through the door. She was furious. The great Dan Forrest, prize-winning writer, darling of the Press and the apple of Martin's eye, was drunk. He was collapsed in the seat beside her like an huge ungainly sack and the smell of brandy rose from him in clouds of toxic fumes.

Helen was too angry at the moment to consider how she was going to get him to his hotel room without considerable embarrassment and a good deal of help. He was as big as a house and tight as a newt. She could just be thankful that he was the sort of drunk who slept. If he had been either offensive or maudlin she would have pushed him out of the car at the airport and let him take his chances. She had not been too pleased to be landed with him at the expense of her own work but she had never expected to be landed with someone who was too inebriated to put one foot in front of the other.

When she stopped at the hotel he made no move to get out of the car. He appeared to be asleep, safely enclosed in some drunken cloud, and Helen left him where he was while she stormed through the falling rain and went inside to get help. This place was costing enough. To her mind, the prices at this hotel were outrageous. If they encouraged celebrities they could just come out and take over when one of them was drunk. Apparently they knew the man a lot better than she did, so they were probably used to it. She refused to tolerate it for one more moment.

At the reception desk she bit back the words that were hovering on the tip of her tongue. She wanted to say, 'Kindly come outside and collect your drunken guest.' It wouldn't do, though. If the Press got hold of it the whole thing would reflect badly on Martin's business. The Press were always interested in Dan Forrest, according to Martin. There were other authors to consider too, and in any case she owed Martin a lot. She didn't owe Dan Forrest one damned thing. She came back out to the car and made an effort to rouse him.

'Mr Forrest! Mr Forrest!'

He stirred when she shook his arm vigorously and spoke loudly enough. It was that voice again, cold as ice and sharp as a razor, making his head ring. He gave her a bleary look through half-closed eyes.

'Can't you quit nagging?' he asked plaintively, and Helen summoned up all the necessary self-control to bite back an acid retort.

'We've arrived,' she informed him stiffly. 'If you could manage to get out of the car, I'll arrange to have your luggage taken up to your room.'

He didn't manage to get out of the car without her help. She had to actually pull him out, and she ended up collecting his key and escorting him to his room while the porter brought the luggage along as if everything were wonderfully normal and sugary-sweet.

Helen felt on the edge of violence. From the lift, down the carpeted passage to the door of his room, she actually found herself holding his important arm very firmly, wondering at what point he would sink to the floor and refuse to go any further. He wasn't silent now either. He was muttering vague complaints under his breath but she wasn't interested in asking what they were. She just wanted to be rid of him with all possible speed.

She tipped the porter, put the keys on the small table by the door and regarded her charge with total abhorrence.

'Your keys, Mr Forrest,' she said frostily. 'I'll leave you to get settled in. I'll see you on Wednesday morning.'

He never answered; he was just standing there in the middle of the carpet looking like a giant with a hangover. Helen gave him one last icy look, put the 'Do Not Disturb' sign on the outside knob and left, closing the door loudly behind her. He was disgusting! How could Martin have him for a friend? Why did Margaret allow it?

The sharp sound of the closing door brought Dan painfully back to the present when his head reeled from the noise, but when he turned she was gone. He only had a vague idea of how she had looked. He only had a vague idea of how he had got here. All he knew was that there was blessed silence, and another thing he knew for sure. He was very much in need of help and she had simply walked out and left him.

'What a bitch!' he muttered.

He made it to the bed, took off his shoes and jacket, loosened his tie and wrapped himself in the quilt. He would ring down to the desk in a minute and get something for this head, then he would ring Martin and give him a lecture on the value of friendship and the inadequacy of his staff. The sort of woman he needed now was a big, strong hospital sister with a cool hand for his head and a strong potion to keep him alive.

He didn't need the sort who had a great skill at slamming doors when she wasn't jabbing at him with a tongue like a wasp. It was probably a good thing that she'd gone, but what sort of woman would leave a man to die? When he choked Martin he would include her in the package. He closed his eyes to stop the room from spinning and tilting.

Next morning Helen tackled her boss when he came in and enquired after his famous friend.

'He was lit up like a Christmas tree – paralytic, totally incapacitated, blind drunk,' she stated indignantly, looking at Martin over the top of her large spectacles. 'He told me to collect his luggage as if I were a servant, then he got into my car and fell asleep – half over my seat, I might add. The smell of brandy was so strong that if there had been a naked light we would have had an explosion and he would have got more publicity than he bargained for.'

'Dan?' Martin looked at her in disbelief. 'But he doesn't . . .' He turned to go back to his office. 'I'll ring the hotel and have a word with him. I hope you picked up the right person because the one you've been describing is definitely not Dan Forrest. He's the most level-headed, self-sufficient person I know.'

Helen gave a snort of annoyance and settled back down to the the manuscript on her desk. Tomorrow she had to start this round of social activity with Dan Forrest and she had no intention of escorting him back to his hotel suite each night like a nurse. If he drank too much she would dump him wherever they happened to be and he could make what he liked of that. Drunk was something she would not tolerate in any circumstances at all.

A face came into her mind, flushed, angry, fists like curled-up lumps of rock.

'*You'll get out and you'll do it! Come back without money again and I'll put you in hospital!*'

'Dan's not answering. He must have gone out.' Martin popped his head round her door again and Helen shook off the memories and raised her brows in surprise.

'A remarkable recovery,' she murmured scathingly.

'Honestly, Helen, this is not like Dan.' Martin shook his head worriedly and then gave a sigh of resignation. 'Anyway, I have too many appointments today to get over to see him. Maybe he'll come round here before we finish. He's probably roaming round London right now, drinking in the sights.'

'Bad choice of verb,' Helen muttered angrily as Martin left. If Dan Forrest was drinking anything it wouldn't be sights. 'May he fall in the Thames,' she thought, and put him right out of her mind. The memory of him infuriated her and she had work to do.

He didn't answer later when Martin phoned again and as far as Helen was concerned, that confirmed everything. According to Martin, Dan would be out on the town. Martin went home happily. Helen went home still fuming.

When Helen presented herself at the hotel next day, the manager came to speak to her the moment she asked for Dan Forrest.

'Are you a friend of Mr Forrest?' he asked in a subdued voice as if he were in a church or in the presence of greatness.

'I'm going to work with him,' Helen said firmly. No way was she going to be classed as a friend of a drunk. 'Dealing with Mr Forrest is part of my job.'

'Then I'm glad to see you – very relieved, in fact. I'm told that someone brought him here from the airport on Monday night and just left him. It was a woman.'

'It was me,' Helen said warily, wondering how many things he had broken in his room as he staggered uncontrollably around, ricocheting from one piece of furniture to another. 'What has he done?'

'Done? Mr Forrest? He's done nothing at all,' the manager told her indignantly. 'Mr Forrest is ill. Didn't you realize when you walked out and left him that you were leaving a very sick man by himself? You even put the "Do Not Disturb" sign on the door. We had no idea.'

'He was drunk!' Helen snapped, furious at being held to account by a smarmy male and contradicted about something she had seen clearly with her own eyes.

'He was ill, very ill. Had the cleaner not decided to use her keys to get into his room when the sign just stayed there, I shudder to think what would have happened to him. He hadn't even managed to get into bed. He was lying on top of the bed almost unconscious, hardly wrapped up at all. We had to send for a doctor immediately. Nobody else seemed to care if he lived or died. I can quite see why he always chooses to stay with us when he's in England if this is the way he's treated by other people.'

'But – but I thought . . .'

The manager gave her a very severe look.

'Mr Forrest *always* stays with us, as I said. We've known him for years. He is never drunk. He was very ill. It was quite obvious.'

'Not to me,' Helen said quietly. She felt devastated by her own actions. The past was too firmly set in her mind to allow for any human foibles. She had judged a fellow human being with no thought of mercy, no thought of a mistake.

'Is he in hospital?' she asked in a subdued voice.

'He prefers to stay here with us. He feels at home here.' The manager gave a tight smile of satisfaction. 'We are taking care of him.'

'I'd better go up and see him.'

'If he's sleeping you should leave him in peace. He's had enough problems.'

Helen choked back a retort at the tone of voice and went to the lift without another word. She could hardly argue with the manager. She was utterly in the wrong and guilt was overwhelming her. She had simply abandoned a sick man without a backward glance because the past still sat heavily on her shoulders, colouring her attitude to other people.

A waiter was just leaving the room when she got there and Helen was able to get inside without disturbing anyone. She was nervous and guilty but the sight of Dan Forrest in bed, resting back against plumped-up pillows, sipping the hot drink the waiter had brought, more than doubled her anxiety.

He was not at all what she had expected. He was, somehow, much more male. She forced herself to meet his eyes. And what eyes! She had not noticed when she had picked him up at the airport because they had been half closed with what she realized belatedly must have been pain. She noticed now. They were amber, unblinking, staring at her fixedly like the eyes of a magnificent hunting animal, and the impact almost took her breath away.

The hairs on the back of her neck stood up with the sudden shock and her hands felt limp as a sort of weak protest welled up inside. She was sure of herself, cool, unimpressed by men, but now she didn't know what to say or where to look. No man had ever made her feel like that in her entire life. She felt trapped by those eyes, forced to stay where she was and accept her punishment. She deserved punishment and she knew it. Here was a man who would not hesitate to administer retribution where it was due.

It wasn't helping at all that he was naked to the waist – at least she imagined it was just to the waist;

23

her mind balked at thinking further than that. He looked pale but he was not in any state of collapse. Not that she was surprised now that she could see him properly. He looked too powerful to collapse.

He stared at her steadily, not saying a word.

'I'm Helen Stewart,' she said uncomfortably, forcing herself to meet the cold, golden-eyed indifference. 'I – I met you at the airport.'

'I vaguely remember. The angel of mercy.' He went on staring at her, making her more uncomfortable than ever. 'What can I do for you, Miss Stewart – not that it will be much in my present condition?'

Helen felt her face going hot with embarrassment but she knew she deserved anything he might say to her. The quiet, cultured American voice was edged with contempt, steadily cutting her down to size, but she could not defend herself because the feeling of guilt was too strong.

'You look better,' she managed unevenly, almost whispering, and dark brows rose sardonically over the golden eyes.

'Better than dead? You're probably right.'

'The – the manager said you were very ill. I expected . . .'

'To have to look after me? Perish the thought, Miss Stewart. I'm strong, but I'm not sure how long I would last left to your care. Fortunately, one injection of penicillin works miracles.'

'Did the doctor say what . . .?' Helen asked

shakily, trying to ignore the fact that every time he opened his mouth he was quietly attacking her.

'Black Death. Obviously you'd better leave quickly.'

Helen felt guilty, frustrated, unable to defend herself with her ready tongue, and that, coupled with the shock of meeting those eyes, left her perilously close to tears. She deserved the sarcasm and she knew it, and he was ruthlessly chastising her without even raising his voice. She half turned to escape but she could not just walk out. She had to offer some explanation and in any case, she had to work with this man, unless Martin gave her the boot for her cruelty to his friend.

She looked at him sideways, horrified that her lips were trembling. The shell that protected her from the world never cracked but it was dangerously close to cracking now under his quiet onslaught.

'I'm sorry,' she whispered. 'I really thought you were drunk. You – you smelled of brandy and – and you just sat there and went to sleep.'

'The brandy kept me upright during the flight, Miss Stewart. Foolishly, I refused the offer to have an ambulance waiting for me. I assumed I would be met with some sort of sympathy. After all, everyone has flu from time to time; they know how it feels.'

'Flu? The manager said . . .'

'My self-diagnosis was wrong. I had a nasty little virus that burned itself out and almost burned me out with it. Fortunately the type of virus is not long-lasting. I survived. The injection was in case of secondary infection. In any case,' he added impatiently, 'I can't remember much about the airport or the time later. And as it turned out, you're not really in any position to fill me in, are you? I owe my present state of increasing health to a cleaner with an inquisitive disposition.'

'I'm sorry,' Helen repeated. 'I really thought you were just drunk.'

'And would you abandon someone who was helpless, even if they were "just drunk", Miss Stewart?'

'*Yes!*' she said fiercely. She turned away to the door. 'I'll tell Martin that you're ill. We can re-arrange your schedule, or even cancel it. Martin will come and see you. He – he was snowed under with work yesterday, that's why . . .'

Helen put her hand on the door, desperately anxious to get out of his sight and restore her shattered self-esteem. She knew she would have to get Martin to have someone else work with him. She would never get over the guilt, and obviously he would never forgive her. Anyway, she couldn't face those eyes. They made her scalp tingle and her breath tighten up..

The golden eyes narrowed at the tone of her voice and his gaze swept over her from head to foot, lingering on the slender figure and the long length of her legs. The cold-hearted bitch who had left him to his fate wasn't quite what he had expected. She almost looked in need of help herself. There was something flowing beneath the surface that he couldn't quite fathom but he instinctively reacted to it, homed in on it.

'Just give me a couple of days, Miss Stewart. I recover quickly. Meanwhile, feel free to alter my schedule. I'm quite prepared to fit in with anything you arrange. I'm sure we're going to get on beautifully.'

Helen heard the disdain. She just left without turning round and Dan finished his drink thoughtfully. He had a feeling that she was trouble. Beneath that efficient, hard exterior was a good deal of vulnerability, and he did not particularly care for vulnerable women. He liked a woman who stood on her own two feet and not on his.

She was beautiful too, delicate features like a china figurine and a mass of short blonde hair that kept trying to curl around her face. She had pushed it behind her ears with enough frequency to prove habit. The spectacles were also a habit, because if they weren't clear glass they were near enough to it. There was nothing short-sighted about the violet-blue eyes.

Helen Stewart had problems. He frowned and finished his drink. He was here to enjoy himself and get a rest. Being involved, however remotely, with a female who seemed to be strung to the point of breaking was not his idea of a good time. That was business. This was supposed to be pleasure. He wondered about phoning Antonia but decided against the idea. He wasn't yet up to her chatter, and anyway she would not advance beyond the door in case he was infectious. Antonia set her own standards and the devil with anyone else. He could not imagine a time when *she* would be close to tears.

Martin arrived during the afternoon, bearing an inappropriate bouquet of flowers and words of regret and sympathy.

'You'll come and stay with us, of course. Mo insists on it.'

'Forget it,' Dan murmured. 'I like it just fine here. I can demand special care with no scruples because I'm paying for it. Besides, I like to be right in the middle of things, though not quite as much in the middle as I was after the flight.'

'Helen is devastated by the whole thing,' Martin assured him, settling in a chair by the bed and looking worried. Dan noticed with some amusement that the worry was all for the Stewart woman. As far as Martin was concerned, his favourite writer was not dead and could therefore cope without anxiety being wasted.

'She seemed to be when she called earlier.'

'I hope you weren't too hard on her, Dan? She can do without your sarcastic tongue.'

'Oh, I'm too sick for combat,' the mocking voice drawled. 'I take it, then, that you're not about to give her a lecture followed by swift dismissal?'

'Dismiss Helen?' Martin snorted in disbelief and then gave Dan a sharp glance. 'Somewhere or other, she's got problems. We don't know what, but we do have the odd worry about Helen.'

'You and Margaret? Concentrate your worries on my health and Jenny's latest exploits. Miss Stewart seemed quite capable of taking care of herself.' Dan felt a flash of renewed irritation when his mind strongly objected to that last statement it had formed. He wasn't at all sure that she was capable. He just refused to be involved.

'Capable physically, perhaps. She's clever, fit and vigorous. I think she's doing judo or something. Anyway, she's at the gym almost every evening.'

The golden eyes blinked in surprise. The gym? She looked as delicate as a wild rose. But Martin went on. 'It's not that at all. It's inside. Something bothers her. We often think it's eating away at her but she just keeps quiet.'

'Look,' Dan interrupted, letting his impatience show. 'Leave me out of this, and if you want advice here's some for free. Give Margaret a good talking to and make a pact to mind your own business, both of you. If Miss Stewart is good at her job that's all you need to care about.'

'She's the best editor I ever had. I can't think how we managed before she came on the scene.'

'Is that why I'm stuck with her, because she's your best?' Dan enquired drily. 'Or are you hoping to interest me by waving her under my nose every day?'

'I hoped she might intrigue you, to be perfectly honest.'

'By all means let's be perfectly honest. I'll give you my professional impression of Miss Stewart right now. She's an irritating female with all the sympathy of a robot. She's snobbish, clever, probably a product of one of your "great" universities. She'll go right to the top by planting her dainty foot on anyone in the way – your own chest if it applies. Mind your business, watch your back, get the hell out of here and let me sleep.'

'You know, you're really good,' Martin muttered with some show of awe as he stood to leave. 'Some of it is right on the nose. She is very clever and she will go to the top, but you're wrong about her character. She's crying inside.'

'I'm never wrong,' Dan assured him imperiously, sliding down in bed. 'She'll only cry if you cut her salary, and even then she might go for you instead. Just remember the judo. It's probably timely preparation. What you have there is one tough cookie. Shut the door as you leave.'

He closed his eyes as Martin left, but his own words seemed to stick in his throat. Liar, he thought disgustedly. He could picture her eyes with the slight sheen of tears of frustration and shock, the way her lips tried to tremble. She had been unduly upset at her genuine mistake about him and the way he had treated her earlier would have had any other female pouring his drink over his head. He knew damned well she had problems but hell, it was nothing to do with him at all! He was here to enjoy his favourite city.

CHAPTER 2

Helen walked out of the gym with Jack Garford. It was dark but the rain had stopped and it wasn't cold at all. She slung her canvas holdall more comfortably on her shoulder and stepped out briskly, matching his pace, her white trainers making no sound on the ground.

'Sure you want to come for a coffee?' Jack glanced down at her and met the clear violet of her eyes. She had left off the spectacles and the difference it made was startling. Her whole unusual beauty seemed to shoot into focus, as if *he* had been the one wearing inappropriate lenses.

'Quite sure, but I'm in a tracksuit again.'

'So am I. I had in mind the usual scruffy café.'

'All right.' She laughed up at him and felt a definite surge of relief. She hadn't really wanted to go straight back home. The thought of the next day was weighing too heavily on her mind.

Things had been put off for a few days because of the unexpected illness of her charge, schedules had been rearranged but time had finally caught up with

31

her. Tomorrow she had to face Dan Forrest. She had to look into the panther-gold eyes and try to be pleasant however badly he treated her.

It would be hard enough facing him at all without having to summon up any sort of friendliness and charm. The resentment of leaving her own job to wait while she did something she didn't want to do was still hovering around in her head, but she was honest enough to admit that there was more to her agitation than that. She dreaded facing him, and it was nothing to do with her inexcusable mistake either. She was more than capable of saying, Look, I've said sorry and that's an end to it.

No. It wasn't that. It was the man himself. Her skin tightened at just the thought of him. In some peculiar way he scared and excited her. He had even scared and excited her when he was ill, sitting up in bed, propped up with white pillows. She was not looking forward to facing him when he was on his feet and fully recovered. He had eyes that seemed to see everything and she didn't really want to be forced to face them again.

At the airport her mind had shut him out. She had barely glanced at him. Her own resentment and her conviction that he was as drunk as a skunk had almost made him invisible. It had been a big mistake, because he was anything but invisible and she had to face him first thing in the morning and escort him to the first book-signing.

For the better part of a week the busy publishers Martin owned would have to function without her whether she liked it or not. Martin had been particularly insistent. It had to be her and nobody else. Her confession of embarrassment had done nothing to soften his attitude. She was stuck with it, he had told her that firmly.

'Here we are,' Jack announced. 'This place is disreputable enough for anyone. You'll definitely be overdressed in a clean tracksuit here'

Helen grinned at him. The gym was not in a particularly salubrious area; neither of them could afford the prices of the top-notch central gyms. People went to Bob's Body Shop to learn to take care of themselves in dangerous situations, not to tone gleaming bodies to even finer lines of beauty. The café was therefore in tune with the neighbourhood. Without Jack she would never have dared to go in through the door and she was always aware of that.

'Fine,' Helen agreed. 'You buy the coffee, I'll buy the buns, if you dare to eat one here.'

'I'm in prime condition,' Jack boasted. 'Backstreet rock buns don't scare me.'

They went in, and Helen saw that they were not the only members of Bob's who had been struck by the idea of coffee.

'Hi, there, Helen, Jack. How is it?'

'Strained and bruised,' Jack muttered, lifting his hand in greeting to the small group who sat at one of the plastic-covered tables.

Mostly they were young, late teens or early twenties, and mostly they were big. Every one of them dwarfed Helen although she was by no means small herself. She waved and sat at a nearby table as Jack went to order. It was incongruous, a far cry from university, a far cry from the place where she now spent her days.

It was like being in different worlds, living separate lives. By day she was Helen Stewart, senior editor at Newman's Publishers. In the evening she was just Helen, a member of this gang of youthful people who accepted her for precisely what she was. At night she was someone else again.

Night. Her mind pushed it away but it came surging back, cutting out the sound of the voices around her.

'Where did you go, Piccadilly? You stupid bitch, it's taken already, real professionals. What did you think you could make there? You get down by the stations, or down by the docks. And try to look pleasant. When I get back in there'd better be some money in that purse of yours.'

'Two coffees, two dubious rock buns,' Jack said cheerfully, sinking down into the chair beside her. He looked at her closely. 'You okay, Helen?'

'Yes. Why?' She pulled herself back into the present and glanced at him with a smile.

'You were miles away.'

'Dreading tomorrow,' she told him quickly. 'I have to chaperon Dan Forrest.'

'Why dreading it?' Jack asked, giving her an odd look as he drank his coffee. 'Get you out of the office.'

34

She wished fervently that Dan Forrest had been like Jack. Everything about Jack was kind, unthreatening, easy-going. If she needed to know a man at all it would have to be someone like Jack or Martin, someone with a smiling face and a quiet voice, someone who respected her just because she was a woman. Dan Forrest had a quiet voice, but it was full of authority and there was something about him that made her nervous.

'I don't want to be out of the office. I've got manuscripts coming out of my ears and it's not fair to my authors. Martin won't consider letting anyone else go. I mean, the place is teeming with life but no, it has to be me.'

'He probably thinks you have more tact than the others.'

'Actually, he knows I haven't,' Helen admitted ruefully. 'I was the one who picked Dan Forrest up from the airport a few nights ago and decided he was drunk. I just abandoned him at his hotel. He was, in fact, very ill. They had to get the doctor. Mr Forrest is not, it seems, a forgiving man. That's why I'm dreading it.'

'I see. The truth at last. Well, as far as I can see you'll have to eat a portion of humble pie and do your job. It's not going to be for long anyway. Dan Forrest doesn't stay too long when he comes over here.'

'How do you know?'

'I'm a journalist, in case you've forgotten. It's my business to know everything about celebrities. Dan

35

Forrest is always news in one way or the other. I've never yet managed to lay hands on him.'

'Hey! Dan Forrest? You know him, Jack? I just finished reading one of his books.'

A lanky youth from the club pulled a chair out at their table and straddled it, looking at Jack with hopeful eyes.

'Not me,' Jack corrected, 'Helen. She's escorting him round this week.'

'Boy! What a job!' He looked at Helen with renewed respect. 'I just finished his latest book, *Gateway to Hell*. It sizzles. I hear he won some prizes.'

'Not for his blood-and-guts work,' Jack corrected drily. 'Dan Forrest is respected for his books on psychiatry. They brought the prizes. The sizzling books simply bring in the cash.'

'He's a psychiatrist?' Helen looked at Jack in astonishment, and in her mind she saw those eyes and understood them.

'A greatly esteemed psychiatrist. He lectures all over the world, is called in as a consultant even by the police when they have a possible nutcase on their hands. And not just the New York police either. He's pretty important over there. I started to read one of his great works once but had to give it up. It was beyond me.' He gave their companion a smile.

'You want to read *Gateway to Hell*, man. You'll not give it up, you'll not be able to put it down.' He went to join his friends to spread the news and Jack made a wry face.

'Actually, I abandoned it because it gave me the creeps,' he confessed to Helen in a low voice. 'There are plenty of weird people around in the world and Forrest seems to have dealt with a lot of them. I prefer not to think about it. Life's tricky enough without having to deal with all the popcorns.'

Helen was hardly listening. Not only had she misjudged Dan Forrest, she had seriously offended an intelligent man of importance. He probably had her classified down to the last full stop and he was very dangerous to her. She would have to be careful, much more careful than she had anticipated. She couldn't do with anyone probing her mind on her way of life.

The thought hung around in her head all the rest of the time and even later, when she was at home, she could not shake off the feeling that she had made a very crucial mistake and gravely affected her own future by being the focus of the strange golden eyes. She wanted no one at all to show interest in her. Part of her life was strictly secret.

She made a great effort to shrug the feeling off. In all probability, Dan Forrest would be coldly polite and not even glance at her while she was escorting him. She had seriously offended him and, cultured though he was, he didn't look the sort of man who would readily forget, or forgive. This brought another worry to mind, and she hastily looked in her diary to make sure she had ordered the car for tomorrow. She had. At least she wouldn't be making any more mistakes or errors of judgement. She must do nothing in future to draw attention to herself.

Helen took a shower and changed her clothes yet again. A glance through the closed curtains showed that it was still not raining, which was a relief. It was bad enough going out without having to brave the endless rain of the past few days. Walking the streets in the rain made things seem much worse.

She realized that she was tired, more tired than usual, and she hoped she had not caught Dan Forrest's virus. She knew what it was without too much thought, though. She was strung up tight, permanently on edge, and the night excursions were robbing her of much-needed sleep. Going out was imperative. She had to search but she was weary, so weary.

She put on her raincoat just in case the rain came back and left the house as silently as usual. It was quiet, dark, but she did not fear the dark. There were other, worse fears. She drove as far as she thought was feasible and then left the car and locked it. From here on she had to be on foot, and she walked steadily down the street. There was no need to rush. Searching was a painstaking business and needed time. She knew all about time. She had used a lot of it already and thus far to no real avail. She seemed to be no closer to her goal. Maybe tonight?

Her lips quirked with no real amusement. She said that every night and the hope was never fulfilled. One night, along some dark, glittering street, she would find what she was looking for.

She took a short-cut down a side-street with no lights but she was not at all anxious about her own safety. She was not defenceless, not now. Defenceless was something from the past, from a long time ago. She stepped back into the lights at the other end of the street and glanced both ways, ignoring the passing cars, her eyes searching the pavements, the pools of light by the shop windows, and then she started to walk. Maybe tonight the search would end, and then what would she do? How would she face the truth if she found it? What would she do with it?

Dan walked through the foyer, extremely loath to admit that he was actually testing his legs. They seemed to have been doing well at holding him upright in his hotel suite but this was the real thing. He was taking them out in public for the first time. If they gave way here he would cancel tomorrow's trip and stay right where he was. The thought of collapsing into the slender arms of Helen Stewart and relying on her better nature did not appeal to him. Full possession of faculties, physical and mental, were required with her or there was no deal.

'How do we feel now, Mr Forrest?' The manager flew gleefully across to speak to him and Dan's lips quirked in amusement.

'We feel fine, Mr Enderby, just fine.'

There was a definite sign of smug satisfaction on Mr Enderby's face.

'We know how to take care of our guests.'

'You sure do.'

'It's fortunate that we do. The young lady who brought you in . . .' Mr Enderby began with pursed lips but Dan intervened swiftly.

'Not to blame at all,' he said firmly. 'I gave every appearance of being drunk. Anything like that is very frightening for a refined young lady, as you can imagine. She's under a good deal of stress at the moment too. I don't blame her at all.'

'Stress? Dear me.' The manager looked hopeful of gossip but Dan nodded to him and walked out through the swing doors, smiled briefly at the doorman and stepped out into the glitter of the city at night.

He felt disgruntled that he had sprung to Helen Stewart's defence so readily. He had given the appearance of being very ill, not very drunk when she had collected him at the airport. He couldn't think offhand of any woman of his acquaintance who would have treated him so callously. But Helen Stewart had not hesitated. She had dumped him swiftly.

Still, she was not a woman of his acquaintance and he was looking at the incident from his own point of view, insider knowledge. For all she knew he might have been a drunken swine waiting to get her into his hotel room, and she had certainly shot out of his room fast. But she hadn't been scared, not till she had seen him in the broad light of day. At the time in question she had just been angry and cold-blooded.

He frowned. Nobody that he could think of was afraid of him; they relied on him. Maybe her fear when she had visited him had been because he was in bed, some sexual hang-up. Or maybe he was just scary to someone like that, all uptight and quivering, although he dealt with them regularly. He'd lay odds to a hundred that she was a virgin.

Margaret and Martin were worried about her and neither of them were fools. Still, they both had the urge to mother people and she looked as if she needed it. The hardness was a shield, he could have sensed that with his eyes closed. He also knew that any attempt to mother her would be met with a very rapid defensive action and a retreat into the woodwork.

He frowned even more. He was not going to psychoanalyse her even from a distance, however much Martin was hoping for it. This was his break in his favourite city. One piece of bad luck was enough and he seemed to have recovered from that. He had every intention of enjoying himself while he was here. He had no idea when he would be able to come to England again so nothing was about to stop his fun now.

He was going to attend these functions with Helen Stewart, be firmly polite, bid her adieu each day when the time came and disappear into the city. She was on her own. Before too long there would be the wide stretch of the Atlantic between them. He couldn't help everybody in the world, and he was too well balanced himself to scoop up every misfit his eyes fell on. Besides, she was too attractive, and that was dangerous ground under these circumstances. If he allowed any interest in her to develop it would not be at all scientific.

The legs seemed to have been doing well. Not that he had noticed at all until this moment. They seemed to have taken him a good way from his hotel while he had been thinking. Dan did a quick mental bodily check. He felt okay. The prognosis was good. He seemed to have recovered and tomorrow could take place after all.

He glanced idly across the street and did a double-take as his attention was caught by a girl on the opposite pavement. Hooker! His mind classified her immediately. She was all in black, a black plastic raincoat that just about covered her bottom, long legs in black stockings and black high-heeled shoes.

Her hair was black too, held down by some sort of band. She was wearing dark glasses even at night and his eyes followed her with amused interest. She only needed a flashing sign strapped to her rear end. She couldn't have been proclaiming her profession more openly.

He noticed a couple of girls in the same trade give her odd looks and he knew how they felt. There was something about her that drew the eye and it wasn't simply her bizarre appearance. She was gliding along the street as if nobody could see her, even though everything about her drew the attention. He followed her on the opposite side of the road to pass the time and was greatly intrigued when a man approached her and planted himself in front of her.

To Dan's surprise she ignored the overture, stepping aside and continuing on her way. If she wanted a customer it wasn't this one. But the man persisted and followed her down the street, importuning, harassing, drawing attention to both of them.

For a few seconds she continued to ignore him and then she turned on him in one swift flash of movement that was almost menacing. The man automatically jumped back and she advanced two threatening steps towards him, looking him straight in the face. Dan was too far away to hear what she said but the man turned and made a quick get-away; he never even stopped to give her any sort of reply. His body language said one word – scared.

Dan's interest grew. A menacing hooker who didn't want a client! This he had to see further. He crossed the road, only getting halfway before having to wait with his life hanging on a thread as more cars swept past him. By the time he reached the opposite side of the road his quarry had vanished. He walked the way she had been going and he knew exactly why he was doing it. His professional curiosity was aroused. But there was no sign of her at all.

There was a small, dark passageway and at the end of it he could see the lights of another major road. She might well have slipped up the alley and be not too far away on the other street, out of his sight. It shouldn't be too hard to catch up with her, not at the slow, measured pace she was walking at. He was fascinated, intrigued to know what she had said that had scared off a big, grown man. He had seen girls of the night on the streets of every city he had visited but never one quite like this. Always they were predictable and he glanced at them with pity or amusement. Somehow those sentiments did not fit this one, and that alone was enough to intrigue him.

He turned into the passageway and then came to an abrupt halt as danger signals flashed brilliantly all through his brain. Normally he would have walked on and given it no thought. He was more than capable of taking care of himself and there was nobody in the darkness. But he balked at going even one step further. Some primeval alert signal inside his head had switched on to red.

He could see right through to the lights and traffic at the other side. Nobody was waiting to mug him; there were just a few refuse bins at the side door of shops that opened on to the dark little lane, nothing else. As side streets went it was tidy. But his instincts said STOP, in large capital letters, and he always allowed his instincts free rein. In New York they acted like eyes in the back of his neck. He was not going into there to follow a hooker for sheer intellectual amusement. He turned back towards his hotel, trying to shrug off the feeling of cold that had suddenly swept over him.

The two ladies of the night he had seen earlier sauntered up, eyeing his expensive suit with interest. Everything about him said money and they looked him up and down, taking in the height and sheer athletic masculinity, the handsome face.

'Interested in company, love?'

They were watching him like female predators and Dan's amusement returned as the eerie feeling of danger passed. The amber eyes turned fully on them, intelligent, calculating and unblinking.

'Information,' he corrected in his soft American accent. 'Who was the lady in black that went past a few minutes ago?'

'Some nutcase,' one of them said acidly. 'Did you see the one that got away? He shot past us like a rabbit, eyes popping out of his head. God knows what she said to him. You want to be careful who you pick up, love.'

'I thought it was ladies of your profession who walked into danger?' Dan drawled, and they perked up at the mention of ladies.

'Not with somebody like you.'

'So who is that dark, mysterious female?' he persisted.

'Beats me. We've never seen her around before.'

'Maybe she wasn't . . .' Dan began, but his budding thoughts were met with high, shrill laughs of derision.

'Come off it, love. It must be because you're a Yank. She was on the game in flashing lights. Half an inch more and you could see her arse.'

Dan nodded in amusement. His thoughts precisely. A prostitute with a neon placard.

'So come on, then. Want some company?' They looked at him expectantly and he grinned, making a sketchy salute with his hand as he sidestepped them.

'Not tonight, Josephine,' he murmured with feigned regret and walked off leaving them laughing, calling after him in a good-natured way before they went back to business.

Interesting. A little mystery to perk him up. A hooker in black with a menacing attitude and no wish for a client. It was something to chase around inside his head and keep the grey cells active.

The smile died on his face when he thought about the next day. He would be spending several hours in the company of a beautiful, uptight, stone-hearted maiden who would rear up and spit fire if he looked at her more than casually. He was spending far too much time thinking about her. She seemed to have got under his skin when he wasn't expecting it. The memory of her face and those blue eyes glazed with tears kept floating into his mind.

If it hadn't been for Martin he would have cancelled the whole shebang and got down to the more serious business of rediscovering London. As for seeing Antonia tonight, he didn't quite feel up to that. Maybe in a few more days. She was good company – among other things.

His mind returned to the woman in black and his earlier flash of animal instinct. Had she been hiding in that dark alley, pressed back against one of the closed doorways? It would have been easy enough, given her slight stature and the dark clothes. And if she had been hiding, why should that have brought him to a halt with cold flooding over him? He could tackle anyone, man or beast, and he couldn't think offhand of anything that scared him. He was used to physical activity. He climbed, sailed, hunted. He often went off alone for weeks into the wilderness to give his brain a rest. And yet the thought of going into that dark little passage still brought a shiver to his skin. Had it been primitive instinct? If not, then what had it been?

Next morning, Helen got into the car and settled back nervously after giving the name of Dan's hotel. To call it a car was an understatement of massive proportions. Limousine, streamlined monster – all it needed was a flag flying from the front, and if Dan Forrest had possessed a coat of arms, the flag would have been there. Martin had stated that only the best was good enough for Dan and this, apparently, was the best that money could hire. The great writer of bloodthirsty novels was seemingly used to style.

She nibbled rather anxiously at her lip and pushed the large spectacles further up on her nose. He didn't just write what Jack chose to call blood-and-guts books. Dan Forrest was important, a clever man, a psychiatrist. Why hadn't Martin mentioned that? For some reason he was keeping Dan Forrest's alter ego a secret, but he must have known she would find out. Or had he expected her to do her job more thoroughly and know all about her charge?

That thought brought even more guilt. If they asked her any questions at the bookshop she was likely to look completely blank and foolish. She had deliberately, wilfully refrained from discovering anything about Dan Forrest because of resentment. What she knew now she had learned almost by accident, and apart from his alarming presence she could not shake off the feeling that he was a danger to her. She had too much to hide and he was frighteningly alert.

When she got out of the car at Dan's hotel, she looked up to find that he was already on the steps waiting, and the sight of him stopped Helen in her tracks. She hadn't realized how big he was, how dark-haired. The last time she had seen him he had been in bed; now he was wearing a dark grey suit with a matching tie against a pristine white shirt. It put him into the ordinary world and he seemed to be more than she could cope with. He was a tall, lithe, handsome man who could never be overlooked at any time, but the eyes were astonishing.

They were fixed on her now in the same unblinking, intense manner, panther-gold, alarmingly intelligent and interested. For a few seconds she received the full blast of unwavering inspection that kept her rooted to the spot. His eyes moved slowly over her as if there were some machine in his head that was taking rapid notes. It was not some unpleasant masculine appraisal, either, it was a deep, fixed interest that noticed everything.

Helen was suddenly highly aware of herself, of how she looked. She knew she looked smart as usual and this morning she had taken extra care. The dark blue suit with the pencil-slim skirt and the yellow and white striped top looked good, she was sure of that, but, with his eyes making a long and detailed inspection of her, her certainty wavered. She wanted to snatch off her spectacles and look better than usual but all she could do was nervously force her hair behind her ears, and when his eyes released her and moved to the long black car she almost slumped in relief.

'You came for me in a hearse, Miss Stewart? Let's not be too hasty about this. I recovered.'

The quiet American voice drawled out the words and Helen just looked at him helplessly for a second. He wasn't laughing at her outright but she could see the amused quirk to his lips, the subtle disdain. Obviously he intended to go on treating her with contempt and there were several days to put up with it. It wasn't fair! Her face began to feel hot with embarrassment mixed with the first smouldering of annoyance.

'Not my choice, Mr Forrest,' she said in a cool, businesslike tone. 'This car is here because Mr Newman insisted on it. *I* am here because Mr Newman insisted on it. Left to myself I would have simply ordered a taxi and told the driver to bring you to the bookshop.'

He gave a tilted smile that was full of derision and then came down the last two steps and motioned her into the car.

'After you, Miss Stewart. Let's get this spectacular vehicle moving before we attract a crowd.'

'I'm sure we won't, Mr Forrest,' Helen snapped as she got into the back and sat down. 'This is London. We're quite used to royalty and visiting heads of state. One more black limousine is unlikely to attract attention, even if you are in it.'

She had hoped he would get in with the driver and leave her in peace but he got in beside her, sitting comfortably and stretching his long legs out in front of him. He was utterly silent in the way that only a big man with complete self-assurance could be, a calm silence from deep inside that made the glowing gold of his eyes more unusual.

He was relaxed, in control, and after fighting down fluttering heartbeats, Helen looked out of the window. She had to put up with this for at least five days. She didn't know how she was going to survive it but she must. She had never been so aware of anyone in her life. If he reached out and touched her with even one fingertip she would scream with shock.

'Why do you dislike me so much?'

The softly spoken words brought back the flutter inside her. Helen shot him a quick glance and then looked hastily away when she found his eyes fixed on her with the same intensity. There was no simple enquiry in them; it was a clinical probing. Good lord, he must scare his patients to death. They probably pretended recovery to get out of his clutches more rapidly. There wasn't much doubt that he could see into their heads; that was what the eyes were for. No wonder he was special and greatly esteemed in his world. He had an asset that no other psychiatrist could possibly have: X-ray eyes. He was like an alien on a secret mission to collect thoughts.

'I do not dislike you, Mr Forrest. In my job I am not allowed likes and dislikes. I treat everyone the same.'

'Unsympathetically.'

'I beg your pardon?' Helen spun round on him and glared through her large spectacles, annoyance overcoming awe. 'I get on very well with my authors and, far from being unsympathetic, I am most encouraging.'

'Even-handed, encouraging and strictly impersonal. You sound as if you're playing a part that you feel is expected of you, Miss Stewart, something you learned, to qualify you for the job. Don't any of these authors get on your nerves?'

'They do not! I enjoy my job. I enjoy working with writers.'

'I'm a writer.' He pointed it out quietly but with a slightly triumphant air, as if he had trapped her in some battle of wits.

'You're not one of mine and this particular job has been dropped on me without my having any choice at all. I have more to do with my time than escort celebrities!'

'Ah! I've got you rattled, Miss Stewart.' The eyes were still probing clinically but they were gleaming like new gold and she suddenly realized just what he was doing.

'Don't you dare start psychoanalysing me!'

She snatched off her glasses to glare at him more potently and was rewarded by a wide grin that lit up the handsome face.

'Much better. You've got eyes like blue-eyed cat, a Siamese. My Aunt Luce had one when I was younger. I used to drive it up the wall, quite literally. It was highly strung, just like you. It used to scratch me.'

'Pity it wasn't a tiger!' Helen snapped, greatly irritated by the fact that her mind was being tossed from one extreme of emotion to another. 'And it's an equal pity that your Aunt Luce, whoever she is, didn't box your ears.'

'She could never catch me. She whacked me with her walking stick more than once, though,' he murmured thoughtfully, his eyes still roaming over her beautiful, angry face. 'Mind you, I've grown some since then. Aunt Luce and I are now firm friends. She's my only family. The cat went to his Maker years ago. Died of old age and hysteria.'

Helen stared at him in astonishment, unable to work out why he was talking like that. He was probing, teasing, working her up into a turmoil, but all the time he was watching.

'I don't suppose you've been drinking again?' she asked, giving him a deeply suspicious glance.

'Sober as a judge. All this is just a matter of breaking the ice. Now that we know something about each other, conversation will be easier. You *do* intend to speak to me during the next few days, Miss Stewart?'

Helen put her spectacles back on and stared out of the window, trying to contain her rage, astonishment and her rapid pulse-rate.

'I shall behave absolutely properly. You need have no fear, Mr Forrest.'

'Well, that's nice,' he drawled. 'It sets my mind at rest, knowing that we're both civilized.'

Helen said nothing. She could not understand why he had won any prizes. Psychiatrists were supposed to be soothing. He had just turned her inside out and left her feeling wild. In all probability quite sane people would be committed to care after a few sessions with him. He had just projected his whole personality at her with very few words and it had left her jaded.

He was quite content now to sink back into his confident, unruffled silence, apparently unaware that Helen was churning inside. She didn't feel capable of facing the day now. She wasn't even sure if she was capable of getting out of the car. It infuriated her. She could have hit him.

'If it makes you feel any better,' he murmured without looking round.

'I beg your pardon?'

'I'm inviting you to take a swing at me if it will help,' he said softly.

'Nothing will help, Mr Forrest, except the passing of time,' Helen snapped, definitely sure now about his ability to read minds. 'I can manage five days, thank you.'

'If you say so, Miss Stewart.' He lapsed back into silence and Helen tried to compose her face and steady her breathing.

This was ridiculous. She never got worked up like that. She seemed to have been on the edge of temper and excitement since she had first seen him and every single bit of it was his fault. And if he thought he could pry into her mind, he could think again. She had her suspicions that Martin had something to do with this. Left to himself, Dan Forrest would never have deigned to take an interest in her.

Helen thought people would never stop coming. They had already been lined up three deep when the car dropped them off at the bookshop. There was no doubt at all about the popularity of his books and normally, Helen would have been very pleased. Books and writers were her job and she liked to see Martin's firm doing well. This wasn't normal, though, and neither was she at the moment.

'Do you think you're going to run out of his books?' she asked the two women at the counter. They were middle-aged, comfortable-looking and obviously thrilled by the event.

'Oh, no, dear. We're well stocked up. We had some idea of what to expect. He's very popular and so good, don't you think?'

54

'Er – yes,' Helen muttered. Did they imagine that every editor read every book put out by the publisher they worked for? He was nothing at all to do with her. She had not read one single word that Dan Forrest had written. She had thought about it a little guiltily when she knew what she had been expected to do, but her time was valuable and she was always too tired to read at home. She wandered round the shop and then hovered near Dan, smiling at his fans and trying to look professional.

He was totally calm, like a warm presence. It seemed to be all around him like an aura, a strange radiance that was coming from inside. She had expected him to be spoiled and demanding but he had asked for nothing at all. He made no complaints and even though he had recently been ill he seemed to be tireless. People were delighted with him. They wanted to stay and that was very obvious. He smiled and talked, putting them at their ease. Helen was the only one on edge.

Lunchtime came around. It had been stated quite categorically that Mr Forrest would be available to sign his books from nine until twelve and from two until four. The customers slackened off as twelve o'clock approached and Dan stood up and stretched like a big, powerful cat.

'Time to eat,' he said, looking at Helen. 'As I understand it, you're here to take care of me. Feed me, Miss Stewart.'

CHAPTER 3

Helen was quite ready for his attitude by now, but in spite of that, every time he looked at her, her heart jumped. It was a bit like being subjected to a series of small electric shocks, and it was keeping her in a state of nervous anxiety. It wouldn't seem to stop, because each time she had herself settled she just happened to meet his eyes and it all started over again.

'I've booked a table for you quite close by and the bill will be sent to our office,' she told him briskly. 'I'm sorry, but I won't be able to have lunch with you because I have a few other jobs to get through. I'll take you to the place and see you settled there and meet you back here just before two, if that's all right?'

She had her little speech all rehearsed and he showed no sign of surprise.

'Quite all right, Miss Stewart,' he assured her sardonically. 'Lead the way.'

She walked stiffly down the street with him, trying not to feel small at the side of his six foot two, and she then actually took him inside the restaurant and introduced him to the head waiter. She was brisk, efficient and icy. It seemed easier to survive like that. She had the feeling that she was talking too much about nothing in particular but she couldn't seem to stop.

Dan suffered it all in a silence that breathed derision. His attitude made her very painfully aware that he was there. It left her time to notice how he walked, how he stood, what his hair looked like, how his aftershave smelled, things she just didn't want to know.

'Exactly what jobs do you have to get through at this particular time, Miss Stewart?' he asked innocently as she made to leave.

'Oh, er – quite a few things. I – I never have much time.'

'Don't you eat?'

'I doubt if I'll have time today.' She looked flustered and escaped as quickly as possible, and Dan watched her hurry through the door and out into the street as if he were chasing her with an axe.

'Okay, lady, scoot,' he said under his breath. 'You've got to come back to the shop and I'll be there again. I believe you're stuck with me, like it or not.'

He frowned as he sat down to look at the menu. He was doing exactly the thing he had sworn not to do. He was taking an interest in her. And it wasn't completely professional either. She was a very beautiful woman. The more he saw of her, the more he realized that.

Those violet-blue eyes were slightly tilted at the edges like a well-bred cat's. The hair, if she would leave it alone and stop scraping it behind her ears, was a shining cloud of honey-blonde. The face was like a delicate porcelain statue, almost unreal, something painted from memory. Her appearance was so much at variance with her attitude that he could hardly keep his mind away from her. She should be sweet, gentle, and yet she bristled at the slightest thing. It was a protective shell and he knew it.

Under normal circumstances he would have gone after her right from the moment she had walked into his room at the hotel, and he knew that too. He also had to admit that, when she was there, a great shock of awareness hit him in the gut like a hammer. He was sexually attracted to her in a big way and he wasn't too pleased about it. It was the first time ever that he had wanted to reach out and touch a woman every time he saw her. He didn't even know this one, either.

She was an uneasy mixture of vulnerability and anger. There was something wrong, deep down wrong. She was carrying a burden of some sort inside that was keeping her permanently on edge, and she was tired. He could see a sad weariness on her face when she was off guard, though she was not off guard very often. Helen Stewart was a complex character. A lady with a secret. He grunted irritably and got on with his meal. The best thing to do was forget her, and the sooner this book business was over, the better.

Out of his sight, Helen dived into the nearest big store, took the escalator to the top floor and went into the self-service restaurant. She couldn't face more than a sandwich and a cup of tea and she could only face that if she was alone. Being with Dan Forrest was turning into a personal nightmare because she found it very difficult to keep her eyes from him. They just wandered to him of their own accord and, having found him, they lingered there until he looked up and seemed to be danger of spotting her.

Nobody had ever affected her like that before, and she had found herself watching his face, seeing every expression, watching his graceful hands as they reached for a book and signed it. The way he smiled up at people in that pleasant, lazy way made her feel odd inside, almost sad. Nobody had ever had such an impact on her and she was astonished that she hadn't felt it the moment she had seen him.

She made a wry face to herself as she ate her sandwich. She had been too busy misjudging him, too tied up with the past, too angry. He was very dangerous to her and she knew it. He was taking a professional interest; whether it was from sheer lack of the ability to let his mind leave things alone or because Martin had spoken to him, she didn't know. She was well aware that Martin and Margaret worried about her and slid round the problem with great care. Was she so transparent? Did the nightmare show on her face? She would have to be more careful in future, especially with Dan Forrest.

The day couldn't end soon enough for Helen. The customers and fans kept on coming, and as they slackened off towards three-thirty, Dan strolled over to charm the two ladies at the counter. And he *was* charming, Helen realized that. There was an unusual warmth that seemed to radiate from him. The customers had felt it and they had been reluctant to leave. Everybody seemed to have been hanging on to his every word.

She watched him surreptitiously. He was elegantly masculine besides being devastatingly handsome. It seemed unfair that one person should have so many physical attributes and brains as well. She found herself looking at his hands again. They were long-fingered, strong. She thought about them touching her and her colour rose as the insidious thought slid into her mind.

When she looked up guiltily he was watching her with those striking eyes and her colour rose even more. What was showing on her face now? She expected some sardonic comment but instead he said quietly, 'How about some tea, Miss Stewart? I'm sure these ladies will oblige.'

He flashed them a smile and they were instantly bubbling with enthusiasm to make tea.

'We've got some champagne,' one of them confessed quickly. 'If you would rather . . .'

'I think we'll stick with the tea, thanks,' Dan smiled. 'I got into the tea habit when I lived here years ago.' He stood chatting to them, making their day, and Helen wished herself light-years away. He was intruding into her tight little world without actually doing anything, and his unpredictable behaviour was putting her more on edge by the second. She had expected him to be frosty, to almost snarl at her after what she had done when she collected him from the airport, but he was quiet, smiling, comfortable to be with.

Someone came in to buy one of his books and he was busy for a while, but the tea duly arrived and Helen sat down with a sigh of relief, wondering if it was so bad after all that he could read her mind. She had really needed the tea, and she had the feeling that he had known without being told. She glanced up and he gave her a smile that almost took her breath away. She was too mesmerized even to smile back.

When they were ready to leave Dan produced a white rose for each of the ladies at the counter and presented them with a flourish. They were thrilled, in fact they gasped with delight, and Helen could see that the roses would be cherished, kept alive as long as possible and then probably pressed in a book – one of his, of course . . .

'How did you do that?' she asked as they went out to the car that arrived exactly on time to collect them. She hadn't really meant to speak to him because she had decided he was too dangerous and that any thoughtless word might alert him, but she was too intrigued to let this pass.

'I got them at lunchtime.'

'But I never saw you with any roses this afternoon.'

'I kept one up each trouser leg,' he assured her solemnly. She just stared at him wildly and he grinned at her innocent astonishment. 'As a matter of fact, they came in cute little boxes that I could keep in my jacket and produce like white rabbits,' he confessed. 'I think my pockets are a bit wet but all in all it was worth it to see their faces. They're "older ladies"; I imagine they've read my books.'

'They have,' Helen said thoughtlessly. 'They think you're good, little short of wonderful. I must say I was surprised at their enthusiasm. Your books are violent.'

'And sexy, Miss Stewart, don't forget sexy. That's what draws the older ladies.'

'But that's disgusting, to imagine that they . . .'

'Disgusting? Is that what you think of sex?' he asked softly, and Helen caught herself before she walked into the trap again. Her ingenuous chatter stopped abruptly.

'Don't start your professional prying again, Mr Forrest,' she warned stiffly. 'I'm fully in possession of my faculties and nothing to do with you at all.'

'Force of habit.' Dan murmured with an altogether artificial look of regret on his face. 'Sheer force of habit. Bone-deep.'

The damned eyes were laughing at her and Helen turned away with a mutter of annoyance. She was not quite sure what annoyed her most, his constant probing or the way her skin shivered at the lazy amusement in his eyes.

* * *

62

Back at his hotel, Dan threw his jacket down on the bed and dropped into a chair, staring straight ahead in a tight-lipped manner. He was irritated, seriously rattled. He had chatted to customers and signed books like somebody on automatic pilot because most of the time he had been watching Helen Stewart. He had been watching her wander around the shop, chat to the two women in charge of the place, glance idly at other books and then come back to stand dutifully by him.

And everything she did had been that, merely dutiful. No smile, no softening; she had just been a cool professional woman who had been detailed, much against her will, to look after him. Considering that he hadn't done a thing wrong it was damned frustrating. She had made a mistake at the airport and had decided that she didn't like him because of that. She was going to continue to be an icy beauty for the whole of his time with her.

And she was beautiful. Her beauty fascinated him. Once or twice she had taken off the huge spectacles and rested her eyes and the transformation had been staggering. The brisk, heartless career-woman had turned into another being, vulnerable, transparent, desirable. He had been more than annoyed by the desire that had instantly pooled in his groin. And the effect had lingered. He had been ridiculously relieved when she had pushed the spectacles back on her dainty nose and assumed her businesslike air again.

He had to face this tomorrow and it would be worse. There was an appearance at one of the big stores and a damned cocktail party in the evening. Fortunately, Martin would be there and with any luck so would Margaret, but it wouldn't stop his eyes from drinking in the sight of Helen Stewart.

He would have rung up Antonia and taken her with him but he was supposed to escort the prickly Miss Stewart. She would be bristling with resentment and his highly charged male hormones would be getting in the way. He would tell Martin that he could take care of himself in future and get a taxi to wherever he was going, because if this continued it was going to get uncomfortable in more ways than one.

He went to shower and then sat at the phone and rang Antonia to bring his mind back into gear. She wasn't there and he slammed the phone down in frustration. He was supposed to be enjoying himself but he wasn't enjoying this one little bit. The trip to London had been a disaster from beginning to end and now he was getting ensnared by an ice maiden. The trouble was that he was more than ready to be ensnared, even if all he got was frostbite.

When he found himself walking round the room like a caged animal he picked up his jacket and went out, locking the door behind him. He couldn't stay in the hotel all evening, bouncing off the walls. He should have taken up Martin's offer to stay with them but he hadn't expected to be restless in London. He had expected to have Antonia's company, for one thing. For another, he had not expected to be angry, puzzled and sexually aroused by a prickly female with a face like an angel and a tongue like a wasp.

Helen landed flat on her back on the mat with one of the boys standing over her triumphantly. She looked up at him with a pained expression on her face.

'You wanna watch that particular throw, Helen,' he grinned, reaching down to jerk her to her feet. 'You're trying to use force and you're too light-weight. You should have used my weight to throw me. Wanna try it again?'

'No way! The breath is still leaving my body. That was ferocious.'

'Well, you're supposed to be good at this. Some-body attacks you, they're not going to say, "Beg pardon," and help you up. They're gonna go for the kill.'

The smile died on Helen's face and she had to struggle to make it return. Kill. The word sent waves through her that she could never cope with. There were words, key words that triggered off both panic and pain, and there was the fear that never went away.

'You okay?'

'Perfectly. It's time to go anyway. I might try that again tomorrow.'

'I'll not go easy on you.'

'Better not. I learn quickly.' She made a smiling escape and collected her things, keeping her head down, horrified at the way just the one word could shake her world so violently.

'Want to come for coffee?' Jack came up after she had showered and obviously expected to have her company, but she shook her head with regret.

'I'm up to my ears. I really have to go straight home.'

'Okay. I'll alert the taxi. How did you get on with Dan Forrest?' he enquired conversationally as he walked along with her later and went outside to meet the taxi.

'All right,' she lied quickly. The mention of him brought the flush of heat to her skin, made her scalp tighten. It took away the other feelings as if they had never been there, but the way Dan Forrest affected her was no more welcome than the fear she had been feeling a few moments ago or the dread she lived with daily.

She told herself firmly that she was too much in control to be feeling like that about any man, but it didn't stop her hands from going limp at the thought of him. It didn't stop her eyes from following him when he wasn't looking. She kept telling herself very firmly that it was ridiculous but it didn't seem to make much difference. She was desperate to get home, to be able to shut the door and hide away from everyone and everything. The quiet American was an added problem but he would be going away. Her other problem would never go.

Shutting herself in the house when she got home did little good, though. There was no hiding from herself. Wherever she went she took the past with her, and it was there forever.

Kill! She had been the one who had made the trip to the hospital mortuary to identify him. She had been the one who had stood there and nodded her head, too afraid to speak in case she shouted out her joy at the sight of him lying there lifeless.

'My stepfather. Yes, that's him.'

She could still hear her own voice now, still hear the control she had mustered. She could still remember the kindness of the people around her and her own knowledge that she didn't deserve any kindness at all because she had wanted to scream out that she was glad, glad, glad.

Somewhere, some unknown person had done what she had wanted to do for a very long time. Granville Burton had been beaten to death and she hoped that the God who would have punished her would let his executioner go free. He had beaten plenty of other people and now he had met his match. She had looked down at him with nothing but revulsion in her heart but nobody had known.

She had been filled with a wild mixture of guilt and joy, fear and delirious happiness. He could never come back now. But the happiness was short-lived. They had not told her everything. He had not died from the beating. Someone had come to Granville Burton later and delivered the *coup de grâce*, delivered it many times, ten stab wounds and the first had been the real cause of his death.

Her mind had spun back to the past then and seen a face, a face she had not seen for years. 'I'll kill him! One day, when he least expects it, I'll be there.'

That memory had come back later in her life when events triggered it into action. That was when Helen started to go out at night, searching, watching, waiting. That was when her secret look hold of her whole life and left little time for anything else. She lived with it, ate with it, slept with it, waking in the night from bad dreams to face it yet again.

Helen forced off the tiredness of a day of tension with Dan Forrest, of an evening spent making herself go through a gruelling routine of attacks and falls, and began to get ready. It was night, dark. She had to search, to face the hostile streets. Maybe tonight she would solve all her problems.

Dan saw the woman just ahead. A few quick steps and he could be right behind her but he held back, infinitely wary. He had not forgotten his burst of awareness of physical danger the night before and he dropped his pace to match hers, the slow, measured, prowling steps. She passed a particularly well-lit window and he had a good look at her. She was wearing exactly what she had been wearing last night, looking as if she had never been anywhere but walking these streets since then.

Her hair was almost too black, brilliant in the lights, and the band on her head was velvet. It was quite clearly defined against the shine of her hair. It was as incongruous as everything else about her. It hadn't rained for ages, the pavements were dry, but she still wore the black plastic raincoat and as she moved he could see the dress, almost indecently short and velvet, black velvet.

From behind she looked just like any other hooker, a type that was recognizable in every city in the world. But sheer instinct and professional certainty told him she was not just any other lady of the night. He would have liked to get a look at her face from close up but caution warned him to put that idea right out of his head. He was following her for the same reason he had followed her last night to exercise the brain cells, because he was bored, because it took his mind off what he really wanted.

He had eaten at a small bistro just off Regent Street and the dim lights and subdued voices had quietened the unusual turmoil inside for a while. Normally he was comfortable inside, an inner assurance that went partly with his profession and partly with the man he was. There was no inner calm tonight. There had been no real inner calm all day.

And he was perfectly aware of the reason for his agitated state. He needed a woman, and not just any woman. He had thought of ringing Antonia from the bistro but he had not made the call. The woman he wanted was probably tucked up in bed with a manuscript, unless she was tossing somebody on their head in a gym.

He could see her in his mind's eye, pushing those ridiculous spectacles higher on her dainty nose, dragging the beautiful hair behind her ears like an uncomfortable schoolgirl. He had had a hard time this afternoon not to get up and run his fingers through the thick blonde tresses until they stood out tangled and wild from her face.

He couldn't get her out of his mind and she hated him. Christ, she hated him for something *she* had done! To add to any other problems she had, there was now a new one: guilt at the way she had simply left him to live or die at the hotel. He wanted to shake her, kiss her, make love to her until she cried out for him to stop, and it had happened so quickly that he hadn't worked out a suitable defence.

The effect she had on him was not only uncomfortable, it was infuriating. He had never felt like that before with any woman. He was too damned clever to let it happen. This woman was probably a case for clinical help and she was driving him wild. He had to suffer this for a good many more days too. And what was he doing about it? He was following a mysterious hooker in black like Inspector Clouseau on the trail of a robber and he was *still* thinking about Helen Stewart!.

The woman walked into a bar and he hung around outside, watching through the only clear part of the window until he saw her sit at a table with a drink. Even then he couldn't see her face clearly. He knew it was beautiful but she still had those dark glasses on and the fringe, weighed down by the band, was heavy and deep. She settled, crossing long, sleek legs, and he walked into the bar and ordered a drink.

He was careful not to look at her as he passed her table, and once again every instinct came to full alert. She was dangerous, he needed no notes or consultation to tell him that. He just knew it inside, and he had been in this game too long to mistake an instinctive reaction.

She never glanced at him and he sat well away from her, watching, summing her up, with part of his mind still on Helen Stewart and the physical ache inside that was not a hunger which food could satisfy. The speed of this attraction to her left him feeling stunned, raw.

He concentrated his mind on the woman he had followed. If he were coding this woman in his notes he would have called her Black Velvet. He let his glance run over her, his mind filing everything away. How was it that she aroused not the slightest bit of interest in him in the physical sense? She was undoubtedly beautiful in spite of a rather bizarre streak, but she was as alien as a Martian and he knew she was more dangerous than any thug with an iron bar.

What was she? Who was she? Could she be a policewoman on a stake-out? Was that why the man had legged it out of her sight so rapidly? He could just imagine her looking through those dark glasses at the poor jerk and saying, 'Police, buster. On your way.'

He was certain that she was searching, looking for somebody or something. Her eyes scanned every man who came into the bar and then looked away with no further interest. She was, as he suddenly realized, very strategically positioned. No doubt he had received the same scrutiny when he had entered, but whoever she was looking for, it was not somebody like him. He was profoundly grateful for that.

A man came in, looked round and spotted her and Dan could almost have written the scenario that followed. The man never took his eyes from her while he was being served and then he sauntered to her table with his drink and sat down, apparently not at all bothered when she ignored him totally.

After a second, he leaned forward and spoke to her. She didn't answer at first, but the man persisted, and when she finally did answer, the man shot back in his seat so fast that the legs of the chair grated on the floor. He snarled something at her and stood quickly to move away. He went back to the bar, his face red, and Dan stood slowly to follow him. If he was going to find out anything at all, this was likely to be his only chance.

'No luck with the hooker?' he asked conversationally.

'The what?' The man looked up aggressively and then changed his mind when he took in Dan's size and physical appearance.

'The hooker.' Dan nodded towards her where she sat with her back to them and the man understood. He leaned closer to Dan.

'She's bloody crazy. Don't try your luck there.'

'She didn't want a client?'

'She threatened to kill me.'

Dan stared at him in disbelief, although he had suspected something like that the night before and then put it out of his mind as being too ridiculous to contemplate.

'You're joking,' he muttered as his mind tried to fit this new information into a well-oiled groove.

'I'm not!' the man protested. 'She never raised her voice. You know how they are with their screeching voices, that sort? Well, she isn't. She whispered at me.'

'Whispered?' Dan looked at him with obvious doubt and the man grasped his arm.

'Whispered! As God is my witness. She told me to get away from her and if I said anything else to her she would wait for me outside and kill me. She called me a filthy pig. Why the hell is she on the game if she doesn't want a pick-up?'

Dan had already asked himself that question. He looked round and she was gone. He dismissed the idea of a police stakeout, a woman private detective, a wife trying to trap her husband and every other thought that had come into his mind. The only thought he allowed to stay in his head was danger, real danger, and the fact that she was a woman did nothing to cancel out the reality of it. He had dealt with dangerous women before, although none of them had been quite so bizarre, nor had they been free to roam the streets.

He left the bar but he turned towards his hotel and decided to forget his file headed 'Black Velvet'. He was not so bored that he had to follow a lunatic. He already had his own clients and he was not in the business of hunting for more. And if he had to deal with her he had the uneasy feeling he would want it to be from the other side of some solid bars, and that action would be a first for him.

As to his other problem, it was still there, banked down but definitely still there. It was a question of, 'Physician, heal thyself.' He walked back to his hotel and phoned Antonia. This time she answered and he ordered the champagne in readiness for her arrival. She liked champagne and expected it. As far as he was concerned she could have a whole bucketful.

The hotel staff had seen her before when he had been in London. She would come straight up to his suite without any problem. Besides, she was not the sort of woman anyone would challenge, although they might just get out the red carpet and roll it in front of her. She really was something.

Antonia Wingfield was there in half an hour and Dan grinned as he let her into the room. She looked like a duchess. He ought to be able to fathom how her brain worked but he had never succeeded. To be quite truthful he had never even tried. He was always amused by her ways and left it at that. All he knew about her was that she came from a very good family and he had privately decided that it was probably some sort of aristocracy. He was sure she was not called Wingfield. She'd probably read that name in a book.

'Well, darling? How are you?' she asked as she stepped close to him.

'Fine.' He pulled her into his arms and looked down at her. 'Have you missed me?'

'God, no! I'm much too busy for that sort of thing.' She smiled up at him and Dan found himself grinning. The only difference, he realized, between Antonia and those ladies of the night was that she was class all the way through and she liked sex. As far as he had been able to make out over the years he had known her, sex was her only hobby.

'So, what's been happening?' She sat down on the settee and crossed elegant legs. 'Have you been here long?'

'A few days.' Dan opened the champagne and poured two glasses, a little disturbed to find that the thought of sex with Antonia suddenly bored him.

'Tell me about it.' She patted the settee beside her, telling him where to sit, looking more at home in this suite than he did himself, and Dan wondered how she was going to take it when he told her that he was not interested in bed at all. She always worked up to it gracefully, but she invariably worked up to it. She wasn't here to listen to his woes and sympathize about the impossibility of his utterly mad desire for Helen Stewart.

And it *was* mad. Every time he saw her it was like a hard blow to the solar plexus and it was impossible to remain detached and faintly amusing with desire coiling and twisting inside him. Right now, at this moment, late or not, he wanted to go and find her. He had as much chance of sleeping as flying off the roof.

Antonia kicked off her shoes and lifted her legs, resting them across his thighs as he sat down beside her, and although Dan absently stroked her ankles,

75

nothing happened inside except that he realized he had never actually studied Helen Stewart's ankles. He had been too taken with her face and hidden vulnerability. He wondered if there was passion hidden too?

'All right. Who is she?'

Antonia withdrew her tempting legs and curled them beneath her. She looked at him over the top of her champagne glass and Dan was relieved to see that she was taking this well, amusement but no annoyance.

'Her name is Helen. Helen Stewart,' he said quietly.

'Do I know her?'

'It's unlikely. I doubt if she would move in your circle.' He glanced across at her wryly. 'Not that I know anything about your circle.'

'The very best, darling.'

'Why do you do it?' he asked. Something he had never given any thought to before.

'I'm good at it. I enjoy it. Sometimes it lasts one night only, sometimes a week, sometimes even longer – a year.'

'Like last year?' He fixed golden eyes on her and she nodded, meeting his gaze squarely. 'What happened to him?'

'He went overseas. I nearly got burned there.'

'Did his wife go with him?' Dan asked, and she frowned at him.

'There are never wives. I'm not a home-wrecker, Dan. And I don't do it for money, just in case that thought is flickering in your brilliantly agile mind.'

'What was his name?'

'He's not dead, darling, just gone, and it's still a bit painful to speak about if you don't mind. His first name is Jefferson.'

'No kidding? He's American?'

'He's true blue British. You are the only American of my acquaintance. Are you going to psychoanalyse me?'

'Not you.' Dan grinned at her and she smiled back, sipping her drink.

'So tell me about this girl.'

'She's a woman.'

'And you want her but she's unavailable.'

'That's about the size of it.'

'So tell me anyway. We have to do something to pass the time. Card games bore me and I'm not walking out of here immediately. It would shatter my reputation with the hotel staff.'

'You're one of the good ones, Antonia.'

'I know it. I don't need my ego boosting. Talk, Mr Forrest.'

Much later, when she left, Dan felt as if he knew his own trade better. He knew how satisfying it was to just talk to somebody about troubles. Not that Helen was a trouble. In a very short time she was becoming an obsession and he was very good at treating obsessive behaviour. But not his own, apparently.

It occurred to him that while he had been talking to Antonia the elusive Miss Stewart had become Helen in his mind. If he called her that by accident she would probably slap his face. Tomorrow at the book-signing he could pretend to ignore her if he really got a grip on himself. There was, however, the cocktail party to follow. Ignoring her there would be impossible.

Getting ready for the cocktail party next evening, Helen realized that she was not at all happy. It did not need any detective work to discover why, either. Dan Forrest had been cold as ice with her all the time they were together, this morning and afternoon.

The amused disdain was gone. The forays into her psyche had stopped. Today he had treated her like a colleague, and she had definitely felt like a colleague who was inferior, way down the ladder. Beside him she had felt intellectually stunted because he had lapsed into that self-contained silence of his, and any remarks or questions he had aimed at her had been very proper and very academic, skating on the edge of highbrow. He had left her feeling like an underling. Today she had really known what he was and who he was: a man who was completely outside her sphere.

She certainly didn't feel like scoffing at his money-making thrillers now. If he chose to do that, then she was quite sure he typed one out in a morning with no effort at all and then got on with his real work. She hoped he wasn't going to be so aloof and superior tonight, because she would have to be a little more sociable whether she liked it or not. She had to pick him up in just over an hour and she was dreading it.

So was Dan. He tied his bow-tie for the fourth time, got it wrong again and glared at himself in the mirror.

'Idiot!' he snapped at his reflection. 'You're a goddamned idiot and you deserve anything that's coming to you. Stop behaving like a boy and forget her. You don't know a damned thing about her.'

He finally got the tie right and strode across the room to get a drink, glancing at his watch as he went. She would be here in twenty minutes, and if she thought he'd been drinking she would be all stiff and icy. He shrugged and poured himself a drink anyway; she was always stiff and icy and his behaviour today would have made her freeze up even more. In fact, she seemed to have been freezing right before his eyes as the day progressed. He wanted to get near her, wanted her with an urgency that astonished him, and yet he had deliberately frozen her out. He couldn't stand any more of these bookish jaunts and he was most certainly not looking forward to tonight.

One thing, though – Martin would be there and so would Margaret. He could talk to them and try to ignore Helen and the disastrous effect she had on him. If she froze even more it would at least be better than if he lost all sense of proportion and pulled her on to his lap.

He had felt like doing that all day. And he wondered how she would have taken it if he had said, 'Come and sit on my knee, honey, while I sign these damned books.' She would have fought him to the last breath.

In retrospect, talking to Antonia about her hadn't been such a good idea. It had brought it all out into the open – which was exactly what it was supposed to do, and if he didn't know that, who did? Having it in the open made it worse. He was getting to feel wounded by the thought of her, throbbing with a need that was beyond anything he had ever known, and with no chance at all of doing a damned thing about it.

Before he could go down to the foyer and wait for the car, she was there early, knocking on the door, and he jerked it open to stare at her, feeling furious with both of them when his muscles tensed in the now familiar way.

'The car is here,' she finally managed a little breathlessly, staring back at him like a scared cat.

'I imagine it is, since you came in it,' he said sardonically, unreasonably irritated by her obvious unease and more than irritated by his own feelings. 'Come in. I'll get my jacket.'

He motioned her inside and walked across the room to pick up his jacket, seeing the rest of his drink on the table and tossing it off in one go. He never tasted it but he was not about to leave it there like a guilty school-boy, hoping she wouldn't notice. What had he expected but unease? He had been treating her badly all day. She was staring at him with those tilted eyes. And he forced himself to observe her.

It was a mistake of major proportions.

CHAPTER 4

She had left the spectacles off for the evening and her hair was not scraped back, it was like a cloud of sunlight around her face. The hammer hit him in the solar plexus again and desire snaked through him like a warm river, twisting him up inside even more with no prior warning.

She looked lovely, flawless; the short, cloudy blue dress she wore was perfect for her slender figure and perfect for her angel's face. There was something about her that was almost dreamlike and he wanted to stride across and lift her up, hold her close but he could do nothing at all. He was in a rage with himself. He resented the effect she was having on him. He wasn't used to feeling rattled and powerless.

She was staring at the glass in his hand too, as if it terrified her, as if it was hypnotizing her, and he put it down on the table with a bang that seemed to echo right through the room.

'I have not been drinking. I am not drunk!' he said almost savagely.

'I didn't suggest that you were.' Her voice sounded small, as scared as her face, and he took a deep breath, unreasonable anger and unreasonable desire fighting together inside him. Some damned psychiatrist he was. He could have handled something like this with one hand behind his back even before he had taken any sort of degree. He was behaving like a boy with the first taste of desire and he knew it.

Her obvious distress stopped him in his tracks, though, and drowned his anger. She had arrived scared and he was setting out to scare her even more.

'I'm sorry,' he said quietly. 'You don't have to put up with this.'

'I think I do,' she managed tremulously. 'It's part of my job.'

'For God's sake! Having someone snarl at you is not part of your job. You were ready to take my head off from the first moment I saw you. Why aren't you taking it off now?'

'We have to go, Mr Forrest,' she said in an agitated voice, backing away from him. 'The car is outside and we're supposed to be meeting Martin before we go into the hotel. He wants us all to walk in together because there are a lot of people there, waiting to see you.'

He swore under his breath and made an exaggerated sweep of his hand towards the door.

'Then let's leave at once by all means, Miss Stewart. Writers should never keep either their fans or their publisher waiting. Thank you for reminding me. How would I manage without you?'

She went out quickly and he followed, snapping the door shut and walking to the lift with her. She was keeping as far away from him as possible. In fact, he had the impression that if she had been able, she would have flattened herself to the wall to put more distance between them than ever. Dan gritted his teeth. This was going to be some wonderful evening, and he only had himself to blame, because acting naturally with her seemed to be beyond him. She needed calm reassurance and he was anything but calm. He was wanting to nuzzle the smooth skin of her neck, to run his hands through her hair, to kiss the softly trembling lips until they were red as cherries.

'Dan!'

Margaret Newman gave him a great hug as soon as she saw him and Helen felt a shiver run over her skin when she saw his arms go around her. They were strong, powerful arms, the sort of arms that would protect you and hold you safe. Nobody had ever protected her. Any protection she had ever had was the protection she had contrived for herself, the disguise she assumed, the hard shell she had surrounded herself with. She turned her face away and Martin noticed at once.

'Are you cold, Helen?'

'I'm fine, thank you. It – it was just a little shiver running over my skin.'

'Oh, I know that sort. When it happens to me, it scares me. My mother used to say it was someone walking over your grave – horrible thought. It lingers in the mind. People used to be very morbid in those days,' Margaret stated. 'What a lovely dress, Helen. You look really beautiful, doesn't she, Martin?'

'As ever,' Martin said, winking at Helen.

'Don't you think so, Dan?' Margaret persisted, and Helen shivered again as the golden eyes were turned on her.

'Like an angel.' He didn't sound sarcastic but Helen knew he was being as disdainful as ever. She looked rapidly away.

'Thank you,' she muttered. 'Should we go in, do you think?'

'Businesslike,' Martin laughed. 'Always businesslike, our Helen. Come on, love,' he added, offering his arm to Margaret. 'I have to take you in. Dan is the official guest and gets to escort the office beauty.'

'Impudence,' Margaret snorted. 'I know there's an insult in there somewhere. Just you watch out when I fathom it.'

They walked in front and Helen almost shrank away from Dan. The thought of him touching her at all was enough to panic her because she didn't know how she would react. She was supposed to go in with him but she wanted to run and catch the others.

'Shall we follow, Miss Stewart?' He was watching her, the golden eyes probing again, and Helen managed to smile and nod. He didn't offer his arm; instead he took hold of her own arm lightly, but there was enough sensuous force in his touch to have her shivering again as tingles ran over her skin.

'Oh, please!' she whispered as the excited, frightening rush of feeling hit her. She hadn't meant to say anything. The words just came out by themselves.

'I don't bite indiscriminately, Miss Stewart,' Dan murmured coolly. 'It's safe to walk beside me. When we get inside you can hide as quickly as you like.'

'I'm sorry. I don't want to hide. I – I know I'm behaving oddly, badly.'

'Why?' He almost breathed the word and she bit at her lip nervously.

'I – I don't know. It's probably because I don't take compliments very well. I never know what to say.'

'A big smile will get you by in most places,' Dan assured her in the same soft voice.

'Is that what women do when you pay them a compliment?'

'I rarely pay compliments to women. They usually know precisely how good they look and normally it sounds a little trite. Tonight was my very first compliment.'

'I'm sorry if it broke some sort of record,' Helen said shakily. 'I know Margaret made you say it.'

He held the door open for her and looked down at her as she stepped into the bright lights of the foyer.

'Nobody makes me either say or do anything, Miss Stewart. I normally think for myself. You look like an angel. I can only repeat my remark.'

They stepped into the room where the cocktail party was being held and it was like being wrenched into another world. After the quietness of Dan's voice and her own subdued murmurs, the noise was tantamount to a physical assault and Helen was shakily glad. His voice had been soft as smoke, almost penetrating her skin. In this room they were drenched in sound and it was much safer.

'What do we do now?' Dan asked wryly in an entirely different voice, and she glanced up at him, knowing he was back to goading. The smoky-dark manner had gone as if it had never been and she felt like a fool. He knew exactly what to do and she knew it. In the first place he had done this many times over in several countries and for several reasons. He was a prize-winning author of four important books on psychiatry and had been fêted the world over.

She had been reading up on him during the last two days and she had found out another thing that she didn't really want to know. He was a professor, the chair of psychiatry at one of the top American universities. It should really be Professor Forrest. There was no doubt at all that he could see through stone and he was amusing himself at her expense, going from seductive to taunting with no pause in between.

'We circulate, as I'm sure you know,' she said tightly.

'Why do you imagine that I know what to do?' he asked sardonically, without even glancing down at her. 'I'm a simple American boy.'

He was calmly looking round the room and Helen felt her temper rising to overcome her tension. He enjoyed tying her up in knots. He was amusing himself, passing the time by winding her up.

'You're a college professor with so much prestige that judges listen to you,' she snapped. 'The police call for your help. You lecture all over the world. You were probably doing this sort of thing when I was still at school.'

'How old are you?' He still didn't bother to look at her and Helen snapped again.

'Twenty-five,' she informed him furiously.

'I'm thirty-six,' he mused in his sardonic way. 'I suppose it's possibly true that I was doing this sort of thing when you were still in school. I'm what is called an older man.'

'You're what is called an inverted snob,' Helen flared and before he could answer she walked off and left him. If he didn't like it, he knew what he could do. She had been in a panic about coming here tonight, just in case he so much as looked at her nicely, and he was just the same, taunting, sarcastic, *patronizing*!

It was Margaret who finally tracked her down and took her in hand.

'I assume that Dan is annoying you?' she said when she had Helen securely at her side. 'Don't let him get to you. He can be a mocking devil when he likes. He slides out of one character into another just

87

for fun, or, as he says, for the hell of it. Right now he's being the reluctant author of racy books.'

'It looks like his real character to me,' Helen muttered crossly.

She was watching him and although she was watching him unwillingly, she couldn't seem to stop. He was standing with two women who were chattering away to him in an animated, adoring fashion and Helen could see his amused boredom from right across the room. He had a cool cheek! She didn't know how he got away with it.

'We've known Dan for a long time,' Margaret assured her quietly, her eyes also on him. 'This is his escape mechanism, the popular books he writes, the act he puts on. In what you might call "real life" he lives with a lot of pressure, his own and other people's. Something has to give him a break from it or he would probably go mad because of carrying so many problems on his shoulders. He seems to have devised this way of slipping into a character without pause. If he ever bothers to be himself while he's here in England you'll get a very big shock.'

'You mean he's worse?' Helen asked irritably.

'I mean he's wonderful. He's a very special man. You get this great desire to tell him every little secret because you just know he'll set everything right. It's quite astonishing really. Jenny, of course, is madly in love with him.'

'She's only fifteen,' Helen reminded her, her tight face relaxing at the thought of Margaret and Martin's precocious daughter.

'I know,' Margaret sighed. 'I wish Dan would come over here to live permanently. When he leaves she'll fall in love with someone else who might just take her seriously. It's been the same since she was thirteen. I age several years when Dan goes back home to America. Luckily the teachers at her school are all women. The last time Dan was here we tried to get her to call him uncle. That was a big mistake. Her reaction was to walk out of the room, put on lipstick, march back in and sit on his knee.'

'How did he take to that?' Helen laughed.

'He was in his racy author mode. He tickled her until she screamed and returned to childhood. Then he took her for a walk. When they came back she was sucking an ice lolly and skipping to keep up with him, chattering away quite normally. I felt years younger. Dan showed me a few grey hairs. He said it was stress from the afternoon.'

Helen found herself looking at him with warmer eyes as she realized how little she knew of him. But of course, once again she had acted rashly, let her tongue run away with her, antagonized him. She couldn't apologize again and she would not. Anyway, however he treated Jenny, he had been awful to *her*.

Martin looked up and signalled to them urgently and Helen felt her heart take off wildly. Martin was with Dan and a few other people and there was a lot of excited talk that didn't seem to be centred on Dan but he was there all the same and she didn't want to go close to him. Margaret went across and

89

Helen had to follow, though she did it very reluctantly.

'Have you heard?' Martin said as soon as they were close enough to hear. 'There's been a murder!'

'I can't see why you're so excited about it,' Margaret protested sharply. 'That's terrible news and nothing to be eager about.'

'I'm not enjoying it,' Martin assured her in an offended voice. 'You never let me finish, Mo. I'm not eager, I'm shocked. It was right here.'

'In this hotel?' Margaret asked in a horrified voice.

'Near enough. You know that little lane by the right of the main front entrance? It was up there.'

'What happened?' Margaret wanted to know, and everybody seemed to try to answer at once.

'It was a man. He was stabbed.'

Helen felt the ground start to sway beneath her feet. Her chest tightened as if a heavy band was being wrapped around it. Heat engulfed her and then cold. She felt sick.

Stabbed. Guilt flooded her whole being. She could see the body again, the bruising, the cuts on his face. They had never shown her the stab wounds but it would be the same, always the same and it would never end. She had been here, all dressed up, being normal, and all the time, out in the darkness . . .

'Helen!'

She could dimly hear Dan's voice and when his hand came to her arm she didn't try to shrug him

90

off. She didn't seem to have the strength, and fright made her want to turn to him for assistance. In spite of the state she was in she could feel the warm strength of him, calming, protecting, safe.

He pulled her away from the small crowd and she went like a sleepwalker, her legs barely holding her up. The turmoil in her head was drowning out sound and all she was aware of was the steadying hand on her arm and her terrible desire for comfort.

'Drink this.'

When the room stopped spinning she found herself backed into a corner with Dan's tall frame hiding her from prying eyes. It made a safe haven for her and she didn't try to move out of it.

He was holding a brandy to her lips and Helen took an unwary gulp before it hit her. She started to cough and struggled to breathe as the fiery liquid slid down her throat, and Dan just waited until she had herself steady. He never moved from his protective position. He never spoke. He was just *there*, as if she had all his attention for a long as she needed it.

The warmth of the drink brought some colour back to her face and she looked up at him gratefully.

'Thank you,' she whispered. 'I felt faint for a minute.'

'I know. Are you all right now?' He spoke quietly and she nodded, giving him another grateful glance and then avoiding his eyes. There was an alert stillness about him, but all the same she felt so secure. If she could tell him he would make things all right, but she could never tell anyone.

'That's never happened to me before. I thought I was going to fall,' she said shakily.

'I noticed. There was no need to be afraid. I wouldn't have let you fall.' His voice was dark and soothing and the astonishing eyes were suddenly warm, molten gold. There was a momentary glow of flame in them and she felt safe, safer than she had felt for a very long time, safer than she had felt in her life. It was fleeting, possibly imagined, but the effect it had on her was steadying and powerful.

'Thank you,' she whispered, staring up at him.

He just nodded and took her arm again to lead her back to the others but she wasn't ready to go yet. She was in a secure refuge with him. She needed him some more and didn't want to leave the safety he had made for her. In this brilliantly lit room there was nothing to fear but she was afraid all the same. Her feet were reluctant to move from him. She wanted to cling to him.

'Please. Not yet. Will you keep me here with you for just a minute more?' she asked.

'The longer we stay away, the more obvious it will be. We should join them before they notice anything,' he advised softly, tightening his hand on her arm.

'They must have noticed already.'

'They're too interested in the news,' he murmured. 'In any case, you simply felt faint. It was the heat. That should hold them.'

'I wanted to stay here with you,' Helen confessed in little more than a whisper.

'You can stay as long as you like,' he told her softly. He moved so that she could see the room. He simply stood beside her but he kept his hand warmly on her arm. 'Nobody is interested,' he pointed out. 'They're too taken with the news. Even Martin and Margaret aren't looking for you and that should tell you how your little feeling of faintness has gone unnoticed. Normally they fuss over you, don't they?'

'Yes. But I never ask them to,' Helen said defensively.

'You would never have to,' he assured her in the same soft voice. 'It would be very easy to fuss over you, a difficult habit to break.'

He glanced down at her and smiled but there was no sarcasm. He looked away again and simply stood there. He didn't ask any questions, didn't even look at her now, and Helen felt herself relax. She was almost back to normal because of Dan, almost back to herself. The secret buried itself inside her and went far into the background where it lived.

'I'm ready,' she said firmly, and by the time they joined the others she *was* completely ready. Dan glanced down at her intently and then let her go, his hand sliding from her arm like a gentle caress of praise.

'Good girl,' he said softly, and went to join Martin.

Later, as they all managed to escape, Martin invited them both for dinner in the hotel dining room. They had been able to leave earlier than they had expected because the news of the murder so close at hand had left most people just talking to each other and Dan had quietly backed away from the limelight.

'I'm really tired, Martin,' Helen said quickly when he issued the invitation. 'If you don't mind, I'd much rather go home. I do hope you haven't booked a place for me?'

'No booking. Spur-of-the-moment decision. We got away much sooner than I expected.'

'Then count me out too,' Dan said. 'This book business is exhausting. I doubt if I'll write any more.'

'If that's a threat it's a good one,' Martin assured him drily. 'You bring in the money very nicely.'

'Then pander to my wishes,' Dan suggested in amusement. 'Set me free this one time.'

'Who could refuse such a request?' Martin asked. 'I'll have to put up with you, Mo.'

'Then I'll go with Helen and leave you to it,' Dan smiled and gave Margaret a quick peck on the cheek. 'Enjoy yourself.'

He led Helen out of the hotel and, at the car, took charge without asking her opinion.

'Take Miss Stewart home first,' he ordered as they got in. 'You can drop me off at my hotel later.'

'But I should see to you. I mean I'm supposed to be . . .'

'Chaperoning me? Not tonight, Helen,' Dan stated quietly. 'This is not one of our afternoon jaunts. It's dark. I'll do the chaperoning on this occasion.'

He nodded strictly at the chauffeur and the car slid noiselessly into the traffic.

'Because of the murder?' Helen asked faintly, not daring to look at him.

'Because you're afraid,' he corrected. 'And don't bother to deny it, Helen. I'm an old hand at this game.'

She didn't bother to deny it. It would have been useless. She was afraid now and she would be even more afraid when he left and the car went out of sight. She felt the loneliness of fear, the loneliness of failure and a deep dread of the future. There was nobody to tell, no one to share her secret.

The driver knew where she lived. He had picked her up each day and she was glad of the security afforded by the huge car and the man at her side. She wanted to sit closer to Dan and absorb his strength but there could be no security from the thoughts in her head. The memories lingered and would always linger. Her reaction to Martin's news this evening had proved to her that she would never be free.

The car drew to a halt outside her house and Helen looked up at the darkened windows. It was a small house in a street but she was proud of it. She had struggled to buy it and it was a monthly struggle to keep it but it was her place where nobody intruded. She wished that, just this once, Dan were coming in with her.

'If you want to tell me anything, tell me now,' Dan said quietly. He was watching her in the shadowy warmth of the big car and she wanted to tell him. She needed the strength she could feel radiating from him. There was nothing to tell him, though, nothing to tell anyone. There was only the guilt, the memories, the searching, the fear inside as soon as darkness came.

'There's nothing,' she answered, unaware of the weariness in her voice.

'All right.' Dan grasped her hand as she prepared to leave. 'Just tell me one thing, and be truthful or I don't move one inch from this place. Are you safe?'

'Yes.' She looked at him with clear eyes and he nodded, partly satisfied as he released her. If she was in any personal danger then he was sure she was unaware of it. But she was shaken, afraid, and there was nothing he could do about it unless she invited him into her life.

'I'll see you tomorrow, then. Where will we be?'

'It's another big store day. Regent Street. It's . . .'

'Don't tell me. Keep it secret. The revelation might make me collapse if it's too grand and then I'll not be able to go.' Helen laughed and he gave her one of his special smiles, a brilliant flash of white teeth and warmth in his eyes that lit up his face. 'Goodnight, Helen,' he said softly. 'You know where I am. Ring me if you need help.'

'I don't, thank you.'

She looked at him a little desperately for a moment and then gave a small smile that was a mixture of anxiety and gratitude. She did need help but she could never ask for it. The car didn't leave until she was safely in the house and then she heard it purr away down the street, taking Dan back to his hotel.

He hadn't had dinner. She wondered where he would go, if he would go with someone. He hadn't backed out of joining Martin and Margaret because he was tired. There had been a strange look in his eyes and it had not been exhaustion. From the moment she had been hit by the shock of Martin's announcement, Dan had changed into another person, just as Margaret had said he could. He had become softer, more gentle, but his strength seemed to have grown more tangible. He had been ready to defend her. He knew there was something wrong but he would never find out what it was. Her secret was well hidden.

Tonight she would not search. It was too late. She would find nothing. It had already happened, and it had happened far more quickly than she had anticipated. It had been earlier in the evening, away from the dead blackness of night. Things would be calm now and then she would start her search again, but not this week. It was too late. She had failed again, and there was no one to turn to for help.

'Drop me off here,' Dan said abruptly a while later as the car took him back. 'I have to eat.'

'I can recommend a place if you like, sir.' The chauffeur leaned back to speak but Dan refused the offer.

'Thanks,' he said shortly. 'I know London.'

He did. This city was like a second home to him but he had never felt about it as he felt now. Somewhere in this city, someone was prowling, dangerous, a killer. Why did he see the shadowy figure as a woman and why had Helen been close to collapse at the thought that some unknown man had been stabbed to death? She was not some weak, fainting female. In spite of her unknown troubles she was tough, but when Martin had made his announcement the shock had hit her like a physical blow.

The car pulled in at the pavement and Dan stepped out, signalled his thanks and then turned to walk back the way they had come. It was completely dark, only the lights of closed shops and the overhead lights of the road holding back the shadows. But he knew he could walk anywhere now. The feeling of menace was gone.

Tonight he didn't feel the chill of instinct. Somewhere in this city a valve had blown and released a deadly tension. There was a quiet, a calm that had nothing to do with the night. For now, things were safe. Helen was safe. Her fear was for someone or something else. She had no personal fear. But she may be wrong.

His mind reached out to her in the same way he had wanted to reach out to her physically. Martin was right. She was crying inside and now he had heard her pain, her fear and her knowledge of danger.

'Oh, Helen,' he breathed softly into the night. 'You're in trouble and there's nothing I can do about it. I can't even hold you.'

And he wanted to hold her. He had not wanted to leave her tonight. He gave a short laugh of self-derision when he realized he would have been quite content to sit up all night in a chair and just watch over her.

'No hassle, no commitments,' he reminded himself softly. 'You're slipping, Professor Forrest. Helen Stewart is an unwanted complication.'

The trouble was, he did want her, complication or not. He was wasting his precious time in his favourite place because of Helen, and for the first time in his life he was lonely. He was lonely for a woman who didn't like him, a woman who didn't know how to handle her life, a woman who carried a burden she refused to share.

And it was something to do with that killing. He frowned and saw her face again in his mind. The mention of a murder hadn't really bothered her; she had been too conscious of him and her own recent verbal assault on him. It was only when Martin had told them that it was somebody who had been stabbed to death that she had reacted like that.

Dan walked into a restaurant to eat and ordered a meal almost vaguely. His mind was marshalling the evidence, tearing things apart. He put himself in a woman's place when such a thing was mentioned. A woman's reaction would have been like Margaret's reaction: resentment, revulsion.

And what about later? If the news had been that a *woman* had been stabbed to death there would be a certain amount of personal fear – a madman running about, dark corners and lonely places, a knowledge of personal vulnerability.

Helen's reaction had been almost violent and yet she had known that the victim had been some unknown man. Unknown because no name had been mentioned. Her reaction therefore had been merely to the stabbing, the knife, the act itself, almost as if she had been expecting it.

Dan ate his meal without even tasting it and almost forgot to pay as he left. His brain was doing what it did best: searching the mind of another person. He always felt pain for them if they were suffering but this time he felt fear. Helen was on the edge of some hidden darkness and she was there alone.

Caroline Brown glanced up as the shop door opened and then gave a little smile that was mischievous and pleased at the same time.

'Good heavens,' Mrs Edgerton muttered. 'If that boy buys any more music he'll be able to set up in business for himself. He's already been in twice this week and it's only Tuesday.'

'He likes music,' Caroline whispered, careful not to let him hear. He was so young that she felt quite motherly towards him.

'He likes *you*,' Mrs Edgerton corrected in a low voice. 'You're costing him a fortune and he's not even taking you out yet.'

'What do you mean "yet"?' Caroline looked outraged. 'I'm not going anywhere with him. He's just someone who comes in here. He might be anybody. Letting somebody just pick you up is dangerous. You only have to see the news each night.'

'Oh, go on, girl! He looks a really nice boy.'

'Boy is just about it,' Caroline agreed, eyeing him secretly from beneath her dark lashes. 'I bet he's no more than seventeen. I'm twenty-three.'

'Twenty-three!' Mrs Edgerton laughed. 'That *is* old. He can be a toy boy, then.'

'Oh, quiet, Mrs Edgerton! He'll hear you,' Caroline muttered anxiously. He was coming to the counter and she didn't want to hurt his feelings. He was blushing even before he got there.

'I'll have this, please.' He put a tape down on the counter and looked at Mrs Edgerton, carefully avoiding any sort of eye-contact with Caroline.

'I'm busy at the moment, dear,' Mrs Edgerton told him, quickly getting out order books. 'Miss Brown will see to you, won't you, Caroline?'

'A pleasure.' Caroline smiled, holding out her hand for the tape.

'Oh, thanks.' He went a dull red and Caroline wondered how she was going to be tactful if he became bold enough to ask her out. Things like this were tricky. She glanced down at the tape and pity surged through her.

'Do you really like rap?' she asked gently.

He stared down at the tape and looked as if he wanted the shop floor to open around him.

'I – I must have picked up the wrong one,' he stammered.

'Oh, it's easily done. Only yesterday a man came in and did exactly the same thing,' Caroline lied. 'I only asked because I thought you liked classical music.'

'Did you notice?' He looked as pleased as a puppy and almost stumbled across the floor to change the tape.

Mrs Edgerton glanced at Caroline with amusement and then manoeuvred herself to another place a good way off. Caroline sighed and then turned back to her admiring customer with a smile on her face as he put the other tape down on the counter. She just hadn't the heart to be starchy with him, but she did wish that Mrs Edgerton would stop trying to get her paired off with some boy.

'I expect you're at the university,' she said pleasantly as she wrapped the tape and took his money.

'Yes. How did you know?'

'You just look like that.' Caroline almost sighed aloud this time. What he looked like was an eager schoolboy. She couldn't remember having been so young and guileless herself. She felt a lot older than twenty-three. 'What are you studying?'

'English. This is my first year.'

Caroline readjusted his age in her head and gave him his change with a wide smile.

'Well, I expect we'll be seeing you again,' she said cheerfully.

'Oh, yes. My name is Peter Saddler, by the way.'

'What a nice name. I'm Caroline.'

'I know. I've heard that other woman speak to you plenty of times. Maybe I'll see you around.'

'I'm sure you will,' Caroline said hastily, quite pleased when Mr Rider came out of the office although he was not her idea of a nice man at all. He was only welcome to her just now because he represented authority, nasty authority, enough to scare off any number of innocent admirers.

'Chatting up the customers, Caroline?' her boss asked in his smarmy way as Peter Saddler left hurriedly.

'He chose the wrong tape, Mr Rider. I was just pointing that out to him. He looks like a nice boy. It saves him having to come back and change the tape.'

'You're a kind girl,' he murmured, breathing all over her. 'You look particularly lovely today, an asset to the shop.' His eyes roamed boldly over her, taking in the slender figure and the pale blonde hair. He stepped a bit closer and Mrs Edgerton walked up briskly.

'I've done all the re-ordering, Mr Rider. If you want to take it away to your office and glance at it, I'll be quite willing to post it tonight.'

'Right. Thank you.' He gave Mrs Edgerton a disapproving look but he took the papers and went back to his office and Caroline's tension eased.

'Thanks,' she said gratefully. 'If ever you leave I'm out of here fast. Lecherous old pig. I bet he's seventy.'

'Fifty-four if he's a day,' Mrs Edgerton assured her drily. 'I'm fast approaching fifty myself so watch what you say, love.'

'You're not lecherous.'

'Oh, I don't know. I could go after your young man.'

'He's not my young man. I thought for one moment he was going to ask me out. I don't know what I'll do if he does. I would hate to hurt his feelings. He's so sweet.'

'Well, go out with him. Ask him yourself and save him the embarrassment.'

'I can't,' Caroline said firmly. 'I have things to do.'

'Then fix the poor boy up with a friend.'

Caroline smiled and shook her fair head. 'I'm sure he wouldn't like my friends. They might make fun of him and I wouldn't like that. I don't like to have people's feelings hurt.'

'You're a nice girl, Caroline. It's time you were married. You need a really pleasant man.'

Mr Rider stuck his head round the door of his office.

'Here's the order, Mrs Edgerton. Get a stamp and take it out of the petty cash.' He turned to look at Caroline. 'It's time to lock up. Can I give you a lift, Caroline?'

'We've arranged to have a cup of tea together at the Centre,' Mrs Edgerton intervened quickly.

'Of course, if you'd rather get a lift home, Caroline?'

'Oh, no, really,' Caroline said quickly. 'I want to do some shopping while we're in the Centre and then I'm meeting Joe.'

Mr Rider just nodded and gave both of them a rather grim smile. 'Well, I'm going. Lock up carefully, Mrs Edgerton.'

'As if I don't every night,' Mrs Edgerton snorted as he closed his door. She looked at Caroline in surprise. 'Who's Joe?'

'I just made him up. Oh, thanks for rescuing me. I don't know what I'd do without you.'

'Neither do I,' Mrs Edgerton assured her, giving her a worried frown. 'You're so naïve, Caroline, and far too good-natured. I don't know about being the manageress, I'm more like a mother to you.'

'Yes,' Caroline agreed with a far-away dreamy smile on her face. She never had any trouble remembering her mother. She hadn't been a bit like Mrs Edgerton.

They both looked up as Mr Rider came out of his office and crossed the shop to the main door. He closed it with a bang, never said goodnight and stopped outside to adjust his coat.

'Stupid fool,' Mrs Edgerton muttered crossly.

Caroline never said anything. She was watching him with a slight frown on her face, a puzzled stare in her eyes. Something was at the back of her mind and Mr Rider reminded her of it but she couldn't quite grasp it. It bothered her.

She went on staring at him, her frown deepening. He looked too brawny to be the owner of a music shop. He looked as if he would be more suitable for rough work. She felt as if she ought to know him from somewhere but she had no idea where. He scared her, though. She was quite sure of that.

When they finally left the shop, the young man who had introduced himself as Peter Saddler was hanging around outside and trying not to look obvious. Mrs Edgerton gave a very grown-up sigh.

'Hello.' His eyes were only on Caroline but he gave Mrs Edgerton an anxious glance.

'Hello,' Caroline smiled at him and stopped. 'Let's see, it's Peter, isn't it?'

'You remembered!' He said it as if it was an astonishing feat of intelligence although it hadn't been more than fifteen minutes since he had told her. 'I – I just happened to be passing.'

'Would you like to walk along with us?' Caroline asked gently. 'We're going to the Centre.'

'Super. I was just going there myself.'

Mrs Edgerton gave another loud sigh and glanced sideways at Caroline. 'I'm still going for a coffee and you're still coming with me,' she said pointedly.

'Coffee. Super!' Peter exclaimed, and Mrs Edgerton rolled her eyes heavenwards. Caroline tried to hide a smile. Now that the anxious young man had plucked up his courage, Mrs Edgerton was irritated because it upset her own plans.

Across the road, standing in the gathering dusk, George Rider stared at the trio with fury on his face.

He had nothing but contempt for dithering young fools but there was a dithering young fool walking along with Caroline, and obviously being encouraged.

His eyes moved to Violet Edgerton. He couldn't stand the woman. She always seemed to be in his way. If it had not been for her, he would be escorting Caroline to his car right now, getting round to fixing up something permanent. She looked the sort who would give in easily. His hands bunched in his pockets and he gave them all one last glare before he made his way to his car.

CHAPTER 5

Helen was late. Her sleep, when she had finally managed any, had been filled with dreams that had kept her tossing restlessly all night. There were faces she had not seen for years, other faces she would never see, and the menacing presence of a violence that should have been swept away long ago.

When her alarm had sounded in the morning she had been almost too tired to get out of bed and now she was rushing, trying to get her brain working and make herself prepare for yet another day with Dan.

She stood in the shower letting the warm water fall over her head and over her skin and she shivered at the thought of those golden eyes watching her. His kindness and his prompt action last night had made her even more aware of him, and she was looking forward to seeing him with a mixture of anticipation and dread.

There was no knowing how he would be this morning. He would probably be back to sarcasm and disdain. But whatever he was, she knew she was drawn to him with an irrevocability that stunned her. As soon as he had softened, she had wanted to stay with him. She had wanted him to come in with her and talk all night. She realized that she loved the sound of his voice, the quietness of it, the soft American accent. Not that it did any good, because she never knew how he was going to be and in any case, there was her secret.

She stepped from the shower and turned it off, wrapping her wet hair in a towel and rubbing herself dry quickly. He would be more than disdainful if she was late. It would put her at a terrible disadvantage. These past few days she seemed to be constantly racing the clock.

Helen glanced back into the shower cabinet. There was still the sound of running water and she half expected to find that she had failed to switch it off. There wasn't so much as a drip of water and she turned her head, listening carefully. The sound was from downstairs and it was getting louder by the minute. She raced from the bathroom in a panic and hurried downstairs with bare feet, shrugging into her short white bathrobe as she went.

The sight that met her eyes pushed everything else right out of her mind. The noise of racing water engulfed her as she opened the kitchen door. Water was pouring out from the cupboard beneath the sink. It was already all over the kitchen floor and rapidly making its way to the next room.

A burst pipe! She stared at the water in horror and then flew into the hall and the telephone.

'Plumber. Plumber.' Helen thumbed through her address pad, muttering frantically to herself, still numb with disbelief. This couldn't be happening. Everything in the house was new.

She found the number of the plumber and got him straight away.

'I've a burst pipe in the kitchen,' she told him frantically when the voice came on the line. 'The water is everywhere, flooding the place.'

'Can't get there for an hour. Shut off the water and it'll be all right.'

'I don't know where . . .!' He put the phone down before she could finish and Helen stared at it wildly. He didn't care. It was just one more address, one more burst pipe. It was all right for him to be calm; it was not his house that was being ruined. Every last penny of her savings was in this house.

After a second or two of panic-stricken uncertainty, she had a brainwave. She raced back upstairs and turned on the shower, turned on the bath taps with the plug out and flushed the toilet. It should take some of the pressure off for the time being. She looked round breathlessly and then glanced at the clock. She was later than ever and there was no way she could leave this chaos and go to collect Dan.

She phoned his hotel from the extension in her bedroom and finally got through to him in his suite.

'I can't come!' she said urgently. 'You'll just have to go alone. I'm sorry.'

'What's wrong?' His voice sounded sharper than it should have done, not at all as it had sounded the night before, and Helen yelled back at him, dancing about from one foot to the other.

'I've got a burst pipe. The whole kitchen is being flooded out. It's going to ruin the house and there's no plumber for a whole hour. He said to shut off the water and I've no idea where . . .' She suddenly let out a wail of frustration. 'The car! I've got to re-route the car!'

'Leave it to me, Helen,' Dan said, and she could hear him actually laughing.

'It's not funny!' she snapped, glaring at the phone.

'It is to me. You're not in any position to hear yourself. You seem to have had a complete change of personality. Anyway,' he added wryly, 'you can't drown in a kitchen.'

'You haven't seen the water and I can't stand here talking to you while the house floats away. I have to phone about the car and then go back down and . . .'

'Leave the car to me,' Dan ordered again. 'Go and deal with your burst pipe.'

He put the phone down and Helen glared at it some more. He had no business to laugh at her tragedy. He was nothing like he had been last night. It served him right that he would have to go to the store alone. She hoped they didn't recognize him. She hoped they tried to make him buy one of his own books. He wasn't quietly kind this morning.

Twenty minutes later she was in a desperate state. She was still in bare feet and her short robe, trying to sweep the water out through the back door, but she couldn't keep pace with it. When the front doorbell rang she abandoned her task with pleasure and threw the brush down into the water. The plumber. He had come early.

It was Dan. A taxi was just pulling away and Dan stood there looking at her in amusement.

'The store,' she began. 'You'll be late if you don't go now.'

'They can wait,' Dan told her firmly, putting her aside and coming in when she left him standing on the step. 'Where's the kitchen?'

He didn't wait for an answer. He could hear the water and before she could stop him he was in the kitchen looking at the scene of her morning's tragedy.

'Why haven't you shut everything off?' he enquired, looking down at the brush and then at her bare feet and her wet legs beneath the short robe. She was too frustrated to be embarrassed.

'I have no idea where the stopcock is,' she snapped. 'I told you that when I phoned.'

'You never seemed to finish one single sentence.' He took off his jacket and put it on the table, which so far had escaped the deluge. 'It's probably under the sink.' He rolled up his shirt-sleeves and waded towards his goal while Helen stared at him in dismay. He was going to be wet. How would he be able to go to the book-signing then? The water would soon be lapping over his shoes and on to the bottom of his trouser legs.

'You can't do it,' she protested.

'Just watch me,' he rejoined smugly.

She was too stunned to stop him, and he reached through the water that rushed from the cupboard and then grunted in satisfaction.

'Problem solved,' he muttered. 'The stopcock is here.' A second later and the water stopped abruptly. Helen stared at him in silence and then turned to race out of the room.

'Now what?' he called.

'I left the bath running, and the shower. I thought it might take a bit of the pressure off but I don't think it worked.'

Dan grinned wryly as she disappeared. It wouldn't. The mains were down here. He looked ruefully at his wet shirt-sleeves and badly splashed trouser legs and then grinned again. It was worth it to have seen another side of her character. The cold Miss Stewart had been submerged, in more ways than one. She was utterly feminine this morning, so helpless that the thought of simply picking her up was almost too much to resist.

She came back, took one horrified look at him and disappeared again. Dan raised dark brows in surprise. This was turning out to be an astonishing morning. He suddenly had a vivid picture of life with Helen if she could get rid of her fears, if she were relaxed and happy. It sent warmth through him that completely obliterated the memory of the cold water.

'Come in here,' she called, and he went out of the kitchen and tracked her down to a small, neat sitting

113

room. She was holding a hairdryer and she looked at him with dogged determination. 'You can't go like that,' she assured him seriously. 'You look bedraggled.'

'I'll go late.'

'Oh, no. You can't do that. When people expect you, you should be there. Being late is really bad for your reputation.' She came forward purposefully and turned the hairdryer on at full, aiming it at his chest. 'We'll start here,' she muttered, going at her task single-mindedly. 'It will take a while but eventually we'll have you dried out.'

Dan looked down at her with something like delight on his face. Her hair had escaped from the towel which was now hanging round her neck. Somewhere in this turmoil she had forgotten to be either scared or starchy. She looked warm, clean, delicious and so unlike the starchy Miss Stewart that he wanted to snatch her up into his arms and hug her.

He kept his mind firmly away from the dangerous thought that beneath the short robe she was undoubtably wearing nothing at all. This was definitely the wrong time to be dwelling on thoughts like that, but it was difficult to keep the thoughts out of his head.

'You're planning to dry me out piece by piece?' he asked softly, and she looked up at him with regretful blue eyes.

'I don't have a dryer. I know it must sound funny to you because you're an American and apparently they have all these gadgets. But I couldn't afford a dryer for the clothes when everything else was settled. I've got a mortgage as high as Everest.' She gave a resigned sigh. 'Maybe next year I'll get a dryer if other things don't keep breaking down. Anyway,' she added, getting on with her task very seriously. 'this is probably more practical. I couldn't put you into a dryer, could I? You would have had to take your clothes off.'

Helen stopped and went rose-red as the words escaped her mouth and met the light of day. Dan's grin stretched across his face and she stood with the hairdryer, not looking at him, aiming it at one part of his chest that had never been near water. A wave of unaccustomed tenderness welled up inside him that had very little to do with the fact that he wanted her physically.

'I hesitate to mention this,' he murmured, with laughter at the back of his voice, 'but you're burning me. If you don't change the position of that thing, my shirt will be scorched.'

'I'm sorry.' She sprang away and looked utterly helpless and Dan reached forward, took the dryer out of her hand, switched it off and put it down on a chair.

'If your authors could see you now,' he said quietly.

'I got into a panic,' Helen confessed with a resigned sigh. 'I'm not very good with things like stopcocks and burst pipes.' She looked up at him worriedly. 'I'll have to do something to get you dry.'

'Get yourself dry,' Dan said almost gently. 'We'll get the car to take us to my hotel and I'll change there.'

'But you'll be late by then.'

'Helen,' he insisted firmly. 'My shoes are soaking wet. What do you propose to do with them, put them in the oven?'

'I suppose not,' she sniffed. 'We'll just have to be late.'

'I already told them we would be late. Now get ready and don't be too long. I might get pneumonia and I already know that you're not very good with people who are ill.'

'I'm very good with them!' Helen protested thoughtlessly.

'As long as it's not me?' Dan suggested quietly, and then regretted the remark when her face fell, almost like a disappointed child.

'I thought you were drunk. You know that,' she reminded him stiffly. 'I'll get ready.'

Dan could have done himself an injury. Just as they were getting close he had to come out with that smart little remark. He was supposed to be a psychiatrist. The trouble was that where Helen was concerned he was nothing more than a man with a woman. Apart from grabbing her and making her want him he was about as prepared for his feelings as a callow youth. They were as new anyway. He had never in his life felt quite like this.

Helen had been ordered to bring him back to the office after their time in the store and she was glad to

116

be able to hand him over to Martin and get behind her desk with some work. It had been a very trying day. She had started off with a catastrophe, made a fool of herself with Dan and then dropped into guilty misery when he had said that about being ill.

The fact was, he was being clever and disdainful again, another change of character at the drop of a hat. She sat at her desk, methodically put her spectacles on and took out a new manuscript, deeply upset when she found that her mind wasn't on it. The time at the store had been fraught with stress, electric emotions that seemed to sing in the air like high-tension wires in a thunderstorm.

She had tried not to look at Dan, and when she had risked a glance he had been looking thunderous himself. She had not been sure which one of them had been giving off all that agitation, herself or Dan. Whoever it had been, it was a relief to get away from him, go to her desk and at least pretend to work, secure in the knowledge that he was safely cloistered with Martin. She resisted the temptation to try to catch a glimpse of him through the glass-panelled door. It wouldn't do a bit of good, and he might see her.

Inside his office, Martin was trying to make his mind up about Dan's state of temper. He had news to impart that might not be taken too kindly by his tall, angry-looking visitor. It was not, however, something he could keep to himself.

'Helen fixed up a reading for you,' Martin said casually, waiting for the explosion.

117

'She did *what*!' Dan turned blazing eyes on him and Martin decided that the best thing to do was press on in the same casual manner.

'There were enquiries and she thought it would be a good thing for you, sell more books, etcetera.'

'Scrap the etcetera,' Dan grated. 'I'll not do any bloody idiotic thing like that and you know it. The book-signing is bad enough. I feel like a damned prima donna. I'm doing that for you because you're a friend. Reading my own words in a theatrical voice and playing each part as it arises is *out*.'

He snatched up one of his books from Martin's desk and gave a hilarious reading of several characters in different voices that had Martin struggling hard to contain himself. He dared not laugh aloud, nor even grin. Dan was furious.

'Forget it!' Dan snarled as he threw the book down. 'And you can tell her yourself. I've had it.'

'Pity,' Martin murmured regretfully. 'She's going to have to go round and apologize. Helen gets embarrassed quite easily.'

'Tough,' Dan said nastily, standing and pacing about with his hands in his pockets and going to glare through the glass of the door towards Helen's desk.

It stopped his rage like a damp squib in the rain. She was sitting there in a sort of unnatural quiet. She was reading a manuscript but he could have laid odds that she wasn't seeing a word. She had those big, unlikely-looking spectacles back on her nose and she was scraping that glorious cloud of hair behind her ears every few seconds. She looked nervous and pitiful and much too vulnerable to be doing any sort of job at all. His strange eyes stopped flashing golden fire and softened.

'Okay,' he said quietly. 'I'll go. But she comes too.'

'What are you up to, Dan? I won't have Helen upset. I know you.'

'You don't know me from a pig's snout, my friend,' Dan assured him softly. I don't even know myself, he added inside his head, but I know what I want and she's sitting there like a beaten child.

'Never mind the pig's snout,' Martin said, looking at Dan suspiciously. 'If you're thinking of punishing her . . . You can just tell me why you suddenly changed your mind – why you're raging one minute and then calmly agreeing the next.'

'Seconds, actually, not minutes,' Dan corrected, his eyes still on Helen's bent head. 'You can calm your fatherly anxiety. I just remembered that she's had a hellish day. She had a burst pipe this morning. It flooded her kitchen. The floor's probably knee-deep in water now. She should be home right this minute instead of sitting there working.'

'You were at Helen's place this morning?' Martin asked in a dazed voice.

'Sure,' Dan murmured innocently. 'I turned off the water for her, but not before the whole kitchen was flooded out. She's got one hell of a mess waiting for her.'

'I had no idea,' Martin muttered. He got up and went out of his office, leaving Dan leaning nonchalantly in the open doorway with his hands in his pockets and his eyes on Helen. Martin went over to Helen's desk and spoke to her, and although Dan couldn't hear a word, he saw her look up and glance in his direction, a most delightful surprise on her face. He looked back innocently, amused to see her blush. But she took off the damned spectacles, and by the time Martin came back to his own office she was hurrying to the door, going home.

'On your way, sugar,' Dan whispered to himself, his golden eyes following her progress. 'Dream about me, but please don't let it be a nightmare.'

'Now,' Martin said firmly as he closed his office door and sat back behind his desk, 'why were you at Helen's house and how did you know where she lived anyway?'

'I took her home after the cocktail party. She was upset, if you recall. Your announcement about the murder wasn't exactly subtle.'

'I know,' Martin murmured ruefully, 'Margaret threw the book at me later. It was good of you to take Helen home.'

'We still had that shocking great limo, if you recall,' Dan pointed out drily. 'He simply went in Helen's direction first. I didn't want to leave her when she was upset.' He did not add that he could feel danger round her too, that he had been anxious about her.

'Why were you there this morning?' Suspicion was back in Martin's eyes and Dan grinned at him.

'Is this jealousy or fatherly concern?' he asked sardonically.

'You know I worship Margaret!' Martin snapped, and Dan nodded, his expression softening.

'I know. As to Helen, she phoned me to tell me to go to the store alone. I asked why and she told me about the burst pipe and that there was no plumber for an hour.'

'Why didn't she turn the water off?'

'She didn't know how to do it. She's not very good with things like that, apparently. When I got there she was ankle-deep in water and looking like a wet cat.'

'You know a lot about her.' Martin said stiffly.

'Only what she tells me, and in case you're worrying about her moral safety, I wouldn't harm a hair on her head, even if I got close enough to touch her head, which is doubtful.'

'She can be a bit prickly.' Martin agreed thoughtfully. He glanced up with an apology in his eyes. 'I'm sorry, Dan. It's just that Margaret and I worry about her, and you've got to admit that over the years you've built up quite a reputation with the ladies, psychiatrist or not.'

'Yeah,' Dan drawled vaguely. That seemed to have been light-years ago. Now all he could see was Helen and her angel face, her worried eyes and her faint, distant sadness.

'So back to business,' he said aloud. 'What about this goddamned reading?'

'Helen will deal with that,' Martin assured him briskly. 'No doubt she'll be in touch.'

'No doubt.' Dan's agile brain started to form a plan and he almost missed Martin's next remark.

'By the way, Margaret and I expect to see you on Saturday about six-thirty. Jenny is dying to see you too and you haven't been over yet. Don't be late. We're having a barbecue.'

'Great,' Dan muttered with no great show of enthusiasm.

'I thought you liked barbecues?'

'Not so you'd notice,' Dan drawled. He wasn't thinking about food. He was thinking about Jenny and how he was going to escape her adolescent talons if she was as bad as last time.

'Helen's coming,' Martin said absently. 'I asked her yesterday. I almost forget to ask you and you're the reason for the whole thing.'

'Don't worry. I'll be there,' Dan said smoothly. Inside the hammer was hitting his solar plexus again. More time with Helen. This time he would watch his tongue. A horrifying thought occurred to him.

'Is she bringing anybody?' he asked casually.

'Don't know. We told her she could. She never talks about her private life although we see her at the house quite a lot. There's this chap called Jack; apart from that I don't know. We'll just have to see.'

Dan's hands bunched at his sides. He wanted to yank Martin over the desk and demand to know more. He had never even thought once about Helen with another man. He could imagine Jenny climbing all over him and Helen smiling into Jack's eyes, whoever Jack was. The thought felt as if it was

killing him. It was too late to back out now, too
pointed. His mind searched frantically and came up
with Antonia.

'A *barbecue*! Obviously something horrendous is happening to that wonderful brain of yours, Dan. You
should see somebody about it. A psychiatrist perhaps?'

'It would only be for an evening – well, early
evening and maybe going on until later.'

'No, darling. It's most unseemly. I would be lost
and embarrassed, to say nothing about the utter
boredom. And anyway, what does one wear for a
barbecue? It's completely out of my sphere.'

'Okay, Antonia,' Dan sighed. 'It wasn't fair to ask
you. I just walked into a leg trap and I can't see
anyway of getting out of it.'

'Oh, don't worry about being fair, darling,'
Antonia said cheerfully. 'I'm only fair when it suits
me.' She gave him a searching look. 'As you're
looking particularly depressed, I assume that this
Helen girl is going to be there.'

'That's what I've been told,' Dan muttered glumly.

'So go and enjoy yourself. Get close to her, woo
her or whatever it is that Americans do.'

'She's probably bringing someone,' Dan told her
with even more gloom, and Antonia gave a resigned
sigh of understanding.

'I see. Honestly. Dan, you look completely hopeless. You're not worth much as a psychiatrist at the
moment.' She sat up briskly in her chair. 'Let's get
this straight. You're going to a barbecue and Helen

might be there with a boyfriend. My mission, if I choose to accept it, is to go as your cover, a sort of, "Well I've got one as well," attitude.'

'That's about it,' Dan agreed, wincing at her forthright manner.

'Very well. I'll do it for old times' sake – but don't expect me to put on an act. I'll be myself. I can't think of anyone I like better than me anyway.'

'Antonia,' Dan said in glad relief, 'you're a treasure. I have nobody else to turn to. I knew you'd do it.'

'You knew no such thing. You relied on my good nature and the fact that you can look gloomy with the best of them. And I still don't know what to wear.'

'You'll come up with something,' Dan assured her. 'We'll order dinner now.'

'I'm going pick the most expensive things on the menu,' she threatened. 'You've just lured me right out of my own background. When is this wretched event, by the way?'

'Saturday, early evening. Starts about six-thirty and we eat around seven-thirty.'

'Wonderful!' Antonia said crossly. 'Bang goes the theatre, then. This is a bigger sacrifice then you imagine. Country bumpkins and burned food. You owe me after this, Dan.'

'I know.' He grinned at her and signalled to the waiter. Whatever she wore, Antonia always looked spectacular. Maybe it would jolt Helen a little and make her notice him for a change.

Antonia refused any offer of an escort to her home. It was no surprise to Dan; she had always refused. He had no idea where she lived. He flagged down a taxi and handed her into it, not one doubt in his mind that she would appear as his partner at the barbecue. Whatever her failings, she always kept her word. There were much worse people in the world than Antonia.

He decided to stroll back to his hotel. It was not too far off and not really worth the effort of trying to get another taxi. It was a nice evening in any case, and he had plenty to think about. He had to plan out a strategy for Saturday for one thing.

For another, he had to remember to restrain his considerable temper when he saw who Helen was bringing. As soon as he got in he would ring Martin and tell him about Antonia. The sight of her would be enough of a shock, without dropping her on them unannounced.

He smiled to himself, indulging in very pointless daydreams about how Helen would feel when she saw him with another woman. He was well aware that the daydreams were pointless; all the feelings were coming from him, nothing from Helen. All the same, he enjoyed doing it. A few wandering thoughts never hurt anyone.

His faint, lingering smile suddenly died on his face when he felt again the chill of foreboding. It swept over his skin like an icy warning, an omen of danger. Until his visit to London this time he had never fell it before, except on one occasion when he was helping the police in Chicago. The man had been a psychopath but he had had all the appearance of normality. It had been the eyes, the fixed stare with the unrelenting coldness of ice that had suddenly blanked out the smiling warmth of moments before. Dan had felt the chill down to his soul and he had never forgotten.

He felt it now, the old primeval signal of peril. He stopped, his eyes searching both sides of the well-lit street. People were passing, hurrying or sauntering, intent on their own lives, but he knew without seeing anything that a hunter was among the flock.

He stood quite still, making no attempt to hide the fact that he too was searching. His eyes moved over every illuminated shop-front, every darkened doorway. Danger was here, close. He made no move to stifle the feeling; he let it guide him.

And then he saw her. She was walking with the same measured, prowling pace, looking straight ahead, paying no attention at all to the beautiful things in the shop windows. But there was nothing aimless about her walk. She was combing the city, searching in patient, persistent silence.

Her clothes were the same, as if she had never shed them since the last time, the high heels, the sheer stockings, the shiny raincoat and the incongruous band of black velvet against her blue-black hair.

He let her walk out of his sight. He would never attempt to follow her again. He was stunned at the wave of premonition that had flared through him at the sight of her and even before he had actually seen her. Nothing like this had ever happened to him before. Everything he did was scientific, and he had no leaning towards premonitions or second-sight, but since he had first seen the woman with the black hair he had felt the premonition whenever she was near.

He could hear again Martin's voice announcing the murder just outside the hotel. A man, stabbed. He could also see Helen's instant reaction to the idea of a knife. There had to be some sort of connection, but nothing he could prove to himself or anyone else.

'Are you all right, sir?'

Dan had been so deeply into thought that the sound of the concerned voice shocked him. It was a policeman and for a second, Dan looked at him, pondering. He shrugged and tried to throw off the feeling of evil.

'Fine, thanks. I'm just watching all the lights.'

'You're an American,' the policeman deduced when he heard Dan's accent. 'You want to come back over here at Christmas. You'll really see lights then.'

He gave a funny little salute as he walked away and Dan wanted to go after him, to tell him, to warn him. He did not, however. What did he have to tell – a feeling, a chill, a conviction with no facts to base it on? A woman was searching the night and she would choose her prey from any of the people who came within her range, but she would not choose haphazardly.

She would choose by some criteria of her own, some yardstick she lived by. Sooner or later some unknown person would die by that same set of rules and there was nothing he could do about it. It was instinct, a feeling backed by his experience, by his profession but still, only a feeling. There was nothing concrete he could say to anyone. But he *knew*.

His attempt to shield himself from having to see Helen with another man now seemed to be puerile, unimportant. But he wondered where she was tonight, if she was safe. There was nothing he could do about that, either, because once again he only had instinct to connect her to this.

He wondered if she knew, as he did, that the valve was once again gathering steam that could not be controlled, and that once again – it would blow.

Martin rang Helen at home that night.

'About Saturday and the barbecue,' he announced. 'Thought I'd better let you know that Dan's bringing some woman or other. He rang me earlier and told me. Maybe you should bring this friend Jack you keep mentioning? It would even out the numbers and make it more of a party.'

Helen went still inside. What he meant was that she would not feel alone if she brought Jack. It was kind but it made her feel even worse. In the first place she had not had any idea that Dan was going to Martin's, and the thought of his bringing a woman upset her. She didn't know exactly how she would take it but it would be hurtful. She wasn't sure that she wanted to ask herself why it would hurt. She just knew it would.

'What woman?' she asked stiffly.

'I've no idea. Dan always plays things close to the chest. It's probably some old friend from when he used to live here ages ago, but who knows? It might be someone he's met since he's been here this time. Not that it matters to us either way, Dan is Dan and does his own thing all the time. I just thought you might like to bring Jack and take some of the wind out of Jenny's sails. She'll be wanting to corner you and discuss Dan's lady friend as soon as she sees her. She'll be green with jealousy too, I expect, but she might just keep it to herself if you've brought a new face. Even Jenny has her pride. She won't make an exhibition of herself in front of a stranger.'

Helen was none too sure about that.

'I'm going to the gym right now,' she said quickly. 'I'll tell Jack. Thanks for asking.'

'Pleasure,' Martin assured her and rang off.

It wasn't a pleasure, and it would not be a pleasure on Saturday. Apart from anything else, she would perhaps be as green with jealousy as Jenny. She knew she did not want to see Dan with another woman. More and more she was wanting to be close to him herself. She hardly knew him really, but it didn't seem to make a lot of difference.

And Martin had told her something during the day that had made her uneasy too. Dan was not pleased about the reading at the bookshop, apparently. If he was annoyed he would either glare at her or go for her with his sarcastic barbs. He might feel restrained about doing that if Jack was there, and she would have to throw herself on Jack's mercy, because there wasn't anyone else she could ask.

'Ah!' Jack exclaimed thoughtfully when she put the matter to him that evening. 'Dan Forrest is going to be there? I might get the chance to interview him if I go with you. Would that be socially acceptable, do you think, cornering him at a family party?'

'Yes, as far as I'm concerned,' Helen muttered. 'Martin dropped me into this with no warning, so if he doesn't like it he'll just have to cope.'

'Actually, I was thinking more about Forrest's reaction.' Jack pointed out drily. 'He might get stroppy if he's confronted at a barbecue.'

'Then he'll just have to cope too and get over it. If you have the nerve to corner him, go ahead and do it. He's bringing a woman with him, so you might pick up more than you bargained for.'

'Really? Who is she?'

'I have no idea and I don't want to know,' Helen snapped.

'I see,' Jack mused, giving her a sideways glance. 'Shall you go for the neck lock or a full toss over the shoulder when you see her?'

'What exactly is that supposed to mean?' Helen demanded indignantly.

'It means that you sound jealous. And don't go advancing on me threateningly,' he warned as she took an aggressive step towards him. 'I was tossing people over my head when you were in knee socks and pigtails.'

'I was never in either,' Helen murmured disgustedly as she turned away to hide her flushed cheeks. 'Let's get into the gym. I'm not paying my fees to waste an evening standing outside the door talking to you.'

'Be pleasant to me,' Jack warned, 'or I might not go.'

'Suit yourself. If you don't go I can always plead a headache.'

'It's okay, I surrender. I'll come. Give me the details over a coffee later and if you want me to pretend to be a boyfriend, I can deal with that easily.'

'Just be yourself,' Helen retorted. 'That's bad enough.'

Jack slapped his hand to her shoulder and burst into laughter and her annoyance vanished. She had her camouflage with Jack and she planned to stick close to him all the time on Saturday. She would just have to watch her tongue and refuse to be upset, whoever Dan brought with him. In any case, there was plenty of time to get herself under control before then.

Helen was more settled in her mind when she left the gym. As usual she shared a taxi with Jack. She never brought her own car and it was too far for either of them to walk. He dropped off a few minutes before her and it was only after he had gone that she suddenly felt the same old depression sinking over her and around her.

The feeling that brought a darkness to her days was back. It hit her without warning like some dreaded pain inside, and she hurried into the house when she got back and locked the door, leaning back against it as if she had been chased all the way home.

It was starting again, the endless nightmare that kept her on her lonely vigils through the streets. It was screaming inside but she tried to ignore it as she had tried many times before. She was inside her own house, safe; she would not go out searching. What good had it done so far? Every night she had returned home feeling hopeless, dispirited. She had not achieved anything at all. She didn't even know if it was real.

But as the evening wore on, she found herself listening to the quiet around her, hearing things that were not there. Mostly though she heard voices in her head, Martin's voice. '*It was a man. He was stabbed.*' She had tried not to look in the papers but it was almost unavoidable. A middle-aged man, a big man.

Voices from the past came too. Voices telling her that her stepfather had died of multiple stab wounds. And how many more? How many had died before she had realized what must be happening? There was no one to tell, nothing to tell anyone about, no facts. It was just a fear, an instinctive certainty, a burden she carried alone.

Helen put on her coat and went out of the house, not even bothering to eat. She could feel the deadly tension rising and tonight it seemed to be almost visible, floating in the darkness, strong. She had little time to waste. It would all happen again. She walked quickly, heading for the lights, lights that attracted the foolish like moths, lights that attracted them to their own death.

132

CHAPTER 6

Dan came out of the theatre and asked himself if he had heard a word of the play. The answer was definitely no. He had also left well before the end. A waste of time and money, because he could have been thinking about Helen in greater comfort in his hotel room. The play had simply interrupted his thoughts about her.

He had never felt alone before in his life but he felt alone now. He also felt like a fraud. He had spent years teaching people how to manage their feelings but now he couldn't even manage his own. He had cured people of obsessions but he was obsessed with Helen and he had no idea how to deal with it.

He walked along looking for a taxi but this evening they seemed to have all gone into some sort of hiding. It didn't bother him too much. He wasn't anxious to be back anyway. Being at the hotel was turning out to have been a mistake, not that he would have been any better off elsewhere. He might have had more room to pace about but that was all the advantage he would have felt.

133

And he wasn't regretting having refused Martin's offer either. If he had been staying with them he would have been seriously tempted to risk talking about Helen and Martin was already casting suspicious glances in his direction. Besides, there was Jennifer. She was still home from that boarding school and she was a year older than when he had last seen her, a year more developed.

He wished she would turn her sexual fantasies in some other direction. The older she got, the more embarrassing it would become. Maybe she would take a shine to this Jack person? If she pestered Jack as much as she pestered him it would leave him free to spend his time with Helen. He made a wry face. Antonia would be there. He had almost forgotten that.

Saturday was going to be a bad day. He never knew quite what Antonia would say or do in any case, and Jennifer was often outrageous. While he was coping with that, he would be screwed up tight about Helen, wanting to be close to her. She was usually unapproachable and he was constantly saying the wrong thing. He knew why too. He wanted her too badly to be reasonable.

He walked round the corner with a black frown on his face and bumped straight into her, almost knocking her off her feet.

'Helen!' He caught her arms to save her from falling and let her go abruptly when she stared up at him as if he was the very last person in the world she wanted to see. He had wanted her to he as glad as he was, and her reaction just screwed him up inside further.

'I'm sorry,' she murmured. 'I wasn't looking where I was going.' She sounded almost frightened and Dan had to fight down the desire to keep hold of her, to pull her close, or even to shake her. Why was she frightened of him? Why didn't she want him? He had never before felt this desperation.

'It's not too easy to see round corners,' he reminded her stiffly. 'I wasn't looking either.'

They went on staring at each other and Dan felt utterly impatient with her and with himself. He was supposed to be able to put people at their ease. She looked pale, anxious, and he was too uptight about her to be normal. It ground into him that she should be anxious with him, although he knew he had given her more than good reason. And what the hell was she doing here at this time of night, all by herself?

'What are you doing here?' he asked abruptly. 'It's nearly nine-thirty.'

'I'm just walking.'

'In the city at night? Alone? What are you looking for, trouble?' He glared down at her and Helen glared back, animosity overriding both fear and embarrassment. He was talking like that again! They stared at each other like enemies.

'You're walking in the same place, so why shouldn't I?' she accused, and his jaw tightened considerably.

'I'm a man, or hadn't you noticed, Miss Stewart?'

'I'm perfectly safe, Mr Forrest,' she told him tersely, hearing the sarcasm in his voice. 'I do judo.'

'A black-belt karate expert would have trouble dealing with a gang of rowdies. And you could meet a gang of rowdies round any corner, just as you met me. What will you settle for, one throw in four?'

'I could throw you!' Helen snapped angrily, suddenly furiously annoyed with him and Dan's panther eyes lit up with instant amusement at her fierce little tilt of the chin as his own annoyance vanished. An angel was squaring up to him in the street. It restored his equilibrium and he suddenly realized that he could never stay annoyed with her for more than a minute or two.

'All right, honey,' he agreed softly. 'Let's go somewhere with a softer landing than the sidewalk, then it won't matter one little bit if you fall down with me.'

'It's a pavement,' Helen corrected unevenly, her cheeks flushing at the subtle innuendo.

'It sure is,' Dan agreed. 'Come on.' He took her arm and Helen panicked.

'Please, Dan. I have to go. I have to . . .'

'Let's eat,' he offered gently, thrilled that she had called him Dan so readily. 'You can throw me some other time when we know each other better. I often eat at this little Italian place across the road. Promise not to send me crashing into a table. They'll shout in Italian and I won't understand a word of it.'

'I have to go home.' She didn't manage to get the stubborn words out until they were halfway across

136

the road, and Dan took her arm more firmly and made her run the rest of the way when the traffic cleared a little.

She stood quite still on the other side, though, and set her feet firmly, because there was no way she could go with him. She needed to search. It was like a desperation inside.

'I have to go home,' she repeated dejectedly.

'Can I come with you?' The golden eyes were filled with gravity and Helen's face went hot again. 'I'm lonely. I want to be with you, Helen,' he added seriously when she stood looking anxious and embarrassed.

'Please!' Helen begged, but he just smiled into her eyes.

'Just eat with me, then. I know you're hungry.'

'You don't,' Helen protested weakly. 'You can't possibly tell whether I'm hungry or not.'

'Oh, I can. It's part of my training. I can see it on your face. I studied it for years. Sometimes there's absolutely nothing wrong with a person once you feed them. We once tested a whole town of six thousand people. They kept reporting strange sightings, lights in the sky, spectral phenomena. A few of them went berserk. Turned out they were hungry. A bowl of soup each and we had them cured.'

Helen just stared at him through her huge spectacles and he stared right back, the panther eyes unblinking and serious. She suddenly felt better, safer. *He* made her feel safer. He always did and in spite of her determination to escape from him, her lips quirked and then tilted in a smile.

'Does that mean you'll eat with me?' he asked like an eager child, the veneer of total innocence still on his face. He had drawn her into his little fantasy with no effort at all. Helen could almost see him in a white coat with a serious expression on his face as he dispensed soup to lunatics. She tried to stop the laughter bubbling up but she couldn't quite manage it.

'Will you, Helen?' he asked softly again.

'I don't seem to have a lot of choice, other than by kicking and screaming and making a complete fool of myself. I think I really believed all that for a second. Maybe you're not safe to talk to. You tell convincing lies. Anyway, I'm not really dressed for eating out,' she added with a sigh, glancing down at her coat and then looking at Dan's elegance.

'The thing about Italian restaurants,' he murmured, taking her arm and steering her in the right direction, 'is dark corners. We'll find one.'

He felt like singing at the top of his voice. Right out of the blue he had her with him. He could almost feel her relaxing, but he had to watch his step and at the back of his mind sat a question that would not go away. Why was she here at this time of night? She had been roaming the streets. Why?

There were few people in the restaurant, as it turned out. The theatre crowds had not yet appeared; those who ate early had gone. All the same, Dan spotted a quiet corner and urged Helen towards it. He took her coat and hung it up and she sat looking vulnerable, her hands clasped in her lap below the level of the table-top.

'I didn't bring my bag,' she said anxiously, glancing up at him. 'My purse is in my pocket, though.'

'When I take a girl out to dinner I expect to pay for the meal,' Dan assured her. 'I hope you're not one of these modern fifty-fifty women. I might turn nasty and cause a big scene.'

'It's just that I feel sort of unprepared. You pulled me off the street.'

'You shouldn't have been there in the first place.' He frowned at her and her anxiety began to come back.

'Plenty of women are.' She looked across at him warily and the golden eyes looked into hers.

'You're not "plenty of women". You're different. And, judo or not, you're not safe out there. You're intelligent, you must be aware of the dangers. London is like any other city at night and, much as I love it, it's dangerous for a woman alone.'

Their eyes locked and then Helen looked down.

'I have to find somebody,' she said quietly.

'You found me. Make do with that.' His hand reached across and tilted her face. 'Whatever it is, let it go, Helen.'

'I can't let it go. You – you don't understand. Nobody would.'

'Try me.'

For a second she looked at him with a weary longing on her face, hope at the back of her eyes, and then she shook her head, avoiding his gaze.

'I'm not even sure if it's imagination. If it's imagination then I'm probably going mad, I expect. If it isn't . . .'

The waiter came, interrupting the conversation, but Dan had already decided to step back a little, This head-on challenge would merely frighten her and that was the last thing he wanted to do.

'I understand you're coming to Martin's barbecue tomorrow,' he mentioned casually. 'Martin tells me you're bringing someone with you.'

'Well, so are you.' She almost seemed to be reproaching him, even her eyes looked accusing, and Dan's insides knotted up with a mixture of desire, hope and frustration. She had just given him the chance to say so many things and with any other woman he would not have hesitated. At the moment, though, he was in the business of watching his step because she could slide away from him as smoothly as he had captured her.

'Because of Jenny,' he muttered, trying to look defenceless. 'I didn't realize you would be there to help me. I pictured a terrible state of affairs, with Jenny having absolute free rein.'

Helen grinned at him.

'What makes you imagine I would have helped? Margaret told me that Jenny is in love with you. That's charming.'

'*Please!*' Dan begged theatrically. 'Don't turn this into a serious discussion of Jenny's delusions. She's like Lolita. Last year it was like being attacked by a young octopus. She's got to be worse now; she's a year older. When I got back to the States last time she wrote to me. It made my hair curl.'

'Why don't you psychoanalyse her?' Helen sat laughing across at him and he adored her eyes. They were so beautiful, so blue, sparkling with laughter instead of being wary and scared. It was difficult to keep his mind on the conversation.

'No way! She would just love it. Don't you know, Miss Stewart, that women get sexual fantasies about their analysts? I dread to think what young girls get. I'm not about to investigate that either.' He shrugged and glanced at her. 'Anyway, Jenny scares me and leaves me in a fix. I can't put her firmly where she belongs because Martin and Margaret are friends. I have to defend myself as best I can. That's why I asked Antonia to come with me.'

He was amused to hear himself lying so smoothly. Desperation it seemed, could lead to many new skills. Helen took him by surprise with her next question.

'What does she look like?'

'Jenny? Surely you know?'

'Antonia.'

Their eyes met and held and Dan wasn't quite sure now how much she believed of his pitiful story. He smiled to himself. Helen was smart. He must be careful to remember that. He was on decidedly slippery ground but they were having a fairly normal conversation, even though his end of it was mostly fabrication.

'Beautiful,' he murmured vaguely, trying to look as if he was giving it considerable thought. 'Very sophisticated. Aristocratic, I think. Of course, that's only an American opinion. You'll judge her much better. See what you think of her and tell me on Monday.'

The mention of Monday reminded Helen about the reading at the bookshop and her face fell considerably. The amusement went out of things. She was silent.

'Did I say something wrong?' Dan asked quietly. 'Is Monday a bad thing to say, or was it the mention of being an American?'

'I know you're annoyed about the reading,' Helen told him a little miserably. 'I thought you might like it. I suppose I should have known better then to arrange it without asking you. It was unforgivable really.'

'Oh, it was, but I'll forgive you if you take off those enormous spectacles,' Dan said as the waiter came back with their food.

'I need them to see with,' Helen protested quickly, and, as the waiter left, Dan leaned forward and gently removed them, folding them and placing them on the table between them.

'No, you don't, Helen. You need them to hide behind. Let's see how you manage without them for a while. If your fork goes into the table instead of the food, I might just be convinced.'

'You keep prying into my mind, don't you?' Helen murmured. Her cheeks were pink and it made the blue-violet eyes shine like stars. Dan knew he could have sat there and just watched her all night, maybe all his life. The last thing he wanted to do was eat.

'It's the only thing I can get away with,' he said softly. 'You won't let me talk about your problems.'

'I haven't got a problem,' she insisted quickly, and he looked at her for a long moment and then smiled that long, secret smile.

'Okay, honey. If you say so. Eat your meal and relax.'

'Do you call everyone honey?' Helen asked a little waspishly.

'Only the sweet ones,' he assured her laconically. He got on with his meal and Helen did the same, after giving him a small glare which he did not see. She had wanted him to say that he only used the endearment with her. Which was stupid, she reminded herself. She knew what he was like. Martin had told her often enough. She hated Antonia, sight unseen.

When they left the restaurant Dan had a difficult decision to make. He wanted to use every trick in the book to keep her with him but he also wanted her safely at home. He surreptitiously glanced at his watch. It was coming up to eleven. Chances were she would have been home by now in any case, but

143

he didn't know. For all he really knew, she was used to walking and searching all night, and he wasn't taking any risks.

He had slipped her spectacles into his pocket and she had not even noticed, and now, as they walked along quietly, Dan could almost hear her tension rise. He had got her into a relaxed state but now that they were out in the street she was tightening up again as if she could feel danger in the air.

The traffic was still heavy; the lights were still bright. If the city ever slept it was not sleeping now. His eyes scanned the road, looking for a taxi, and at any moment he was expecting her to insist either on walking off or on getting a taxi for herself. He wanted her safe, and he had a deep, certain conviction that she would only be safe with him.

Maybe it was because of the way he felt about her. It was difficult to simply walk beside her, to be amusing, friendly and brotherly. He was aching to touch her, to put his arm round her, to taste the soft lips. Every male instinct in him wanted to devour her, but he had to play it cool and she had to be safe. If he was to get close to Helen he would not be able to use his normal smooth charm. In any case, this was different. She was more important to him than any woman had ever been.

Two things happened simultaneously. He spotted a taxi cruising along looking for a fare and he saw the woman in black. Every nerve in his body seemed to shoot to alert and he threw up his hand for the taxi and grasped Helen's arm tightly, his body blocking out the sight of the woman across the road. He knew she must not see the other woman. He had no idea why he knew it, but he did.

The taxi swooped in towards them and effectively did what Dan had been trying to do. Helen could not now see anything.

'I'm taking you home,' he said firmly when she looked up at him in surprise.

I can get there by myself. I was going to . . .'

'You've had dinner with me, I'm taking you home. You promised you would stop this walking about.'

'I didn't!' Helen protested, but he handed her into the taxi and gave her address.

'Promise me now, then,' he commanded. 'How do you expect me to sleep if I think you're walking around by yourself?'

'You don't know me well enough to lose sleep over my activities.'

'Okay. Let me get to know you better and then I can claim legitimate sleep-loss.' He looked down at her, his expression softening when that helpless expression came back into her eyes.

'I never know how to take you,' she complained warily.

'Straight. Just as I come. I mean everything I say with you.'

Helen gave a little sigh of frustration and Dan sat back, smiling. A difficult manoeuvre, executed faultlessly.

The taxi managed to pull out and take off and Dan glanced keenly through the window. The woman in black was on the opposite pavement, level with them and walking with the same prowling pace. He made a quick decision. It was a risk, but he had to know if his feelings of unease for Helen were based on fact.

'Weird-looking hooker,' he murmured casually. 'I mean . . .'

'I know what you mean. I know what a hooker is, thank you. I watch American films,' Helen assured him tartly. She glanced out of the window too and stiffened like a horse at the starting gate. Her hand grasped Dan's as it lay on the seat between them, her fingers biting into him. Shock raced through her. He could actually feel it.

'Stop the taxi!' she ordered in an urgent whisper.

But Dan leaned forward and slid the glass partition closed and then turned her hand so that he was holding it firmly.

'No, Helen. I'm taking you home.'

'I have to get out! I have to . . .'

'No, Helen,' he insisted quietly. 'I won't have you in danger.'

'You have nothing to do with me!' she said wildly, staring at him and shaking her head from side to side. He grasped her chin, making her keep still.

'Only because you won't let me,' he told her softly. 'Given half a chance I would have everything to do with you and I think you know it.'

'I don't,' she whispered. She moved her hand from his and looked wearily out of the window as she gave in. The lights were behind her now. It was too late in any case. It was the closest she had ever been and it was too late. It would all happen again, and maybe she could have stopped it tonight.

'I've been looking for a long time,' she said almost to herself, 'and just then I could have done something.'

'No, Helen,' he said implacably. 'You couldn't.'

He steadfastly ignored the tears that had started in her eyes. Now was not the time, not the place. She was safe for the time being and that was all that mattered. In any case, he had nothing to go on but instinct and he knew she would tell him nothing. The fact that their instincts were running on a parallel course was significant but not proof of anything. She had already said that she might be imagining things

He got out with her at her house and told the taxi to turn round and wait for him. He wanted to see her safely inside with the door locked. She turned to face him, looking up at him in the lights outside her front door, her expression puzzled and vaguely reprimanding.

'I know,' he assured her quietly. 'I'm a bully. I interfere when it's none of my business. I got the better of you by brute force. I'm everything you're thinking. But promise me you won't come out again tonight, Helen.' She just looked up at him, saying nothing and he took her arms, grasping them insistently. 'Helen. Promise me.'

'All right.' She seemed to come out of a small trance and nodded tiredly. 'I wouldn't anyway. It's too late. It's taken so long and now my chances of finding . . .' Her voice trailed off and Dan spoke to her urgently.

'Tell me about it. Share it. Let me help.'

'I can't.'

'It's that woman,' he stated. 'How do you know her?'

'I might not. I don't know. I can't tell you. It might be all untrue, don't you see?'

Funnily enough, he did see. He had had the same feelings, the same instincts, and he might also be imagining it. Only years of experience had convinced him it was not imagination. But what was the woman to Helen? How did she fit into this?

For now he had to leave it. He had to let her go even though he wanted to dismiss the taxi and go inside with her, to stay with her all night and hold her safely.

'Promise you'll tell me when you can?' he asked.

'You always want a lot of promises,' she said fretfully.

'I'm a very demanding sort of guy. You'll realize that when you get to know me better.'

'I won't get to know you better,' Helen said rather sadly, and his hands slid round her face tilting it to his.

'Oh, yes, you will, honey,' he whispered. Before she could even guess what he was thinking, his lips closed over hers gently, his hands cradled her head and every bit of breath seemed to leave her body as sensation shot through her like a strike of lightning.

For those few seconds she forget every other thing, her misery, her guilt and her fears. There was only Dan, his lips claiming hers, the scent of his skin in her nostrils, the feel of his hands on her face. A wonderful being was holding her close and Helen was in a dream world she had never entered in her life before. She just wanted to stay there.

He lifted his head and looked down at her, smiling when he saw that her eyes were still blissfully closed.

'You'll know me better. Helen,' he promised softly.

When she looked up at him with dreamy questioning, his eyes almost drowned her, blazing like fire, compelling and urgent, desire crackling through the gold, darkening it to deep, rich amber. But he pressed matters no further.

He reached into his pocket and carefully took out her spectacles and she stood, unable to move, as he gently slid them back on her face and arranged them in place. He kissed the tip of her nose and looked down at her.

'All the better to see me with, my dear,' he misquoted softly. 'Goodnight, Helen.'

'Goodnight.' She watched him for a minute and then said almost vaguely, 'Dan?'

'What is it, honey?' he asked softly.

'I left my car behind. I went in it and you made me come back with you. I simply forgot about it.'

'Which just shows how you feel about me,' Dan told her quietly. 'I can make you forget everything if you let me. Do you want me to bring your car back now?'

'No,' she assured him shakily. 'It's in a safe place. I can get it tomorrow.'

'Shall I come for you in the morning or shall I stay with you tonight?' Dan asked seductively.

'I – I can manage,' she whispered, and then almost flew into the house.

'I wonder if I can?' Dan murmured wryly as he heard her lock the door. He walked down to the taxi and grinned at the driver.

'Home, James,' he ordered cheerfully.

'And where's that?' The taxi driver turned to grin back at him. He had seen that nice little parting. He liked a romantic glimpse of life from time to time.

'I'll tell you when I remember. Let's go before I change my mind.'

Dan leaned back and took a few steadying breaths. The flames of desire he had been fighting for days had leapt into life when he had kissed her. He was honest enough to admit that, had it been anyone else, he would have been in there with her now, making love to her, staying the night. The way she had reacted to him made that certain, but he had also felt the urge to protect her.

The spellbound look on her face told him as nothing else could that she was defenceless. He might be all sorts of things but he was no wolf. And she had problems, greater problems than he had dreamed of when he had first seen her. There was a connection between Helen and a woman he knew to be dangerous.

He knew for sure about the danger, and not by sheer instinct. The woman was young and slender and yet she had frightened off two grown men, and it could not have been just by her words. Normally a man would have laughed at her. Those two had beat a hasty retreat.

He knew now that Helen had been looking for her, searching the streets. If he hadn't seen Helen earlier and scooped her off for dinner, she might have found what she had been searching for. And even if it had all been a mistake she would have been confronting a woman who moved in the dark as if she had been born to it. A woman who filled him with apprehension. Somehow he must help Helen whether she liked it or not. He had to keep her safe.

Caroline walked into the bookshop on Saturday morning and saw at once that Violet Edgerton was not there. Her heart sank. It meant a day alone with Mr Rider. Mrs Edgerton was never off work, and she had to choose this time to be away, when Caroline felt awful herself. She had a queer, oppressive headache that refused to go. She had had it for two days and it seemed to burn right into her head.

She had to face the whole day and she had to face it with *him*. She would have been able to manage alone much better, but she was not sure how she would manage the shop and George Rider at the same time.

As the day progressed her headache intensified and she was on edge about him every minute. He was watching her all the time. She could feel his eyes on her even when she wasn't looking. Today he would do something. She had escaped it so far because of Violet Edgerton's friendship, but it was asking too much to escape now.

Luckily it was Saturday and there were plenty of customers. Caroline put some beat music on to encourage even more of them, and although the music tore into her head until she felt it would burst, she kept it going and kept smiling. He never came out to help her with the crowds. He was like a loathsome, slimy creature crouched in his hole, waiting.

He called her into his office when there was a slack period just after lunch. There were no customers in the shop and she felt almost sick at the expression on his face. Lecherous bastard! He made her skin crawl.

'Come round here, Caroline,' he ordered when she stood just inside the door. 'Tell me what you think of this new poster for the window.'

It was turned so that she couldn't see it and she had to go round his desk and stand beside him, everything inside her stiffened and ready for escape.

'It's good,' she said quickly, hoping to make a hasty retreat.

'You hardly noticed it. Take a better look.' He slid his chair closer and when she pretended to look she felt his hand come to her leg, stroking her, moving up beyond her knee, his fingers tightening hotly.

'Mr Rider!' She tried to pull away but his other hand slid round her hip and he pulled her even closer.

'Don't be shy with me, Caroline. I know what you're really like inside. It would have been like this ages ago if that old bitch hadn't been with us every day in the shop. I'm going to get rid of her and then it will be just the two of us. We can stay after the shop closes every night.'

His hand was moving higher up her leg and he was pulling her towards his lap and Caroline wrenched herself away.

'Not here, Mr Rider,' she said quickly when he looked angry and red-faced. 'Somebody might come into the shop at any moment.'

He gave her a lascivious smile and let her go completely.

'Tonight, then, when we close,' he insisted in a slurred voice. 'We'll lock up and stay here.'

She thought fast, trying to keep the cold out of her eyes.

'Let's go somewhere else,' she suggested. 'Somewhere more private. I'll leave a bit early and get changed and you can pick me up just down the street, where it's dark. By that bit of park opposite the church.'

'If you're having me on . . .' he threatened and she summoned up a smile that had his face reddening again.

'Why should I be doing that? You're the boss. Don't think I haven't thought about it. I can always see you in your office when I'm working.'

She made it to the door, thankful when the shop door opened and a customer came in. She could hear the bell.

'What did I tell you?' she said slyly. 'It's a customer. Don't forget that there's a clear glass panel between this room and the shop. What would they have thought, Mr Rider?'

He glanced into the shop and then frowned and stood up.

'It's that bloke who was here chatting you up.'

Caroline looked too, almost sinking with relief to see that it was Peter Saddler, looking as embarrassed as ever.

'Oh, him,' she scoffed quickly. 'He's only a boy. He's not like you.' She deliberately let her eyes run over him slowly, sickness welling up inside her again when she saw his aroused state. 'I'll get off early and get changed,' she promised. 'I'll leave at four-thirty. You'll be able to manage the rest of the time by yourself.'

'Four-thirty?' He was back to suspicion again.

'I have to get home to change,' she cajoled.

'You look all right as you are. Anyway, you live close by, don't you?'

'These are my working things. I want to take time getting ready. We're going to have a date, aren't we? Wait till you see me later. You'll not be able to keep your hands off me.'

'I knew you would be like this,' he said, his eyes running over her breasts and rounded hips. 'I'd like to get my hands on you now.'

'Well, we wouldn't like your wife to see us, would we?' she asked archly.

'She knows my car,' he said, looking worried. Doris had warned him that if anything like this happened again she would divorce him and take every penny he had. Caroline watched the anxiety racing across his heavy face and her eyes hardened like ice but she kept on smiling with that same coy, encouraging smile.

'How can she see it in the dark?' she asked. 'It won't be here by the shop, will it? Does she go up on the old common on the grass? She'd have to go right up there to see us. It's lovely and soft on the grass and it's dark. I bet she never wants to take you up there, Mr Rider.'

'Four-thirty, then,' he said, his breathing fast and heavy. 'I like the way you always call me Mr Rider. It gets to me. You can call me that tonight when we're in the grass. I'll pick you up by the park at seven o'clock. Gives me time to get home and back again.' It would also give him time to see Doris and tell her he had a meeting. He would think of something. It would also be darker by then, less chance of being seen by the park when he picked her up. 'It's a long time between four-thirty and seven. If you're a good girl tonight you can leave at four-thirty and meet me later regularly.'

'Oh, I'm a very good girl, Mr Rider,' she said, giving him an encouraging look. 'You'll see.'

He was actually licking his lips. Her stomach turned over but she smiled. She had been thinking all week that she knew him. Now she remembered who he was. His big red face reminded her. All this time and she hadn't realized. She didn't know why she hadn't remembered before. It was funny how she sometimes forgot things like that. But he didn't know her, he didn't recognize her. The fool.

'Hello, Peter,' she called cheerfully as she stepped back into the shop and closed the office door behind her. 'Good job you came in now. I'm leaving early today.' She looked at her watch. 'You can stay and chat to me if you like. In fact, if you feel like it you can walk me to the bus when I go.'

He beamed at her and went bright red and she gave her another smile that never reached her eyes. She could get him to stay easily. It would mean a safe escape at four-thirty without any further need to have those foul hands on her. After that it didn't matter. She wouldn't be seeing Mr Rider again after today.

'Do I look all right, Margaret?' Helen asked anxiously as she helped Margaret in the kitchen. She was on edge, waiting for Dan to arrive, longing to see him but dreading it in case her face gave away her feelings.

'You look lovely, Helen; you always do. I've never seen you in anything like that before. You usually look extremely businesslike. You don't wear jeans much, do you?'

'Only around the house. It seemed to be a suitable way to dress for the barbecue but I didn't really know. Maybe the woman Dan brings will be looking glamorous.'

'I should hope not. I never achieve glamour myself. Anyway, so long as you're comfortable,' Margaret said, looking comfortable herself. She lowered her voice. 'I don't know what Jenny intends to wear. One shudders to think. She's treating the whole affair as if it's an important social event. I didn't quite have the nerve to tell her that Dan's bringing a woman with him. I suppose it was unfair of me, but if she's going to kick up a fuss there's safety in numbers. She won't fuss with Dan here.'

Helen looked down and nibbled at her lip. She was having problems of her own about the fact that Dan was bringing a woman in spite of what he had told her in the restaurant. She had never for one minute stopped thinking about the kiss he had given her the night before. It had been gentle, but she had felt the leashed-in heat behind it, and heat wouldn't seem to stop flooding through her too every time she thought of him, which was most of the time.

He had said he wanted to get to know her but she wondered if he really meant it. She had spent the better part of the night and this morning reminding herself about his reputation. He would be gone soon, and this interest in her could only be a way of passing his time.

And even if he meant it, she dared not let him get close. She dared not let anyone get close. She was safe in her work, safe when she went to the gym, but she had a secret that was too terrible to allow her anything other than a casual acquaintance with anyone.

She knew that Dan already suspected her. He knew that something was very wrong, and the fact that he seemed to still be interested in her in spite of his suspicions made her legs feel weak. She knew that she wanted to be closer to him. He was rarely out of her thoughts.

It was no use, though. He had uncannily pinpointed the subject of her quest the night before. If she let him get closer he would find out everything. Already the guilt weighed heavily on her, and if he found out, Dan would be disgusted. She would rather he went back to his own country and thought about her pleasantly. If she saw the horror in his eyes that she knew she would see when he found out, she would not be able to endure it.

'What did you say his name was?' Margaret asked, breaking in on Helen's thoughts. 'Jack Garford? He seems nice, and he's good-looking in a very pleasing homely way. How long have you been going out with him?'

'I haven't,' Helen assured her, hiding a sudden smile at Margaret's attempt to be subtle, Margaret would love to get her married off. She liked things all nicely arranged and rounded, no rough edges showing. 'We go to the gym together, that's all. Martin asked me to bring someone to make up the numbers, so I brought Jack.'

'Goodness, I hope you didn't tell him he was just making up the numbers,' Margaret said anxiously. 'That's no way to intrigue a man.'

'Er – no.' Actually she couldn't remember whether she had said that or not. She tended to say exactly what she thought with Jack. She had been too busy being jealous about the woman that Dan was bringing to take much notice of Jack's finer feelings. 'As a matter of fact,' she added, 'Jack is a journalist. He's hoping to get a sort of interview with Dan while he's here tonight. I hope you and Martin won't mind.'

'We won't mind. Let's just hope Dan is in a good mood,' Margaret murmured. She looked up at the clock. 'They should be here soon. Would you mind just nipping upstairs and having a look at Jenny, Helen, while I finish off here? Honestly, I daren't go myself. If she's up to anything, I'll scream, I know I will. She just gets more difficult every time I see her.'

'She might not like it if I go up,' Helen pointed out.

'Nonsense! You've known her for ages and she likes you. Just saunter into her room casually and tell her she looks awful, because if she's dressing up specially for Dan, that's exactly how she will look.'

'That's *your* job,' Helen laughed. 'I'll go up, but any telling comes from you. I refuse to drop even a hint.' She peered through the window. The kitchen looked out over the swimming pool and Martin had the barbecue set up near there. Jack was listening to him and nodding his head vigorously, passing him things. 'Jack and Martin seem to be getting on well.'

'I'm not surprised. Martin will be telling him how to fix a barbecue. He tells everybody. If Jack's listening nicely it just proves he's a pleasant man and not to be dismissed out of hand when you're thinking about marriage,'

'I'm not thinking about marriage, though,' Helen assured her with a grin. 'I never give it a thought.'

'You should.'

'I'll go upstairs. I think I'd rather face Jenny than this.'

CHAPTER 7

Helen stopped to look at herself in the long mirror in the hall. She was rarely uneasy about her appearance. She knew how she was supposed to look for work and during the trips with Dan she had stuck steadfastly to a businesslike image. Now she was nervous, and she knew it was because it mattered to her when Dan looked at her.

Her hair looked too curly and there were faint blue circles under her eyes. She moved her head to see if it was a trick of the light but it wasn't, and she hadn't really expected it to be the light because she knew what it was. It was lack of sleep. Worry about her guilty secret and excitement about Dan.

She wondered now if she should have come in something different. The dark blue jeans fitted snugly around her narrow hips and the blue checked shirt looked all right. She could roll up the sleeves. Maybe it would look better then. She wished she hadn't come in white trainers. She looked altogether too casual. The woman Dan was bringing would probably be in something flowing and feminine. If she was, then Helen knew she would feel like a frump, a frump playing at having a good time.

She hurried upstairs. She had to get to Martin before Dan came, and then she had to stick to him all evening and try not to look too often in Dan's direction. One look of amused disdain from those panther eyes and she would curl up with embarrassment.

Helen knocked on Jenny's door, a little alarmed when Jenny snapped out at once, demanding to know who it was in a sharp voice that was quite ready for an argument.

'It's Helen, Jenny. We're nearly ready to start the event.'

'Oh come in, Helen. I thought it was Mummy coming to check my clothes. She's been creeping around earlier looking sideways at me. What do you think of the outfit?' she asked when Helen popped her head round the door.

'Very modern,' Helen managed diplomatically. It was all she could come up with on the spur of the moment. What did one say to a fifteen-year-old in a long skirt that was just about at her ankles and skin-tight all the way down, especially as it was topped by a cut-off cotton jumper that left a good deal of midriff bare. The footwear made a startling finishing touch that had Helen staring, heavy-soled boots with white socks turned over the tops.

'It's the rage,' Jenny informed her smugly, leaning towards the mirror and applying a thick coat of red lipstick. She glanced at Helen and did a rapid inventory of her appearance. 'Why don't you go for something like this? You're not really old. It would brighten you up.'

'Er – I thought everyone would be wearing jeans,' Helen said hastily. 'I've probably done the wrong thing but I'm stuck with it now.'

'Oh, you look all right really,' Jenny condescended airily. 'Bit stiff perhaps, but you've got a nice face, all dreamy and misty.'

''Thank you. I'll tell Margaret that you're coming, then,' Helen said faintly, beginning to back out.

'Soon,' Jenny promised with a little smile of satisfaction as she turned before the mirror and admired the finished product. 'I'm going to wait until Dan comes. I'll let him have five minutes to miss me and then I'll be down. But don't tell Mummy that,' she added sternly. 'She thinks I'm a child. It's ridiculous.'

'Not a word,' Helen vowed as she made her escape. She didn't know whether to laugh or be filled with pity. Poor Jenny. When Dan came with a glamorous woman, Jenny would be in tears. Dan was in for a bad time, but then again, so was Antonia, whoever she was. Helen's lips quirked in amusement. She could rescue Jenny easily if it became necessary. She wouldn't dream of rescuing Antonia. She peered at herself in the mirror on the passage as she hurried past. All dreamy and misty? Until now she had been labouring under the impression that she was always crisp and efficient.

Apparently she looked like someone staring through water. If it had been meant as a compliment it was very unnerving.

Helen had just made it downstairs when Dan arrived. She knew because Martin yelled out the fact to Margaret at the top of his voice.

'Dan's here!'

'Good,' Margaret muttered. 'I thought he just might think about sneaking out of it. Hope he's in a good frame of mind, because he's going to need all his skills tonight. Maybe I should have packed Jenny off to some sort of holiday camp. What did she look like?'

'She's on her way down,' Helen said quickly, escaping to the outside and making a beeline for Jack. She wasn't getting mixed up in this until she had to. Martin had a fiery temper and Jenny had inherited it. She had the feeling that things might just explode when Martin saw his daughter in her outfit. And Dan hadn't come round the side yet, so she just had time to make it safety.

She was a few beats too late. The side gate opened before she could get to Jack and Martin. It was too late to go forward and too late to retreat to the kitchen.

'Hello, Helen.' Dan's quiet voice held her rooted to the spot. It sounded seductive and it sent waves of heated feeling through her, making her legs go weak and she turned slowly, too shaken to even pretend to smile. Last time she had seen him he had been kissing her. A shiver ran all over her skin and she

164

had no alternative but to face him and face the glamorous Antonia.

And she was glamorous. Helen found herself staring, quite unable to stop. Antonia looked like something off the front of an expensive, glossy magazine. She was dark-haired, her hair just touching her shoulders. It was straight, thick, heavy and beautifully groomed. The eyes were dark too, full of intelligence and wry amusement, as if she'd seen it all and nothing was going to astonish her.

The dress was a work of art, silk by the look of it, draped round her figure, almost sculpted to her, and Helen felt gauche, clumsy, and terribly dismayed, even if the dress was far too elaborate for a suburban barbecue.

How could Dan say that the only reason he had asked Antonia to come with him was because of Jenny? Helen knew without being told that he spent every spare moment with this woman. When he had said last night that he was lonely he had just been playing one of his games, amusing himself.

'I'm wearing the wrong thing, darling,' Antonia said, looking up at Dan as she tucked her hand in his arm. 'I should have been wearing jeans. I shall feel out of place all evening.'

'I doubt it,' Dan drawled sardonically.

'You look lovely,' Helen said, quietly because she really meant it. 'Margaret is wearing a dress. It's what you're comfortable in that matters.'

Antonia gave her a close look that was a mixture of approval and surprise and then held out her hand.

'Introduce us, Dan.' she commanded. 'Or shall I guess? You're Helen. I've been hearing about you.'

'About how I walked out and left Mr Forrest all alone when he was ill, I expect,' Helen murmured miserably.

'Did you? He never told me that. It was very wise of you. I can't bear illness. I'm always afraid of catching something. I wouldn't even have been there in the first place. To even approach him was very brave indeed.'

'Helen is headstrong,' Dan assured her. His eyes had not left Helen since he had come through the gate. They were pinning her to the spot. He was fighting desire with every breath he took. 'How about me?' he asked quietly. 'Do I look lovely too, Helen?'

'Very nice,' she pronounced somewhat glumly. He looked handsome and at ease. He was wearing light casual trousers and a dark polo shirt that looked as if he had paid a fortune for it. He probably had. He looked very American, too, and he wasn't playing any of his games. He was just being himself, and nothing could draw her to him more than that. She wanted him to reach out and touch her and it was all so stupid. He was with the sort of glamorous woman he liked. It would be the sort of atmosphere he lived in. Helen felt very plain and miles distant from his world.

'I'll introduce you to Martin and then Margaret,' she offered quickly, looking at Antonia and avoiding Dan's eyes. 'Martin is by the pool but Margaret is in the kitchen, making the rest of the salads.'

'And you've been helping her,' Dan surmised quietly. 'Is Jenny there too?'

'Not yet.' Helen remembered Jenny and felt considerably better, her amusement growing in spite of her disappointment. There was a look of apprehension on Dan's face, and the thought of the entrance Jenny planned to make had her relaxing in anticipation. 'She plans to be down in five minutes.' She couldn't stop her smile and Dan narrowed golden eyes on her, suspicion on his face.

'Tell me what to expect.'

'And spoil her surprise? That would be unfair.' Helen's smile widened and Dan ushered Antonia through the gate and then took Helen's arm, pulling her close against him as he followed Antonia.

'Come here. You're supposed to help me, you blue-eyed little cat,' he muttered.

'You'll be all right. You have Antonia. Jenny will just be in a rage when she sees how beautiful Antonia is, but I expect she'll get over it. Just sit and eat and let things wash over you.'

'The only thing I want to eat is you,' Dan whispered seductively against her ear. 'I've been awake all night thinking about you. Don't imagine that anyone is going to keep me away from you. I only came because of you.'

'Dan, please!' Helen said anxiously, her cheeks flushing, and although she had told herself that this was all wrong and impossible for her, she felt her knees go weak at the seductive whisper.

'Help me to ward off Jenny or I'll make an embarrassing scene,' Dan threatened in a low voice. 'I'll kiss you in public.'

'Jack would object,' Helen managed with shaky triumph. 'I expect Antonia would too, but Jack does judo.'

Dan released her arm, and when she risked a glance at him his face was fairly thunderous. He felt thunderous too. He had forgotten about her escort. When he was with her she seemed to belong to him. He had to get a good look at this Jack character. There were too many advantages for the opposition. They went to the same club, he remembered, and Helen had probably known him for a long time. He was English too.

His jaw tightened and his frown grew with each second. All this *and* Jenny. He wouldn't get a chance to be near Helen. She probably wouldn't want to be near him either. Then he remembered the way she had looked when he had kissed her and changed his mind rapidly. She had wanted to be near him then, and she had looked devastated at the sight of Antonia.

'Right,' he drawled. 'Lead the way to the slaughter. I'll just have to be grown-up by the look of it. All I can say is that this makes me feel my age.'

'I expect it does. Jenny says *I'm* not all that old, though,' Helen said brightly. 'She doesn't really mind my jeans either.'

'Well, they sure fit snugly in the right places, honey,' Dan murmured, letting his gaze skim slowly over her until she was blushing again.

'Antonia is beautiful,' Helen whispered to get herself out of the situation, and Dan shot a quick look at her. She was looking downcast. He smiled enigmatically.

'I know. She's just the thing for a man to drape on his arm.'

Helen's face fell even more and he hid his satisfaction. Maybe the opposition didn't have it all going their way? She was jealous, not with the green-eyed angry jealousy of some women he knew, but with a sad little jealousy, as if she thought she could never compete with someone like Antonia. He wondered what she would say if she knew about Antonia's hobby. He hoped she never found out.

'Okay,' he said resolutely. 'I'll get the meeting with your boyfriend over before Jenny springs one of her surprises on me. I'll get round to you later.'

George Rider pulled the car close in to the kerb and switched off the lights. It wasn't quite dark yet but it was close enough to it. You had to be near to someone to really see them clearly, and that suited him fine. Doris hadn't taken it too well when he had pleaded a meeting and prepared to leave the house. She didn't trust him. It would mean a row sooner or later, but he would put up with that just to get his hands on Caroline at last. He had been planning it for weeks, and he had been really surprised at how easy it had turned out to be.

He wasn't giving it up now, whatever Doris had planned for when he got back. All the same, he was impatient for Caroline to come, impatient to get out of the area where he just might be spotted. He wouldn't put it past Doris to have a private detective on his trail. There had been a look in her eyes tonight that made him suspicious. The sooner he got Caroline on to the common she had spoken about, the better.

His body stirred in anticipation. From the first moment he had seen her he had known it would end like this. It would have been sooner if that old cow hadn't been there, always ready to step in like a mother hen. It was impossible to do anything without her seeing. He would get rid of her some time during next week, then he could have a great time with Caroline with nobody the wiser. He would start shutting the shop at lunchtime.

He glanced at the clock on the dashboard. It was getting darker by the minute. It was almost black now. There were very few lights round here, which was a good thing for him, but it made it difficult to see anyone clearly even close up and he would have a hard time watching for her. It was time she showed up. If she'd been having him on, being a little tease, she would pay for it on Monday.

He looked in the mirror when he heard a slight noise and he saw a woman come out of the gate by the church behind him on the opposite side of the road. She was very dark-haired, though. The light by the church gate shone on her for a second as she moved under it and it only gave him time to notice her hair. It wasn't Caroline. She was late. If she didn't come . . .!

He jumped in surprise as the passenger door opened noiselessly and the woman he had noticed by the church slid into the seat without a word.

'What . . .?' he began angrily, and then he started to grin as his eyes roamed over her. 'This is what you meant by getting changed? I like it!'

He started to reach for her, but she moved out of his way and glanced round anxiously.

'Not here,' she whispered. 'I went to a lot of trouble to get you alone. It's not dark enough here. Drive off.'

He obeyed immediately. He wanted to get away from here and up to the common for more reasons than to escape Doris's surveillance. His body was tight with anticipation. He didn't care how long he would be out tonight, and he didn't care what Doris said; it was going to be worth it. He glanced at her out of his eye-corners.

She had gone to a lot of trouble for him. She had meant it when she had enticed him in his office. His sense of anticipation grew. He would get a flat for her and then she could dress up for him every night, lunchtime too, perhaps, instead of staying in the shop. He could see her then, watch her get changed to look like this. He couldn't see her properly here because she was sitting pulled away from him and it would be too dark on the common. It was exciting, as if another woman had suddenly come chasing him.

The way she had whispered as if she hardly knew him had aroused him even more. He would make her whisper all evening. He wouldn't go back home. He would stay out all night with her, go to some hotel room if she was as good as he anticipated.

'Here.' she whispered. 'Turn off on to the grass.'

He turned the car and bumped it along for a few yards and then stopped, reaching to grab hold of her, even though the engine was still running.

'Wait until we're on the grass,' she whispered urgently. 'It's better. More room.'

He could hardly hear her voice and it excited him. It was driving him mad; his fingers were shaking as he switched off the engine and he got out of the car quickly. But she stayed where she was, waiting for him to open the door for her. She was playing, working him up, making him more excited. He loved it. His heart was beating like a hammer.

He went quickly round the bonnet and leaned forward to help her out, participating in the game as if she were a real lady out for the night with him. It suited him. He liked this sort of game and she seemed to know exactly what he wanted. He stood back with mocking gallantry as she moved. In a minute he would have his hands on her.

He was already glancing round, looking for a good place. They could stay near the car, perhaps, get in the back. The grass might be wet at this time of the year and he would have a hard time explaining wet clothes to Doris.

They wouldn't be here long, anyway. He'd made his mind up about the hotel room. This was too good to hurry. It would be the best he had ever had.

Even in the shop Caroline excited him, but the way she was dressed up now was even better. It would be like having two women in future, Caroline in the shop doing just what he wanted and then how she looked now, a different person, making him wait. He could take to that, easily.

She put her legs out to stand up, long, slender legs in black tights, and he looked down at them as she bent her head to get out of the car. She had stunning legs and she was letting him get a good look at her, making him hold back the raging sexual turmoil she had built up. He was more excited than he had ever been in his life.

'Come on,' he said roughly. 'Let's get started. We've played enough. I want it now.'

She moved quickly, lithely, one smooth, agile movement that brought her to her feet facing him. He never saw what was coming, never suspected.

'Here it is, then,' she whispered. 'I was going to give it to you now. You didn't have to ask.'

'Who . . .? he began in a startled voice, but he had no chance to say anything else. The thin knife never flashed in the light. It was too dark. It slid into him without warning, giving him no time to cry out. And even if he had shouted, there was nobody. There was the deserted common, darkness, the car, nothing else.

His mouth opened in shock and he was falling long before the pain hit him. He staggered against the side of the car, his hand clutching for support, and the knife slid into him again before he fell, one expert blow followed by another.

He fell on to his back by the car and lay still and silent in the darkness, and she stared down at him coldly for a second. It was done at last, finished, over. Now there would be peace in the house. She dropped to her knees beside him to perform her terrifying ritual.

'For her! For her! For me! For me!' she whispered. She went on until the ten blows were delivered, but he was dead long before then. He had died at the second blow. Her skill was well practised. She had never missed yet, and this one was perfect.

Her shoulders relaxed as she stared down at him, and then she wiped the knife on his jacket and stood slowly. 'Pig,' she whispered. 'Dirty bastard. Did you think you'd get away forever?'

She walked across the grass to the road they had just left and turned towards the nearest lights, never even glancing back. There was nothing to see because it was too dark. A few steps and even the car was invisible. There was no sound but the noise of her own footsteps in the high-heeled shoes. The lights ahead were not too far away now. She would clean the knife carefully. She never forgot that, because each time was the first time and the knife must be new again. She would go home and sleep when the last ritual was over, and everything would be pure, undefiled, cleansed.

She walked from the common, across the deserted

wasteland, and came to the long street. It hadn't been raining so the road did not glitter in the lights. It was ordinary now, with no special magic, a road like any other road. The house at the end was in darkness still and she opened the gate and closed it methodically behind her. A moment later the front door closed behind her too, with a hollow tone that echoed through empty rooms.

Dan was talking to Jack and showing no sign of resentment. Apparently this was the interview, and as they both laughed frequently Helen assumed it was all going well. She glanced round at the others. Everything was calm. Martin and Margaret had surprised her with their ready acceptance of Antonia, and although Helen hadn't spoken to her much she was obviously easy to get on with. They were sitting by the pool with Antonia now, laughing at something she was telling them, and Helen glanced up at the lighted window above.

Poor Jenny. She had made such a fool of herself, had horrified Margaret and infuriated Martin. Antonia had taken it in her stride, as if things like that happened every day. Jack had found it hard not to say something appeasing but he had managed to keep silent. And Dan had looked mortified and sorry, sympathetic but knowing better than to intervene when Martin had flown into a rage. Dan's initial attempt to be calm and friendly with Jenny had been used in a way that had stunned him, and now she was by herself, no doubt crying her eyes out.

The whole thing had been more than anyone had bargained for and Helen's personal problems were pushed to the back of her mind as she tried to work out a way to help Jenny to regain her dignity. What could she say? She had never have anticipated that Jenny would walk down to them and ignore everyone but Dan. She had never anticipated either that the small cut-off top would have been pulled down from her shoulders after she had seen Jenny in the bedroom.

Dan had reacted perfectly. He had shown no surprise and had held out his hand with a smile of welcome.

'Hello, Jenny. I was wondering where you were.'

Jenny had taken the hand he held out and pulled it round her waist. She had flung her arms round his neck and kissed him full on the mouth and Martin had erupted immediately. He had been angry, embarrassed and, frankly, shocked as Helen had seen. Margaret had told her about Martin's temper but she had never witnessed it before.

He had snatched Jenny away from a startled and embarrassed Dan and spun her round in front of everyone.

'Go back to your room and stay there!' He had pulled out a tissue and wiped the lipstick off almost savagely and Jenny had screamed at him, twisting uselessly to get away.

'No! I won't! I'm grown-up and I love Dan.'

'You look like a tart and you're behaving like one. Dan is my guest. He's old enough to be your father and if he were he would probably put you across his knee and belt your bottom until you got some sense. Now go to your room.'

Jenny had fled and Martin had been too angry to make apologies to anyone. Margaret had been in tears and when Helen had jumped up Martin had snapped at her instantly, telling her to keep out of it.

Antonia had been utterly unperturbed. She had stood up with one smooth movement and picked up the champagne bottle.

'Can we start this now?' she asked in her rich throaty voice. 'I always find it calming.' She had proceeded to pour out glasses for everyone and gave Margaret a wide smile as she raised her own glass. 'Here's to a young lady with spirit. I was just like that at her age.'

'Were you?' Margaret asked shakily.

'Exactly. Well, come to think of it, not the boots. I liked high heels, the higher the better. The sentiments were the same, though.' With her standing there smiling and looking like a duchess it was impossible to imagine that she would ever have put on such a juvenile display, but it eased the embarrassment, and the champagne did the rest.

'*Were* you like that?' Dan asked quietly later when they were out of Margaret and Martin's hearing.

'Good gracious, darling, no!' Antonia whispered. 'My father would have flayed me and sent me to a convent.'

She walked off rather grandly and Dan muttered, 'Her father the duke.'

'Was he?' Helen asked, feeling dazed.

'God knows! You've got to admit, though, that she's got style.'

Helen nodded. She admitted it readily. Things had been smoothed over. Jack had started talking in an animated way to Martin, asking idiotic questions about the barbecue, and then they had all chattered to cover up the embarrassment.

Now they were settled and all was back to normal, although slightly subdued. Things were not back to normal for Jenny, though. She was still in her room and no doubt suffering teenage agonies. Helen stood quietly and slipped away without being seen. Maybe Jenny would scream at her, but she had to try to make her feel better.

'Go away!' Jenny shouted as Helen knocked on her door.

'I can't, Jen.' Helen said. 'I feel too guilty.'

'Why should you?' Jenny's voice was thick with tears and Helen risked walking in without an invitation.

'Well, it was my fault really,' she confessed, standing in the doorway.

'Why?' Jenny raised red-rimmed eyes and looked at her mournfully. 'Dan brought that woman. I never noticed her until it was too late. I knew you were with a man, I saw you come but I didn't know about her. That's why everyone was embarrassed.'

'That's not true – well, not exactly,' Helen said, venturing further in and sitting on the side of the bed.

'Daddy was furious.'

'I know, but it wasn't because of the woman that Dan brought. It's my fault. I should have told you when I came up, when you were getting ready. No father wants to see his little girl being so grown-up, especially as you're not quite grown-up yet. He wants to see her make the best of herself, and the best thing you have going for you is youth.'

Get more make-up on! Who do you think is going to take any notice of you if you look like that? And get that blouse on that shows your back. Do I have to dress you myself?'

The voice rang in her ears, making a mockery of what she was saying, but Helen fought it off, pushing it where it belonged, back into her nightmares.

'I was making the best of myself,' Jenny said miserably.

'No, Jen. You were trying to look too old and I should have told you. I suppose I didn't have the nerve. That makes me a coward.'

'Oh, no, Helen.' Jenny sat up and wiped her eyes. 'I know you're not a coward. Daddy says you're a real fighter.' She looked down miserably. 'Daddy hates me now and so does Dan.' She looked back up mournfully. 'I love Dan.'

'No, you don't, Jenny. The fact is that you're at a school full of girls and women. You don't see many men. Dan is rather glamorous. He's clever, amusing and very kind. He attracts people.'

'Does he attract you?'

'Even me,' Helen confessed, trying to smile and make it a source of amusement. 'He brought Antonia

179

because he's known her for ages. I brought Jack for the same reason, to make it into a real party. You should really have had a boy to bring with you. It would have made all the difference.'

'It's too late now. I can't go down.'

'Maybe not, but we could try. Antonia stuck up for you straight away, even though it was none of her business. She said she used to be like that, to dress like that. Of course she's too sophisticated to do it now.'

'I wanted to be sophisticated,' Jenny muttered. 'That's what I was trying for.' And Helen knew she was almost there.

'What have you got in your wardrobe that's suitable?'

The search revealed jeans, a rather nice sweater and a wide belt with a spectacular buckle.

'Let's go for high heels,' Helen suggested when Jenny stood looking at herself dubiously. 'Young *and* sophisticated. You'll have it both ways.'

'What do you think?' Jenny asked as she stood with white high-heeled sandals and white earrings dangling from her ears.

'Excellent. You're a very pretty girl, Jen. Now, just a bit of lipstick, and stick to pink.'

'It's useless,' Jenny muttered. 'If I go down now, Daddy will have a fit again, and anyway, I'm too embarrassed.'

'Do you know what Dan said to me once?' Helen said quietly. 'He told me that a smile goes a long way and covers just about everything. And a nice apology,' she added, keeping her fingers crossed.

'I suppose I could try. What will Dan think?'

'He'll be quite proud of you,' Helen assured her, and she was absolutely certain that it was true.

They went down together and Helen kept her arm around Jenny's shoulders as they walked out to the pool. There were lights around it, all lit now and the two of them made a sort of reluctant grand entrance as everyone turned to look at them.

'If you're annoyed, Martin,' Helen said firmly, 'take it out on me for interfering. It's just that – well – tomorrow seems to be such a long way off.'

'I'm sorry, Daddy, everyone.' Jenny said bravely. 'I made an idiot of myself. Sorry, Dan,' she added. 'Helen explained everything to me. I thought it was a good idea but I can see it was stupid. I hope you'll forgive me.'

Dan's smile was brilliant.

'Of course I will. I would much rather have you as a friend, cupcake.'

'What does that mean?' Jenny turned to Helen for support.

'It's one of those things Americans say, I think. They're very strange people. Just say thank you and forget it.'

Dan's smile grew wider, his eyes flaring warmly over Helen, and Antonia waved Jenny across to her like a queen.

'Sit by me, Jenny,' she ordered. 'I've been hearing all about your school. Do you know, I nearly went there myself when I was younger.'

'Daddy?' Jenny asked anxiously, and Helen was relieved to see Martin smile.

'It's all right, love,' he told her quietly. 'Nobody can do more than say sorry, and you did it very nicely.'

Margaret hugged Jenny and gave Helen a grateful smile, and when they were all talking again, Dan came over to Helen and handed her a glass of champagne. He smiled down into her eyes.

'You are one sweet lady,' he said softly. 'You want to come back to the States with me and join my clinic? I could use somebody with that sort of skill.'

'No, thanks.' Helen laughed, wanting to sink down with the wave of pleasure his quiet voice gave her. 'I would be much too scared.'

'Not you, Helen,' he told her gently. 'In any case. I would take good care of you.'

'I have a job, thank you,' Helen informed him shakily.

'I'll keep the offer open. Maybe you'll change your mind.'

'I never will,' Helen whispered.

'Why?'

'I have things to do, things I couldn't leave behind.'

'Whatever it is, you would be safe with me,' Dan said quietly. 'You do feel safe with me, don't you, Helen?'

She looked up at him quickly and her gaze was held by the golden eyes.

'Don't you?' he prompted softly.

'I – I don't know.'

'Yes, you do, honey. You're safe with me and you know it. I want you with me and you know that too.'

'Oh, Dan! Don't!' Helen pleaded.

'Chance, as they say, would be a fine thing,' Dan pointed out with a wry grin that grew wider when she blushed furiously

'Martin!' Jack called a little frantically. 'I think I'm burning things.'

'Turn them over and then we'll eat. Come on, Jenny, get the salad bowls. Helen can get the potatoes.'

'I'll help Helen,' Dan offered loudly with a small frown in Jack's direction in case Jack wanted to step in and take her away from him. Jack never even noticed. He was too busy trying to get control of new skills.

Martin marshalled his guests and showed Jack how to cope with burning meat. Everything was back to normal and Helen felt quite proud of herself. Antonia sat languidly, waiting to be served, and Helen glanced across at her and then met Dan's amused and caressing eyes.

'What do you expect of a duchess? She's done her bit; now she's resting on her laurels.'

'She has done her bit,' Helen agreed. 'She smoothed things over wonderfully. I like her.'

'Yes, you would,' Dan breathed against her ear as his hand tightened round her arm. 'I had great hopes of you being jealous but, as I said, you're one sweet lady.'

'You won't be thinking that on Monday when you're reading out your own words,' Helen reminded him ruefully.

'It's a long time to Monday,' he drawled. 'One whole day and two long, lonely nights.'

In the semi-darkness, Helen's blushes faded. For a little while she had forgotten about the night. She had been normal, talking to other people, doing her bit to help, allowing herself to be thrilled because Dan was there, paying attention to her. She should have been out there, searching the darkness, stopping the nightmare, doing the duty that fate had placed on her as a burden. Instead, she had been involved here, looking at Dan, helping Jenny, being happy, and all the time, at the edge of the lights, the night was waiting like a watching beast of prey.

Dan saw the expression on her face change. From sweet confusion she was now emptily forlorn. What had he said? The only thing that occurred to him was the mention of one word, 'night'. Did she dread the nights so much? He wanted to be with her tonight, every night, but there was a long way to go. He slid his arm round her shoulders no matter what anyone thought.

'Okay,' he said tauntingly. 'If all I get to do with you is serve potatoes, I'll make the best of it. Let's go, honey. We can't have our team coming in last.'

He almost felt the warmth come back into her, and it warmed him too. Whether she knew it or not, Helen needed him, and he had no doubts at all about how he needed her. It was pretty close to driving him mad.

CHAPTER 8

When Caroline went in to work on Monday morning Violet Edgerton was there, looking a trifle watery-eyed and pale but back on the job nevertheless.

'Oh. Mrs Edgerton. I'm so glad to see you,' Caroline cried as she walked in and found her companion and safeguard checking the shelves. 'It was really awful without you. Are you better?'

'It was just a touch of flu, I think, Caroline. I stayed in bed and I was a lot better on Sunday. I did let Mr Rider know but he didn't seem to be bothered whether I lived or died. He's not here yet,' she added, glancing towards his office. 'I had to use my own keys to open up.'

'He wore himself out staring at me on Saturday, I expect,' Caroline sniffed angrily as she put her bag behind the counter. 'I bet that's why he's late. He'll be too busy trying to make his eyes stop popping out of his head. Anyway we had a lot of customers so it was all right. And guess what? That nice, well-mannered boy walked me to the bus.'

'There, I told you,' Mrs Edgerton murmured with satisfaction. 'It's time you started going out with a boy like that. It seems to me you don't go out often enough. You'll not always be young. This time of your life is quickly gone.' She glanced at her watch. 'If Mr Rider doesn't come in by ten o'clock I'll have to ring his wife. There's a bit of petty cash in the drawer but we'll need the safe if we get a lot of people. Apart from the takings there'll be no change.'

'I'd rather put my own money in for change than have him here,' Caroline confessed with a deep frown. 'He's getting on my nerves more every day. If it weren't for you, I'd leave this place and find another job.'

'I know it's trying for you, Caroline, but jobs aren't all that easy to come by. If he gets too bad then just you tell him. And if he talks about dismissing you then you can remind him that he could be sued for sexual harassment.'

'Oh, yes!' Caroline exclaimed gleefully. 'That would wipe that smarmy smile from his face. When he starts again, I'll do it. I bet he'll start as soon as he comes in. Just you watch.'

But at ten o'clock there was still no sign of him, and when Violet Edgerton rang his home she came back looking puzzled.

'He's not at home, Caroline. And from what his wife said he's been out all weekend. She sounded absolutely furious, snapped my head off. I bet he's always chasing after women and I bet she knows it.

He looks that sort of man.' She frowned and the puzzled expression on her face grew. 'All the same, it's really strange. I've never known him miss work. I've been here a long time and sometimes he's come in looking as if he's had a night out, but even so, he arrives at work and he's always on time.'

'Well. I'm glad he's not here,' Caroline stated firmly. 'I had a bad head on Saturday and he didn't even come to help in the shop. The place was crowded all day and he just sat there, staring at me and doing nothing to help at all. I hope his wife chokes him when she sees him.'

The day settled to normality, customers came and went, but George Rider never put in an appearance. It was a pleasant day without him, everything calm in the shop without his stares at Caroline and his snappy remarks to Violet. They even got a good, long break for lunch and sat in the back with coffee and sandwiches.

'It's a bit like a holiday,' Caroline mused. 'If it were like this every day I wouldn't even bother to go home. I feel really happy.'

'Enjoy it while it lasts,' Violet advised drily. 'He might miss one day but he'll not miss another, mark my words.'

She was very wrong. At four o'clock a police car drew up outside and then they found out why Mr Rider had never been in. He had been found on the common and he was dead – murdered.

Violet Edgerton sat down abruptly, white-faced.

'I can't believe it,' she whispered. 'He was a big man, not the sort to get murdered or mugged or anything. He looked as if he could take care of himself. There must be some mistake.'

'There's no mistake, madam. His wife has identified him. We knew who it was because of the car and the things in his pockets. Mrs Rider confirmed it when she went to look at the body.'

'Poor woman,' Caroline said quietly. 'What a thing to have to do. It's too terrible to think of. I hope she's going to be all right?'

'She's very shocked, miss. She was the last to see him, apparently. That was Saturday evening. What we want to know is how he was when he left here. Did he look upset? Anything you can think of might be useful.'

He looked at both of them but Violet Edgerton shook her head as if she was in a daze.

'I'm not going to be any help at all, I'm afraid. I was off work on Saturday with a touch of flu. Caroline was the only one here.'

'How was he, miss?' The policeman turned to Caroline and she made a small, helpless gesture with her hands.

'Like always, I suppose, at least I never noticed anything different. He was in his office for most of the day.' She frowned. 'I think he was here when I left. Well, he must have been, because I haven't a key and he had to lock up. I left with a customer who walked me to the bus.'

'Could I have his name, then, miss?'

'It's Peter – er – Saddler, I think.' She glanced across for confirmation and Violet nodded.

'That's right. He's a young man from the college. He comes in here a lot. A nice, quiet boy, just the sort who would walk Caroline to the bus.'

'Right, we'll contact him as soon as possible. If you think of anything else that might help, let us know. Of course, we'll be in touch again. Sorry if this has upset you, ladies.'

When they both looked at him rather blankly, still too stunned to make any comments, he nodded and turned to leave.

'When did you find him?' Caroline asked in a dazed voice.

'Just before lunchtime today. A man saw his car and went to investigate. Apparently he had been out all night before, so Mrs Rider hadn't reported him missing.'

He left and Caroline sat down close to Violet.

'What's going to happen now, do you think?'

'I'm not sure. I expect we'll carry on for now. I ought to ring Mrs Rider about the safe keys but I don't really like to, with all the shock she's had. I should have mentioned it to that policeman, I suppose, but I was too stunned. Maybe we can get through the day and then see what happens. They might want to close the shop or something.'

'Should we lock up now and go home?' Caroline ventured. 'You know, as a mark of respect?'

'I honestly don't know. I think we'll just have to wait. There's probably a lawyer to talk to Mrs Rider.

He'll think of the shop in all probability. We'll just have to hope something happens soon to let us know what to do. Fancy,' she added vaguely, 'a big man like that. You would have thought he could take care of himself, wouldn't you? And what on earth was he doing on that common? Nobody goes there at night. It's just asking for trouble.'

'Maybe he was up to something,' Caroline muttered, biting at her lip. 'He was a big, rough sort of man, though. He must have been taken by surprise or he would have fought back. I would have thought he could fight anyone. He was a very frightening man, when you come to think of it.'

'I suppose he was,' Violet mused with a quick look at Caroline. 'I never thought of him like that. I just thought he was sort of uncouth but I can see how he would have frightened you, Caroline. I'm sorry. I should perhaps have spoken to him more firmly, protected you more.'

'Oh, no, Mrs Edgerton. Don't you start feeling guilty about me. I've always been able to look after myself. I'm not big but I'm quick. Anyway,' she finished, 'it doesn't matter now, does it? He won't be coming back here. Did they say how he was killed?'

'I don't think so.' Violet stood up with a sigh. 'Well, we'll have to carry on until somebody tells us to stop. I feel really guilty now about all the bad things I've said about him but you don't expect anything like this.'

'I know,' Caroline agreed. 'Who would have thought? It's terrible. But you shouldn't feel guilty about anything. We both know he was an awful man, and so rough. I've never been able to understand why he had this sort of shop. He had no sort of feelings, did he?'

'He didn't seem to have. Perhaps his wife made him buy this place, or maybe he had it left to him. You never know what life will bring.'

'I know,' Caroline mused seriously. 'It's terrible when you come to think about it.'

'Where do you go to do your judo?' Dan asked casually when Helen called for him on Monday afternoon.

'Bob's Body Shop.' She was sitting a trifle uneasily in his suite as he proceeded to get ready in a very leisurely fashion. He seemed to be filled with a sort of unholy glee about something and she was definitely uneasy. The excitement she had grown used to feeling when he was near was somewhat banked down by anxiety about today. He seemed to be taking this reading trip very casually, not at all as she had expected him to take it.

He was just fastening his tie in the bedroom, and as she answered he stuck his head round the door.

'Bob's *what*?' He was grinning at her and Helen tried to look severe and dignified.

'Body Shop. The name isn't important. It's a good place and it's cheaper than some glossy place in the centre of the city. Neither Jack nor I could afford that. We don't go to be fancy. We go to train and the training is good.'

'It sounds as if you're restoring cars,' Dan called, going back to his task, and Helen frowned at the half-open door. She was still in the state of glancing at herself in mirrors and comparing herself with Antonia. The comparison always came out to her own disadvantage. She was ordinary, Antonia was glamorous, and Dan came from a glamorous world, New York, a university, flights all over the world to lecture. He was glamorous himself.

He walked in a moment later, looking immaculate and very handsome, his dark hair brushed and gleaming and his golden eyes on her in the usual steady, assessing manner as if he had been watching her through the wooden door with no trouble at all. The memory of how he had been on Saturday was still uppermost in her mind in spite of her small worries about today, and she wondered if he knew in his almost magical way.

'Want to try for that throw now?' he murmured with all the appearance of seriousness.

'Don't patronize me,' Helen threatened, giving him a slight glare of annoyance. 'I can take care of myself in all circumstances.'

'I'm not patronizing you,' he protested with every outward sign of innocent surprise. 'Why would I do that? Didn't I promise to let you try it when there was a softer landing than the sidewalk?'

'Pavement,' Helen corrected automatically, and when he walked towards her purposefully she stood up and backed off in a panic. 'It's time to go,' she finished quickly.

'Sure.' He smoothly changed direction, the seductive look wiped from his face in an instant. He opened the door and waved her through with an elegant sweep of his hand. 'We wouldn't want to keep them waiting.' She rushed past him with a nervous glance in his direction that had his grin widening and while he was locking the door she stood well back.

'It's very kind of you to go through with this,' Helen told him quietly as they went down in the lift. He hadn't touched her and her confidence was slowly coming back, although there was a definite gleam in his eyes that made her nervous.

'It sure would be kind of me, if I intended to do it,' he agreed nonchalantly. He was watching her and leaning like a relaxed tiger against the side of the lift, and Helen's eyes opened like saucers as she stared at him.

'What do you mean? You said you'd forgiven me. We're on our way.'

'I always forgive you, sugar. You know that,' he assured her quietly. 'I guess I've got some books to sign, therefore.'

'And the reading,' she insisted, watching him warily.

'I doubt if I'll manage that with my voice,' he warned, giving her a mockingly mournful look.

'There's nothing wrong with your voice. It's perfect!' Helen snapped.

'Thank you, Helen,' he murmured softly, letting his eyes run over her in a taunting masculine way.

'You're perfect too. We'll be fabulous together, won't we?'

'It's too late to back out. You've *got* to do it,' Helen told him urgently, ignoring the sensuous words and looks, trotting to keep up with him as the lift opened into the hotel foyer and he strode off purposefully. 'Listen to me!' she insisted.

'I never miss a word you say, babe.'

'You've got to do the reading,' she pleaded. 'And stop calling me those – *things*!' she added sharply.

'Okay, Miss Stewart.' He handed her into the car and looked at her in apparent surprise when she just sat there staring at him. 'Want to give the driver the address or are we going to sit here cosily for the afternoon?' he asked. 'If we are, it suits me.'

'It's a very nice place,' Helen told him agitatedly when she had finally pulled herself together sufficiently to give instructions to the driver. 'It's very old. It dates back to the nineteenth century. In those days, all the nobility used to go to the shop for their books. It was famous. Now it's a strange and interesting mixture of the old and the new. You'll really like it,' she went on frantically when he sat and said nothing. 'The books are on galleried floors with lovely old black wooden rails and beams.'

'Safe, I hope? No rot?'

'Oh, Dan, please,' Helen begged in great agitation. She went so far as to grasp his arm and he caught her hand before she could move it and raised her fingers to his lips.

194

'The only reason I'm going is to save you embarrassment,' he told her softly. 'It also gives me the excuse to be with you all afternoon.'

'So you're going to do the reading?' she asked with a look of great hope on her face.

'Nope.' He let her hand go and sat back with an infuriating smile on his face and Helen knew she was going to get not one step further.

'What am I going to say?' she muttered, with such a look of despair that Dan's face softened.

'I'll do most of the talking at first,' he assured her. 'I'll have to do that to let them hear the voice. If I don't they're not going to believe it.'

'But there's nothing wrong with your voice!'

'Laryngitis,' he said seriously. 'I've felt it coming on all morning. It's nearly here now. Another five minutes and it's going to be really bad. I guess they'll understand, especially as the place is so old. In those days there was plenty of disease. They've probably got it all tabulated in one of the antique books.'

Helen sat back and refused to say even one more word, and when she finally decided to take him to task again, Dan looked at her mournfully and shook his head. He put his hand to his throat and smiled weakly. She had a great desire to hit him and keep on hitting him until she was exhausted but she knew she had lost the fight. He was not going to read anything. She was going to look like an idiot.

Helen left it to him. He had talked himself into this and she would let him get himself out of it.

When the car dropped them off she walked with him into the shop, maintaining a hostile silence until she had to introduce him to a very eager-looking man who was waiting.

'This is Mr Forrest,' she said, indicating Dan and giving Dan a glance of utter distaste as she did it.

'I'm so glad you could come,' the man said, pumping Dan's hand vigorously. 'There's a whole room full of excited people upstairs. The reading will be there and then you can sign books down here.'

'I'm so sorry. Devastated, in fact. It's impossible to read when my throat is like this. It couldn't have come at a worse time but the pain when I speak is excruciating. I would never have even left my bed but I know what this means to everyone.'

The man stared at Dan in dismay and Helen stared too, disbelief and outrage on her face. If she hadn't known better she would have said that Dan was really feeling ill with a terrible throat. His beautiful, quiet voice with the soft American accent was now just a weird croak. He looked as if he was bearing up steadfastly under a good deal of misery. He was even managing to look brave. Her desire to fly at him and beat her fists against his chest was almost overwhelming. Her blue eyes were flashing sparks at him.

'Oh, what a terrible thing. It was really very good of you to come at all,' the man said. 'I wonder what we can do? Of course you mustn't even think of reading in your condition.' He brightened and looked at Helen. 'We can't let them all down, though, can we? Perhaps you could read a bit, Miss Stewart? Then you can answer their questions and Mr Forrest can walk round if he feels well enough and then sit and sign the books. They wouldn't be disappointed. At least they will be able to look at him, and if you could read out the words . . .?'

He sounded comfortably sure that things would work out nicely. Dan was smiling benignly and Helen opened her mouth to give a very acid refusal. She closed it again. She was well and truly trapped, boxed in. She could hardly protest and say that the great Dan Forrest was playacting. It would be little short of scandalous. Martin's publishing house would be ridiculed and Dan would slide out of it somehow and disappear in a blaze of glory.

'Of course,' she murmured, summoning up a smile with a great effort. 'Please lead the way.' She turned to glare at Dan on the way upstairs but all he did was give her a slow and sexy wink.

'Just wait,' she whispered in a threatening voice. 'You wanted me to throw you? When we're coming back down these stairs, I'll toss you to the bottom.'

'When we get home, honey,' Dan murmured seductively, and just grinned at her even more.

Helen was furiously silent as they left later, even though she had become so absorbed in the story she was reading that Dan had been forced to touch her hand and shake his head at her to warn her she was going on too long.

That hadn't done much to stop her temper either, because she had been embarrassed and had wondered uneasily if at any time she had been so absorbed that she had just been reading to herself. The books had been almost sold out.

'Great,' Dan said cheerfully as they left in the usual limousine. 'Practically a sell-out. Martin will be rubbing his hands. More money for the old firm.'

Helen said nothing. She would have liked to rub Dan's face into the seat very violently. She would have liked to rain blows on him and scream into his ear. She was filled with fury and hate. He had got the better of her as if she were little more than an idiot, and he was so damned smug!

Dan glanced at her stiff, angry face and his lips quirked with amusement but he did nothing to try and appease her. When she was like this, shaken out of her crisp businesslike image, she delighted him. He could watch those blue eyes flash fire all day.

When the car stopped at Dan's hotel and he got out, Helen slammed the door behind him and snapped out an order to the driver.

'Take me home!' She imagined she had been expected to get out with her important, irritating companion and shake hands with him, make arrangements for another amusing excursion to pass his expensive time. She flatly refused to be even civil. The car swept away and, after staring after it for a second, Dan smiled to himself and went into the hotel to change into something more suitable for the evening. He had no intention of staying inside all alone. Things were going his way and he intended to roll them along some more.

As the car dropped Helen at home, a taxi drew up and Jenny got out and came running up to her with a wide smile on her face. Helen curbed her temper with difficulty but she managed a smile of welcome. Jenny was almost a protégée by now and she understood her much more than she had done before.

'I'm going back to school in the morning, Helen,' Jenny explained. 'Half-term is over. We don't get long. I just wanted to say goodbye to you.'

'Come in for a coffee,' Helen invited. 'I could do with one myself. I've had a trying time today.'

They went inside and Helen finally calmed down as she sat for a while and talked to Jenny. She was glad that everything had worked out all right. It would have been terrible if Jenny had been going back with the shame of the barbecue evening still hanging over her. Today she looked just like a girl, and pretty as a picture.

'I feel as if I've had a good shaking and come to my senses,' Jenny confided, sitting on the end of Helen's kitchen table and swinging her long legs. 'In fact, if it hadn't been for you, I think Daddy would have given me a good shaking when everyone left. I deserved it.'

'You did go a bit over the top,' Helen murmured, pouring another cup of coffee.

'Do you think Dan will forgive me? I was terrible. Does he think I'm an idiot?'

'Dan is a psychiatrist,' Helen reminded her. 'He understands a lot of things, much more than other people.' She tried to keep an even, cheerful voice. Dan understood far too much and he had not had much difficulty in manoeuvring her. He had certainly managed to make her feel like an idiot. She fought down the temper again and kept on talking cheerfully.

'This is a nice little house,' Jenny said after a while as she looked round and peered into the sitting room. 'There's no pool, though. It's lovely having a pool. Why don't you get a house like ours? You could live near us then. We'd all like that.'

'Oh, how I wish,' Helen laughed. 'I'm only just managing to pay for this house. Yours is in an expensive part of London, and I hate to say this in case you let it go to your head, but your father is very wealthy. After all, he does own Newman Publishing. I just work there.'

'Dan's wealthy too,' Jenny murmured with a quick glance at Helen.

'No doubt, but that doesn't do *me* a lot of good. Anyway,' Helen added with a wide smile, 'you told me I was not too old. I can work up to it.'

'Actually, you're beautiful,' Jenny mused giving Helen a long glance of inspection. 'You've got a lovely figure but it's your face that does it, it's sort of misty, dreamy.'

'So you said,' Helen reminded her, trying not to laugh.

'Why do you wear those spectacles? They spoil you.'

'I wear them to see with. Does that sound reasonable?'

'Hmm. Pity,' Jenny murmured. 'They hide you.'

Which was more or less what Dan had said and more or less true, Helen thought. She only needed them for reading, and then not too much. They were a sort of disguise but she never admitted it. The world was too cruel to be without a disguise. The world had always been cruel.

Jenny was just looking at her watch later when the front doorbell rang. She jumped down from the table and gathered her bag.

'You've got another visitor, Helen, and I've got to go in any case. I honestly don't know how I come to have so much to pack when I've only been here a few days.'

'Washing?' Helen suggested wryly, getting up to see her to the door and find out who else was there.

'I expect so,' Jenny grinned. 'Mummy does a great batch for me every holiday. But I do my own ironing,' she added hastily.

'And lucky for you,' Helen pointed out with a mock frown. 'One day you'll have a place of your own, my girl, and Mummy won't be fussing round then to keep the washing up to date.'

'That's not going to be for ages,' Jenny laughed. 'I've decided not to grow up yet. I know a good thing when I see one.'

Helen smiled and opened the door. Dan was standing on the step, his hand just raised to ring the bell again, and the smile died on Helen's face at the sight of him. She glared into his golden eyes and Jenny went a deep shade of pink.

'I came to say goodbye to Helen,' Jenny explained quickly as if he would think she had come to waylay him. 'I'm just leaving. I – I have to pack.'

'There's my taxi just turning. You'll need it if you're leaving,' Dan concluded. He looked round, put his fingers to his lips and gave a piercing whistle that had the taxi pulling back in for Jenny. She looked up at him in awe, nothing but childish admiration on her face.

'Gosh! Can you do that? I would have thought you were too important. I'm always trying to whistle like that. Bettina Smythe-Jones can do it but nobody else can.'

'I'll teach you next time I'm over here,' Dan promised, smiling down at her. 'Goodbye, Jenny.' He leaned down to kiss her forehead but she held her hand out in a manner that would have done justice to Antonia and shook his hand politely.

'Goodbye, Dan,' she said in a demure voice, and went off to get the taxi, waving to Helen as she got into it.

'Must be losing my touch,' Dan muttered as the taxi drew away.

'You've never had one. Goodbye, Mr Forrest,' Helen said acidly, closing the door.

'Oh, honey, let me in,' he begged, and before she could quite get the door shut he was inside and it was closed behind him.

'Go!' Helen ordered furiously. 'You are not invited. I don't like you and I don't care for the tricks you play on unsuspecting people. You're mean, chauvinistic and totally without principles. The normal codes of conduct do not seem to apply to you. You make up your own, always to your decided advantage. I do not want you in my house. Please leave it at once!'

Dan said not a word. He let her rave on and then reached forward and pulled her into his arms, catching her lips with his almost before she could take a breath after her furious speech. It was so quick that Helen was taken completely by surprise but even so she resisted him automatically, her hands coming to push at his broad chest. She was angry and she thought frantically of bending her knees and rolling backwards to throw him over and on to the floor, because he certainly deserved it.

She wasn't quite sure she could do it, though. She could feel iron strength in him and he wasn't some boy at the club, fooling around. He was six foot two of raw masculinity. It was no game and she knew it. Dan wanted his arms round her, wanted to kiss her. She didn't really want to fight him, either, because his kiss was like magic again, and before she could decide what to do, every bit of strength had left her body.

'Fiery little cat,' Dan whispered against her skin. He cupped her face in his hands and placed swift, hot kisses all over it before coming back to claim her mouth. And Helen had no will to resist at all. She just floated down in the tide of it, and when he pulled her back into his arms she went so willingly that he knew the battle was over.

He lowered his mouth to hers, this time kissing her deeply, parting her lips with ease and sliding his tongue slowly into her mouth in a possessive gesture that made her gasp for breath. He groaned, tightening his arms around her, and Helen was soft and submissive, clinging to his shoulders as if she would drown, completely at home in his arms as if she belonged there.

Dan was almost dazed at the perfection of his victory. She was always in his thoughts but now he couldn't think of anything but Helen. His mind went blank. There was just this desire he had been feeling since he had first gone anywhere with her. It was raging inside him now and he stroked his hands down her back, urging her closer, knowing he could never get her close enough. She had him spellbound and he was beginning to feel utterly lost without her.

He raised his head and looked down into her entranced face, and as he gently removed those big, unlikely-looking spectacles she didn't even open her eyes. His face became almost harsh with desire and he swung her up into his arms, moving with her into the small, neat sitting-room where she had tried to dry him out after the flood.

'Dan.' She murmured his name in a weak protest but he was already sitting down, cradling her on his lap and his lips cut off any further sound. The banked-down fire of the past few days leapt into life as her mouth moved with growing fervour beneath his. She wanted him. She was trying to move closer, and even if her mind didn't know what was happening inside her, her body was dictating her actions with a will of its own.

He pulled his mouth away from hers to make seductive forays against her throat, her ears, the line of her jaw, his teeth gently nipping her skin, and Helen was lost. She felt languid, weak, her arms and legs useless as she lay against him. She couldn't think beyond this second, because all her world was feelings, warm, trembling feelings that she had never experienced before.

She never felt his fingers at the buttons of her blouse until his hand slid away her bra and cupped her breast possessively. She opened her eyes then, shocked and delighted, refusing to collect the messages her brain was sending. He was looking down at her, the golden eyes, darkened with passion, watching the slow journey his fingers made around her hardened nipple.

'You're beautiful, Helen,' he said thickly. 'I want you more desperately than I've ever wanted anything in my life.'

His fingers closed around her breast, moulding it gently, and his eyes came back to hers, waiting, questioning.

'I can't.' The words seemed to be torn from her although she only whispered. 'I can't, Dan.'

'Why, baby? You want to. We both know that.'

They stared into each other's eyes, losing themselves, and Dan's breath was an ache in his throat, every muscle in his body taut with the need to contain his desire.

'Nobody can get close to me. I can't let anyone . . . If you knew exactly what sort of person I am . . .'

She sounded so close to tears, so weary that Dan suddenly felt only the urge, the necessity to protect and comfort her. He slowly buttoned her blouse again and put his arms right round her, holding her tightly against him.

'I know what sort of person you are, Helen,' he told her huskily. 'I know you're brave, sweet and loyal. I know you have some great problem, some grief that you keep to yourself, but nothing could change my mind about you, whatever the problem is. I couldn't stop wanting you no matter what you told me.'

Helen looked up at him with a mixture of hope and pain on her face and then she moved forward with a soft little cry and wound her arms tightly round his neck, burying her face against him, searching for the safety and strength that was such a tangible part of Dan.

She had never felt such safety before and she longed to hang on to it, to wind herself round him and cling forever. Dan just held her close, his face resting against the top of her silky head. He thought ruefully that he had never been in quite this sort of situation before. She wasn't a patient. She refused help and anyway, he never wanted his patients. This was a new state of affairs for him and he had to accept whatever rules Helen laid down.

'Are you any good at making coffee?' he asked after a while, dropping a kiss on her forehead.

'I've only got instant.' To his relief she smiled up at him, the few tears she had allowed blinked away, and the golden eyes looked into hers with mocking sincerity.

'I didn't know there was any other sort. You've got to make it, though. I couldn't get as far as the kitchen. I need to recover.'

'I'm sorry, Dan.' She looked at him wistfully and his hand caught her under the chin in a playful gesture that robbed the moment of stress.

'Don't worry,' he said softly. 'That was just the beginning. Lose the battle but win the war. It's the family motto. It's embroidered on my baseball cap.'

'By your Aunt Luce?' Helen smiled as she got up and he looked at her with fake astonishment.

'Hey! Who told you about her?'

'You did, when you were describing your terrible youth and your disgraceful behaviour towards the cat.'

'Oh, yeah. I remember.' He gave her a lopsided grin. 'Don't hold it against me. I was young at the time.'

He stayed where he was while Helen made the coffee and it gave both of them time to recover. Her legs were still shaking and heat kept flashing through her, curling inside, reddening her cheeks.

It was no use pretending she didn't want him. He had left her stunned from the first, and since then the feelings had just grown.

She had never had to fight feelings like this before. It had been easy to distance herself from people and guard her secret. Now, though, she wanted to be close to Dan. He had given her the chance and she had been forced to let it go. And he had never pressed the advantage. A great rush of feeling went through her. He was a wonderful man, a man she could cling to all her life if things had been normal.

Things were not normal, though, and in any case, she reminded herself, Dan wanted her and only that. She would be foolish to read anything else into it. He would be going back home to America soon and then she would never see him again. The thought hit her hard, making her feel almost sick. Never to see him. To be left in this darkness by herself all over again. Helen closed her eyes and tried to pull herself together. It was useless to dream, useless for her. All her dreams were nightmares.

Dan was sitting with his head back, staring at the ceiling, doing two things. He was trying to assert his will over his body, trying to erase the soft feel of her skin from his mental image. And he was thinking in the way he usually thought: quickly, logically and intuitively. She wanted him. He ought to be making love to her right now; at the very least he should be feeling wildly triumphant. Instead he was fighting a battle with his body and trying to probe her mind without asking anything outright.

For the first time in his busy, full and active life he was crazy about somebody, and it had to be somebody who thought she was not worthy of his desire. She was too scared to be closer to him because she thought he might find out something that would shock him. What had she said? 'If you found out what I was really like.' He knew what she was really like. He could see it in her eyes. What terrible guilt was weighing her down, spoiling her days, forcing her out at night? Somehow he had to find out.

'Speaking of my misspent youth,' Dan said casually as Helen took the coffee in, 'tell me about yours. I don't know a thing about you.' He was watching for the stiffness that would come and he had not been mistaken. She had a lot of trouble putting the tray down quietly and the cups shook.

'My parents died when I was sixteen,' she told him with, strain in her voice. 'I went to live with my aunt. End of story.'

'I can't take responsibility. I have children of my own and when this all gets out it would embarrass them. I can't keep her here. You'll have to find somewhere else. I'm sorry, but I have to think of my own.'

It had not been the end of the story. The story had been long and pain-filled, and it had never ended. She still heard the sharp, cold voice in her head, still remembered the feeling when she had discovered what alone really meant.

'Then you went to university?' Dan prompted.

'Yes. When I came out I got into a publishing house as little more than the tea girl. I was lucky. I worked my way up quickly and then, last year, I came to work for Martin.'

'You were clever and worked your way up quickly,' Dan corrected. 'Martin never stops singing your praises.'

'Martin and Margaret like me,' she confessed quietly, not looking at him. 'They've been good to me.'

'I like you,' Dan said softly. 'I want to be good to you too. But you won't let me.'

'Sex isn't being good to me,' Helen murmured, still not looking at him.

'Hey! Don't knock it till you've tried it,' Dan said softly.

He was getting exactly nowhere. At the mention of her home life she had clammed up tight. He watched the glitter of her curls for a minute and then said, 'My old man died last year. He was seventy-one and even then it took an accident to kill him. My Mom died a couple of years ago. I've got a brother, though.'

'I thought you said your only relative was your Aunt Luce?' Helen pounced, and he was back to grinning at her again.

'I just wanted to get your sympathy. I thought it made me sound lonely and pathetic. You've got to admit it was a good tale.'

'What about the cat?' Helen asked, finding it impossible to stop the smile growing on her lips.

'That is as true as I'm sitting here,' Dan assured her as he lay stretched back on the settee. 'We had a dog too, a funny ragged sort of breed. We all used to go to Aunt Luce's place in Maine in the summer. Dad taught Bill and me to fish. We had great times.'

'Bill is your brother?'

'Yeah. The dog was called Jasper but he had to stay in the barn at night, Aunt Luce having an hysterical cat and Jasper being inclined to go for it.'

'Where did you live?' Helen asked, suddenly finding that she was almost hungry for information about him. She wanted to know everything, to see photographs, listen to his quiet voice talking all the time.

'We lived in New York, always. Dad was in the banking business. Mom was an artist.'

'What does your brother do?'

'Bill? Now Bill grew up to be stuffy. He's a lawyer. He's got two children and a very beautiful, long-suffering wife.'

Helen was silent, thinking sad thoughts. Family, continuity, happiness in memories, all the things she did not have. There was her secret and that was all. Even the mention of the word 'lawyer' sent alarm signals down her spine. She drank her coffee, sitting on a low stool away from Dan and he watched her silently for a few minutes, his intelligent golden eyes roaming over her face and seeing far more than she realized.

'What are you doing tomorrow?' he suddenly asked, and Helen looked up, almost startled at the

211

sound of his voice. She had been sinking into her problems, trying to find a way out of the dark maze that had held her for so long.

'I'm staying here at home. I've got a day free and I'm going to catch up on a few manuscripts.'

'Want to help me look for a house?' Dan asked casually, and she shot a look at him that contained a mixture of expressions; he was almost sure that one of them was hope. He found himself almost holding his breath. He wasn't sure if he could face the next day without the sight of her.

'You're going to buy a house?'

'Rent. I can't stay here long enough to go to the trouble of actually owning one, but there are plenty on the market to rent.'

'I thought you were going back to New York?' Helen said breathlessly.

'I am. But not this minute. Now that the book business is finally over I've got time to do what I came here to do in the first place: enjoy myself. I can do that a lot better if I'm in a house.'

'Do – do I come under the heading of enjoying yourself?' Helen asked quietly, her face flushing at her own temerity.

'No, honey,' Dan told her seriously, fixing her with his startling eyes. 'I want you badly, and at the moment I'm not enjoying myself at all. I think you know that.'

'I – I can't be close to you,' she whispered.

'You sure made a good start,' he reminded her with a slanting smile that made her heart take off rapidly. 'But in case you're suspicious, I'm not trying to lure you to any empty house. I've picked out three and I've got the agents lined up to show me round. All I want is your advice and your company.'

'I'll come,' Helen pronounced, giving him a beaming smile. 'It sounds exciting.'

'What about the manuscripts?'

'I'll catch up later. In fact, I'll do them at night. I think better then.'

Dan nodded and got up to leave. He wanted to stay but he was not going to push her at all. He was well satisfied. If she was working at night she could not also be roaming the streets, and if she was tired during the day it was better than being in danger at night.

CHAPTER 9

Doris Rider came to the shop herself before the end of the day. Neither Violet nor Caroline had seen her before and she was something of a surprise. She was tall, dark and well-dressed, not too bad-looking. She was red-eyed with crying, but Violet thought she looked a hard woman all the same.

'I've brought the safe keys,' she told Violet. 'I've talked it over with my solicitor already because it was urgent, and we've agreed that for the time being you should take charge here and keep the shop open. This is a good business and half of it was mine in any case. Now I'll own the lot. There's no point in closing and losing customers so I'm leaving it to you for now. You've got keys to get in with and lock up at night. Now you've got the keys to the safe, so the full responsibility will be yours for the time being. I'll see that you get extra pay for it straight away, and later we'll have a talk about the future.'

'We'll both do anything at all to help, won't we, Caroline?' Violet said sympathetically.

'Oh, anything, Mrs Rider.'

So far she had been ignored, but when she spoke, Doris Rider turned to look at Caroline and her tight mouth tightened even further as her eyes ran over the slender shape and the clothes.

'I'm not too sure about you,' she said sharply. 'Are you the girl my husband was seeing after work?'

Caroline just stared at her in shock, and Violet Edgerton cut in immediately.

'We know you're upset, Mrs Rider, but Caroline is a very nice girl and you shouldn't say things like that. There was never anything at all between Mr Rider and Caroline. She has a boyfriend from the university and your husband was a much older man, old enough to be her father by the look of him.'

'It never stopped him in the past,' Doris Rider assured them bitterly, 'and she's just his type with that blonde hair and those short skirts. He was very excited on Saturday night before he left home. I've seen it all before. He didn't fool me. He was going to meet some girl.'

'Well, it wasn't me,' Caroline stated angrily. 'I know he's dead and I know you'll probably fire me for speaking out, but for your information, Mrs Rider, I couldn't stand your husband. He was a mean man. He was always snappy to both of us. On Saturday I was here by myself because Mrs Edgerton was ill. The shop was absolutely full and I had a bad headache and he never once offered to help me. He was never nice and I just didn't like him. I often thought of leaving because of his attitude. He made me miserable.'

Violet was biting her lip a little anxiously at this frank disclosure, but Doris Rider stared at her and then nodded slowly before she turned away.

'You can stay. You're only saying what I think myself; I don't hold it against you. All I can say, though, is that you're lucky. You're just the sort of girl he chased. He probably drew the line at doing it at work.'

'Only because I was here,' Violet muttered as Mrs Rider handed her the keys to the safe and left. 'That was pretty brave of you, speaking out like that, Caroline. She had no business to accuse you of anything. It's bad enough as it is.'

'I still shudder when I think about him,' Caroline said. 'I know he's dead and it's awful, but he wasn't nice at all.'

'He wasn't.' Violet agreed firmly. 'A nastier man I've never met.'

'Do you know,' Caroline murmured quietly after a second, 'I went on like that at her, but truthfully, I can't even remember his face? It's funny, isn't it? I mean, it was only Saturday and I can't picture him at all.'

'Just as well, love,' Violet told her comfortably. 'Just put it all out of your mind. Don't even try to remember his face. He's nothing to do with us now, thank goodness.'

'Thank goodness,' Caroline repeated, a puzzled expression on her face. What *had* he looked like, though? Who had he been anyway? If it hadn't been for the police and then his wife, she would not have thought of him at all. He was like a dream, a ghost at the very back of her mind, and she couldn't even picture his face in any way at all. She felt as if she had been shouting lies at Mrs Rider about a man she had never met.

'Customer, Caroline,' Violet pointed out quietly, and Caroline brought her mind back to the present as Peter Saddler walked in.

'Yes, Mrs Edgerton. I'll see to him,' she said with a smile. It cheered her up at once because she could remember Peter Saddler very well and she hadn't seen him since Saturday either. It was funny about Mr Rider, but it must just be a blank spot or she wouldn't have been able to remember Peter, or Mrs Edgerton for that matter.

'Hello, Peter,' she said brightly. 'Spending some more money? You don't have to. You can just call in and talk to us whenever you like. Mrs Edgerton is the boss now and she's my friend.'

Dan called for Helen next morning and he was driving a brand new car, a bright red Porsche.

'Did you buy this here?' Helen asked, admiring the lines and the colour.

'The temptation was great, but I hired it,' Dan told her. 'I might buy one when I get back to the States, though. I'll keep this while I'm here, especially if I like one of the houses and take it. Besides, I can't come to collect you in a taxi every day.'

'You won't be collecting me every day,' Helen said quickly.

'Don't bank on it, Miss Stewart. You're my girl.'

'Dan, I'm not!' Helen looked up at him with a mixture of happiness and despair on her face and he caught her chin with his hand, tilting it up and dropping a quick kiss on her mouth.

'As far as I can see, you don't have a lot of say in it,' he told her softly. 'You can't decide things for other people and I've made my own decisions. You're my girl even if I never get the chance to see you.' He held the car door for her and settled her in the passenger seat. 'Now, with this beauty,' he added, leaning in to look down at her, 'I can hang around regularly. You'll finally take pity on me because, as I said before, you're one sweet lady.'

She didn't know whether to laugh or cry. Dan was saying the things she wanted to hear, but although it caused a great burst of happiness, Helen knew it was impossible. And if he was always with her, how would she continue her search? A treacherous voice inside said, Give it up. Be with him while you can. But she knew it was impossible; the pulling power of dread was too strong and the habit was too well established. So was the guilt.

At least there was today. She smiled at Dan as he got into the car and sat back, basking in happiness as he smiled that wonderful smile and sent the car roaring down the street like a chariot taking her away from her nightmares. There was today, and for today she would live like any other person of her age. She was with Dan, and if it was just a day out of her whole life she would enjoy it to the full.

The first house they saw looked good from the outside, but inside it was a disaster. Ultra-modern had been mixed with antique, chrome against old mahogany, and Dan's eyebrows shot up in surprise. Helen made a wry face and he turned to the agent and shook his head.

'I think not,' he said firmly.

'You would be allowed to refurnish,' the agent began, but Dan took Helen's arm and began the retreat to the front door.

'Sorry, out of the question. In any case, she doesn't like it, do you, honey?'

'Er – not really,' Helen murmured. 'Sorry.' She gave the agent a look of regret and Dan had her out of the house and into the car before the door was locked.

'Try not to blame everything on me,' Helen complained, laughing as they left rapidly, and Dan grinned across at her.

'Why do you think I brought you? You're my quick get-out. Next stop you can get that frosty look on your face, just in case.'

She needed it, because the next house was equally bizarre and none too clean. But the last one was perfect. The agent was a woman and she took them round with a pride that showed her own pleasure.

'This is the one,' Helen whispered as they walked round. 'It's even better than Martin's house. It's got a lovely private garden and the furnishings are almost new.'

'The owner is overseas for two years,' the agent said, overhearing Helen's approving whisper. 'He wants professional people. Mr Forrest would be ideal, of course. I think you would both enjoy living in this house. Oh, I should perhaps mention,' she added, 'the contract states no barbecues.'

'That settles it, then,' Dan announced. 'This is the perfect place. I have bad memories of barbecues. We'll happily eat indoors.'

When they left after making arrangements for Dan to sign the lease, Helen looked across at him worriedly, the bubble of her happiness wavering on the edge of bursting.

'You said we,' she pointed out quietly. 'You said "We'll eat indoors."'

'Happily,' Dan corrected. 'Don't forget that word. I fully intend to be happy.'

'Are you – is Antonia going to be with you at the house?'

Dan glanced across at her and then braked sharply and pulled into the side of the road, turning to look at her and catching the sad expression on her face.

'Antonia is not my girl,' he reminded her softly. 'You are.'

'But I can't! I can't be with you . . .'

'I'm not pushing you, baby,' he said gently. 'I'm just daydreaming. Keeping you out of the daydreams is too difficult to manage. I stopped trying soon after I met you.' He tilted her anxious face to his. 'Don't let it worry you. I'm no threat at all. I'll be with you when you allow it and I'll go away when you order it.'

He pulled her into his arms and kissed her slowly and gently, and Helen didn't make the slightest attempt to resist. She had daydreams too, so strong that sometimes they drowned out her nightmares, and Dan was always at the centre of any dreams.

'You're going home to America,' she whispered mournfully, and he looked down at her with the same intent golden gaze she had become so used to now.

'Not this minute,' he said softly. 'I'm staying with my girl.'

'I – I've never actually been anyone's girl before,' Helen murmured, and he just went on looking down at her, holding her in his arms and ignoring passing traffic.

'With that angel face? Are Englishmen blind?'

He was making a joke of it, but he had surmised almost from the first that she had never been close to any man. She had her secret and she lived with that. His golden gaze flooded over her, encompassing her. She was going to know him. She was going to live with him, sleep with him, learn to be happy. He wanted her enough to fight any dark menace.

He tilted her face and kissed her passionately, letting his hands run over her, learning the shape of her body. She melted into him because she could no more help herself than he could. But the secret was in her head, breaking her heart, and he was as aware of it as if he could see it.

'Let's get you home,' he said thickly, sitting her up and starting the car. 'If we get arrested for loitering here, Martin's going to throw one of his rages and come after me with a club.'

'You're his friend,' Helen said shakily, trying to throw off the drowsy feeling of warmth that made her ache inside. 'He won't go after you with a club.'

'He will if you're involved,' Dan growled. 'I've already had one lecture. If he has to bail us out he'll come after me with one of those clubs giants use, the sort with nails stuck in them.'

Helen giggled, visualizing the picture he painted so swiftly of Martin in a rage. She settled back with a sigh. She never wanted to leave Dan, never even wanted to get out of this car. She could sit beside him and go on and on to the end of the world and leave her dark maze behind forever.

'Happy, honey?' Dan asked softly and she couldn't lie.

'Yes,' she whispered. For now, for now she was happy.

'Then be my girl.'

'I can't, Dan.' He glanced at her and her face was no longer smiling. The weary sadness was back. The panther-gold eyes turned cool and determined. Whatever happened to his job, his tours, his writing, he would stay here until he had this thing beaten. If anyone hurt her he would probably kill them, and yet she was being hurt now by some dark, intangible danger that seemed to be impossible to control. His eyes narrowed with a danger of their

222

own. He *would* control it! She needed him, it was as natural as breathing and it was going to happen. Maybe then he could set her free.

It seemed completely normal for Dan to park the car and come in with her when they got back to her house much later. Helen was happy again. The shadow had gone. She couldn't remember being completely happy before, but a day spent with Dan when he was in this mood was the nearest thing she could think of to perfection.

'I can cook if you want to stay for an evening meal,' she offered shyly, and Dan looked at her very seriously for a second and then nodded.

'I'll chance it if you will,' he said quietly, 'and I'm not talking about the food.'

'I know.' Helen looked away, biting at her lip as her face flushed.

'I can't stop wanting you, Helen,' he admitted huskily, 'but I'm not about to spring on you. Just tell me you feel safe with me.'

'Very safe.' She looked across at him with clear, trusting eyes and Dan's face softened.

'Then I'll stay. What do you want me to do?'

'Just sit there,' Helen ordered cheerfully. 'You can open the wine and make a start on it.'

'Not before the meal. If you're trying to get me hazy it's impossible. I like to keep my wits about me. I'll watch the news. I like the English news, it's more interesting than ours.'

Helen switched on the television and then went into the kitchen to start the meal. She could hardly believe her own courage. She had actually asked Dan to stay. The fact was that she didn't really want him to go at all. The day had passed in a warm glow that she wanted to keep and hug close to her. Without him she was going to be lonely again. She had lived with it for so long that it had become part of her, an accepted fact, but Dan had banished it with his humour, his warmth and his desire. 'Cling to it while you can,' the little voice inside said, and this time she didn't try to silence it.

She was just walking in to start setting the table when the news came on, and there was no way she could miss the first item.

'The police have just released details of a man who was found stabbed to death on Thurley Common. The body was discovered by a man walking his dog on Monday morning, but according to reports, the body had been there since Saturday night. He was identified as being Mr George Rider, aged fifty-two, the owner of a music shop. There was no apparent reason for the attack and police are said to be linking it with the murders of other middle-aged men over the past three years. All have been killed with a similar weapon . . .'

The dinner mats fell from Helen's lifeless hands as the room seemed to swim in front of her eyes. It was here, back, right inside her own house, threatening, almost goading her, as if it was making a promise never to go away, never to give her peace.

Dan jumped up as he heard the sound of the mats falling and saw that Helen was in the room listening. He switched off the television but it was clearly too late.

224

She had heard everything. Her face was white, waxy, and she just stared straight ahead, wrapped tightly in some personal nightmare. Before he could reach her she fell slowly to her knees, her head bent over as she rocked herself soundlessly, her hands over her ears.

'Helen!' Dan dropped down beside her and forced her to move her hands, holding them tightly in his. If she had seemed to be shaken by the news of a stabbing at the cocktail party when Martin had made his overly blunt announcement, it was nothing at all compared to the state she was in now. She was looking straight at him but she was not seeing him. Her mind was somewhere else, seeing other things, things of dread.

He stood and lifted her to her feet, putting his arm round her and helping her to the sofa where he had been sitting a few moments ago. She came with him but he was pretty sure that she had no real idea of what was happening.

'Helen.' He bent over her, speaking quietly, but her eyes had never moved and they didn't move now. It was the same flat stare.

There was a burst of hissing from the kitchen as something boiled over on to the cooker but Helen didn't seem to hear it. Dan grimaced and left her for a second as he strode into the kitchen and methodically turned off all the rings. The hell with dinner. He had a case of shock on his hands as far as he could see.

She was sitting exactly where he had left her, staring into space, seeing nothing, and he made no attempt at all to speak to her. He simply lifted her up and sat down himself, pulling her on to his lap and holding her close. She was stiff, not shivering. He took her icy cold hand in his and gripped it tightly.

'Come on, honey,' he whispered urgently. 'Come out of it. Come back to me.'

He rocked her against him, slowly, warmly, his face against her hair and gradually the stiffness went, the shivering began and his hold on her tightened, surrounding her with safety and comfort.

'It's all right,' he whispered. 'It's all right, Helen.'

She gradually began to soften, lean against him, and the warm voice kept on with a soothing rhythm, coaxing her out of shock and back into the world. But his mind was racing, however much his voice soothed. The golden eyes stared straight ahead as his cheek rested on her shining hair.

A knife. Again it had been a knife and again he saw the shadowy figure of a woman, saw the darkened alley between two major roads and felt the chill of premonition. What did he do now? Did he go to the police and tell them that he knew who they were looking for but had not one shred of hard evidence? He had not seen the woman in black do anything at all to invite police scrutiny.

She walked in the night and the men who approached her walked in the night too. Theoretically she was the one at risk, but the two men he had seen making advances to her had literally fled. And what about the victims? He knew only of two. Both had been middle-aged, big men, men of the same type. If it was her, she chose them because of the type of man they were, because something about them rang a loud bell of violence in her mind.

Neither of the men he had seen approach her had been in that category, and they had been dispatched with ferocity. She didn't need them. They had not been suitable victims and it had saved them. She hunted in the night but she hunted carefully. How many others had there been, and over what period of time? During his relatively short stay in London he had seen her surprisingly often. Was she getting worse?

The golden eyes narrowed and he hugged Helen against him. On Saturday night, while a man was being killed, Helen had been with him at the barbecue. She had been normal and sweet, confessing a liking for Antonia even though Antonia's presence had hurt her. She had been helping Jenny to save face and make peace with her father. She had shown no sign at all of knowing that somewhere in the darkness a man was losing his life.

She seemed to follow the way his own instincts led, but she had not known that the fuse had blown again. What *did* she know? What did she suspect, and why was it so important to her? So important that it could reduce her to this state of shock?

She began to cry quietly and Dan knew she was coming out of it. She buried her head against his shoulder and he held her as the weeping shook her body. Crying was the best thing she could do and he just let her cry, his hand stroking her hair as he rocked her gently. And after a while, when the tears became subdued, dry sobs, he lifted her face and kissed her trembling lips, pouring his warmth over her until she sighed and the trembling stopped too.

'How many have there been, Helen?' he asked quietly as he dried her tears. He made no attempt to look into her eyes and he kept his voice very even, calm. She made no attempt to dodge the question either.

'Three that I know of,' she whispered. 'But maybe I'm wrong. Maybe I don't know at all.'

'The hooker. The woman in black.'

'I think so.'

'How many times have you seen her?' he asked carefully with the same even intonation.

'Just once, when I was with you. I've been looking for a long time. It was the nearest I ever got to her.'

'You know her?' Dan looked down into her eyes now and she looked straight back, shaking her head.

'I don't know whether I do or not. I couldn't tell. I was too far away. You made me go with you.'

'Thank God,' he muttered, pulling her protectively close again. He leaned back and looked down at her after a second. 'You think it was someone you knew before, some time ago?'

'Yes.'

'Who?'

'I can't tell you.' She struggled to get up and he shook his head, clasping her close.

'All right, all right. I won't ask you anything else. But listen to me carefully, Helen. You are not responsible. Whoever she is, whatever you know, you are not responsible for the actions of another person.'

'But if I could stop her . . .'

'You can't, Helen.'

'How do you know?' she asked miserably. 'If I could see her, talk to her, persuade her . . . You don't know her either, so how do you know I can't stop her?'

'Because she's a psychopath. Nothing and nobody can stop her. If she's doing this, she needs to be caught and taken care of. You must never approach her. She's as deadly as a rattlesnake and she has no understanding of right or wrong.'

'She would never hurt me,' Helen said, and Dan gripped her arms tightly, fear for her safety when he was not with her surfacing rapidly, chilling him.

'Because you're not a big, middle-aged man? Don't bank on it. She will kill anyone who endangers her. And if you approach her she'll not hesitate.'

'She would never hurt me,' Helen repeated quietly, and Dan's eyes held hers as if he was trying to see into her mind.

'Who is she, Helen?'

'I can't tell you,' she whispered.

He frowned in frustration. He was no further forward. And he dared not make the next step to challenge Helen with the fact that her silence was probably putting other lives at risk. In any case, like him, she was guessing. They were both making assumptions based on instinct, and the fact that his instincts were highly trained and channelled made him, if anything, the more guilty.

Helen made no attempt to move away from him. She seemed to be quite content to stay close, nestling on his knee, resting her head, and Dan sat quietly, absently stroking her hair, thinking. He glanced down at her but her eyes were closed, as if she was worn out with the shock that the news item had given her. She had this ability to suddenly become a tired child, completely at variance with her crisp, hard image when she was working.

She hadn't worn the spectacles today and that gave him a burst of pleasure. She trusted him and found no need to hide behind any sort of disguise. But she held some secret that was crushing her. From where? Her childhood, or more recently? He felt as if he was walking on a very thin line with Helen, afraid to push her too far, afraid for her safety and afraid of losing her. His arms tightened as the thought came into his head. He damned well wasn't going to lose her.

His involuntary action made her stir and she looked up at him and then looked quite stricken.

'The dinner!' she exclaimed. 'I left it on.'

'I switched it off,' Dan informed her complacently. 'I know how to turn off a stove, even when it's an English one.'

'I'd better get it going again.' She made a move to get up and Dan let her go, but his voice was extremely firm when he said,

'No. We eat out. You don't stand on shaking legs and cook a meal tonight. We eat out and that's an order.'

'I feel a little bedraggled for going out,' Helen protested, but he could see that she was not entirely opposed to the idea.

'Go and freshen up, then, and be back here in ten minutes. I know a cosy place where there are plenty of dim corners.'

'You seem to know a lot of places with dark, cosy corners,' Helen pointed out, and he grinned up at her, relieved to see that she was recovering rapidly. Even if she was still thinking about the news they had heard, she was fighting it.

'I sneak about a lot,' he said. 'I have to have somewhere to hide and watch the world go by.'

'Are you always working?' Helen asked, looking at him seriously.

'It depends on exactly what you mean by working,' he murmured cagily. She suddenly seemed to be on guard and he wanted to keep her relaxed, but he knew what she was getting at. She couldn't divorce him from his profession and the recent incident had reminded her of just what he was. He knew that in the present circumstances it was something she would fear.

'Do you ever forget that you're a psychiatrist?'

'No,' he told her honestly, holding her worried eyes with his. 'When I'm with you, though, I come very close to forgetting – most of the time.'

'Until you think about the woman,' she surmised, looking wary and downcast. 'She reminds you and . . .'

'She intrudes,' he intervened quietly. 'I automatically start doing what I do best. Having a trained mind means that it jumps into action almost of its own accord.' He smiled across at her. 'Mostly, though, I think about you, and that's problem enough.'

'I don't need a psychiatrist, Dan,' Helen said quickly. 'I know I have worries but . . .'

'Oh, you *do* need a psychiatrist, honey,' he said wryly. 'You need me but you don't quite know it yet, and pretty soon I guess I'm going to need one myself. I want you,' he finished softly. 'I need you in my arms, in my bed. If this goes on much longer I'll really need help in a big way.'

'You could just go away and forget me,' Helen whispered, as colour flooded her cheeks.

'I've never been suicidal. Going away is a medication that would probably finish me off. Besides,' he added drily, standing and looking down at her, 'I haven't given up hope of the cure.' He kissed the tip of her nose and turned her to the door. 'Get ready, Miss Stewart; quit while you're ahead. I'm bigger than you are, and if you throw me I'll pull you down with me. I give that idea a whole lot of very pleasant thought.'

Helen fled and Dan smiled ruefully. Talk about many a truth being spoken in jest. He was crazy about her and he didn't really know the first thing about her. Who she was on the surface was not at all who she was inside. Not that it seemed to make much difference. He wanted her anyway, as he had never wanted anyone before. He was even content to wait, because when she came to him he wanted it to be real, with no regrets later.

They ate at a quiet restaurant that Dan spotted by sheer chance and Helen was silent for a lot of the time. He didn't try to make her chatter and smile. She had to work out things for herself. As far as he could judge, she had an almost insurmountable problem. He could guess that her conscience was troubling her much more than his own troubled him.

He was practical, scientific. There was no evidence at all. How many people raced off to the police with wild theories? Plenty, and he knew that for sure. He had been there and heard them. It merely threw spanners in the works. And his theory was as wild as they came. But Helen knew a lot more than he did, at least she thought she did. Somehow he had to stop her from taking matters into her own hands and confronting a woman he knew to be dangerous.

Even if she had nothing at all to do with the murders, the woman with the black velvet band in her hair was very dangerous. That was a fact that needed no evidence at all. He had seen it for himself, out on the street and in the bar. He had felt it by the quiet, dark alley between two busy roads, felt the chill and the warning signals. Until this was over or until he had Helen safely with him every night, she was walking into peril with every excursion she made into the darkness of the city.

When Dan drove her home, Helen invited him in for coffee. She was obviously nervous and reluctant to see him leave, and Dan was happy enough to stay with her. They sat with coffee and managed to make a normal conversation without too much tension. There was a limit, though, how long he could make a cup of coffee last, and finally he stood and made an obvious move to go. He was determined not to crowd her in any way at all, and if leaving made that obvious to her then he was prepared to simply leave.

'I don't want you to go,' Helen said in a rush of sound that almost seemed to be hurting her. Dan turned to look at her and his face softened at the anxiety on her face. 'Please don't take it the wrong way,' she pleaded breathlessly. 'Don't think I mean that . . .'

'Helen, with you I've just about given up thinking altogether. I wait for orders and try to obey.'

She knew it wasn't true but she was grateful that he was keeping everything calm. She had this terrible desire to cling on to his hand, to beg him to hold her. When he left, the darkness would come rushing back, and it was getting too bad to face.

'I suppose – I suppose I'm a little frightened,' she confessed, avoiding his eyes. 'I don't mean that I really feel in any sort of danger because I know I'm not in danger but – well . . . I feel nervous.'

'And you want me to stay the night,' Dan concluded.

She looked up at him quickly.

'Will you? But . . .'

'Okay,' he said wryly. 'As far as I can make out, you want me to stay as a companion. You want me to keep guard through the night but you can do without a lover. Is that about right?'

'I shouldn't have asked you,' Helen muttered, hastily looking away from the mocking panther-gold eyes. 'I'm sorry. It was childish. I don't know why I'm behaving like this. I'll just lock up when you've gone.'

'Where's the spare room?'

'You'll stay?' She gave him such a look of hope that he had a hard time keeping his hands to himself. Stay? He never wanted to leave.

'Sure. I'm not about to drive off knowing you're uneasy. So where's the spare room?'

'Oh, I didn't want you to . . . The spare room is right at the back of the house. I thought if you would stay in the same room with me I might feel safer. I don't think I'm going to be able to sleep, but if you're there where I can see you . . .'

'You're trying to push me over the edge, Helen?' he asked quietly. 'Keep pushing. I'm more than ready to go.'

'I can't, Dan! You know I can't.' She was panicking and he relaxed, grinning at her with a wolfish grin that took all the heat out of things in some miraculous way.

'Okay, lady,' he said with a strong accent like a gangster. 'You don't touch me, I keep clear of you. I protect myself, see?'

Helen gave him a wavering smile and then looked at his beautiful clothes.

'You haven't anything to wear.' Her mind was slightly numb with her own boldness in asking him to stay but she was afraid of the shadows that would come when he left. He was like a wonderful light in the darkness of her life.

'So where's the problem? Tomorrow you go to work and I go back to my hotel as if I've had a night on the tiles. Who's to know? I'll not tell if you don't.'

'You're very good to me,' Helen whispered.

'Not yet, Helen,' he said softly. 'Any friend could do this for you. I want to be a lot more than your friend. Then you'll know how good to you I am, how it feels.'

CHAPTER 10

Helen looked at him helplessly and Dan couldn't stop himself from walking forward and taking her in his arms to hold her close. He rubbed his cheek against her hair and gave a rueful smile. He wondered if all this was going to make him better at his job. England had never been like this before. She was utterly vulnerable and he was treating her like a good buddy, holding down a raging desire that was tearing him apart. Sooner or later, something had to give or he was going to start banging his head into the nearest wall.

Helen went to sleep quickly, curled up in bed with her back to him, and Dan stood watching her. She hadn't told him precisely where he was to sleep but he had figured it out for himself. He was to lie on top of the bedclothes like an amiable watchdog. He was to keep one eye open and not move more than an inch in any direction. He shook his head ruefully. She seemed to think he was some sort of superman with iron control.

He had stayed downstairs, making an effort to read until he was fairly sure she was fast asleep, and now, as he watched her for a minute, his face softened into a wry smile. She looked totally different from the crisp Miss Stewart he had first met. She was like another character and her face was peaceful in sleep. There was a childlike droop to her soft mouth, thick eyelashes rested against the peach of her cheeks and her hair was a halo of gold round her head in the light from the lamp. In some obscure way she belonged to him already, and the crazy thought filled him with pride.

Dan took off his shoes, his jacket and tie, and then went quietly back down the stairs. He made sure the door was locked and then put the key in his pocket. He didn't expect intruders; that wasn't the problem at all. The problem was Helen, and if she woke up in the night and thought about going out searching she was going to have trouble getting out through a locked door. From now on she was not going anywhere without him. He intended to stick to her like her shadow until this thing was resolved. The lecture tour could wait indefinitely.

He went back to her room, unfastened the top two buttons of his shirt and then gingerly climbed on to the bed, well away from her. He could hear her quiet breathing and it filled him with a sort of painful tenderness. If this was as close as he was could ever get to being in heaven it was going to be pretty harrowing. He couldn't resist tucking her in more carefully and then he lay on his back and stared at the ceiling for comfort and inspiration.

He had a decision to make and he had to make it soon. What would he have done about this if Helen had not been involved? Would he have flown back across the Atlantic and put it right out of his mind? He didn't really need to think about it. He would have taken action and risked looking like a fool if it proved to be a mistake. It was no mistake. Everything he knew, had ever learned, everything he had seen made him deep-down certain. He understood about Helen's battle with her conscience. His own was prodding him unmercifully.

The room seemed to be getting colder and he took a chance and stole some of the quilt, trying not to disturb Helen and moving to get more comfortable. She murmured and snuggled towards him in her sleep, and he could feel the soft warmth of her body through the rest of the bedding.

'Oh, honey,' he groaned softly, 'you sure know all about torture. There's no other girl in the world I would do this for. I hope you realize that I deserve a gold star on my card.'

Next morning when Helen woke up she felt slightly disorientated, and then she remembered and turned her head quickly. Dan wasn't there, but she could see where he had been sleeping, if he had slept at all with about one foot of quilt and his head on the outside edge of the pillow. She felt terrible about it, more so since he had obviously gone back to the hotel. Why had she been so stupid, so childish? Now that morning was here the dark shadows seemed to

239

be a long way off. She could have managed without putting him in this awkward situation.

He put his head round the door at that moment and then came in with a cup of tea when he saw that she was awake. He looked red-eyed and tired.

'You look really bad,' Helen said regretfully, pulling herself up in bed and tucking the sheet as high up as she could. 'I should never have asked you to stay. It was selfish and incredibly stupid.'

'Oh, I don't know about that,' Dan murmured, setting the tea down on the table by the bed. 'There's some sort of reward in everything when you look at it closely. I can say I slept with you. In my diary I'm going to put "September sixteenth, slept with Helen, tired next day". That should stir some interest in the academic world.'

Helen blushed wildly at this teasing and he stood looking down at her. She looked soft and warm and he wanted to reach for her and lift her into his arms. He had never wanted to make love to her as much as he did now. He was aching for her. It showed in his eyes and Helen quickly looked away.

'I'll get up and make some breakfast,' she said shakily.

'I'll start it,' he offered, iron control making his voice cool. He turned and went out of the room and Helen never gave a thought to the tea, she swung her legs out of bed, saddened by the thought that her own selfishness at asking him to stay had put Dan through all this torment. Somehow there was a difference now, as if they had taken a step forward

240

and could never go back, could never just be friends. She didn't really know what to do.

He came back in at that moment, taking her completely by surprise.

'Shall I make toast . . .?' he began, and then his eyes darkened as he took in the soft allure of her in the silky nightie she wore. It was riding almost up to her thighs as she moved to get out of bed. She looked warm, still sleepy, her hair tousled around her angel's face, and uncontrollable desire hit him inside, hardening his body into instant arousal.

'I want you, Helen,' he said thickly. 'You're torturing me.'

She stood up, unable to take her eyes from him, and he walked forward slowly, a drawn look on his face that turned her heart over.

'Let me hold you,' he whispered. 'Just let me touch you. I'll go mad if I don't. Let me hold you and then I'll go away.'

Helen never said anything. She was mesmerized by his obvious longing and by her own. When he reached for her she flung her arms tightly round his neck and let him pull her close into him without any resistance at all. She was warm, pliant, silky-soft, pressed against his hardness with so little between them that he could feel the swollen ripeness of her breasts through the thin material of his shirt.

The tender contours of her womanhood fitted into his taut muscular body as he brought her closer with one heated movement. She was so willing, so warm that his iron control snapped completely as the need to possess her overwhelmed him and he tumbled her onto the warmth of the bed and came down with her, kissing her wildly, groaning against her mouth, drinking in the little whimpers of pleasure that escaped from her lips.

It was a fire that had been waiting to happen, a burst of flame that bonded them together with its scorching power, and they were both blind to anything but passion as they rushed headlong to the only conclusion that could be reached.

The nightie had ridden up to her waist and Dan pulled it impatiently over her head, tossing it aside and covering her warm body with heated, urgent kisses. His hands cupped her breasts as his mouth explored her skin and Helen threw her head back in an agony of pleasure.

'I'll be late for work,' she moaned, knowing she would make no move to leave him.

'No. Don't go,' he groaned, his tongue tracing her swollen breast. 'Tell Martin you're sick today and can't go anywhere. Stay here with me, Helen, while I make both of us better. You can't leave me. We'll both die if you do. Say you can't leave me.'

'I can't,' she whispered tremulously. 'I can't leave you.'

He groaned with pleasure as his mouth found her breast and she gave a little cry of pain and enjoyment as his lips pulled at the hard, darkened peak. He took it soothingly into his mouth and she wanted to touch him too, her fingers began to frantically tear at the buttons of his shirt. She wanted his skin

242

next to hers, wanted it with a heated desire that left her with no other thought. It was something that had never entered her mind before but now it was bursting inside her urgently

'Dan!' she ordered fretfully, and he tore the shirt over his head, ignoring the sound of ripping buttons. He shrugged impatiently out of the rest of his clothes and moved completely over her, crushing her on the softness of the bed. She could feel his hardness against her, pressing into her, and she moved with sensuous pleasure against him as her hands threaded into his dark hair, tugging the thick, shining strands with impatient fingers as his lips burned over hers and his tongue moved possessively into her mouth.

She was kissing him back wildly, and when he moved demandingly against her she parted her legs by sheer instinct, ran her hands down the powerful muscles of his back and wound herself around him. They never spoke, but the invitation of her body was unmistakable. Nothing else mattered. There was only heat, passionate arousal and an intense desperation that drove them both onwards.

'I want you, Helen,' he said thickly. 'I'm so hungry for you.'

His hands moved heatedly over her breasts, round her waist and then beneath her to lift her into him, and then he slid powerfully inside her at once, cutting off her wild cry with his lips, holding her fast until she relaxed and adjusted silkily around him.

She was a hot, moist sheath holding him, her body pulling him further inside her, and Dan lifted his head and looked down at her flushed, wild face. His eyes were molten, glowing, unblinking and unsmiling, his face taut with desire, and Helen stared back into his eyes, losing herself in the gold. She had no thoughts in her head except the knowledge that he had taken her body. He was above her, watching her, none of the humour left in him. He was claiming his mate, primitive, and she closed her eyes slowly, accepting the fate that had been waiting for her since she had first looked into the panther-gold eyes.

Helen tensed when he began to move slowly inside her, her mind suddenly alert to the strange reaction of her body. It was like listening for something with her whole being, not knowing what to expect, and then pleasure began to build up inside her that brought a startled cry from her lips, tiny ripples of heat that spread rapidly through her.

She opened her eyes and looked into glowing gold and her hands clutched at his shoulders as everything exploded into a rhythm as old as time. She called his name in a far-away voice and he silenced her with his mouth; arms like steel held her, his lips ravished hers and the powerful rhythm increased until she fell off the world into a spinning vacuum of flashing lights, a dream place with no reality except Dan's harsh breathing and her own trembling limbs.

Spirals of sensuous pleasure curled inside her, coursing around her, sending her arms and legs into a limp, relaxed softness that accepted the weight of his body over hers. She was unable to move or think, and when Dan lifted his head and looked down at her she lay there with her eyes closed as if she were lifeless.

'Helen.' When he spoke she opened dazed eyes and looked up at him with a sort of wonder on her face. She had never dreamed of anything like this. She was warm through to her soul, belonging to the man who looked down at her with steady, unblinking eyes. She wasn't alone. She would never be quite alone again.

He watched her for a second, reading her expression, and then he slowly withdrew from her. She gasped at the ripples of pleasure that this action sent through her whole body and Dan misread the sound completely. He moved to the side and reached for her, holding her close and pulling her head to his shoulder. Helen needed no encouraging. For a while she had been free, deliriously happy. She never wanted to move away from him.

'I didn't mean it to be like that,' he said tautly. 'I hurt you.'

'You didn't,' Helen told him softly. 'You didn't hurt me at all.' She gave a little sigh. 'I was free then, you know. For the first time ever in my life I was free. I just stopped thinking about anything else. I only thought about you.'

Dan turned towards her and looked into her eyes.

'I wanted it to be beautiful for you, slow, gentle.' He grimaced wryly, self-disgust on his handsome face. 'I was too hungry. I wanted you too damned much to be slow and gentle.'

'It was my fault,' Helen began quickly, and he smiled down at her, stroking her hair back from her face.

'You sure had a whole lot to do with it. I've been lying beside you all night like a big, dumb guard-dog. I nearly made it too, but you just had to get out of bed looking as if you'd fallen from heaven, didn't you? I suppose we could say it was your fault if we were making excuses, but we're not, are we?'

She looked at him shyly and shook her head.

'I was happy.'

'That's because you're my girl,' Dan told her huskily. 'We could have got around to it a whole lot sooner but we finally made it.' He cupped his hand round her face and tilted it towards him, kissing her gently. 'Any regrets, Helen?'

'No. Not one.' She snuggled against him with a contented sigh and then stiffened and gave a small cry of anxiety. 'I'm late for work!'

'You're not going,' he said assertively, clasping her firmly to him. 'When my mind rights itself, I'm going to make love to you.'

'You just did,' Helen reminded him tremulously, but he shook his head and smiled.

'No, I didn't. Making love is slow and peaceful, healing. What happened just then blew us out of our minds. Sooner or later we'll have to eat and then I'll go back to my hotel and change into something I haven't slept in.'

'I think you tore your shirt,' Helen pointed out regretfully.

'Yeah. I think so too. I've no idea what the rest of the outfit looks like. Maybe I'll go back in a black plastic bag if you can find me one.'

Helen giggled and he smiled against her hair. The next step was going to be tricky, because he had no idea how she would react when he asked her to move into the house with him. If he could get her there she would be safe, and if Martin wanted to blow his top like an outraged father, he could damned well get on with it. Helen was all that mattered.

He bent over and began to kiss her slowly, and after a second she sighed against his mouth and wound her arms round his neck. She was soft, pliant, the most sweet, willing girl in the world, a girl straight from heaven with the darkness of hell dogging her footsteps.

'Helen,' he said deeply. 'You're my angel, my girl. I hope you know that.'

'Yes,' she whispered, ignoring all the small spiteful voices that tried to get into her mind. Dan held the darkness at bay, vanquished the night like a knight in white armour. She smiled against his lips and he lifted his head.

'What?' he asked gently, looking down at her. Her hand touched his face as she smiled again.

'You don't look a bit like Sir Galahad.'

'I should hope not. All that cumbersome armour. All I had to do was tear my shirt when you were complaining and trying to get close to me.'

Helen blushed wildly but held her mind on the theme.

'You rescue me, though. In a way you are like Sir Galahad,' Her fingertips traced his dark brows. 'I don't suppose he had panther eyes.'

'Is that what I've got?' Dan asked, grinning down at her.

'That's what I thought when I first saw you. Your eyes scared me.'

'Do I scare you now, Helen?' he asked seriously, and she shook her head, looking straight up at him.

'No. You make me feel safe. Safer than I've ever felt before.'

Dan pulled her close and began to kiss her with tender passion. He knew where she got her blue eyes. She had brought them with her when she fell straight out of heaven. He tightened his grip on her and his kisses became passionate, his body more demanding. Nobody was going to pull her into the darkness. Wherever she went, he would be one step behind her.

Violet Edgerton turned her back on the shop and smiled secretly. Peter Saddler was in as usual and this time he was speaking earnestly to Caroline and looking as if he was quite determined. She hoped he was going to ask her out, because the girl didn't seem to have any sort of life outside this shop and Violet was worried about her. For the past few days there had been an almost dazed look on Caroline's face, a sort of daydreamy look, but if she was daydreaming it was not a very pleasant dream. She had changed a lot recently, since George Rider's death in fact.

Of course, Violet didn't really know much about

Caroline, other than that her parents were dead and that she had a flat of her own. There were supposed to be friends that Caroline went out with but somehow Violet doubted that, because there was never any chatter about what she had done the night before. Violet had talked about her own husband and family to try to draw her out but she had never succeeded. Maybe Peter Saddler had summoned up his courage and she certainly was not about to interrupt. If a customer came in she would dive forward and serve them before Caroline could move.

'Can I go a bit early tonight, Mrs Edgerton?' Caroline asked when they were by themselves in the shop and Peter had left. 'Peter asked me to go to the matinee at the cinema and I could just make it if I go about ten minutes early.'

'You can go whenever you like, love,' Violet told her with a wide smile. 'I knew he'd get round to it. Go whenever you want to.'

'Oh, ten minutes will do. It won't take me long to get there.'

'Are you going for a meal afterwards?' Violet asked, trying not to sound interfering but very anxious to know if this was something that would go on for a bit longer then one matinee.

'No. It's going to be really dark by then. I shall go straight home.'

'You're not a child, Caroline,' Violet pointed out gently. 'You can do exactly as you like. I mean, it's not as if anybody was going to check up on you and ask you where you've been.'

'I have to go after the matinee,' Caroline said flatly. 'Peter should be indoors when it's too dark anyway.'

'He's not a baby,' Violet laughed. 'I shudder to think what some of these college boys get up to after dark. They are men, after all.'

'Peter is only a boy,' Caroline insisted stiffly. 'I'm only going to the cinema with him because he plucked up courage to ask me and I didn't want to hurt his feelings. When it's really dark he has to be inside. It's dangerous in the dark.'

She walked off as a customer came in and Violet watched her in surprise. She had never seen Caroline like that before, all stiff and cold. She was a nice, good-natured girl. All the same, she had been different lately, as if she was thinking about something else, something far away. Maybe Mr Rider getting killed like that had reminded her of something from the past.

Violet shrugged and went into the office to get on with some work. More money meant more work but it didn't bother her. She glanced at Caroline through the glass of the door. Normally she would have asked outright what was wrong, but Caroline had been really different this last week, quite unapproachable. She frowned and got back down to work. Perhaps there really was some trouble from the past that had caught up with her? There was nothing she could do unless Caroline chose to tell her, though. It was strange. Even when Peter Saddler had been asking her out she had not once seen a smile come to Caroline's normally cheerful face.

'Can I go now, Mrs Edgerton?' Caroline asked when it was just on the ten minutes before closing.

'Oh, yes, love,' Violet said, getting up from the desk and walking through to the shop to start counting up for the day. 'If you're out late after all, you know you don't have to worry about being in on time tomorrow.'

Caroline stared at her without smiling.

'I'll be out late myself, but not with Peter. I have to go somewhere straight after the matinee. I'll be in on time tomorrow. I always am.'

She walked off without saying goodnight or anything, and Violet watched her go with a very worried frown on her face. Something was definitely wrong with Caroline. She had never seen her look like that before, unsmiling, glassy-eyed. It was almost like looking at a different person. She shook her head and went to count the day's takings. Maybe the girl was ill and not saying anything about it?

The thought worried her. Who was there to see to her if she collapsed or something? That was the trouble with these young people living by themselves. If anything happened to them, nobody knew for ages, and if anybody tried to help they were classed as being interfering busybodies. Well, she wasn't going to be that, but she intended to keep an eye on Caroline all the same.

Meanwhile, Caroline was walking along the street and she glanced at herself in a shop window. There wasn't really time to go and change if she was to be there to catch the matinee. She looked reasonably all

251

right, though. All the same, she stepped into a shop doorway and took out her compact, looking at herself in the mirror and carefully applying the pale pink lipstick she normally wore.

She stared at herself, blinked her eyes and looked again more closely. It was funny. She knew this was her face but somehow she looked all wrong. She had no idea why. It had been troubling her for days; as if she had forgotten who she was. It was a bit like when she had heard about Mr Rider and couldn't remember his face either. She still couldn't, and she couldn't remember his name sometimes.

She had never told Mrs Edgerton that, though, and it was all right because they both tried to avoid speaking about him. She was sure that Mrs Edgerton remembered his name because she often started to say it when there was something or other to do with the shop but she always caught herself in time and stopped. She said it was upsetting, and Caroline couldn't understand that, because it didn't upset her. She had hardly known him. She didn't even know how long he had been there.

She gave her hair a quick comb in the reflection from the side window of the shop. She would just about do. Peter wouldn't notice. He was too young, easily satisfied and always pleased. He was a nice boy, and she had to be on time because they had to catch the beginning of the film. It would be dark when it was over, but not too dark, and she had to make sure that Peter went away quickly.

He said he shared a house with three other people from college. It would probably be all right if he came out again when she had left him, providing they all went out together. She wondered what the house was like, if they messed it up? She seemed to have memories of living in a house herself at one time. It had been dark as far as she could remember. She couldn't actually remember a lot about it but she knew she hadn't liked it. She must have sold it or something.

'Excuse me, please.'

The voice made her jump. She was blocking the doorway and a woman was trying to get out of the shop. Caroline hurried off without saying anything, wondering what she had been doing, standing there when she was in a hurry to meet Peter. She remembered putting lipstick on and combing her hair, tidying herself up. That was what she had been doing, of course!

Caroline smiled with relief. Everything was back in focus. It must be tiredness but she didn't really feel tired. She was quite pleased to be going to see a film and it had given her a nice feeling to make Peter happy. He was a really sweet boy. What he could do with was a nice girl, someone really young who would look up to him and make him feel important. It was a pity he seemed to have picked on her.

She glanced at herself in another shop window and smiled even more. Not bad. She felt cheerful now. She liked this yellow skirt and blouse. It suited her and she hated dark colours anyway. Even when it was really deep winter she dressed brightly, like a canary. She gave a little laugh that had people turning to look at her. Somebody used to call her that. She could hear a voice calling her 'Canary' as if it were her real name. Somebody gentle, with a lovely face. It was terrible to keep forgetting things and she had no idea how long she had been doing it. The lovely face stayed in her thoughts for a while but by the time she met Peter she had forgotten it, at least it was hazy, somewhere hidden in her mind.

When the taxi called for Helen she was still trying to make up her mind whether or not to go to the gym. She was all ready but for the first time ever she wasn't particularly looking forward to it. Dan had told her he was coming back but he hadn't come after all, and she was torn between staying in case he came and going to the gym to show him that she expected nothing from him at all. She wasn't going to cling to him and make a nuisance of herself. If the small time with Dan was to be her only bit of happiness she would hold it close and never forget it.

She got in the taxi and then saw that it wasn't the usual man.

'Where is my normal driver?' she asked, not able to shake off the uneasiness she felt whenever something was even slightly different.

'Two flat tyres, would you believe?' The man half turned to speak to her as he gave this information. 'He limped back into the depot just as I'd been detailed to collect you. No accident either. Somebody stuck a couple of nails in his tyres while he was helping a woman with her suitcases. West End too. Don't know what things are coming to, what with these murders . . .'

'We have to collect somebody else,' Helen cut in quickly. 'He goes to the gym. We share a taxi.'

'That's okay, love. They told me.' He reeled off Jack's address and then settled to driving. Helen sat back in the shadows of the back seat. She didn't want to talk. He was speaking about the murders as everyone else would be doing, and it was only natural. They would be saying things all over London, all over the country. It had been in the morning paper that had been lying in the hall when they finally got up to have breakfast, and Dan had quickly folded it up and taken it with him. But not before she had seen the headlines. 'Serial Killer in London.'

What was Dan thinking about her? Was he secretly horrified that she had made no move to stop all this? She *had* tried. She had searched night after night, praying that she was wrong but knowing deep inside that she was not. The damage she would do, though, if she spoke out mistakenly would be incalculable.

A pretty face with blonde hair swam into her mind. Karen. She hadn't seen her for years. For all she knew, Karen had made a new life. She might be married, with a family. There was no way she could accuse without proof, and even with proof, what would she do? There had been destruction enough in the past. But it was still going on if her terrible suspicions were correct. Violence begetting violence, an endless cycle of ferocity that would not end until the deadly circle was broken.

Dan knew something, but not in any way the terrible reality of it all. There had been a face on the front page of the morning paper, a photograph of the man killed on the common, and there had been a dreadful recognition in Helen's mind although she had never seen him before. It had made her silent and depressed. No wonder Dan had not come back.

'Here,' Helen said, coming out of her dark thoughts.

'I know, love. Know this place like the back of my hand.'

Jack wasn't waiting on the front doorstep as usual, and Helen had to get out and knock. When Jack finally came to the door he was in his dressing gown and he looked terrible.

'Oh, hell. I forgot,' he said in a muffled voice. 'Keep clear of me, Helen. I've got flu or something. I should have rung you but I've been too wrapped up in my own misery.'

'Can I do anything?' He looked quite ill and Helen didn't know if he had anyone to help him.

'No. The doctor came and told me to go to bed. He's coming in the morning, if he gets the time.'

'Who's going to look after you, though?'

'A whisky and two aspirins. Doctor's orders,' Jack said with a twisted smile.

'That's some funny doctor,' Helen started indignantly, but he waved her away and pointed to the taxi.

'It suits me. The meter's running and I'm freezing at this door. Count me out for a few days.'

'But Jack, who . . .?'

'I do have a girlfriend, Helen,' he said after a fit of coughing. 'Why do you think I haven't chased after you in all this time? She'll be here soon, so don't start worrying about me.'

Helen got back into the taxi when he had closed the door and they went on to the gym. She was beginning to think she should have stayed at home after all. Besides, if Dan did come back he was going to be pretty annoyed that she had just walked out. She could ask to be taken back home but it would look as if she needed somebody to hold her hand, going back just because Jack was ill.

She decided to go on and stand on her own two feet. The taxi had to come back to fetch her. Everything was ordered and it was a well-established routine. When Helen got out at the gym she reminded him about coming back all the same. Being in an area like this with Jack for company was one thing; being here alone after the session was another thing entirely.

Dan drove round to Helen's house feeling quite irritated with himself. After the glorious euphoria of this morning he had managed to behave like a delirious schoolboy for the rest of the day. He had gone back to his hotel, changed and packed and then had spent a long time on the telephone making transatlantic calls. After that he had set about browbeating the agents into letting him take over the house on the spot.

It wasn't exactly how they went about things, they told him, but finally, after he had threatened to look elsewhere and had offered to pay six months' rent in advance, they had agreed to hand it over to him at once. They had saved face by saying that as they knew exactly who he was it would be all right to waive any thought of immediate references. They knew everything about him, the woman at the office had said complacently.

Dan had managed to look superior and cool. If they had known *everything* about him they might well have had second thoughts. They didn't know that he was desperate to get into the house so that he could scoop Helen off to comparative safety where he could watch over her all the time. They didn't know that he was probably concealing the identity of a killer. With every day that passed he was more sure that the woman with the black hair was the person the police were looking for. When he had Helen safe he would have to deal with it.

He drew up at Helen's house and realized at once that she wasn't there. Her car was there but there was no sign of Helen at all, no lights, nothing, and his feeling of behaving like an idiot grew. He had never rung her once because he had been intent on keeping things secret, presenting her with a *fait accompli*, hoping that the surprise would help to persuade her to live with him.

He had never once looked at it from her point of view. They had spent the morning wrapped in passion and then to all intents and purposes he had simply driven off and put it right out of his mind. He had let an almost juvenile enthusiasm to complete tasks push the really important thing out of his head. Helen needed him.

He sat in the car for a moment and asked himself where she would be. Was she roaming around looking for the woman in black? The thought sent shudders down his spine but common sense and his own observations told him that it was too early. It was dark because of the time of the year, but it was not dark enough for the woman who prowled the streets to be out and ready. Helen knew this too. He was sure of that.

He managed to get his mind back into gear and the very obvious solution came to him. The gym. He drove off quickly, looking for the first telephone kiosk with a Yellow Pages. He had the name. All he needed was an address. He knew London almost as well as a taxi driver and he would be able to find her. He was puzzled that she hadn't taken her car but he would take that up with her later.

When Helen came out of the gym after the session, the darkness after the bright lights inside was something of a shock. With Jack there she had not given it a thought, but as she was alone it reminded her that she was extremely vulnerable. The others had left while she had been showering and changing, and although the lights were on inside because Bob himself would be the last out, she really felt alone.

She hated to feel so uneasy, and after all she had been coming here for ages in order to face any sort of situation. She was supposed to be able to take care of herself physically. The new taxi driver was not on time and she stiffened her resolve and decided to walk to the entrance to meet him. Standing about could only make her more nervous and after all, these past few months she had walked through many dark places alone.

There was a rather gloomy yard to go through with no lights at all, but the main road was not far at the other side; she could see the street lights. It was only as she was walking through the yard, halfway between the safety of the lighted gym and the road, that Helen remembered why the taxi was not here. It never came until they called for it.

Jack had set up a regime to suit himself. He liked to have a coffee after the session and he phoned the taxi to say they were ready as soon as they went into the dismal café that was fairly close by. She had simply left it to him. If she didn't feel like joining him he always phoned the taxi from the gym.

Helen turned round to go back, hoping that Bob had not already locked up by the time she got there because she would have to phone the taxi for herself tonight. It wasn't very far back to the gym. She could see the lights as soon as she turned, and although she knew she was getting a bit panicky she forced herself to walk normally.

Without warning, a man lurched at her out of the shadows. He was almost up to her before she saw him, and everything that Helen had learned simply left her head. All she could see was someone rushing at her and she simply froze. Fear robbed her limbs of movement, even took away her ability to scream, and just as the man grabbed her, a car came round the corner into the yard, the headlights picking up the scene of the struggle in a white blaze of light.

The man never stopped, even though they were bathed in light now, but it brought Helen to her senses. She tried to fight her attacker off but she was already at a disadvantage. She had let him close in and he was big. He was also drunk. She could smell it on his breath; in fact she could smell it all over him, as if he had been washed in it.

'What's a nice girl like you doing here?' he questioned in a slurred voice, panting for breath in the struggle with her.

He never got another word out because hard hands hauled him away and Helen stood shaking as Dan spun the man round, hitting him so hard that he was knocked against the wall.

'Are you all right?' Dan turned to Helen and took her shoulders in a punishing grip, and when she just stare at him with wide open eyes he tightened his grip even more. 'Helen!'

'I – I'm fine,' she managed shakily, and Dan let her go to turn his rage on her assailant again. It was too late, however; the man was already on his feet, making his getaway as swiftly as possible, lurching out of the yard and into the lights of the main road.

CHAPTER 11

Dan swore fluently under his breath and started after him, but he was loath to leave Helen alone. He was torn between two things: the desire to offer violence to anyone who tried to harm her and the necessity of keeping her safe.

'It was just a drunk,' Helen said in little more than whisper. She was considerably shaken, and not only because Dan had appeared like a tornado and punched the man. She was stunned at her own inability to defend herself. She had been walking the streets at night very secure in the knowledge that she could hold her own in any circumstances, and the first time she had been put to the test she had frozen.

Dan turned on her, his eyes blazing so much that she could see them in the very dim light.

'What the hell are you doing, walking about in a place like this?' he thundered.

'The – the gym is here. I came out for the taxi but . . .'

'What's the use of having a car if you leave it at home?' he roared. 'What do you think you're doing

262

walking through a dark yard all alone when you've got a perfectly good car standing at home?'

'It would get vandalized here,' Helen protested, still shaken and now thoroughly subdued by the power of his voice.

'You'd rather be vandalized yourself?' he snarled.

'What's going on here?' Bob loomed up on the edge of the shadows and Dan instantly went into an alert stance. He was ready to hit anyone by now, and Helen had to hold his arm.

'It's all right,' she said quickly. 'This is Bob. That's his gym over there.'

Bob was black and looked like a wrestler. He was easily as tall as Dan and under his tracksuit he was obviously rippling with well-trained muscles.

'So this is where you come to waste your money?' Dan said scathingly. He turned baleful eyes on Bob. 'What sort of a gym do you run here anyway? She was just attacked in your own damned yard and she froze up like a mouse. She's be better off having boxing lessons.'

Bob stiffened with annoyance and Helen looked from one angry male to the other, feeling a little like the cheese in a sandwich. It was Bob who kept his temper, though.

'I'm really sorry, Helen,' he said quietly. 'Come inside for a minute.'

'I'm taking her home,' Dan snarled. 'She can call to get her money back tomorrow.'

Bob's mouth set in grim lines but he managed a smile at Helen.

'Just come in for a minute, Helen. I'll sleep a lot easier if I've seen you in the light and know you're okay.'

Helen glanced at Dan and then followed Bob towards the gym. It would give Dan time to calm down before he had to drive, and Bob was asking nicely in spite of considerable provocation. It wasn't his fault that she had failed to react to danger when she had faced it for the first time.

Dan followed, and he was so obviously still in a fury that Helen avoided looking at him. So much for her threats to throw him down the stairs at the book shop. He had hit her assailant with all the power of his tall, athletic body behind the blow and she had stood frozen with fear.

Inside it was still brightly lit, and Bob walked casually across the floor with Helen following in a daze. Dan stood grimly in the doorway looking ready to pull the whole building down, in no way recovered from his fury. It was going to be a silent trip home as far as Helen could see.

'What's the idea of making a fool of me?' Bob suddenly turned on her with every semblance of violence, raising his voice and glaring at her threateningly. 'You been coming here for months and now you let a mugger take you without a fight? You're completely stupid, girl. Maybe I should throw you out of this place.'

He made a dive for her, not looking at all like his good-natured self, and he was so obviously going to attack her that Helen acted without thought at all.

She met his forward momentum and then suddenly gave ground, tossing his powerful body across her own and standing threateningly over him when he hit the floor with a crash. Everything about her stance was alert and menacing, and Dan who had leapt forward at Bob's tone, stopped halfway towards them, astonishment on his face.

Bob lay on his back and grinned up at her, pointing one finger in her direction.

'Training,' he reminded her smugly. 'You don't freeze, you react, and the training does the rest.' Helen relaxed and took a steadying breath as she held out a hand to help him up. Bob shook his head and got to his feet without assistance. 'Don't tempt me,' he warned. 'I can feel every bone in my back. The next time I go for you, I get out a mat.'

Dan came closer and glowered at him.

'Did you have to scare her like that?' he grated angrily.

'Yes, I had to scare her like that, man. What is it that rich folk say? When you fall off a horse, get right back up there. Doing things in the gym with people you know is a whole lot different from self-protection on the street. Helen is a dainty lady. Out there it's mean. She's got to react. Tonight was the first time she had to put things into practice. Next time she's scared she might not just go down under it. She's good. All she has to do is believe it.'

'Sorry,' Dan muttered. 'I guess I tend to act first and think later.'

'Not if you're this psychiatrist bloke they're all talking about here.'

'How do they know about Dan?' Helen wanted to know as her face began to grow pink.

'Jack,' Bob told her with a sceptical look in her direction. 'He's been going round like the bellman.' He glanced towards Dan who was pacing about angrily now. 'You better take him home.'

'I have to cancel the taxi,' Helen said as she remembered.

'Give me the number, I'll do it,' Bob offered with another glance in Dan's direction. 'This place is for sport. He still looks ready for a battle.'

He did, and Helen went with Dan to the car rather uneasily. There was not much about him now that was amused and gentle. He was taut and silent, still with that air of anger about him that had really scared her. Now that the whole thing was over she wasn't feeling too good herself anyway. There was this tendency to feel shaky and a definite feeling of weepiness. She settled in the car and tried not to look at Dan at all. It was a far cry from the bliss of this morning.

He didn't speak to her at all. He just started the car and stared grimly ahead, and she couldn't quite believe that the strong hands on the wheel had held her so possessively this morning. It seemed a long time ago, and she wanted him to hold her now, to be gentle, to make everything all right. She was still shivering and a few tears had come into her eyes.

Helen let them stay there because if she wiped them away he would notice. She blinked rapidly but she felt them roll on to her cheeks and slowly trickle down. She gave a miserable little sniff and Dan turned his head to glance at her. It was easy to see how unhappy she was, how shaken.

He pulled into the side of the road and unfastened their seat belts before reaching across for her.

'Come here, honey,' he said quietly. 'Come here to me. I'm taking my temper out on you and I shouldn't.'

She buried her face against his shoulder and felt all her misery start to ease as his hand stroked her hair. She was back with Dan, wrapped in his warmth, her tears damp on his sweater. She bunched her hands in the soft wool to try and draw him closer.

'I was frightened,' she confessed in a whisper. 'I wasn't quick and efficient or ready or anything. I was just frightened.'

'Shh,' he murmured softly, rocking her against him. 'You weren't the only one who was frightened. When I drove round that corner and saw what was happening, I thought it was . . .'

'You thought it was the person who had killed those men,' she finished for him.

'For a second,' he confessed. 'I thought I might have been wrong all the time. I never considered that it might be a man. I've got damn all evidence one way or the other but I've been convinced it was a woman. When I saw you struggling with him, though, I went crazy. I could only see that you were in danger.'

'It was just a drunk. I don't imagine I was in all that much danger. If I hadn't frozen I could have got rid of him easily. I expect he was just trying to get my bag.'

'Probably,' Dan muttered. It hadn't looked like that to him. When he had seen the man pawing her, trying to hold her, his rage had been uncontrollable. He had wanted to go for Bob too. If he hadn't already known how he felt about her he would have known now. Having her out of his sight was sheer hell.

'Let's go home,' he said quietly, sitting her up and getting ready to start the car.

'Which way are you taking me?' Helen asked. She fastened herself in and looked round for the first time. 'I don't recognize this road at all.'

Dan's hands stilled on the keys.

'I got the house today,' he told her with a wary glance at her face. 'I moved in this afternoon. That's why I didn't come back. I was checking out of the hotel and making sure there were all the necessary things at the house. I should have called you but I wanted to get it all done. This is the way to the house. That's why we're on this road.'

'Are we going to look at it now, at this time of night?' Helen asked in surprise. It was late; she wasn't exactly up to viewing houses.

'I hope we're going home,' Dan said quietly. He turned so that he could face her. 'Come and live with me, Helen. I want to be with you every minute.'

'Oh, Dan. I don't think . . .'

'Why not?' he asked intensely. 'We both know how we feel about each other. You can drive to work from there. I know it's further away but it's quiet too.

You'll be able to bring your work home and curl up by the fire with it. I won't interrupt you, honey. I'll just be there with you, looking after you. At night I'll hold you close and neither of us will be lonely.'

'Oh, Dan,' Helen whispered. Her hand came to touch his face and he turned his cheek against the velvet softness of her palm.

'I'm not trying to kidnap you. I won't lock you in and try to keep you.' He looked at her with passionate eyes. 'I need you, Helen. Say yes to me.'

'Yes,' she said tremulously, and for a moment he just looked at her as if he didn't believe it and then he pulled her back into his arms, holding her close and then kissing her hungrily.

'Oh, God!,' he whispered. 'I've been dreading this all day, sure you'd say no.' He held her face to his and covered it with burning kisses. 'Helen, Helen, you're driving me crazy. I can't be without you.'

'What would you have done if I had said no?' Helen asked shakily when he finally let her go.

'I would have moved in with you,' he assured her unsteadily as he started the car.

She laughed softly but he wasn't actually smiling. It was just about true. He wanted her safe. At the house he had rented she would be too far away to be constantly making trips into the city at night. Besides, he would be there with her, able to watch her, able to either stop her or go with her.

He would make love to her until she was just too tired to go anywhere because he knew deep inside him that the woman she was seeking would kill her without hesitation if the need arose. And if Helen confronted her, the need would arise immediately, because the woman would feel threatened. *She* wouldn't freeze as Helen had done tonight. She would react to the danger and strike out.

He was fairly certain that if it was the woman he thought then she had no real recollection of the things she was doing. It was a madness that allowed her to live two separate lives. He had seen it all before, and now that he had Helen safe he would have to do something about it.

When they finally got to the new house and went inside, Dan switched the lights on and then turned to look at her. She was trembling, looking uncertain, and he walked towards her, his golden eyes holding hers.

'Want to change your mind?' he asked quietly.

'No.' Helen shook her head. 'It's just that I can't believe it.' She looked up at him almost as if she was in a daze. 'I hardly know you.'

'Very few people know each other as well as we do,' he said softly, 'and if you're thinking I just mean sex, I don't. There's a lot more between us than that. If you want to go back to your own place, I'll take you,' he added seriously.

'I want to be with you. I think I'll always be lost without you.' She gave a helpless little shrug, a delicate gesture with her shoulders and hands. 'I suppose I've always been lost, anyway.'

'Not any more, Helen,' he assured her deeply, catching her to him with an almost desperate movement. 'You're not lost, not now. You'll never be lost again.'

She surrendered gladly to his kisses, her body yielding when his hands became demanding, but her mind went winging away for a second, seeing the dark streets, the future. He would go back to America and leave her. No matter what he said, she knew she would be lost again but she loved him and he was here now. She gave a soft little cry against his lips and he swept her up into his arms, carrying her out of the lighted hall and into the soft warmth of another room.

'Come back to me,' he whispered. 'I know when you go away from me. I feel it inside.'

She wound her arms round his neck and began to kiss his face, warm, urgent kisses that brought a renewed tautness to his body.

He changed direction and began to mount the stairs, holding her closer than ever.

'The first thing I did here was make the bed,' he told her huskily. 'That's where we need to be.'

'My things are at home,' Helen whispered between her heated kisses against his face.

'Tomorrow,' he promised thickly. 'Tomorrow I'll do anything you ask. Tonight we're here, together, and it's a long time to tomorrow.'

'I hope it doesn't come,' Helen whispered when he put her on the bed and came to take her back into his arms.

'We'll ignore it,' Dan said deeply. 'We'll just stay here and let the world go by.' He silenced her with urgent lips and soon Helen forgot about the darkness outside and the darkness that tried to creep into her soul. She was with Dan in a world that was safe, and she would hide in it for as long a time as Dan could give her.

He was the only steadfast thing she had ever known in her whole life. He might swing from mood to mood to amuse himself or, as Margaret had surmised, to protect himself from the stress of his work, but his moods were never cruel and when she needed him he was himself instantly, there for her, caring for her.

He looked down into her eyes and she smiled, knowing how much she loved him but saying nothing. She would never trap him as she had been trapped by life. She wanted him to stay as he had always been since she had known him: a wonderful being with golden eyes whose kindness reached out to everyone.

'Sometimes you hide from me,' he said thickly. 'Those beautiful eyes smile but you hide inside.'

Helen reached up to kiss him, to silence him. She had too much to hide to allow him into her mind completely, too much to hide from him forever. Even if he wanted to stay with her always she would have to refuse.

Over the next few days they brought the things that Helen needed over to the house. Nobody at all knew that she was living with Dan because Helen kept it to herself. It was in any case habit to keep silent on anything private, and for another thing, she still couldn't believe it. But she was happy and it showed. She raced home at night and flew into

Dan's arms; her world revolved around him and nothing intruded.

Even Dan felt the relief of being further away from the city. At the back of his mind the dark figure prowled but she was more distant, less likely, and Helen made no attempt to go out at night unless he was with her. She never even wanted to go to the gym now, and Dan did not encourage her. She was with him all the time unless she was working. She was safe and in any case, they needed each other. Helen showed it so sweetly, so gladly, and Dan had never before felt as he did now.

They were invited to spend an evening with Margaret and Martin. The invitations came separately: a phone call to Dan at home because Martin had his new number, and Helen was asked while she was at work. They both said yes without consulting each other and as far as Dan was concerned this was the crunch. It was time people knew they were together, and an evening with Margaret and Martin would bring things out into the open because there was no way he could be with Helen and not reveal his feelings.

They met at a smart restaurant and naturally, Dan and Helen arrived together in his car. He could see that this did not go unnoticed. Margaret and Martin glanced at each other and Dan had a pretty good idea about what was to come at some point during the evening.

'Would you like to dance?' Martin asked Helen as the meal was finished. He had noticed the happiness, the dreaminess for the past two weeks and tonight she was glowing. He knew why and it bothered him greatly. Dan would simply go home and leave her.

'I'm not very good at dancing,' Helen laughed, 'but I'll risk it if you don't mind ending up with sore feet. I'm sure to step on your toes.'

'I'll chance it,' Martin told her, trying to be a little more light-hearted than he felt.

Margaret started as soon as they were out on the floor.

'It's none of my business,' she murmured, turning to Dan.

'But you're going to make it your business anyway?' Dan asked drily. The ploy was fairly obvious. Get Helen out of the way and question him on his intentions. He had seen it in Martin's face all evening. He just hadn't known quite what tactics they would use. 'Fire away, Margaret,' he continued. 'It's bothering both of you. Let's get it over and done with before Helen gets back here. I don't want her to be upset.'

Margaret's face flushed uncomfortably.

'We thought it would be better coming from me.'

'In case I gave Martin a black eye? Sound judgement. So what is it?'

'Are you sleeping with her, Dan?' She looked very uncomfortable but very determined, and Dan turned the forbidding power of his amber gaze on her before answering.

'In normal circumstances I would tell you to mind your own goddamned business,' he said quietly. 'I know, however, that you both care about

Helen so I'll tell you. Yes, we're living together and obviously we're also sleeping together. She's happy, Margaret. You can see it on her face.'

'Yes, we can see it,' Margaret muttered uneasily. 'For how long, though, Dan? Things have never lasted long with you, have they?'

'No, but I'd never met Helen before,' he reminded her softly. He turned his head and his eyes followed Helen as she danced with Martin. Her face was glowing and she glanced across and met his gaze. His eyes devoured her and for a moment nobody else was in the place. Martin spun her round and Dan looked back at Margaret. 'What happens next will depend entirely upon how long Helen will stay with me.'

'You'll be going home, Dan.'

'We'll cross that bridge when we come to it. For now we're living every day. What we do in the future will rest with Helen.'

The other two came back to the table and Dan immediately swept Helen on to the floor again, He wanted to leave Margaret time to impart the news, but more than anything else he needed to hold Helen close. He had never before noticed how people intruded. He liked people. They intrigued him. It was all with good intentions too, but it had partly violated the world he had built around Helen. She was safe in the world he had made and now the danger seemed to be closer, waiting, because Margaret and Martin represented normality. They made him realize clearly that he and Helen could not stay in their dream world indefinitely.

'I wish we'd never come,' he growled against her hair, and Helen looked up at him in surprise.

'I thought you liked Margaret and Martin? Anyway, we can't live in a time capsule.'

'Why?' Dan asked almost angrily. 'We're happy in it.'

Helen glanced across at the other two and drew her head back to look up at Dan.

'They wanted to know about us,' she stated astutely. 'Did you tell them?'

'I told Margaret. She was asking for both of them. They were banking on my gentlemanly ways with ladies.' He gave a resigned sigh and pulled her close again. 'Let's go home, Helen. People are a pain in the neck.'

'They're your friends,' she reminded him, and he looked down into her eyes, holding her gaze until she felt weak.

'I only need you,' he said huskily.

He could feel the malevolence edging closer. He could almost see it and he was terrified that Helen would know too. So far she had given no sign that she had, but she would feel it sooner or later as he was doing now. She was not as alert to it as she had been because he had surrounded her with emotion. If the world intruded she would sense the threat again, and he had the feeling that it was more real now than it had ever been.

During the following week Helen bumped into Jack Garford as she was leaving the office to have

276

lunch. He pounced on her at once and fell into step beside her.

'What happened to you?' he asked. 'I was just coming to see you at work. I hope you're not avoiding the gym because of that drunk who attacked you when I wasn't there?'

'No,' Helen assured him. 'I quite recovered from my own foolishness as far as that was concerned. I just haven't had the time to come.'

'Or to answer your phone? I've been ringing every day and there's no reply. Don't you even pick up the messages on your answering machine?'

'I'm not living at home at the moment,' Helen told him in as casual a voice as she could muster. Here was one journalist prying, and the fact that he was a friend wouldn't make a lot of difference because Dan was involved.

'So where are you living?' he persisted.

'Further out – er – a better area.'

'So why is it only for the time being?'

'Jack, will you stop this interrogation!' Helen ordered. 'When I come back to the gym you'll know it because you'll see me there.'

'Okay, keep calm.' he said in an aggrieved voice. 'Just fatherly interest. If you're going for lunch, I'll join you. I was about to give up my lunchtime to seek you out.'

'Nice,' Helen murmured. 'See that you don't spoil lunchtime with irritating questions, then.'

'Not one more. I was a bit worried, though. Bob was telling me about the drunk. Don't let it take your confidence away. Maybe I'll freeze up if anyone attacks me.'

'You mean they don't attack you all the time?' Helen taunted. 'As far as I can see you're in a very dangerous profession.'

'I've got a different technique with other people. I only come straight out with things if it's you.' He was silent for a while as they went into Helen's usual restaurant and ordered and then he said. 'I hear that Dan Forrest flattened the drunk and then considered going for Bob.'

'He was there, yes,' Helen confessed quietly, waiting for the next question.

'Has Dan moved in with you?' Jack asked, trying to look unconcerned.

'That's not a thing you can ask with such a casual air,' Helen pointed out. 'Am I facing a journalist here or is that a purely friendly enquiry?'

'Friendly,' Jack said with an earnest look. 'I would never try to dig my way into your private affairs, Helen. Besides, I got my interview with him and he was pretty decent about it. I don't write for a gossip column. In any case I have no real desire to be taken apart. So are you going to answer? Has Dan moved in with you?'

'No,' Helen said carefully. 'I moved in with him.' She looked at Jack firmly, and he shrugged and started eating as the meal was served.

'Don't look at me like that. I'm making no comments. I just hope it works out okay.'

He quickly changed the subject, but as they were going from the restaurant later, Jack put his hand on her arm.

'Look, kiddo, I don't want to see you hurt. I can understand that he's everything you think he is but have you considered the future? This is not just any guy who lives in America, this is Dan Forrest. I mean, he's famous, he's in demand and he holds down a pretty high-powered job. For now he may be hanging around here and worshipping at your feet, but sooner or later he has to pick up the reins again.'

'I know that, Jack,' Helen said quietly. 'I'm not a fool. I know he'll go finally.'

'Don't look so tragic, girl,' Jack ordered with a laugh. 'Nothing's final until it's over.'

Helen smiled and they went their separate ways, but she wished she hadn't bumped into Jack today. It only served to remind her that one day soon it would be over. She had taken a chance and believed in her own dream but one day it would end. It would have to.

When she got back to work, Martin asked her to come into his office and started with great enthusiasm to tell her that she would be going to Wales in a few days' time to represent the firm on a television programme. It wasn't something she would have been glad to do at the best of times and he knew it, but now it was out of the question. She refused to leave Dan and cut their time together by as much as a day.

'No,' she said flatly, and she saw the first warning spark of Martin's temper.

'What do you mean, no?' he asked tersely. 'It's all arranged.'

'Without consulting me at all? You can send someone else, Martin, and if you want to know what no means, it means definitely not.'

'This is because of Dan,' Martin snapped, glaring at her. 'If he hadn't been in the picture you would have been off like a shot.'

'You know perfectly well that I wouldn't,' Helen pointed out sharply. 'I don't like things like that and you know it. And if Dan hadn't been here you would never have asked me. You may as well drop it, Martin, because I'm not going. In any case, we both know why you're sending me.'

'It was just an idea,' he muttered.

'Not one of your better ones.'

'I suppose if I really insisted, Dan would go with you anyway,' Martin grumbled on.

Helen was amused by his ability to become a bad-tempered little boy if it suited him.

'If you really insisted, I would leave and get another job,' she warned. 'I will never be pulled into that sort of limelight and you knew it when you gave me the job here.' She suddenly smiled widely. 'And about Dan, yes, if I went he would go with me. He wouldn't be too thrilled either. He might take his books elsewhere.'

'Margaret and I are only trying to protect you, Helen,' Martin said contritely. 'Forget about Wales. I'll go myself if necessary, but just think what you're doing. We don't want to see you hurt badly. We told you about Dan's reputation before he ever came here.'

'I remember,' Helen conceded quietly. 'I'm happy, Martin. Can we just leave it at that?'

He nodded in a very gloomy way and Helen did not feel too cheerful herself when she left his office. Being warned twice about her uncertain future in one day was a little hard to take. She had decided when she had gone to Dan that she would live for the moment, but with every passing day the time was drawing closer to his leaving, and she was well aware of that without being warned by all and sundry. She knew about his past, too. It didn't seem to make much difference. She just wanted to be where he was. When he left it would be time enough to be unhappy.

Caroline was unnaturally quiet. Whatever it was that was wrong was getting worse, and Violet was worried about her. She hardly spoke at all and the normal smiles now seemed to have gone completely. She came each day like a stranger and her attitude was making things more uncomfortable with each day that passed. It was making Violet uneasy. Caroline even looked different in some obscure way, and Violet was not the sort of woman to let things go on indefinitely.

'Look, Caroline,' she said one afternoon, 'I know there's something wrong. If it's me then say so outright and let's get it settled.'

'There's nothing wrong,' Caroline stated in a curiously wooden voice.

'But there must be! You've changed completely.'

'Have I?' Caroline looked at her as she had been doing lately, with a cold stare that sent shivers of apprehension down Violet's spine.

'You know you have,' Violet snapped, beginning to lose her temper for the first time in years.

'I can't remember how I used to be, so I could hardly know if I've changed, could I?' Caroline gave a strange sort of smile and turned to walk away, something she had been doing more and more lately.

'One moment,' Violet said angrily. 'I thought we were friends but obviously I was wrong. Now you can tell me if something is troubling you or you can keep it to yourself, but whilever you work here and whilever I'm in charge, you will not turn your back on me and walk off when I'm speaking to you. If you want to keep working here you'll have to be a little more pleasant to the customers too.'

Caroline turned back slowly and stared at Violet as if she didn't know her at all.

'You're going to get rid of me?' she asked in the same wooden voice.

'It might just come to that, Caroline. I do hope not, though.'

'I hope not too, because I like it here.' The words were whispered and Violet suddenly felt a shock of fear. A customer came in at that moment and relief flooded through Violet that they were no longer alone. For a moment there she had actually felt threatened, and by this slip of a girl. Violet was a big woman who felt herself to be capable of tackling anyone, but this was different and she knew it. She had no real idea what to do.

It was almost closing time when Peter Saddler came in and even he was subtly different. He still watched Caroline in that boyish manner but he seemed to be more wary as far as Violet see. She watched surreptitiously from further down the shop.

'Would you like to go for a meal later?' he asked Caroline straight out, and Violet listened unashamedly.

'No,' Caroline stated flatly and got on with the things she had been doing before, mechanically straightening shelves; whereas previously she would have been singing under her breath, she was now behaving like a robot.

'It would be early,' he pleaded. 'I know you don't go out late so we could go early.'

'I do go out late, but not with you,' Caroline said without even looking round at him.

'I could meet you here after work,' he persisted, and Caroline spun round so quickly that he took a step back.

'I don't want to go. I said no and you heard me. I went out with you because you pestered. Don't pester me again. Don't come into the shop again either.'

Peter looked devastated. He glanced at Violet and then walked quickly out of the shop and before Violet could say anything, Caroline had picked up her bag and was walking to the door too.

'Where do you think you're going?' Violet asked sharply and Caroline didn't even turn round.

'Out. Home.'

'It's not closing time by a long way, Caroline, and while we're about it, how dare you tell a customer not to come in here? You actually frightened that nice boy.'

'Do you think so?' Caroline asked blankly, turning to look at her.

'Yes, I do,' Violet snapped, 'and if you leave now I'm going to have to get rid of you. This has gone on long enough. Anyone else and I would have got rid of them days ago.'

'Get rid of me? How?'

'If you go now,' Violet said more steadily than she felt capable of being, 'you can't come back again.'

Caroline stared at her coldly and then turned back to the door.

'I'll see,' she promised. 'I shall probably want to come back. I like it here. I told you that.'

She just walked out of the door and Violet stared after her, wondering what to do. She knew she should call Mrs Rider and get her backing in this. She felt like walking forward and putting the bolt on the door but she had no excuse for that except her instincts.

She ran Caroline's words through her head and felt more anxious than ever when she realized that Caroline had been whispering at the end. Something was terribly wrong, dangerously wrong. Violet didn't know what it was but she had always had a well-developed sense of self preservation and she knew she had to do something about Caroline.

When Helen got home she could hear Dan on the telephone in the sitting room. She smiled to herself. It was wonderful to come in silently and hear that beautiful, quiet American voice. She took off her coat, went to put the kettle on and then walked across the hall to join him. Just the thought of seeing him set her pulses racing. He always greeted her with the same passion, as if she had been away for months. He always swept her up into his arms and held her tightly. Her cheeks flushed when she remembered that they usually ended up making love before she had even had a cup of tea.

She walked in and he was sitting at the small walnut desk by the side window. He had not heard her and she was glad to be able to watch him for a minute, to drink in the sight of him.

'I know,' he was saying. 'I'm aware that the lecture tour can't be put off for much longer. It can be put off for a while, though. No actual timetable was set and I don't care if they are clamouring for me, I'm not coming yet.'

The smile died on Helen's face. They were calling him back, ordering him home. The happiness died inside her.

'All right,' he said after listening for a while. 'I'll give it some thought but don't expect me to come tearing back yet. I've got something important here and I'm not leaving it.'

He put the phone down and then turned and saw Helen.

'I've never been called "it" before,' she joked shakily, 'but I like being called something important.'

Dan never said anything at all. He walked steadily towards her and stood looking down at her seriously.

'You are something important,' he told her quietly. 'You're the most important thing that has ever happened to me in my whole life.' He tilted her face to his and looked deeply into her eyes. 'Sneak up on me and you're likely to hear a whole lot of things you would rather not know.'

'I – I wasn't actually sneaking up on you,' Helen said. 'I thought you must have heard me come in. I didn't mean to eavesdrop.'

Dan just went on looking down at her and then suddenly gathered her close with an almost savage movement that took her breath away.

'Sooner or later I'll have to go back,' he murmured against her hair. 'You've always known that, Helen. I've got months of things planned ahead for me and I can't go ducking out of them indefinitely.'

'I know,' she sighed. 'It was never a big secret. When you go, I'll just take up my life again as if you'd never been here at all.'

It was unhappy bravado but Dan didn't seem to realize it. He drew back to look at her and his golden eyes were blazing in his face. There was anger, hurt, and Helen's eyes fell before the power of them.

'You'll just forget about me?' he asked tautly. 'You'll put those damned spectacles back on your nose and take up where you left off?'

'I expect so,' she whispered, and he tilted her face with hard punishing fingers, only then seeing the tears on her cheeks.

'Oh, Helen,' he said softly. 'Oh, baby. You can wind me up without even trying.' He began to kiss her cheeks, her eyes and her nose, tiny little kisses that melted her pain. 'I'm even jealous of your spectacles because they'll be close to you when I'm not there.'

'It's all right,' she said tremulously, smiling through her tears. 'I know you have to go. It's just that I never expected it to be so soon.'

'It's not,' he assured her roughly between kisses that were growing more heated by the minute. 'They'll have to drag me away from you. I'll shout and fight and hang on to the doorknob.'

Helen tried to laugh but the tears kept falling, and Dan covered her mouth with his, his fingers spearing into her hair as he held her face up to his.

'Don't cry, honey,' he begged urgently. 'Everything will be fine, I promise you.'

'It won't,' she sobbed, 'but it doesn't matter. I'm with you now, and when you've gone, I'll remember.'

CHAPTER 12

Dan drank in her tears, holding her face to his, covering it with passionate kisses that were hot and urgent. No woman had ever cried for him before; no woman had ever given herself as Helen gave, with a sweet warmth that held nothing back. He had never had this urge to protect before either, this uncontrolled passion that seared through him whenever he saw her.

He wrapped his arms round her and pulled her close, his mouth hot and demanding, his tongue sliding into the sweet darkness when she parted her lips willingly. He pulled her tightly against him, making no attempt to hide his need. He wanted to take her like a man claiming his mate, he wanted to comfort her and soothe her, he wanted to make her happy. The frustration that he could not achieve all those things at once made him more urgent. His fingers slid away her blouse and skirt as his lips moved hungrily over her own, and she softened against him as her tears gave way to an almost primitive passion.

They sank to the floor together, kneeling, facing each other, burning each other with kisses, and Dan slid her last garments away as he took her breast into his mouth and pulled at it strongly. Helen cried out and her fingers laced in his hair as her back arched in excitement.

Dan lifted his head and she had never seen him look like that before, not even the first time. He looked hard, fierce, almost untamed. He drew back and discarded his own clothes swiftly. He wanted her now with a wild urgency that left him without any thought but of being inside her. It seemed to be the only way he could keep her, the only way he could stamp his mark on her so that nobody else would doubt who she belonged to. She was his, *his*.

He pulled her down to the carpet with him and when she came so willingly he softened, but only momentarily. The desire to own her was too strong to be denied.

'I can't stop, Helen.' he breathed into her mouth. His fingers traced her body, gauging her readiness, and then slid gently inside her soft, hot feminine centre. She moved against his hand and her excited gasp of breath snapped what was left of Dan's control. He parted her legs and entered her with one swift movement that rocked both their worlds.

'Dan!' She gave the little cry he had grown accustomed to and he covered her mouth with burning lips as he began to move inside her, increasing the rhythm until Helen's world was spinning on the edge of fierce sensation. He had never taken her so desperately and she had never before lost all semblance of control. She felt as if she was losing her grip on sanity, the pleasure and excitement was so great, and Dan felt her body pulsing around him as he too rocketed off the end of the world.

'Helen,' he said softly when their breathing had steadied and she had relaxed in his arms. 'Did I hurt you, baby?'

She smiled up at him almost shyly, her lips red and swollen, still throbbing from his kisses. She ran the tip of her tongue round them experimentally.

'I don't know. I wasn't there for some of the time.'

Dan groaned and his arms tightened round her as possessiveness surged through him. She was the sweetest girl in the world, and she had just admitted that he had taken her so far, so high that she had almost drifted away. She was so much his that he felt like the other half of her.

'I'll never let you go, Helen,' he breathed against her lips, but she knew he would. There would be no choice. He would go back and she would search. There was no hope for Dan and herself, even if he meant every word he said so passionately. She had a dark, secret past that he must never know anything about. She wanted him to remember her like this.

Caroline walked down the street but it was different. It was fairly light. She knew she had to go to the house but everything seemed strange because she had never been there so early before. Odd snippets of memory came back, of times when there had been lights in the house, but she pushed them away. They were bad. She hated them. There had been a lot of noise, a lot of shouting and fear; there had always been fear.

There were children playing in the street and she had never seen that before. All the same, she knew she was in the right place and she knew she had to come here to the house at the end. She had a key and it must be her house, because it went straight into the lock and worked first time.

The rooms were empty. She had never looked round before. It had always been dark. Even now it was getting later, getting darker, but she had more time. She walked round all the rooms but there was nothing there at all. Each room was empty, reverberating to the sound of her own footsteps. She could hear voices but she knew somehow that they were in her own head.

'No! I won't go! She's coming back, she's coming back. She would never leave us like that. We've got to wait for her. Please! Please!'

The voices were far away, from a long time ago but she saw a face, a lovely face with tears on it, and she saw another face too, a man sobbing in despair – but he was lying. They had both known he was lying. He had known and she had known. Lying would not help him now. She would find him tonight.

She climbed the last staircase and opened the door to the room. The curtains were still closed, and with the dusk outside and absence of any light the room was in complete darkness. She gave a sigh and smiled. The voices stopped and she knew where she was, knew exactly what to do. Today seemed like a dream, but the days of a long time ago were as close as if they had just happened.

She switched on the stark overhead light and then the lamp. In the mirror she was looking at a face that did not belong to her, but she was neither puzzled nor alarmed. She took off her clothes and went to the old wardrobe, and when she was dressed she sat at the scarred dressing table and began to prepare. The black velvet band was hanging by the mirror. She lifted it down and brushed it with great care. It was smooth and dark like the night outside.

Helen slid carefully from the bed. Dan was sleeping beside her and she couldn't resist touching his face. He was so wonderful, so handsome. Love filled her and she wanted to lean over and kiss him, but if she did he might wake and she didn't want that. The fear was back, and she wanted to save Dan from the knowledge of it.

She went on bare feet to the window and drew back the curtains a little. It was completely dark outside, with only the light from the street-lamps to lighten the road. This was a nice road, tree-lined, the gardens of each house sheltered by high hedges that were thick and trimmed neatly. She had noticed today that the leaves were turning to autumn colours but they were still on the trees, rustling softly in the slight night breeze, making dancing lacy patterns on the pavement with the lights behind them.

It was restful, peaceful, safe, a good place to be with Dan. But the night was calling strongly, calling her to the endless mission, and she could not resist the call. She had often fought against it but it always won and it had won tonight, even with Dan sleeping beside her, even though she loved him helplessly.

She turned to look at Dan and he moved in his sleep, reaching for her although she was not there. His hand closed on her pillow and his breathing steadied. Helen smiled and then started to collect her clothes. When she had them, she silently left to dress in another room where she would not disturb him.

If he woke up he would try to stop her, and if she insisted then he would also insist on going with her. If Dan were there she would never succeed. Karen would take fright. In the back of her mind she also knew that Dan would be in danger. He was a man, and Karen might mistake him for the man she was seeking.

Helen left the house with no noise. Her car was parked round the side and she took off the brake and let it run towards the road. It moved soundlessly on the slight incline, and when she had it there she closed the door and started the engine. It made very little noise and she was speeding towards the city in seconds. Closer in, she would park and then she would walk, search, pray that tonight she would find the truth.

It was easy to park at this time of night and Helen chose a place where she felt reasonably sure that her car would be left alone. There was no guarantee, but the lights were bright and there were people around.

It was worth taking a chance. She locked it up and started to walk, knowing that all this might be to no avail. She might be looking in the wrong place, but after her encounter with the man at the gym she no longer felt secure enough to go to dark places. In any case, the only time she had seen the woman had been near here when she was with Dan in the taxi. This was where she would try again.

There were girls in lighted doorways, men walking past, and she ignored them. She knew without being told that the person she was searching for would be alone. If she was to see her she would notice her at once. It would be in the distance and she would know the walk, the clothes, the black hair.

A slight rain started and Helen turned up the collar of her coat. Within minutes the wide, busy street was wet and shining but people still walked, men looking in every shop doorway, girls enticing them with shrill laughter and promises. Helen knew all about it. She had learned it long ago.

The drizzle kept on and although it was slight it was nevertheless making her wet. Dan would wonder where she had been and she would have to hide this coat when she got back. She felt as if she was betraying him, sneaking off while he was sleeping, but she was also betraying him if she did nothing. She had to stop all this fury that roamed in the night.

She lifted her head and her heart hammered as she saw the woman some distance in front of her. It was the same woman, without doubt: the same black hair, the same prowling walk she had expected to see. For the first time in all the nights of her searching, Helen felt a burst of hope.

She quickened her pace, trying to overtake the woman without actually running. She was nervous in spite of her elation at spotting her quarry. Suppose she was wrong? Suppose when she got closer she realized that she had never seen this woman before except the one time through a taxi window?

Helen looked down at the slow, prowling walk and in spite of her fear she smiled.

'I'll walk like this. I'll be so good by then that as soon as they see me I'll be offered a part in a film. It will be a sort of trademark. I'll be called The Walk.'

'You'll be called The Canary.'

'I never will, and don't you dare tell anyone.'

Helen stepped out more quickly, and before she even reached the woman she was sure that this was the end of her searching.

'Karen,' she called loudly. 'Karen, wait for me. It's Helen.'

For a second there was no response and Helen stopped her headlong rush to catch up, a wave of doubt coming into her head. Had she made a mistake after all?

'Karen?' She said the name again a little more quietly and the woman in front turned very slowly to face her.

It was almost impossible to tell who it was. It had been years since she had seen Karen and this woman had dark glasses on, hiding her eyes. The clothes were quite bizarre too, but, more than that, she had an attitude of menace about her that was totally unlike anything that Helen remembered about Karen.

As far as Helen could tell, this woman was simply staring at her coldly; certainly there was no smile on the brilliantly red lips, and the urge to back away from her was very strong.

But she had searched night after night, and if this was not Karen then at least she should stay long enough to make certain,

'It's Helen,' she repeated quietly. 'Surely you know me? I haven't changed all that much.'

There was a long pause while Helen almost held her breath. She was also stunned at the shiver of fear that swept over her skin. She had been sure that this was Karen, certain, but now there was doubt and she was afraid of the absolute cold stillness in the face in front of her.

'Go away,' the voice said as the woman continued to face her, to stare at her through the dark glasses.

'I've looked for you for a long time,' Helen said steadily, fighting down the almost superstitious fear that was struggling to take control of her. 'Perhaps I've made a mistake after all, but at least tell me who you are and then I'll be certain.'

'Go away. You don't know me.' The voice was lowered and even more cold.

'Are you Karen? Please just tell me that. If you're somebody else it doesn't matter. Just tell me the truth, then I can go away and forget all about it. I had to find you.'

'Why?' the woman asked coldly.

'Because this has to stop, Karen. You have to get help.'

'I told you to go. I'm not Karen.' The woman was whispering now and Helen fought down real fear. It was something more than a physical fear. There was a feeling that she was facing someone who was not and never had been quite human. She realized however, that she was alert, ready for danger, and she was sure she would defend herself if it became necessary. The knowledge gave her a fresh burst of courage.

'All right, I'll go. But I think you do know me. I think you're Karen.' Helen dived into her shoulder bag, still keeping a wary eye on the woman in front of her. 'This is my telephone number and my address. If you want to talk to me, if you need help, you only have to ring.'

She held out the card and for a moment it seemed that it was going to be ignored. Angry frustration welled up inside Helen.

'Take it!' she ordered sharply. 'Searching for you is ruining my life. If you need me I'll be there, but I'm never going to try to find you again. If you are Karen then you recognize me, and if you're not Karen then what does it matter? Take the damned card!'

It was raining steadily by now and the black plastic of the woman's raincoat was shining like a cheap beacon. She reached out one hand and Helen watched it with an almost fatal fascination. The fingers were long and the nails were painted the same red as the lipstick. With a suddenly upsurge of

297

fright, Helen realized that the hand was considerably darker than the face.

It dawned on her then that the woman's face was unnaturally pale, as if she had covered it with white make-up. In her anxiety she had not noticed it before. It was colourless, more of a mask because of the brilliantly red lips.

Was it a disguise or merely bizarre? She looked up quickly and in that second the card was removed from her hand and she could see the eyes through the flat reflection of the dark glasses. They were staring at her coldly and steadily, like a predator.

'Go away.' The words were whispered again, the whisper more pronounced, and Helen backed away quickly.

'If you need me . . .'

'I don't know you. Go.'

Helen turned and walked off quickly. Her spine was tingling with the realization that the woman was behind her, watching. It couldn't be Karen, because she would never have been frightened with Karen. She knew too that this was the woman Dan suspected. And he was right, she had no business to be walking at night, searching the streets on the outside chance of finding someone she had not seen for years. Karen had disappeared a long time ago, disappeared without trace, and this was crazy. She should be home now, safe with Dan, lying warmly in his arms. She had wasted a part of their small time together to chase after a dangerous stranger because she had sentimentally thought it was someone she knew.

Helen glanced round nervously and the woman was still standing there, watching, silent and dark like a hunter in the night. There was an absolute stillness about her, and it was not in the way that Dan could be comfortably quiet and still. The woman was poised for some sort of action, her stillness like a preparation, as if she was collecting herself to be ready. She had not taken even one step since Helen had moved away. The rain came down and she must have felt it but even so she just stood there, her eyes on Helen's retreating figure.

Helen turned the corner and, knowing that she was out of sight, she ran. The car was still a good way off and there were plenty of side streets where anyone who knew the city well could take a short cut and appear in front of her. She had the feeling that, like her, the woman would move fast when they could no longer see one another. The rain was falling more heavily and it seemed that fewer people were about and that there was therefore less safety. Helen knew she would be in a lighted area right up to the car and she knew she had really very little to fear, but all the same she was afraid.

By the time she reached her car the rain was lashing down heavily and she had her keys in her hand ready. It was not the rain, however, that was responsible for her rush to lock herself into securely. She almost fell into the driver's seat and immediately locked all the doors. Too shaken to drive off at once, she sat for a moment to get her breath, to steady her nerves, and although the place was brightly lit she found herself watching every corner of shadow, rechecking the doors and still expecting to see the woman come at her from some angle she had not thought of.

She just wanted to be home with Dan, and at the thought of home she gave a gasp of dismay. She had given her address to someone who might very well be a stranger. It was her own address and she wasn't there at the moment, but when Dan went back to America she would be in her own house again. She could scarcely believe her own stupidity.

Helen knew she had almost fully made her mind up that she was facing someone she did not know by the time the woman had taken the card, but she had still let the card go. She had still put it into the outstretched hand. It had been one last, forlorn hope and she had allowed it to follow through because she was still clinging to the days of the past, hoping to set things right when in her heart she knew they could never be set right.

Dan had told her she was not responsible for other people's actions but she had not really listened. She knew now that he had been right and she knew she would never search again. If it was Karen then she no longer knew her at all. In any case, Karen might be miles away from here. She might be in another country. She might even be dead.

Helen started the car and made a vow that her nights of wandering the city were over. Every minute of her time from now on would belong to Dan until he left. But as she drove along, she remembered that slow, prowling walk. She remembered Karen's words when she had practised it day after day. And the hand, though it had shocked her, had still brought back memories. Nothing was solved, the doubts and the nightmares were still there, but now she would leave them behind, would reject them and only think of Dan. In any case, she knew she would never dare to search again.

When Helen drove up to Dan's house the lights were on in almost every room and her heart sank. Dan was awake and he had been looking for her. She pulled into the drive and got out quickly, but as she was running up the steps the door was flung open and Dan came out fast with his car keys in his hand. He was just shrugging into a jacket, but as he saw he stopped and Helen was shaken at the look on his face. He was pale, almost drawn, and he just stepped back without a word and motioned her into the house.

She stood wet and shivering in the hall and Dan simply stared at her, the same intense, unblinking golden gaze that had held her captive the first time she had seen it. She expected him to be angry but he didn't look like that at all. It was difficult to account for the look in those eyes, and Helen found her rehearsed excuses dying on her tongue before they could even be spoken.

'You're very wet,' he said slowly as his eyes ran over her. 'Get a shower. I'll make you a hot drink.'

'Dan . . .' she began, but he just moved to take her coat and ignored her words.

'Get a shower, Helen. Anything that has to be said can wait until later.'

She hurried upstairs, aware all the time that he was watching her quietly. The feeling that she had betrayed him, somehow hurt him, made her bite her lips together to stop the tears from falling. He had protected her, made her safe, warned her, and she had wilfully gone out into the night to face a woman who was probably a stranger. She had ignored Dan and gone off alone, sneaked out while he was sleeping. It seemed as if his caring meant nothing to her. That was how it would look to him.

Helen stood under the hot shower as long as she dared and then she put on her dressing gown and went down to face him. It was no use putting it off. If he had been angry she could have faced that better, but he had not been angry. He hadn't come up to the bedroom either.

He was in the sitting room, stretched out in a chair, and a hot drink was on the coffee table by the settee. Helen sank down and curled her legs beneath her, afraid to look up and meet his eyes, afraid of the reproach she would see there. She sipped her drink and waited, but Dan was silent for a long time and when she risked a glance at him he was not looking at her at all. His head was thrown back and his eyes were closed.

As she moved uneasily, the eyes opened and pinned her to the spot.

'Did you see her?' he asked quietly.

'Yes.' He said nothing for a second and the expression on his face never changed. There was no sign at all of emotion.

'Tell me about it,' he said softly. 'Tell me right from the beginning, right from the moment you left here.'

'I'm sorry,' she whispered, but still his expression remained the same.

'You survived the experience,' he pointed out in the same quiet voice. 'You're here now. Tell me about it.'

Helen clasped her hands in her lap and concentrated on them. She was dreading seeing any hurt on his face and the only way she was going to be able to get through this was by avoiding looking at him.

'It was a long way, so I took the car and parked fairly close to where you and I saw her when we were together. I never went anywhere where it was dark. There were plenty of people around even though it started to rain.'

Dan made no comment at all and she went on,

'I saw her almost at once. After all the searching I've done, she was suddenly there and it was quite easy to catch up with her.'

'You went up to her?' Dan sounded cool, calm, but he was remembering how he had balked at the idea of approaching the woman as soon as he had realized that she was dangerous. What drove Helen to do such things?

'Yes. I spoke to her and at first she didn't take any notice, but when I persisted she turned round.'

'And then?' Dan asked when Helen hesitated. The two men he had seen who had persisted with the woman had fled rapidly. How had Helen escaped? He felt cold inside at the peril she had walked into.

'I asked her if she knew me, told her my name, and she stared for a long time and then she told me to go away.'

'And did you? Did you go away then?'

'No,' Helen muttered with a slight indignation in her voice. 'I've been searching for ages, Dan. I wasn't going to run just because she was hostile.'

'Hostile? Dear God,' he breathed. 'She's not just hostile, Helen. She's a killer.'

'You don't know that. You don't know for sure.'

Dan moved impatiently and signalled her to continue, and Helen told him the rest after a wary glance at him. The anger she had expected seemed to be just under the surface now.

'So you persisted,' he prompted.

'I – I just told her that I had been looking for her and if she needed me I would be there.' Helen frowned and then looked down at her hands, wondering just how much more she should tell him. It seemed to be wise to hold back the part where she had foolishly handed over her own address. 'Anyway,' she continued, 'when I saw her close up I really didn't know her – at least, there was something about her but I couldn't be sure, and she denied knowing me. It started pouring with rain and when she told me to go again, I went.'

'You simply walked calmly away in the rain?' Dan asked with his usual astuteness.

'Not exactly. I walked away calmly enough, but when I looked back she was just standing in the pouring rain staring after me. It was somehow more frightening than all the other things. She seemed to be poised in some way, almost like a dangerous animal. When I got round the corner I ran.'

'Why?' Dan queried softly.

'Instinct, I suppose. I just had the feeling that when I was out of sight she would run too.'

'Run after you?'

'Yes. I was probably just scared but I really felt it. Even when I was locked in the car I expected her to appear.'

'You expected to be attacked.'

'I suppose so,' Helen sighed.

He leaned forward, his forearms on his knees. He concentrated his attention on her so much that Helen felt almost mesmerized.

'What frightened you the most, Helen? What was there about her that really scared you and made you decide to go and then to run?'

'Two things, really, apart from the fact that I suddenly made my mind up that I didn't know her at all and realized I was being stupid.'

'What two things?'

'In the first place it was her face. It was a sort of dead white, as if she had deliberately coated herself in white make-up. Not exactly like a clown but getting on that way. It disguised her completely. With bright red lips against the white it was rather horrific when you got a close look at her, I mean really close. I don't suppose a man would have gained the same impression as a woman, but she really had gone to a lot of trouble to make her face pale and blank. On top of that she wore sunglasses, so I couldn't see her eyes. You can tell a lot about a person by looking into their eyes and I wasn't able to do that. For a minute at the end I could see her eyes watching me through the glasses, but they looked flat and empty. I expect I decided to go at that minute.'

'And what was the other thing that scared you?' Dan asked. 'You said there were two things.'

'Yes,' Helen looked up at him and then bit at her lip worriedly. 'The other thing is silly really.'

'I've listened to silly things often enough,' Dan assured her. 'I can cope with anything silly now. What was it?'

'It was her voice. It might have been anything really. She might have had a cold or something, but . . .'

'But what? Tell me everything, Helen.'

'She never actually spoke to me properly. I could hear her with no difficulty but – but she was whispering all the time.'

Dan stood slowly and took both her hands, pulling her to her feet. He held her hands tightly and stood looking down at her.

'Since I've been in London,' he told her softly, 'I've seen that woman many times, an astonishing number of times. I thought she was a hooker. And the first time I saw her, I followed her.'

'What?' She looked amazed and not a little annoyed, and Dan's lips quirked in amusement for the first time since she had come home.

'Not for the obvious reasons,' he assured her. 'You once asked me if I ever forget what I do for a living. The answer is no. A policeman doesn't forget his training if he sees something suspicious, and neither do I. There was something about her that triggered alarm bells. I didn't follow her for long.'

'Why?' Helen asked again. 'If you were intrigued and suspicious . . .'

'I stopped following her because I was scared.' Dan tilted her face with one firm finger and looked into her eyes. 'Scared, Helen. I've dealt with a lot of dangerous people but I knew that if I had to deal with her, I would want her fastened up before I started. That would be a big first for me. I've seen her scare off two grown men, big men. They literally fled, and they were lucky to get the chance in my opinion. They weren't her type. Her type are big, heavy middle-aged men and I believe she kills them. I have no proof, nothing but instinct, training and observation.'

Helen was silent. She looked at him for a moment and then looked away.

'Did you know her at all?' he asked, forcing her to meet his gaze again.

'No.' She hesitated and then decided to be more firm. After all, there was that walk, but it was not in any way unlikely that plenty of people walked like that. She had seen it on films lots of times. There were the hands but she had not studied them. It had only been a brief flash of memory. 'No,' she said again. 'I didn't recognize her as anyone I knew.'

'Then you've followed up the feeling right to the source. You've settled your mind. Now I want a promise that you will never break. I want to know for sure that you will never go out again at night searching.'

'I won't, Dan,' Helen said earnestly. 'I made my mind up about that when I was safely back in the car. It was stupid, thoughtless. I've allowed it to drive me on for so long that it's become a habit. I'll never do it again.'

He cupped her face in his hands and looked at her seriously, searching her eyes, reading her mind.

'All right,' he said when he was satisfied with what he saw. 'You've had a fright, you've managed to get soaking wet, but you're back safely. Let's forget about it.'

'I'm sorry, Dan,' Helen murmured regretfully. 'I feel as if I've let you down.'

'You placed yourself in danger but you escaped unhurt. That's all that matters.' He bent his head and kissed the tip of her nose. 'I forgive you for being a pest, for giving me the biggest fright of my life. Let's try to get some sleep now'

Later, when Helen had fallen into a troubled sleep, Dan lay quietly beside her. This was the final thing as far as he was concerned, the last straw. Tomorrow, when Helen went to work, he would also leave the house and he would go to the police. They would look at him as if he was a lunatic but he would have to risk that. His conscience would no longer bear the weight of the guilt.

Tonight, Helen had innocently and foolishly placed herself in the power of a woman whose mission was death. She had escaped because she had been in the light, or because there were people about or because she had had the sense to run. For whatever reason, she was safe again, and he wouldn't face another day with the thought of there being any danger to her at all. He could not watch her all the time, and when he was gone there would be nobody at all to watch over her.

She snuggled up to him in her sleep and he tightened his arm around her. Tomorrow he would make someone believe him, and if he was wrong, then fine. At least the woman in the black velvet would get a good long scrutiny if he could persuade the police that she was a possible murderess, the serial killer that they were all searching for.

In any case, he couldn't go back home and leave this unsolved if he could help in any way at all. And he knew he could not go back home with the thought of any danger dogging Helen's footsteps. Soon, he would have to go. His time here was running out. There was more work piled up for him than he cared to contemplate, but his first duty was to Helen and to his conscience.

'What makes you think you know this killer?' The man at the desk looked tired and, at the moment, possibly bored. Dan knew how he felt. In all probability, over the past few months, a whole parade of people had been in here and other stations like it and their tales would have had one steady similarity: the serial killer. There would have been serious confessions, stories of sightings, murmured convictions that it was the man next door, their brother-in-law, the barman at the local pub and the man at the nearest supermarket. He had been in on this sort of thing plenty of times and had helped to sift out the improbables. It was ironic that he was now doing the same thing himself.

'Right,' the sergeant sighed, pulling the necessary sheet in front of him. 'I'll take your name, sir.'

Dan stifled a smile at this stoical attention to civility and gave his name.

'Forrest. Dan Forrest.'

'And your address.'

'I'll give you the address but it's only temporary. I'll be going back to the States pretty soon.' Dan took control of the sheet and wrote his address and telephone number, hoping that assertive behaviour might just lift him out of the category of being another idiot with a mission.

'And this person you imagine is the killer, sir, can you describe him?'

'It's a woman,' Dan said quietly. 'I've followed her a few times and I'm pretty much convinced that she's the one you're after.'

'Why did you follow her?' The attention Dan received was now much more acute; the boredom had vanished from the sergeant's eyes.

'Instinct and training,' Dan said decisively. 'I'm used to watching people. I'm a psychiatrist.'

'An American psychiatrist.'

'That about sums me up,' Dan murmured wryly.

'You're over here on holiday then, sir?'

'Not exactly. I'm here to promote one of my books.'

'Ah. A book on psychiatry.'

'Not so you'd notice,' Dan said quizzically. 'I also write thrillers, crime stories, blood and thunder. Don't underestimate it, it pays well.'

'Can you describe this woman, then, sir?'

Dan went through the description and added everything he could think of that had happened, only omitting any reference to Helen. Even while he was saying it, it sounded pretty thin. Running it round in his head was an entirely different matter from this hazy catalogue of facts that were going down on paper. It sounded as unlikely as he had thought it would, and while it was interesting to be standing on the other side of the fence it was also frustrating.

'If you could wait there for a moment,' the sergeant said, pointing to a very uncomfortable-looking bench. 'I'll just see about this.'

Which meant he was going to go to some superior and tell him that there was another nuisance out here, an American nuisance this time.

Dan waited for a considerable time and then he was asked politely to 'go through'. He got up with every sign of resignation. He was either going to have to go through the whole thing again with more astute eyes on him or they were going to arrest him on suspicion of anything they could think of.

He found himself in a room with three detectives, the seat was more comfortable, and the eyes that looked him over contained no sign whatever of boredom.

'Detective Inspector Swift,' one of them said holding out his hand. 'Sorry to keep you waiting but we had to check on you.'

'How did you manage that?' Dan asked, shaking hands all round and then sitting down to face them.

'Your embassy, sir. They wanted a description. They sent us a photograph through. All we need to see now is your passport.'

'The photograph there looks like a thousand other people,' Dan assured him, handing his passport over.

'Oh, we're already fairly certain that we know who you are, Professor Forrest. When we got the photo through we all had a good look at you through the crack in the door,' Swift said drily. 'This is just the final check.' He handed the passport round and then returned it to Dan. 'Now, tell us about this woman,' he finished seriously.

CHAPTER 13

Dan went through it all again and it still sounded thin, but they listened.

'I haven't one damned ounce of proof,' Dan finished. 'It's sheer instinct. I might well be wrong altogether, but even if she has nothing to do with the murders, she's dangerous.'

'What makes you say that, Professor Forrest?'

'Again, mainly instinct. I've felt the chill myself and I've seen two grown men almost run from her. She's all wrong. There's a coldness about her, a menace. She's never looking for clients, she's simply looking, searching. Whether she's doing these killings or not, you've got a tiger in the city.' He gave a disgruntled mutter and scowled. 'I suppose this sounds stupid?'

'No,' DI Swift assured him. 'Your embassy gave us a fairly complete description of you besides the photograph. You're used to helping the police in America and you're well respected. We would have to take you seriously whatever you said. And, clues being pretty thin on the ground, we're listening carefully, even though it is unusual.'

'So what are you going to do?' Dan wanted to know.

'We'll find her and bring her in for questioning. If she's on the game that's enough excuse to have a good look at her.'

'I feel as if I've got a personal stake in this,' Dan said casually. 'Will you let me know what happens?'

'You can be sure of it. We might even need you,' Swift told him grimly.

'Anything to help,' Dan assured then, adding. 'Whilever I'm here.' He did have a personal stake in this. It was Helen. There were too many coincidences.

Once outside and on his way home, Dan went through his words to them. It would have carried more weight if he could have told them about Helen's conviction too, but there had been no way at all that he was going to do that. Besides, she was now quite sure, apparently, that she did not know the woman in black velvet.

All the same, there was something. The state of shock she had been in when she had heard the identity of the murdered man on the common had been traumatic. There had been more information about the man in the paper he had so carefully hidden from Helen. The man's name had been George Rider and he had owned a music shop called 'Smile and a Song'.

Dan glanced at his watch and then turned the car at the next road junction. It sounded as if he needed the phone book again, because he knew he would not rest until he had seen the place. He was sure the police would already have gone over it with a fine-tooth comb if they had been suspicious. Maybe they were not as suspicious as he would be with Helen's safety at risk. He wanted to see for himself.

Violet Edgerton looked up worriedly as the door opened and Caroline came in. She had been worrying all night about the girl and, if she was to be quite truthful, she had been worrying about her own safety with Caroline like this. It was with an enormous feeling of relief that she met Caroline's eyes and found them smiling and normal.

'Good morning, Mrs Edgerton. I'm not late, am I?'

'No, Caroline, you're a bit early,' Violet said as cheerfully as possible.

'Oh, thank goodness. I nearly overslept. In fact I've more or less thrown myself together. I bet I look a mess?'

'You look very pretty, as usual,' Violet told her.

'Well, you always say nice things about me. I'll not be sure until I've looked in the mirror.'

She hurried through to put her coat away and Violet stood there feeling stunned and puzzled. Caroline was speaking as if nothing had happened at all, as if they hadn't parted with angry words the day before. It looked as if she didn't remember anything. All sorts of explanations flashed through Violet's mind – amnesia, brain tumour? She searched her slim medical knowledge to come up with some sort of reason for this but she was no further forward when Caroline appeared again, smiling and normal.

'Right,' Caroline said brightly, 'Let's get on with the day.'

Violet was lost for words. It was fairly obvious that the girl remembered nothing at all of the last few days of strain. Should she tell her? Should she point out that after walking out against orders Caroline had come dangerously close to losing her job? Should she remind her that it had been very wrong and very cruel to ban Peter Saddler from the shop?

She listened to Caroline singing at the other end of the shop and decided to leave it. She hadn't told anyone about the other night, not even her husband, and now she was glad she had kept quiet. Violet was beginning to think she had imagined everything; there was only the lingering uneasiness with Caroline that told her she had not imagined it at all.

Violet got on with her office work but she could not help glancing uneasily into the main shop from time to time. The feeling that something was very wrong was uppermost in her mind and it would take some time for it to settle and leave her as comfortable with the girl as she had been before.

It was well into the afternoon and they were both in the shop when a startlingly good-looking man walked in. Even if the place had been full, Violet knew she would have noticed him at once. It was not his height and his superb masculinity, either. It was the eyes – clear gold, steady, they looked right at you. He stood glancing through the classical music and Violet felt embarrassed that she couldn't seem to stop watching him. This was something she wouldn't tell Herbert when she got home. In all the years she had been married she had never done more than glance at the male customers as she served them, and here she was, mesmerized by a man who didn't look a day over thirty-five.

When he came to be served she edged out of the way and let Caroline deal with it, because she was quite certain that her own face would be bright red.

'Cheerful place, this,' he said casually, glancing across to smile at her, almost ignoring Caroline. 'You must get plenty of tourists.'

'Quite a few,' Violet managed, pulling herself together. 'You're an American.'

'Sure.' He grinned at her. 'I guess it's not easy to disguise the fact.'

'Are you here to make a film?' Caroline chipped in eagerly.

'Now why would you think that?'

'Well I just thought you looked like a film star, doesn't he, Mrs Edgerton?'

'Oh, really, Caroline!' Violet muttered, embarrassment sweeping over her again.

'Now don't be annoyed with her,' Dan urged. 'She's quite made my day. I'll go back and tell my girl that. Maybe she'll see how lucky she is.' He grinned at them both and paid for his cassette. 'Hey!' he exclaimed as he turned to leave. 'Isn't

317

this the place where that guy worked who was killed? Gee, I guess it is. The name's the same, "Smile and a Song". I read it in the paper.'

'Er- yes,' Violet said stiffly. He wasn't the first person who had come in because of the murder. Mrs Rider seemed to think it was all right, she said it brought business, but Violet thought it was terrible. She could do without notoriety, and to think she had been almost mesmerized by this man. He was nothing more than a prying tourist after all.

'I think he was the boss,' Caroline put in brightly. 'I can't remember his name, though.'

'It was Rider,' Dan said conversationally. 'Well, it's a small world after all.' He walked out and Caroline turned to Violet excitedly.

'Wasn't he just *gorgeous*? I bet he is a film star even though he didn't admit it.'

'He's a prying tourist,' Violet said disgustedly, going back to the office.

Dan walked to his car with a thoughtful expression on his face. It was quite a change to be playing the gaping tourist, and what had he gained? Well, for one thing the woman in charge had resented it strongly, not that he blamed her. Since the murder there must have been one person after another going into the shop to stare and ask questions. For another thing, the girl had looked vaguely familiar and he wasn't sure why.

He had seen her somewhere before and it had been nothing at all to do with this. She was a scatterbrained sort of girl and obviously liked the limelight. She would have been thrilled to learn that he was some wandering film star who just happened to have come into this area to buy a tape.

She was odd too. It had greatly surprised him when she'd said that she thought the murdered man had been her boss but she couldn't remember his name. Even if she was new on the job, she couldn't fail to know that the man who owned the shop had been killed not too long ago. Maybe she was a bit dim-witted? It was possible, but he had to admit that she hadn't looked like that.

He got in his car and decided he had been wasting his time visiting the place. The woman in charge looked as if she would only gossip if tortured, and the girl looked as if she would gossip all day, making things up as she went along. The only advantage he had was that he now knew what the shop looked like, and that was no advantage at all. He couldn't get to the common without directions and he was not about to ask anyone which way to go. He had played the idiotic tourist and gained nothing. He was not, after all, a detective.

Dan turned for home. Helen would be back soon and he hadn't yet decided what he was going to tell her. He hadn't even decided what he was going to do about her. One thing he did know was that very soon he would have to go back to the States and a life he had left behind. And supposing that this was still unsolved? He would be leaving Helen in danger, because he had a deep-seated feeling that she would eventually go back to her night-time searching. She had confronted the woman and decided that it was not the person she was looking for. But did that mean she would stop looking altogether?

He had no idea who she was searching for, and when he went away she would have nobody to watch over her. She had made him a promise but he knew that the searching she did was almost compulsive. He wasn't at all sure that she could stop until she found whoever she was looking for. He had to do something about this now. He couldn't wait for the police. Any small thing he could do would help.

He stopped the car and pulled into the side of the road where a man was walking his dog and Dan called out to him,

'How do I get to Thurley Common?'

'You mean where the murder was?' This time, Dan did not meet resentful eyes as he had done in the shop. 'It's up there. Turn round here and go straight on for about three miles. You'll pass a church on your right, just keep going straight. I expect you're with the police?' the man finished hopefully.

'Not exactly with them,' Dan confessed, looking conspiratorial.

'An expert,' the man concluded. 'You're an American. Did they bring you over?'

'I happened to be here at the time,' Dan said seriously, starting the car and preparing to get himself out of this.

'That's a bit of luck for them,' the man assured him. 'Hope you catch whoever did it.'

'Oh, we will,' Dan assured him as he drove off.

He suddenly felt cold. It was nothing to do with playing the idiotic tourist and then dropping into the character of a mysterious expert. It was the man's idle remark about it being lucky that he had been here.

If he had not been here, what would Helen have done? Would she have escaped so fortuitously when she had confronted that woman? Had any of his previous warnings to her alerted her to the danger? Was that why she had had the sense to run?

If he had not been here he would never have known about the danger, never have known Helen perhaps. She might have just walked into a trap without any warning as she searched the city for someone she thought she knew, someone she thought needed help. The woman did need help, but not from Helen. Helen might now have been dead, another victim, the reason inexplicable because she was not some middle-aged man.

Dan's face tightened grimly. He would not leave her. He couldn't. She was part of his existence now and she needed him. Whoever else needed him back home, Helen needed him more. And he needed her. He needed her more intensely every day.

He glanced at the church on his right and kept on going, straight on as the man had told him. He was probably wasting his time but he felt so helpless. He could actually feel the danger and he would feel it until this woman was caught, because he had not one doubt at all that she was the one the police needed to catch.

She had escaped for so long because she struck at random with no apparent motive. There *would* be a motive, as he knew perfectly well. There was always a motive even if it was imagined. What did the woman in black wish to avenge? What incident in her past life had led her to murder, repeated murder? And did Helen know the reason too, even if the woman was the wrong one? Why had Helen been so sure that the murders had something to do with her? Why had she collapsed when another man had been killed?

He was sure that, in the far distant past, someone had started a chain of events that had led to these killings. That it had been a man was certain, a big, rough-looking middle-aged man. Was the woman with the black velvet headband seeking retribution for herself or for someone she had loved?

And what about Helen? Why did Helen think that the murders had been committed by someone she used to know, some woman? Helen must know the underlying reason too. Until he had sorted this out he was stuck here in London, because he could never settle and work at home with the thought, the memory of this haunting him.

Thurley Common was a bleak place, and not because it was endless miles of cold moorland. It was a derelict area that had somehow managed to survive in the heart of houses and old factories. The whole of the surrounding was run-down, seedy, except for one or two streets where the inhabitants had made a brave attempt to be neat in the midst of dereliction.

The common began at the end of a long street and Dan drove down the street and skirted the common on the road that ran past it and through it. Houses and factories had been pulled down, the bricks and foundations left to nature, and grass had sprung up amongst the ruins. There was a wide stretch of rough grassland that might have been playing fields in happier times, and perhaps in days of long ago this had indeed been a common stretch of land, open to the people.

Now it was like any other run-down area of any city in the world – a forbidding place, not a place to go at night whether you were male or female. Yet a man had come here, driven here in his own car and been killed. A woman had come here to kill him.

Dan stopped the car and sat looking at the area. The place where the murder had happened had been cordoned off with police tapes and two officers were on duty now. He didn't go any closer. If challenged he could refer them to Detective Inspector Swift, but they would probably not challenge him unless he went too close. They would take him to be some prying person who was ghoulish enough to want to visit the scene of the crime.

Nobody else was there. There were no sightseers hanging around. This was not in any way exciting, even to the most morbid person. Any members of the Press and public who had been here had long since gone. The atmosphere was bleak, chilling, rather tragic. A few days ago a man had come here for reasons of his own and now he did not exist any more.

How had the woman approached Rider? How had she managed it without arousing his suspicions? There was only one way really. He had seen other men approach her, and maybe this man Rider had approached her too and had been led to his fate. He would have been welcome where they had not been welcome at all. He was exactly the type she had been seeking. The man she had killed while they were at the hotel cocktail party had met his fate in an alley. Perhaps this one had driven himself to his own destiny in his own car and brought her with him.

Had she sat beside him quietly? Had she whispered to him as she had done to the man in the bar, as she had done to Helen? She seemed to possess a charmed life because the police had been stunned when he had mentioned a woman. He had seen two men approach her, and yet nobody had reported her dangerous attitude.

Dan grimaced to himself. What man would report her? Unless they had been approaching her they would not have noticed her prowling about, or perhaps they would have merely noticed her in passing. No potential customer was going to bring it to police attention. They would be putting their own actions on the line.

Whether knowingly or not, the woman with the black headband had it made. She was safe unless she was actually caught in the act, and she was too careful for that; some animal cunning, some instinct protected her. She wandered about in the night, camouflaged as a woman of a certain type, a type of woman who was expected to wander about at night, a type of woman who was either scorned or ignored – a hooker. She was probably no such thing, and if his surmisings were correct she lived another life, an ordinary life, like Helen or any other of a thousand women in this city.

And she would protect herself too. She would protect her identity. Anyone who approached her was inviting danger or even death. Helen had been lucky. She had insisted on talking and yet she had managed to escape. It made him feel colder than ever. He turned the car and headed home, speeding up to get back to Helen. He was only happy when he could see her and know she was safe.

Caroline went to get her coat when it was close to closing time. She was in no sort of rush; in fact the desire to linger was strong. It had been a good day and she had felt like singing all day. She hadn't once felt strange and restless.

'Do you want me to help with anything?' she asked as Violet came out of the office and locked the door behind her.

'No, thank you, Caroline. I'm going myself now. There was no need for you to stay to the last minute.'

'Well, it's one of those days when I don't really want to go.' Caroline gave one of her sweet smiles. 'I'm really happy here and something exciting seems to be happening all the time, like that man coming in today. I bet he was a film star,

Mrs Edgerton. Ordinary people don't look like that.'

'And film stars don't come into this shop either,' Violet pointed out, still feeling a little disgruntled about her own reaction to their unusual customer.

'Did you see his eyes, though? I keep thinking about how he looked, so impressive, so handsome, sort of calm and quiet.'

'Hmm,' Violet muttered, picking up her own bag and making for the door with Caroline behind her.

'Shall we go to the Centre and get a coffee?' Caroline continued hopefully, and Violet hesitated and then shook her head. She no longer felt comfortable with the girl and it was no use denying it. She didn't want to prolong contact in any way at all. She was even a little anxious that Caroline was walking behind her. She had taken care all day to place herself where she could see without being too obvious about it.

'I have to get home straight away, dear. I have washing to do and a lot of other things. Perhaps another day?'

'All right,' Caroline agreed cheerfully. She stood waiting while Violet locked the shop. 'Peter hasn't been in today, has he? It's funny when he's been coming in daily for ages. I've quite missed seeing him. He's a nice boy. Maybe he'll come in tomorrow.'

She said goodnight and turned to go her own way home and Violet stood watching her in stunned silence. It was obvious that Caroline didn't remember anything about the other day. It had been on the tip of Violet's tongue to say, 'What do you expect when you told him not to come in again?' But she kept silent and now she stood and watched Caroline walk briskly and cheerfully away.

She knew she would have to do something about this, but she was not sure how she should go about it. Mrs Rider was a very heartless sort of woman and would probably just dismiss Caroline so that there would be no problem facing her at all. And Violet knew that if she confided in her husband, if he knew the real depths of her anxiety he would worry all the time, might even ask her to give up her job.

She turned in her own direction, hurrying now to catch the bus. Somehow she didn't feel quite safe any more. The feeling of being a rather indulgent adult had quite gone, and even when she was on the bus, safely seated and on her way home, Violet's thoughts still lingered on Caroline. She knew that something was terribly wrong, but apart from this ability to change character completely and the way she forgot things, it was almost impossible to put a finger on the problem.

Caroline needed help and it seemed that she had no one at all to help her. It made Violet feel terribly responsible. All the responsibility and not one shred of authority. She ran the shop and that was as far as her authority went. It was impossible to pry into other people's lives without accusations of interference.

All this had started when Mr Rider had been killed. Was it possible that Caroline had been so shocked that it had upset her to this extent? In any case, Caroline had not liked the man at all; he had been a nuisance to her since she had started working at the shop and, uncharitable or not, Violet knew that if she had been in Caroline's place, far from unhinging her, it would have been a great relief to know he would never be coming in again.

When Dan drove up to the house, Helen was already there. She was sitting on the doorstep looking rather disconsolate and he was out of the car as soon as it stopped.

'I couldn't get in,' she reminded him with a small smile, and Dan reached down and pulled her to her feet.

'I forgot to give you a key. I'm sorry, honey. I'll give you one the moment we get inside. I should have thought of it straight away.'

'Well, you're usually in,' she reminded him quietly. 'I didn't quite know what to do but I didn't want to go home to my own place and have you wondering where . . .'

Her voice was filled with insecurity and Dan shut the door behind them and then pulled her close to him.

'We live here,' he told her urgently. 'It's my fault that you don't have a key but I never expected to be out for so long. Don't say you were going back to your own place. It makes everything seem very temporary.'

'It is temporary, Dan.'

'No!' He tilted her face and looked into her eyes. 'It can't be temporary. I can't let it be temporary. We need each other.'

'You'll be going back to America. You work there. It's no use pretending that this is going to go on and on because we both know it's going to end.'

'Come back with me when I leave here,' Dan pleaded urgently. 'Sooner or later I've got to go home but I don't want to leave you.'

'You should have been gone by now, shouldn't you?' Helen asked, reaching up to touch his face gently. 'You can't go on putting off the inevitable, Dan, not for me.'

'Come with me, then,' he said seriously, catching her hand and bringing it to his lips.

'I can't, Dan.' She turned away and began to put her things down, her bag, a pile of manuscripts. 'I don't want you giving things up for me.'

'You're giving things up too,' he reminded her. 'You've just abandoned your own home, you never go to the gym . . .'

'I've merely put it off.'

'So that's what I'm doing,' Dan said irritably, beginning to pace about frustratedly. 'I'm putting off my departure, taking a long break.'

'You're just leaving your life over there,' Helen reminded him quietly.

'My life seems to be here at the moment,' he said tautly. 'My life is wherever you happen to be.'

'Oh, Dan!' She turned and ran back into his arms, flinging her own arms round his neck. 'Go home. Get on with your life.'

'Then come with me,' he repeated stubbornly, and she gently extricated herself from his arms and turned away again.

'I can't. I'm trapped here. There's something I have to sort out.'

'Like who is murdering those men. I know who's doing that, Helen, and you don't know her at all, didn't recognize her when you saw her close up. Let it go.'

'You don't know for sure that it's her,' Helen pointed out as she walked into the kitchen to put the kettle on. Dan walked in behind her and decided that it was time to tell her how he had spent his day.

'I'm sure enough to have reported my suspicions to the police,' he said flatly.

Helen spun round, staring at him rather frantically.

'You've been to the police? But you've got no evidence at all.'

'I've got my instincts, my observations and my suspicions, all of them from a trained mind. I thought it was enough to go on at the moment. Plenty of people report their suspicions to the police; if they didn't, a lot of criminals would get clean away.'

'Did they believe you.'

'They listened politely at any rate. I got the chance to put forward my notions. They got in touch with my embassy to find out if I was an amiable nutcase.'

'And they were told that you were nothing of the sort.' Helen murmured. She took a deep breath and then dismissed the whole conversation as if it had never happened. 'I'll cook tonight. What do you fancy?'

'I fancy you,' Dan said softly, 'but I somehow think that the time is not right so I'll go for sweet and sour chicken. I'll set the table and get the wine ready.' He walked out and left her in peace and Helen leaned against the sink, trying to get herself together again.

She knew that Dan had done the right thing and she felt guilty that she had not done something similar before now. The police would catch the woman. She wandered around quite openly and they would get her easily. It wasn't Karen. She told herself that very firmly but inside she knew that she was not exactly certain. Karen used to playact a good deal; it was her way of escaping the darkness. Had this been Karen playacting now?

The police would catch her and then everything would be out in the open. Dan would find out. He would know all about her past life and he would be disgusted. Dan was wonderful, famous, respected, and who was she? Her background was bad, a secret. Helen sighed and stoically got on with the meal. She was nobody. Karen had always playacted but she playacted too, pretending to be someone with a normal background, living up to her job. She lived two lives all the time. While she had been with Dan she had been happy but all the time she had known that one day it would end.

Helen tightened her lips grimly. Whilever he was here she would stay with him, try to make him happy so that he had something to remember that was good. And even if it was wicked she would pray that the police would not find the killer until he had gone home. That way he would never know if everything came out into the open.

The next day, Dan came from seeing Martin and stepped reluctantly outside. He hadn't even caught a glimpse of Helen, although he knew she was somewhere in the building. Initially he had wanted to take her for lunch but she had told him that she would be escorting one of her writers to a luncheon date. A working lunch, she had said firmly, and Dan had let it go. He was finding it difficult not to hang around the office all day merely to catch a glimpse of her, but it would not have endeared him to Martin and he rather imagined that Helen would have objected in any case. He had her with him at home and he told himself to be content with that. The trouble was, he was not content with that. It was constantly on his mind that he would soon be going back and that Helen would not be going with him.

His spirits lifted just a little when he saw Antonia. She was waving to him from the other side of the road and he went to join her.

'Dan! He's come back!' she exclaimed as soon as they were standing together. 'He came back the day before yesterday and I've been longing to tell somebody.'

'And I'll do as much as anyone,' Dan commented drily. 'It would help a little if I knew who you were talking about.'

'Jefferson. I told you about him, Dan. I do believe you weren't listening, and after all the attention I paid when you were miserable about Helen. What's happened there, by the way?'

'We're together, for now,' Dan informed her.

'Why only for now? I thought you were crazy about her.'

'I am,' Dan said gloomily. 'I just don't know where it's all going to end. Sooner or later I have to go back home and I'm not sure if she'll go with me.'

'Of course she will,' Antonia stated emphatically. 'She's a sensible girl and one of the sweetest people I've ever met. You're supposed to be a psychiatrist, one of the best. Work on her mind. Unless she doesn't care enough about you, of course.'

'She does. She's living with me.'

'Oh, Dan, I would never have believed anyone could be so stupid, and you with all those working brain parts! A girl like Helen doesn't just go and live with someone unless she's deeply committed. Of course she'll go back with you. Now do stop bothering me with your little miseries and listen to my wonderful news.'

Dan grinned down at her.

'You always cheer me up, Antonia. So tell me about Jefferson.'

'He came back to me,' she said, glowing as he had never seen before. 'Take me to lunch and I'll tell you the rest.'

'How can I resist such an order?' Dan murmured wryly. 'Let's go before I collapse with the sheer suspense.'

Helen was in the office and looked out of the window, quite casually, her heart sinking when she saw Dan talking to Antonia. Immediately she felt again the flood of uncertainty that had swept over her when she had first seen the woman Dan had brought to Martin's house. She was so beautiful, so sophisticated. The clothes she wore had obviously cost the earth and on anyone else they would have looked too much. But on Antonia they looked perfect.

As Helen watched they walked away. Dan was holding Antonia's arm as she laughed up at him and they looked exactly right together, two handsome people, cultured, beautifully dressed, nothing to hide; they made a good couple and once again Helen was comparing, seeing herself as unworthy. They were probably going out to lunch and then they would spend the afternoon together.

Helen turned away and managed to keep her face straight. She looked down at her plain business suit. It was the sort of thing she wore for work most days. Dan had seen her in it this morning and the next woman he had seen had been Antonia. He wouldn't be able to help making comparisons either.

Helen was still subdued when she left work and Dan noticed as soon as she came into the house. He ignored it until after dinner and then, when she got out the pile of manuscripts she had been intending to hide behind, he took them from her firmly and stood over her as she sat in a chair and tried not to meet his gaze.

'Okay. Let's have it,' he commanded. 'Since you came in I've had one peck on the cheek, a lot of incoherent muttering as you tried to avoid speaking to me and now you're about to hide. You may as well tell me what's wrong because you're doing nothing at all until I know.'

'Nothing is at all wrong,' Helen assured him quietly, but with things out in the open her eyes began to glaze over with tears and Dan pulled her to her feet and into his arms.

'Come on, honey,' he whispered. He rested his face against her hair and rocked her in against him. 'Whatever it is, I promise to make it better.'

'I saw you today.' Helen confessed miserably. 'It was lunchtime.'

'You refused to have lunch with me, Helen,' he reminded her. 'I asked you this morning when I knew I had to come in to see Martin. Why didn't you join me if you were free?' He drew back his head and looked down at her, and Helen tried to sound nonchalant and failed miserably.

'I wasn't free,' she said quietly. 'In any case, you were with Antonia and I didn't want to intrude. It's simply that I happened to look out of the window and saw you both. It's not important.'

'Ah,' Dan murmured. 'You think I'm still seeing Antonia on the side? This is where I confess my sins, is it?'

'No,' Helen protested quickly. 'I didn't mean that. I have no right to ask . . .'

'You have every right,' Dan told her quietly. 'You're the only person who does have a right.' He sat on the sofa and pulled her down with him, keeping his arm round her. 'There's no one quite like you, Helen. You're silently, sadly jealous. Any other woman would have been waiting with a thick stick but you, all you do is confess quietly, as if you're the one in the wrong because you happened to see us.' He hugged her close, kissing the top of her head. 'I expect I have to tell you about Antonia. Perhaps I should have told you before but it seemed to be so unimportant. You may as well know about my dark past.'

'All the women? Martin told me.'

'Yeah, he would,' Dan muttered. 'I suppose I've built up a reputation over the past few years. I never get attached to women. I have too much to do, too many other responsibilities, and I've never felt the need to be with one woman for life.'

Helen's heart sank but she said nothing at all. She couldn't be with Dan for life anyway. She had too much to hide.

'So there was Antonia, whenever I was in London,' he said calmly. 'I don't go around breaking hearts; I'm too busy mending them usually. Antonia has normally been good for me because she doesn't form attachments either. It's just her hobby.'

'Her hobby?' Helen looked up at him with puzzled blue eyes. 'What hobby?'

'Sex,' Dan said blandly.

CHAPTER 14

For a moment Helen sat staring at him, her lips parted in surprise.

'Antonia? You mean she – she's . . .'

'A hooker?' Dan asked wryly. 'No. She's not. She does everything for sheer pleasure. I don't know what you would call Antonia. To me she's just a good friend – and Helen,' he added softly, 'I have not slept with Antonia since I first saw you. I took one look at you and couldn't stop looking. I wanted you, nobody else.' He curled his hand round her face and tilted it to his. 'I can't change my past, Helen. But I'll never want anyone but you again.'

'You will,' Helen said quietly. 'When you've gone . . .'

'I won't go. I'll only go when you agree to go with me.'

'Oh, Dan. Please don't say that. You know it's impossible. You can't stay here and I can't go with you.'

'I have to stay with you somehow, sweetheart,' Dan whispered against her lips. 'I need you. I'm not going away from you even if I have to give up everything. I've thought about it a lot. I couldn't work if I could never see you. I couldn't sleep if you weren't there.'

'But why?' Helen asked miserably.

'Because you're my girl,' he said as his mouth captured hers.

'Antonia wanted to tell me some news,' he went on later when Helen was lying breathlessly in his arms. 'There's this man who went away and now he's come back. He wants to marry her.'

'Does he know?' Helen asked seriously. 'About her past, I mean?'

'She told him,' Dan assured her. 'There's nothing about Antonia that isn't straight down the line. She would never hide her past like that.'

Helen tightened up inside with guilt. She was hiding her past from everyone, but most of all she was hiding it from Dan.

'And he still wants to marry her?'

'He does. They're fixing the date. If I'm still here we're invited.'

Helen was silent. Antonia was open about things, did not keep secrets even though the temptation must have been great. She thought of her own life, her own secrets and the shock it would be to Dan if he ever found out.

'Would you?' she asked tentatively.

'Would I what?' Dan laughed down at her but she was serious, her blue eyes fixed on him.

'In the circumstances. Would you marry Antonia?'

'No,' Dan assured her blandly. 'I would never marry Antonia. Didn't I just finish proving that I would never want anyone but you?'

He was laughing but Helen felt cold inside. He must never find out anything. He was offering her bliss but she knew she could not accept it. He knew nothing about her background and she never wanted him to find out. It was best to just let him go because, however he felt now, he would change when he knew about her life. When people found out she would be stared at, unacceptable, and in Dan's glowing world she would be more than that. It would make a scar on his life. She knew she would have to let him go, however much it hurt.

The following evening, Helen wanted a few more things from her house, and when she mentioned going to fetch them Dan immediately got up and collected his car keys.

'I'll drive you there,' he stated emphatically.

'I can manage by myself,' Helen protested. 'I'm only going to be a short while, straight in and out again.' She stopped and looked up at him reproachfully. 'I promised never to go searching again.'

'I know. I also know that you'll keep your promise, but I want to go with you all the same.'

'I'll be straight back, Dan.'

'We'll both be straight back,' he corrected. 'You may as well give in because I'm going with you and anyway, it would be cruel to leave me here. I would worry and worry.' He put his arm round her waist and started for the door and Helen let the protests die. It was wonderful to have someone so caring when there had never been anyone to care before. In any case, she treasured every moment with Dan.

Just as they were leaving, the telephone rang, and when Dan answered it was Detective Inspector Swift.

'I thought we'd just let you know, Professor Forrest, that we decided to leave the woman free. I've got two men following her. We know where she lives now. It's one of the streets near Thurley Common. There's another girl who might be living there too and she seems to be perfectly okay. Maybe she doesn't even know what our suspect is doing at all. The woman we're following only comes out at night. It's a bit of a puzzle actually, because they don't seem to be there together very often. The girl seems to stay in to watch the house while our suspect goes out. The girl leaves then, no matter how late it is.'

'You decided to try to catch the woman in the act?' Dan enquired. 'That's going to take some doing,' he added doubtfully

'We're aware of that, Professor Forrest, but I think it's going to be the only way. In any case, we're pursuing other enquiries; this woman is only one of several suspects. We've been watching her since you came to us with your suspicions and so far she's done nothing at all except walk about. She doesn't even talk to the other girls on the streets; in fact, according to our chaps, she rarely stops walking. At midnight, she goes home and she doesn't come out again. Sometimes she doesn't even leave the house. We'll give it a week and then I'll have to put my chaps on other duties. When that time comes, we'll bring her in and have a good look at her.'

'What about this other girl?' Dan asked thoughtfully.

'She seems normal, a cheerful girl according to the two chaps watching. I can't spare the men to follow her too. As you can imagine, we're spread pretty thin at the moment.'

Dan put the phone down slowly when the conversation was over. It was one bizarre thing after another. A woman he was sure was dangerous to almost anyone who approached her, and yet she had a friend or acquaintance who visited the house.

He was silent as he drove Helen to her own house, but one thing was certain. The woman was being watched, and that made her less dangerous for Helen. In any case, Helen was now out of it. She had taken her life in her hands when she had approached the woman, but she had managed to get away. It was finished for Helen now. All the same, the small pricking of unease stayed in his head.

'Was that the police?' Helen asked quietly when he said nothing.

'Yes. The detective rang to tell me they were watching her. If she tries anything at all they'll catch her. If they're quick enough,' he added quietly.

Helen thought back to her encounter and went silent. She saw again in her mind the walk, the hand,

the feeling she had had as she went behind the
woman that it was Karen, playacting again, trying
out her walk, dreaming about bright lights. She was
still not perfectly sure about anything.

She remembered her terrible fear too. Whoever it
was, even if it really was Karen, she had to be
caught. She shivered, someone walking over her
grave again, as Margaret had said so morbidly.

'What is it?' Dan asked immediately.

'I was just remembering how scared I was,' Helen
told him quietly. 'You don't need to worry at all,
Dan. I'll never go roaming around at night again. I
still remember how she looked at me, so flat and
cold, as if she wasn't exactly human.'

'She's human all right,' Dan muttered. 'She's a
very sick human being, though. She has to be
caught and treated whether she committed those
murders or not.'

'But you're sure she did, aren't you?' Helen asked.

'Yes,' he said without hesitation. 'I'm sure.'

As far as Helen was concerned that was all he
needed to say. To her, Dan was infallible. The
woman in black walked like a plague in the night.
Dan was light, warmth and certainty, a superior
being who was never wrong.

She gave a small laugh and Dan turned his head to
glance at her,

'Now what?'

'Nothing really. I was just thinking that I look
upon you as a superior being, greater than the rest of
us, a shining example.'

'I'm normal and I've got the same faults as anyone else. I don't want you to put me on a pedestal, Helen.'

'I can't seem to help it,' she sighed. 'I don't know any other way to think about you.'

'Just love me,' he suggested quietly.

'I do,' she admitted without giving it a thought.

They pulled up outside her house and Dan turned and took her into his arms, looking down at her when she turned her face up to his.

'You can't just walk off when you've told me you love me,' he said thickly. 'I need at least one kiss.'

He began to kiss her tenderly, gently, with none of the overwhelming passion he usually showed. It was different, as if he was worshipping her, and Helen felt tears come into her eyes. There could be so much happiness with Dan. He was so perfect.

'Hey,' he remonstrated softly as he lifted his head and wiped away the few escaping tears. 'You're sorry you said that now?'

'No. I'm not sorry. You must have known anyway. I wouldn't be with you if I didn't love you.'

'I know, honey,' he told her quietly. 'I figured it out all by myself. Angels don't just move in with anybody for the fun of it. They've got to care a lot to take the chance.' He stroked one gentle finger down her face. 'You've put yourself completely in my power now, though – I hope you realize that. Getting rid of me will be impossible.'

Helen gave him a quick kiss and then got out of the car. She couldn't talk about the future because there wasn't one.

'I'll not be a minute,' she said.

'Want me to come in with you?' Dan asked, leaning forward to hold on to her hand until the last second.

'No. I'll manage fine. I just have to grab a few things. I'll be right back.'

Dan relaxed and switched on the radio. There was soft music playing and he kept it low, a background for his thoughts. He had found the girl of his dreams and she loved him. He had known for a long time how he felt about her and life should now be happy and smooth, but he knew she would try to make him go away.

There was something inside her that was eating away at her desires, her happiness, and he had no idea what it was. He could take her just so far but she would draw back and sink into some secret world that excluded him. He should be able to make her better, to solve her problems, because he had solved problems for so many people before, but it was different with Helen.

He was afraid of losing her. Their relationship was fragile, the beauty of it balanced on the knife-edge of her nightmares. The darkness was always with her, the distress, the fears. When he was there he could feel it like some malevolent force, and unless she told him willingly she faced it by herself.

Now that she had confessed to loving him, would she be willing to share her problems with him? He thought not. He had known for a long time how she felt about him. It was in the sweet willingness of her

345

surrender, the joy she showed in his arms. It was not just sex with Helen. It was beautiful, a glimpse of heaven, something he had never known before. But she kept her secrets inside and never told him anything. He knew no more about her now than he had ever done.

If it had been anyone else he would have tracked down her background but he would never do that with her. Until she wanted to tell him, her past life and her secret fears were hers alone. He would never violate her wishes even if she refused to stay with him.

He glanced towards her door. She had left the outside lights on and he could see clearly. Even so, he knew he would be anxious until she was back in the car. His fear was nothing he could explain to anyone, not even to himself. They were not in the bright lights of the city. This was a small development of modern houses in a quiet street, but wherever Helen was, there seemed to be danger close to her.

Probably it was only in his mind. She had been safe in her little house long before he knew her. He was overprotective and he acknowledged it. All the same, he found himself glancing up every other second, and he had just decided that it was more than body and soul could stand and that he would go and collect her from the doorstep when he saw her come out.

Dan smiled to himself. She was being briskly efficient again. All the bits and pieces she had been to collect were now in a neat cardboard box. She methodically put it down on the step at the front porch and turned to close the door. Most women would have tried to do both things at once and been juggling the box around while they reached in for the door. Helen did things neatly. He adored her precise little ways. He adored everything about her. He sat watching her with a smile on his face.

Suddenly, a shadowy figure appeared round the side of the house. It was a woman, and he did not need two glances to tell him who that woman was. She came out of the darkness quickly, making straight for Helen, and the smile died on Dan's face as fear leapt in his throat. Helen had not seen her, not heard her, and even if she did, she was defenceless against the ferocity of the woman who approached her so silently and swiftly.

He leapt out of the car but he knew he would be too late. There was the pavement to cross and then a path to the house and the woman was almost up to Helen already.

'Helen!' he called out in an agonized voice and Helen turned. She could see what was happening as soon as she turned her head, and Dan saw her go perfectly still. The keys fell from her hand and he knew she had frozen again. She would not be able to defend herself. He was running but he would never be in time. The woman in black was too close to Helen and she would strike without waiting.

Helen faced the woman who came at her so swiftly. The sound of Dan's voice was still ringing in her ears, the anguish, the pain and fear, but her whole attention was on her assailant. She knew what would happen – the woman meant to kill her – and she also knew that she could deal with it. She opened her hand and let the house keys fall to the ground but her eyes never left the figure in black. She saw the knife but there was no fear inside her. She had been trained to deal with exactly this situation. They had practised it many times. It would be just like any other evening at the gym.

There was no sound, no whispering this time; the face in front of her was expressionless and, strangely enough, that helped more than anything else. It turned the whole thing into an exercise. In the seconds since Dan had called and since she had looked up and realized what was happening, her own brain seemed to have gone into overdrive. She was thinking coolly and quickly and she was ready.

As the knife flashed down towards her, Helen heard Dan call out again. He was close, almost there, but she ignored him. She sidestepped and reached for the hand that held the deadly knife, grasping the wrist and twisting; she braced her legs and threw as she had been taught to do and the woman seemed to sail through the air, falling on her back with a crash that knocked the wind from her. Helen sprang forward and brought her heel down on the woman's wrist, and the outstretched hand that held the knife lost its power; the knife fell from her fingers and clattered on the ground.

The woman was obviously stunned. She never moved at all, and as Dan reached them he pulled her to her feet, holding her arms behind her back.

'Quick, Helen,' he said urgently. 'Let's get her inside while she's still in this state. When she comes round completely she'll not be so easy to handle.'

Helen realized that and she obeyed at once. She found her keys and opened the door, and Dan brought the woman into the kitchen and placed her in a chair. She began to move in a dazed manner and Helen knew what to do without even being told. She dived under the sink and brought out her clothes line and, before she recovered further, the woman was tied to the chair, trussed up like a chicken, unable to move at all. It was only then that Dan had time for Helen, and it was at that moment, when it was all over, that Helen began to tremble.

'Oh, God, darling!' Dan said in a shaken voice. 'I knew I couldn't get there in time. Oh, Helen, Helen. I thought I'd lost you.' He hugged her close, almost hurting her.

There was no time to say more, because their captive began to move violently and Helen could see how wise Dan had been to make sure she was immobilized before she could come round properly. She began to struggle against her bonds, trying to kick out her legs, trying to rock the chair over.

'Stop that!' Dan ordered sharply. 'You can't get free. Struggling will only hurt you, and if the chair goes over, you go with it and you stay down with it. It's more comfortable where you are now.'

She went still as he spoke to her and just stared at them both coldly. By some miracle the glasses had stayed on her nose, and again all Helen could see were eyes that looked at them with no expression at all. Now, in the light, she could see the skill that had been used with the make-up. It was contoured to the face, applied without a blemish, blending in to the hairline and neck, and the only colour was the brilliant red of the lipstick.

Dan took out a large white handkerchief and handed it to Helen.

'Take this and pick up that knife,' he said quietly. 'Take care not to touch it with your fingers and try not to let the knife rub against the handkerchief. We need the fingerprints. I'll phone the police. I can keep an eye on her all the time from the hall if I leave this door open. In any case, she can't move.'

Helen went out, but as she went, her eyes lingered on the woman in the chair. She was still and silent now and she still stared back at Helen with no expression on her face. She was utterly unreal, but even so, there was something about her that brought back vague memories.

Helen came back in and handed the knife to Dan who put it on the table.

'They were supposed to be watching her,' she reminded Dan. 'How did she manage to get here?'

'She gave them the slip,' Dan murmured, his eyes on their captive. 'What really puzzles me is why she came here to try to kill you. How in hell did she know where to come?'

'I gave her my address,' Helen stated calmly.

'You did what?' Dan spun round and stared at her and Helen bit her lip anxiously.

'It's no use being annoyed, Dan. I did it. As it turns out, it doesn't matter. She's captured and also caught in the act, as you stated.'

'I didn't want her to be caught in the act trying to kill you!' Dan pointed out thunderously. 'Why did you give her this address? Why give her anything at all?'

'I thought I knew her, and by the time I began to have doubts it was too late. All I wanted to do then was get away. It doesn't matter anyway,' she repeated. 'Everything turned out all right.'

'If I'd let you come here alone tonight, you wouldn't have seen her until it was too late,' Dan reminded her starkly. 'You could have been dead by now.'

'Please, Dan. Don't,' Helen begged when he pulled her close. 'There's something I have to do before the police get here.' It was the first time she had ever asked him not to touch her since they had been together and Dan let her go with something approaching shock on his face.

She went up to the bathroom and seconds later came back down with a face cloth. Before Dan could stop her, Helen began to wash the woman's face.

'What are you doing?' he asked sharply, taking a step forward to stop her, but Helen shook her head, motioning him to keep away.

'I want to see who she is. I want to know for sure.'

'Helen! The police have to see her like this.'

351

'I don't care. I *have* to know.'

She removed the dark glasses and then, even though the woman tried to duck her head out of the way, Helen grasped her firmly and proceeded to wash her face with a certain amount of vigour that quite stunned Dan. There was nothing at all gentle about Helen at that moment. There was just determination. Her lips were set grimly and she had nothing on her mind but completing her self-appointed task.

The result was more startling than he had expected, and as he stared in fascination, a subtly different face appeared. Helen took hold of the woman's hair and gave a sharp tug. The hair came away in her hand, a black wig, something Dan had never once suspected. Pale blonde hair spilled out and fell to her shoulders, the black velvet band dropped to the floor, and Dan gasped in astonishment.

'It's the girl at the music shop.'

'It's Karen,' Helen said quietly.

'You mean you actually know her?' He was almost holding his breath. If this was the woman she had been searching for then all her troubles were over. She would stay with him, go back with him. He would never have to let her go again.

'Yes, I know her,' Helen said in a curiously brittle voice. 'She's my sister.'

'Oh, my angel,' Dan whispered, stricken for her sake, but Helen ignored him. She came round the chair and faced the woman who was trapped there.

'Karen,' she said quietly. 'You must know who I am. It's Helen. Surely you recognize me.'

To Dan's astonishment the woman became animated, her face totally changed as she smiled and looked across at Helen. She looked cheerful, almost sweet, her eyes were laughing, normal.

'I'm Caroline,' she insisted. 'I'm sorry if you're disappointed but I can't pretend to be somebody just because you want me to. You've got the name wrong and I don't know you at all.' She looked down at herself in the black clothes and then raised her eyes to Helen again. 'Why have you dressed me up in these things? I hate dark clothes, I like bright colours, pinks and oranges and flowered things. I like yellow best of all. I hate black. Get my own things and let me put them on.' She suddenly tried to move again and looked up at Helen quite piteously. 'Why have you tied me up?' she asked plaintively. 'You've got no right to tie me up and take my clothes.'

'We tied you up to keep you safe,' Helen said gently. 'You were trying to hurt yourself. You've not been well, Karen. We're going to make you better.'

'There's nothing wrong with me,' Caroline said. 'I don't know how I got here but that's nothing. Sometimes I forget little things but mostly I remember. I can prove it,' she finished triumphantly, looking across at Dan. 'I know who that is. He came into the shop and talked to me. He talked to Mrs Edgerton too. Mrs Edgerton says he's a tourist but I think he's a film star and I told her so.'

'Yes. You were right,' Helen agreed in the same gentle voice. 'He is a film star. He's over here from America to make a film.'

'There! I knew it! Wait till I tell Mrs Edgerton. She'll be so excited. Will you get me his autograph?' she asked, looking hopefully at Helen.

'Of course I will, dear. I'll get it the moment I know you're all right.'

They heard the police car with the sirens going and Dan went to the door to meet them. He stayed where he could see into the kitchen though and his eyes were mostly on Helen. His throat felt tight with emotion. All this was something he could never have envisaged. If Helen had not been involved he would have been fascinated by the case, but all he could think of now was the agony Helen must be feeling, the bravery she was showing.

He knew now why he had thought he had seen the girl in the music shop before. There was the very faint resemblance to Helen. The same fairness, the same shape to the face, the same glowing smile. But the girl who called herself Caroline did not have Helen's angel looks and she didn't have the violet-blue eyes. He didn't know where this would end or how much Helen would allow him to protect her from the forthcoming publicity. She could have pretended not to know the girl but she had not pretended at all. She was talking to her now in the same gentle voice.

Detective Inspector Swift was with the car and he stopped at the door and looked in on their captive.

354

'I'm sorry about this,' he said in a low voice. 'It must have been a terrible shock.'

'It was,' Dan stated grimly. 'Miss Stewart dealt with her. I was too late to help until it was all over. If Miss Stewart had been defenceless she would have been dead now.'

'I can't think why she came all this way out to attack Miss Stewart,' Swift muttered, and Helen heard him as he walked with Dan into the kitchen.

'She's my sister,' Helen said clearly.

'Sister?'

He gave her the same look of utter disbelief that Dan had shown and she added, 'Half-sister really. We had the same mother. Her name is Karen Burton, my stepfather's surname. I kept my own name.'

'I'm Caroline Brown. She keeps calling me Karen even though I've told her.' Caroline gave a little laugh and looked across at Helen. 'I don't mind really. She can call me that if she wants to. I like her. Isn't she pretty? And she knows this film star. I know him too and she's going to get me his autograph.' She glanced down at her clothes and frowned. 'I wish she'd not dressed me like this, though. I like bright clothes. Can you get her to give me my clothes? I think I was wearing something yellow.'

'Yes, you were,' Helen assured her. 'You always liked yellow, didn't you, Canary?'

The girl went totally silent and stared at Helen and Dan wondered if Detective Inspector Swift felt as he did at that moment, completely out of things, watching from the edge as Helen reached out for a mind that was probably unreachable.

'I think I remember your face,' Caroline said slowly at last. 'Sometimes I think I've seen your face, so beautiful and kind. Do I really know you?'

'Of course you do,' Helen said gently. 'I'm Helen. Don't worry. You'll remember soon. Just go off with these people now and I'll see you later.'

'And you'll bring me my clothes?'

'Straight away,' Helen assured her.

'Will you be here?' Swift asked Dan as they prepared to take Caroline out to the police car.

'No. We'll go home,' Dan said slowly. 'You can reach us there if you need us.'

'Sooner or later, this girl is going to need someone, Professor Forrest. As you're involved . . .'

'Sure,' Dan agreed without thinking much. The girl needed help, but then so did Helen. She had taken it almost calmly and at the moment she was silent. He hadn't had much time to think about the implications himself yet, but even so, definite things came to his mind that would not be avoidable. There would be Helen's eventual pain. Obviously she had had some reason to suspect all this for some time, but now it was not suspicion. This was fact, out in the open.

If he was right in concluding that the knife would tie the girl who called herself Caroline to a series of killings then Helen had to face that fact too. Her half-sister was a murderess. There would be publicity. He had seen things like this before when one member of a family had committed some crime that the rest of the family had to live down. Sometimes they never managed it.

If it was possible to return Caroline to normal, then both she and Helen would have to face the enormity of her crimes. For himself, he very much doubted if Caroline would ever return to normal. Perhaps it would be better if she didn't.

'Let's go home,' he said softly as Helen just stood there staring into space. 'You need to rest.'

'I live here, Dan,' Helen murmured, and he knew he would have to be firm from this moment on.

'Not now you don't, Helen. You live where I live. I gave the police the address and telephone number when I saw them. That's where they'll contact us.'

'I should be with her,' Helen began, but Dan took her arm very firmly and led her to the door.

'They wouldn't allow it at the moment,' he assured her, not caring whether that was true or not. 'She's calm, and while she stays like that she'll be easy to handle. You saw her earlier, Helen. You know what she can change into.'

'I know,' she whispered. 'She's not just two people, she's three, but she doesn't remember being Karen. She doesn't seem to remember that at all.'

'Maybe she doesn't want to remember,' Dan speculated. There was a lot that nobody knew, he realized that, and he wondered if, now that it was in the open, Helen would tell him. She needed to share her burden, and he would not allow anyone else to help her but himself.

By the time they reached the house, Helen was showing signs of distress. During the dramatic incidents at her own house she had discovered an inner strength that Dan had only suspected was there before. He had seen her face fear calmly and seen her face the consequences with equal calm. Now she was silent, shivering in little bursts of movement that had him speeding up to get her into the house.

Once inside, he switched on the fire and poured her a brandy. She never said anything, she simply sat down and behaved like someone in a trance.

'What are you thinking?' he asked quietly after a while, sitting to face her, watching her carefully with his usual intent gaze.

She looked up in a vague sort of manner.

'Nothing really. I can't say with any truth that I'm even thinking at all. My mind seems to be skipping from one subject to the next without pause.'

'Then get control of it,' Dan ordered. 'Talk to me. Tell me about Caroline.'

'Karen,' she corrected in the same detached manner. 'She's my half-sister, as I told you. We both had the same mother. My mother remarried before I was two. Karen is almost two years younger than me.' She stopped talking and started staring into the fire. She was sipping her brandy, however, and Dan was prepared to wait. This had taken a long time to happen and perhaps it would take a long time to come out. He could wait. He could wait a lifetime for Helen.

'He always disliked me, you know,' Helen murmured thoughtfully. 'That's why I still have my own name. He never wanted to adopt me, to give me his name. He rarely spoke to me, even when I was little. As I got older, he ignored me even more.'

'How did your mother feel about that?' Dan intervened quietly.

'At first I think she was hurt. Later she was too scared to care.'

'Why was she scared, honey?'

'He drank. Perhaps he always had done. I don't know. I was too young to know and Karen was even younger. My mother never talked about it. I think perhaps he kept it quiet when they first got married but it wasn't long before he was out in the open with it. Things just went along, I suppose, and then he went bankrupt.' She glanced up at Dan. 'We lived in a fairly good area, but after his business went we had to move. We moved to a house in a long street. Karen and I hated it. It was one of those long streets near Thurley Common.'

Dan said nothing. He just sat very still and went on looking at her. The police had been watching such a house because Karen or Caroline had lived there. He wasn't even sure of how to think of her. She seemed to have so many personalities that he would not have been at all surprised to find that there was more of her somewhere. It wasn't exactly unheard of.

359

'So you lived there,' he prompted when Helen sat silently.

'Yes.'

'Go on, Helen. Tell me about your life in that street.'

'I don't want to,' she whispered. 'I never wanted you to know. I never wanted you to know about me, about how I really am.'

Dan got up and went to sit beside her. He put his arms around her and held her close. At first she was stiff and resistant, but after a while she relaxed against him and he was able to speak to her.

'Listen to me, Helen,' he ordered deeply. 'Nothing you can say will change the way I think about you. I want to be with you. I just can't imagine being away from you. Whatever you tell me, nothing is going to change that. If I'm to help Karen, I have to know all about her life, and if that includes your life too, then you must tell me.'

She was still silent but she had softened against him and Dan waited.

'I didn't do anything,' she suddenly burst out in an anguished voice. 'It's what I should have done that's so unforgivable.' Dan said nothing and she went on, 'Things got worse. There was no money but he drank more all the same. I didn't know it at the time but he made my mother go out and . . .'

'And what, sweetheart?'

'He made her go out – out on the streets,' she whispered. 'I was fourteen, old enough to know, but I didn't know. It was Karen who found out, and at

360

first I wouldn't believe her. I asked my mother outright and she denied it but then I started listening and I heard his orders, threatening her, demanding money.'

Dan squeezed her tightly to him, fury inside him at this brute of a man who had destroyed so many lives.

'Why the hell didn't she refuse? Why didn't she contact the police?'

'Why do so many women allow their husbands to beat them?' Helen asked quietly. 'They always expect that things will get better.'

'I know,' Dan said. He did know. He had seen it so often, kept cool about it, dealt with the aftermath, but when it was Helen he felt only fury. There was nothing scientific about his feelings if she was involved.

'So what happened finally?' he asked.

'I came in one evening a bit earlier than usual. I used to stay at school to do extras for my exams. It was difficult to study at home because there were always rows, sharp words, threats.'

'To you?' Dan asked fiercely.

'No.' She shook her head. 'He simply ignored me, as if I wasn't there at all, and when I was there he never shouted at Karen. I used to look at him and he knew I thought he was contemptible. It got through to him.'

Dan allowed himself a small smile. He knew how those blue eyes could look.

'This particular evening,' she continued, 'I came home earlier. My mother was out as usual and as I went through the door I could hear Karen screaming. I raced upstairs and I saw him.'

'Beating your sister?'

'No. He was trying to – to rape her.'

'God!' Dan muttered, pulling her closer. The thought of Helen, his methodical, fastidious Helen being in the same house with such a man drove him to distraction.

'I hit him,' Helen said quietly. 'There was a lamp by the bed and I hit him with it. I didn't really care if I killed him either, but I didn't kill him. He just staggered away. I don't suppose he even knew what he was doing because he was as drunk as ever.'

Dan understood then why she had behaved as she had done when she had thought he was drunk at the airport. No wonder she had abandoned him to his fate.

'Karen and I sat on her bed, huddled together,' Helen went on. 'It was very late when my mother came in and in all that time we'd never heard a word from him. When we told Mother she cried and cried, we all did. We heard him leave the house and as far as we knew, he didn't come back. Mother sat up all night so that we could sleep. She persuaded us to go to school next morning and we never saw her again.'

'Why?' Dan asked quietly, holding her close.

'They said she went out and never came back. Later that same night the police came and told us she'd been drowned but I never believed it. I thought then and I still think that she confronted him when we had gone to school. I think that's why she sent us off even though we were so upset. I think he killed her and made it look like an accident.'

'How did Karen take all this?' Dan asked when Helen stopped talking for a minute.

'Badly. She refused to believe that Mother was dead. She kept shouting that Mother would never have left us to him, that we just had to wait until she came back because she would come back. The police got interested and the whole story came out. He was crying and denying it and Karen said, "One day, I'll kill him. When he's not expecting it, I'll kill him." I made her keep quiet. I should have listened more carefully.'

CHAPTER 15

'How old were you, Helen?' Dan asked.

'I was sixteen by then. I should have known.'

'No, honey, you should not,' Dan assured her steadily. 'You were a girl and Karen was distraught, little more than a child. How could you have known?'

'Because she meant it. I could see it in her eyes. Anyway,' she went on with a sigh, 'the social workers wouldn't let him keep us at the house. They took us away to my aunt.'

'And you settled there,' Dan concluded.

'For about a week,' Helen corrected with a bitter laugh. 'Aunt Mary was my mother's sister. When she heard about everything and about how he had tried to attack Karen, she assumed it would be in the papers. She seemed to blame Karen, not him. She told the social workers she couldn't keep Karen – I could stay but not Karen. She said she had children of her own and she couldn't have them knowing what had gone on at our house.'

'So you and Karen were split up when you were sixteen and Karen was fourteen?'

'No,' Helen said bitterly. 'I refused to stay. It was both of us or neither of us. The social workers found a couple who were willing to take us both but Karen was always quiet, distant. She knew what had been said at Aunt Mary's and she felt guilty for no good reason. One night, when we had been at the new place for a year, Karen disappeared. I never saw her again until I saw her in the street when I was with you.'

'Oh, Helen, my sweet,' Dan murmured. 'You've been looking for her for so long?'

'I looked for her at first. Everyone looked. She wasn't found and after a while I stopped looking. Nobody knew where she was or what she was doing, or even if she was still alive. I was angry with her for causing even more grief and I stopped bothering. The couple I lived with were very good to me. I was getting ready to go to college. I could have moved into a place of my own, but they wanted me to stay and it was the only settled place I'd ever been in.'

'So that was the end of it until now,' Dan concluded.

'No. One night, the police found my stepfather dead in some alley. I was eighteen. I went to identify him. Nobody else seemed to know him by then. He was just any old drunk, I suppose. I don't know where he had been living. The house had been let again long before then. He was still at the hospital where they'd brought him. He was in the mortuary and I was glad, Dan!'

Helen started to cry very softly and Dan kissed her tears away.

'There's nothing wrong with that,' he said firmly. 'If ever a man deserved it, that bastard did.'

'I had to keep careful control of my face. They were so sympathetic and I felt like a criminal. I thought he'd been beaten as he used to beat my mother and it seemed like justice. It was only later that I found out he'd been stabbed. Ten times, just like all those others. I thought about Karen then but I refused to go on thinking about it. I wanted to get on with my life. It was only later, when other men looking like that started to die, that I began to search for her again.'

Dan rocked her in his arms and said nothing. He could not think of anything to solve this grief right out of the blue. It would take a long time, and even then the scars would live on and on. He understood all her fears and he understood Karen.

'Maybe I'll go mad too,' Helen whispered after a while. 'Maybe it runs in the family.'

'It doesn't,' Dan said firmly. 'You're made of different metal from Karen. You're tough, lady. There's nothing wrong with your head and that's a professional opinion.'

'How do you know, Dan?' She looked up at him worriedly and the panther-gold eyes looked back into hers.

'Because I've studied you since I first saw you,' he told her softly. 'I can see right into your soul and what I see is little short of wonderful.'

They were still sitting, holding each other, looking into the fire and thinking their own thoughts when the telephone rang. It was Detective Inspector Swift.

'Is Miss Stewart there?' he asked, and Dan could hear the disgusted weariness in his voice that he had heard plenty of times before when a good policeman had failed.

'Tell me,' Dan said. 'I'll pass anything on.'

'Maybe it's as well coming from you. She's dead, Professor Forrest.'

'How,' Dan asked quietly.

'God knows,' Swift said with the same weariness in his voice. 'Apparently she was calm, even cheerful. She just seemed like a nice girl, almost as if we'd collected the wrong person. She was chatting away about the shop where she worked, the woman she worked with, some young man who fancied her. Apparently she hardly stopped talking. Then suddenly she went silent. Then she shouted, "Helen! It was Helen!" They didn't have her restrained. I think nobody could quite believe how violent she was when she was that other person. All the evidence was in the process of being sorted and I really think it was in their minds that this was a mistake.

'Anyway, this time she was somebody else entirely – Karen, I suspect. She jumped up and ran out. She turned tables and chairs over and dodged like a rugby player, they said. Nobody could catch her. She was through the main door in seconds and before anybody could reach her she was in the road. She ran straight under a police car that was coming in. I can tell you, Professor Forrest, there are plenty of people here tonight who could do with a few stiff whiskies.'

Dan put the phone down when the inspector had finished talking. His own mind was reeling from the impact of everything that had happened that evening. He had no idea how Helen would take this latest news.

'What is it?' she asked when he came back in and she saw his face.

'She's dead, honey,' he told her, dropping down beside her and taking her in his arms. 'She got away and ran under a police car.'

'Why?' Helen cried in an anguished voice. 'How could they have let it happen?'

'They were too relaxed with her,' Dan said. 'They liked her. She was chattering away and they just failed to realize exactly how she could be. Nobody who hadn't actually seen her as we did could possibly believe that when she was Caroline she was just playing another part in her head.'

'But why did she run away?' Helen wanted to know.

'She remembered who you were. She suddenly went quiet and then called your name. Swift thinks she suddenly became Karen and I'm sure he's right. When she was Karen, she wanted to be with you.'

'I should have gone with her,' Helen wept. 'I would have been there then and she would never have tried to run away.'

'Helen,' Dan said seriously, 'you don't know what would have happened. Nobody knows.' He cupped her face in his hands, gently wiping her tears away with his thumbs. 'Listen, baby,' he insisted quietly. 'The chances are that she would never have got better, and that would have meant being confined for life: no happy times in the shop, no bright clothes.'

'I could have visited her all the time,' Helen protested tearfully.

'For a lot of the time she would probably have been the woman who attacked you, the woman in the black velvet hairband. You wouldn't have been allowed to visit her then and nobody would ever have known when she would suddenly change. She would have been restrained, Helen.'

'She might have got better,' Helen whispered, looking up at him with pleading eyes.

'She might,' he agreed seriously. 'I don't think so, but nobody ever knows. If she had ever got completely better, though, she would have carried a burden for life. She killed a lot of innocent people, Helen. There is no way that she would have been able to simply shrug it off and live normally. It would have been with both of you, night and day for the rest of your lives. And nobody would ever have been able to be sure that she would stay cured.'

'You're saying that the best thing happened?' Helen asked, looking up at him, and he looked back into her eyes.

'Yes, Helen. I'm saying that,' he confessed quietly. 'I'm thinking of what her future would have been in any of the circumstances I've mentioned. Life has to have a quality to be worth living. What quality would Karen's life have had?'

Helen nodded and said nothing more. He held her close and rested his head against her hair. He had told her what he thought, but when all was said and done it was what Helen thought that mattered. She was the one who had to live with it. He tilted her face to kiss her, to try to offer her comfort, but as he looked down at her he found to his surprise that she had fallen asleep in his arms.

Dan felt again a great rush of tenderness. She was safe with him and she knew it. She trusted him completely. Would she be able to simply let him go back alone? He just didn't know, in spite of Antonia's inspiring words. How would Helen face the trauma? Would she withdraw again into a shell that would now contain even more guilt and grief, or would she realize that she needed him more than ever? Only time would tell, and there was so little of that left.

He carried her upstairs, undressed her and put her into bed, and she was so worn out that she hardly stirred. Her small murmurs of distress touched his heart as nothing else could have done, but he knew that if she could sleep it would be best for her. There was nothing she could do. It was all over, if she would let it be over.

Dan went quietly back down and phoned Detective Inspector Swift, who still sounded wearily depressed.

'What happens now?' Dan asked.

'The usual things. Post-mortem, enquiries, especially for us. How she managed to escape from police custody and so on. Of course, now that there can be no trial, questions will be asked about our proof in the first place.'

'Proof?' Dan muttered angrily. 'I should think that being caught in the act would be proof enough. It's only because I was there to alert Miss Stewart and because she was able to take care of herself physically that Miss Stewart is still alive. What more proof do you need? Presumably she was wearing the black clothes when she was killed and you already have the wig. You know where she lived. If you need any more proof then just call on me. I was there.'

'What about Miss Stewart?' the inspector asked. 'How is she taking it?'

'She's exhausted. She's fallen asleep. I want her kept out of this as much as possible. She's suffered enough.'

'We'll do our best, Professor Forrest, but I can't promise anything specific.'

'Why will you need her?' Dan asked fiercely. 'I can do any necessary identification of the body.'

'You're not the woman's sister, sir. Miss Stewart is that.'

'I know,' Dan agreed wearily. 'I just want to save her any more pain.'

'There would have been even more pain if this had come to a trial.'

'I know that too,' Dan murmured.

'She seemed to become normal right at the end,' Swift said thoughtfully.

'Temporarily,' Dan stated with certainty. 'How long any normal state would have lasted with her is something I wouldn't like to bank on. She was facing either a lifetime's incarceration in an institution or a murder trial and permanent imprisonment. Don't feel too bad about things, Inspector.'

'I suppose not,' Swift agreed with a sigh. 'They say that God works in mysterious ways. I'll let you know when we need Miss Stewart.'

Dan put the phone down and walked away thoughtfully. He went to pour himself a drink. He dared not sleep. If Helen woke up she would need him, and if he was sleeping she might just let him sleep on. He couldn't bear to imagine her sitting alone with her grief.

He wanted to get her away from here, away from the memories, away from the publicity. There would be plenty of that, he was sure, even if Helen was kept out of it. The police had been searching for a serial killer. The papers would be full of the final act in the drama. People would want to know that there was no more danger. They had every right to know – but nobody had any right to pry into Helen's life.

Helen insisted on doing everything herself, and although Dan stayed by her side he could not persuade her to back out of anything she considered to be her responsibility. She would not even talk to him about it. All he could do was be there.

It was more or less what he had expected. Years of anxiety did not pass away so quickly.

'Listen, Helen,' he said urgently. 'At the post-mortem there's no need for you to say more than necessary.'

'To spare myself?' Helen asked scathingly. 'What about Karen? There was a reason for her breakdown. I suppose some people could have risen over it and carried on. Karen couldn't. She needed help then and there was no one to offer it. I can't help her now, but I can offer explanations, tell them why she did what she did.'

'The Press will hound you,' Dan warned quietly.

'I know. I've thought about that. I just don't care.' She turned to him with an urgency of her own. 'I never wanted you to know all this. I never wanted you to be mixed up in it either. If I'm involved you need not be. You have work waiting for you. You could just give the police your statement and go home to America.'

'You think I'd do that?' Dan asked with a touch of anger. 'You think I'd take the easy way out and skip, leaving you to take all the limelight?'

'The notoriety, Dan,' Helen corrected seriously. 'You could pick up a character smear that would travel with you wherever you went.'

'So could you,' Dan reminded her, and she gave one of her soft, bitter laughs.

'I don't matter.'

'You matter to me,' Dan said quietly. 'I love you.'

She turned her face away, hiding the sudden glow that his words had brought to it, and she never gave any sort of acknowledgement that she had even

373

heard him. He knew she had, though, and she had not been quite quick enough to hide her expression.

'You love me too,' he said. 'Even if you hadn't told me, I would have known.'

'What does it matter?' she asked sadly. 'You know deep down that nothing can come of it.'

'I know no such thing,' Dan contradicted sharply. 'I'm taking you back with me. We're going to get married.'

'No, Dan. You know it's impossible for a lot of reasons. I would never allow you to make such a sacrifice. It would ruin your life, your future. I couldn't marry anyone else, either, because there would always be a doubt about me.'

Dan swore savagely under his breath and pulled her into his arms.

'Damn you, Helen,' he grated. 'You're the one setting out to ruin my life. I can't live without you and you know it. I worship you. I could never look at another woman. And as to this idiotic idea of any doubt about your future. I've told you it's nonsense.'

'You don't know that for sure, Dan.' she said sadly, and the panther-gold eyes stared down with hostility into her own.

'That's exactly what you said before. You told me I didn't know for sure that the woman was a killer. But I knew, didn't I, Helen? And I know about you. There's nothing wrong with you that a few months in my arms wouldn't cure. You know it too. You accuse me of knowing deep down that nothing can come of how we feel about each other. You're the one who knows deep down, Helen. You know deep down that we love each other and need each other. You know deep down that we'll never be happy apart.'

He let her go and turned away angrily, but Helen had made up her mind and he did not know how he was going to change her attitude.

She went upstairs and he went into the sitting room to collect his temper and think things out. When he finally walked out into the hall she was coming back down the stairs with the last of her things.

'What are you doing?' he asked sharply.

'I'm going home,' she told him with a quiet determination. 'I don't want to live here with you any more, Dan. Forget about me and go back to America.'

'You think it will be that easy?' he asked bitterly.

'Not at first. Time heals things, though.'

'And did time heal things for you? Did time wipe out the past?'

'No,' she conceded. 'But then again my past was traumatic, violent and dirty. Your past is wonderful and so is your future. You'll forget.'

'You're not going to give me a chance, are you?' he asked with weary resignation.

'We had a chance and it's gone,' Helen pointed out. She turned at the door and looked at him in the old sweet way. 'I've never loved anyone else, Dan,' she told him softly. 'I never will.'

She walked out without saying goodbye and Dan felt as if the bottom had dropped out of his world. He heard her car pull away and the house was silent, empty, useless. He stood for a while, not quite believing this had happened, and then he phoned America.

'I'm coming home,' he said quietly. 'I have a few things to tie up here and then I'll be on my way.'

He didn't pay any attention to the jubilation. He had other things to work out. He would not let Helen go because he couldn't. But no amount of forceful words or threats would move her. She believed she would ruin his life, his glowing future. As far as he was concerned, there was no future without her. It was time to use his brain instead of his emotions.

He went to sit down, put his head back and stared at the ceiling. He always thought better like that, and he had the most important thinking to do of his life. He had to set a trap to catch an angel, an angel who thought she was a curse.

'Oh, I'll get you, my love,' he murmured, staring at the light fitting with thoughtful eyes. 'If sugar won't trap you, maybe pity will, because angels are full of that commodity and I want you any way I can get you.'

Helen gave her evidence in a clear unemotional voice and she left nothing out. She painted a picture of the home that Karen had been brought up in, the brute of a man who had been her father. She spoke of the shock of the loss of their mother so soon after Karen's ordeal at the hands of her father. She told them how Karen had almost literally been turned out by their aunt, the one grown-up they should have been able to rely on. There was complete silence in the room and complete sympathy from the coroner. By the time Helen had finished, everyone there understood the mental turmoil that had driven Karen on.

Everyone had been tracked down and Violet Edgerton sat at the back of the court, her eyes swimming with tears. She had really cared about Caroline, and even though she had known that something was very wrong, she had never expected this, the final chapter in Caroline's life. She knew she was going to miss her. When her turn came to give evidence she could only say what a nice girl Caroline had been and how she had changed slowly into someone else towards the end.

Dan just told exactly what he knew, playing down Helen's part as much as he could. He could feel her eyes on him but he took care not to look at her, and when it was over, Helen turned for support to Margaret and Martin who had come to be with her. Dan just left. He was playing for high stakes, for his own future happiness and Helen's, and the urge to take her into his arms had to be curbed.

He had been treated with a lot of respect and his help had been acknowledged by the police. He had been given the chance to say what he wanted to say and it had not been solely for the ears of those present. It had been aimed at Helen.

'I'm leaving for America as soon as possible,' he said. 'Probably this week. If I'm needed I'll be in New York. The police will have my address and number.'

'I doubt if you will be needed, Professor Forrest. You've been most helpful. As a matter of interest, not really for this hearing but more on a personal basis,' the coroner asked. 'If Karen Burton had lived, would you have been willing to take an interest in her case?'

'Yes. I would.' Dan told him firmly. 'Though I must add here, since you have asked the question, that I doubt if she could ever have been totally cured. Her options were few: an institution or prison. When she was rational – and she would have been rational frequently either as Karen or Caroline – either option would have been unbearable.'

'Thank you, Professor Forrest. You have been most helpful.'

As Dan left he saw Helen turn her face against Margaret's shoulder and his heart was heavier than it had ever been in his entire life. But he knew her by now, his angel. She would stick to her guns, stand by her principles, however misguided. He would have to leave her now if he wanted her to be with him for the rest of his life, and he wanted that more than anything else in the world.

It was all in the papers next day as he had expected, and he bought as many of them as he could. He wanted to know how they would deal with Helen, and all things being considered they dealt with her very lightly.

Even so, her face was on the front of every morning paper, along with a picture of Karen – how they got the latter he did not quite know, but they were good at digging up things from the past. The headlines were also expected. 'Serial Killer Dead.' All about the city breathing a sigh of relief, about the complicated life that Karen had led. There were photographs too of the house she had lived in and it was headed 'The Family Home.'

Helen's home, a place of nightmares and restrictions. He started to dream of the house he would buy for her, the light, the laughter, the love. He needed something to keep up his own spirits, and if he had to build a house in his head he would do so.

He knew that Helen was staying with Margaret and Martin and that she was not at work, and the last thing he did before leaving for the airport was to send her a huge basket of red roses with a card that simply said, 'I love you.'

When he got to the airport the past came rushing back to almost choke him. This was where he had first met Helen. This was where her fear of the past had driven her to be cruelly indifferent to him. This was where he was leaving her behind.

At the last minute, Antonia came rushing up and flung her arms round his neck, quite leaving aside her usual contained behaviour.

'Dan!' she exclaimed. 'I thought I'd missed you. I can't believe you're leaving Helen and going back home. You love her, don't you?'

'I love her,' Dan agreed huskily.

'If you hadn't said that, I doubt if I would have trusted anyone ever again for the rest of my life. So why are you going? Why isn't she with you?'

'She's afraid of ruining my life,' Dan told her morosely. 'I've got to work this out.'

Antonia looked at him closely and then smiled.

'You're thinking,' she announced. 'I can always tell when that splendid brain goes into action. Will you come back for her?'

'When she needs me completely, without any worries about the future,' he replied.

'You're taking a chance, Dan.'

'I'm playing it by ear. I've never loved anyone before and with Helen I truly think it's more than love; it's my life and I'm fighting for it.'

'I'm in your corner, don't forget,' Antonia said urgently as his flight was called, and Dan kissed her cheek as he left.

'Where's Jefferson?' he shouted to her as he moved off.

'Waiting in the car,' she called back with a wide smile. 'You'll miss the wedding but we'll both come to yours.'

He waved to her and went out of her sight. He hoped she would be at his wedding, but there would never be a wedding without Helen. He had never fought for his life before and now he was banking everything he cared about on his instincts. He needed more people than Antonia in his corner.

* * *

Over the next three months, Margaret and Martin acted like bodyguards. Their instinct to protect Helen had always been there but now they ran riot, almost refusing to let her breathe alone. Dan never phoned or wrote, and gradually Helen allowed the despair to wash over her as she realized just what she had lost.

All the same, she knew she had done the right thing. He would be getting on with his important life and learning to forget her. She had been lucky to have been with him for a time and she would clutch that to her always.

The Press had let her off lightly but she had had ghosts of her own to lay to rest. She had visited the house where she had lived with Karen. The inspector had arranged it and allowed her to go at night when there was nobody standing around to stare at her.

She had visited the shop too and talked to Violet Edgerton, learning more about Caroline and her happy ways. It all helped with the healing process, but nothing could wipe Dan out of her mind and most nights she cried in her sleep, longing for him and knowing she would never see him again.

It was Margaret who brought up the subject of Dan after the time had passed.

'He asked me not to tell you this,' she said carefully, 'but I really must. Dan phones every week, you know. He always times it for when you're at work.'

Helen's heart leapt but she managed to hide her shock.

'Well, of course he would phone you,' she said as lightly as she could. 'You've been friends for years.'

'Oh, true,' Margaret agreed drily. 'Normally he phones us at Christmas.' She looked seriously at Helen. 'He phones to ask how you are. He wants to know every little detail.'

'How – how is he?' Helen asked shakily.

'I think he's ill,' Margaret told her thoughtfully. 'He never says as much, mind you, but I can hear it in his voice because I've known him for so long.'

'What's wrong with him?' Helen asked urgently, not caring about betraying her anxiety.

'I don't know. He always say he's fine when I ask, but over the time since he's left, he's changed. He's not the same any more and he doesn't even sound the same. He's talking about giving everything up and just going away to some place where he can spend his time fishing or something.'

'He's *what*?' Helen exclaimed. 'He can't give everything up. It's his life.'

'Well, Martin and I think it's not enough for him, not now.' Margaret said quietly. 'We think Dan needs you more than his work, more than anything.'

'Dan's the psychiatrist, not you and Martin.' Helen reminded her sharply.

'Oh, I know. All the same, remember when I asked Dan about you and he looked so sad. You remember when we all went for a meal and you were dancing with Martin? Dan just turned to look at you and said that his future depended on what you would decide to do. He didn't think even then that you would stay with him. I think he's always known at the back of his mind that you would leave him.'

'I didn't leave him. He went back home,' Helen said in a tremulous voice.

'No, Helen. You sent him back home,' Margaret corrected. 'And don't tell me that I can't possibly know that, because Dan told me. He said, "She's sending me away, Mo, and there's nothing I can do about it." I thought then that he might just get over it, knowing how steady he is, but obviously I was wrong. I think he really means to give everything up.'

'He can't,' Helen whispered. 'I'll feel as if I've ruined his life after all.'

'Well, you have,' Margaret assured her.

She left the matter to rest, but she knew a good deal of satisfaction when she saw Helen's tragic face. Being a practical women herself, she could never understand why two people should put each other through hell. She also had a good memory and she remembered how glowing Helen had looked when she was living with Dan. As far as she was concerned, it was never too late to set things right. When Martin came home Margaret told him firmly to keep out of things.

During the next week, Antonia called in to see Helen at work. She told her she had been passing and had stopped for a chat and to ask her to the wedding. Helen thought her heart would actually break when she saw how happy Antonia was and when her imagination pictured the wedding. It also pictured her own wedding to Dan, something that could never happen now.

'Have you heard from Dan?' Helen asked anxiously just before Antonia left.

'Yes, as a matter of fact, I rang him to ask if he could come back for my wedding.'

'Is he going to come?' Helen asked breathlessly.

'No. Apparently he's going off into the wilds. I shudder to think of it, all those dangerous rapids and things they have there. He did say something about going to actually *live* in the wilds too. He must be crazy. Imagine just having bears for company! I can't even think about it. I never thought Dan would do anything like that.'

Helen went home that night and simply locked herself in. When the telephone rang she didn't answer it. It couldn't be Dan, and if it wasn't Dan then she didn't care who it was. She went to bed and cried as she had never done before. After all her sacrifice in giving him up, all she had succeeded in doing was taking his life apart.

On Christmas Eve, Helen drove home with great care. It was snowing and although it had only just started she knew it would get deep very soon. The big, fat flakes were falling like tiny white clouds, touching the windscreen and melting, resting on the bonnet and then falling off. She had always loved snow, and things were more poignant this evening than ever. She knew she wanted to share it with Dan but he would be in New York, probably attending some Christmas Eve party and watching the snow fall from the same sky.

She had bought the presents she had set out to get and she had also bought a present for Dan. She knew she would not send it. If he was managing to get over this idea of going off into the wilds to live, any card or present from her would only start him off again on his road to unhappiness.

She pulled up by the house and bent into the car to collect her bag and the gifts that were already wrapped, and as she straightened she saw a dark figure standing at the side of her porch, obviously sheltering from the snow. She could not help the burst of fear when she remembered another dark figure, the figure of Karen who had meant to kill her. She remembered, too, Dan's agonized call when he saw what was happening.

She stood perfectly still, not daring to go any further, no longer willing to take the risk, and as she stopped, the figure detached itself from the shadows and stood where she could see.

'Merry Christmas, honey,' Dan's quiet voice said. 'You can come on up here if you promise not to toss me on to the ground. It's cold down there.'

'Dan? It really is you?' Helen asked in a dazed voice.

He came to meet her and stood looking down into her eyes.

'It sure is, babe,' he said softly. 'Are you going to throw me out, refuse to speak to me, send me away for my own good? It's not good, sweetheart. It's hell.'

Helen just stood looking at him. He never attempted to kiss her, never tried to take her parcels, and when she simply walked towards the house he followed in silence. He was still silent when she opened the door and walked into the hall and as she turned round to speak to him, she found that he was bringing in his luggage.

'I once said that if you wouldn't live with me, I'd move in with you,' he reminded her. He looked across at her, the wonderful eyes capturing her soul. 'Don't send me away, honey,' he begged. 'I can't live without you.'

Helen said nothing. She just flew into his arms and he wrapped her tightly against him, burying his face in her hair and whispering her name over and over.

'How long can you stay?' she asked in a second when he allowed her to breath again.

'For as long as it takes,' he said quietly. 'This time, when I leave, you're coming with me, aren't you, Helen?' He tilted her face with one gentle finger and she smiled her happiness into his wonderful eyes.

'Yes, Dan,' she promised, and he swept her close and gave her the kisses she had been pining for all these weary, lonely months.

Later when they were curled up in front of the fire Helen asked why he had known she was ready to go with him when she had been so adamant before.

'Sound judgement,' Dan told her smugly. 'I knew it was going to be tricky. I had to give you time to realize you can't live without me.'

'I really can't live without you, Dan.'

'I know, honey,' he assured her softly, kissing her deeply again. 'I can't live without you either.'

'I got you a present but I wasn't going to send it,' Helen confessed later.

'That sure shows a streak of meanness,' Dan stated severely. 'Let's have it right now.'

Helen went to her parcels and he watched her with lazily smiling eyes. It was all right. They were together again. Nothing would part them now.

'It's a sweater,' Helen said eagerly before he had even opened the box, and Dan hid a grin at the wonderful change in her since she had seen him. She was back to normal, his very own.

'I brought you a present from New York,' he told her after a few minutes. 'And I'll tell you what that is too. It's a very splendid nightie, only to be used in case of fire. I brought something else too,' he added when Helen's face was covered in blushes. He took out a velvet box and opened it. The ring sparkled like fire and Helen looked up with the same shine in her eyes.

'Now will you marry me?' Dan asked huskily. She didn't answer. She did the thing he had always preferred to words: she threw herself into his arms.

'How did you know when to come back for me?' Helen asked later when they were lying together, warm and happy.

'I told you. Instinct and a little help from my friends.'

'What friends?'

'You think I haven't any?' Dan asked with mock outrage. 'Let me tell you, my girl, that they've been working hard on my behalf, telling you I was giving everything up and going wild.'

'You mean you weren't going to do anything of the sort.'

'No,' Dan assured her, grinning down into her flushed face. 'I'm a psychiatrist, honey. I know how to work on minds. Although,' he laughed when she began to rain blows on him, 'I knew I would never be good enough to manage it alone. I really needed help this time, because it's not at all easy to catch an angel.' He turned to look at her, his face suddenly serious. 'And I had to catch you, Helen. My life depended on it.'

Helen gazed at him with more love than he had ever seen.

'You'll never know the comfort I find in your voice,' she told him softly. 'I love you so much.'

'And I love you, my darling,' Dan said huskily. 'When I look at you I'm looking into heaven. It's right there in your eyes and I could look for a thousand years. Will you come back with me this time?

'Oh, yes, Dan,' she whispered. 'I couldn't bear to be away from you again.'

'And you never will be,' he said as his lips closed over hers.

THE EXCITING NEW NAME
IN WOMEN'S FICTION!

PLEASE HELP ME TO HELP YOU!

Dear *Scarlet* Reader,

The end of July will see our first super Prize Draw, which means that **you could win 6 months' worth of free Scarlets!** Just return your completed questionnaire to us (see addresses at end of questionnaire) before 31 July 1997 and you will automatically be entered in the draw that takes place on that day. If you are lucky enough to be one of the first two names out of the hat we will send you four new *Scarlet* romances every month for six months, and for each of twenty runners up there will be a sassy *Scarlet* T-shirt.

So don't delay – return your form straight away!*

Sally Cooper

Editor-in-Chief, *Scarlet*

*Prize draw offer available only in the UK, USA or Canada. Draw is not open to employees of Robinson Publishing, or of their agents, families or households. Winners will be informed by post, and details of winners can be obtained after 31 July 1997, by sending a stamped addressed envelope to address given at end of questionnaire.

Note: further offers which might be of interest may be sent to you by other, carefully selected, companies. If you do not want to receive them, please write to Robinson Publishing Ltd, 7 Kensington Church Court, London W8 4SP, UK.

QUESTIONNAIRE

Please tick the appropriate boxes to indicate your answers

1 Where did you get this Scarlet title?

Bought in supermarket ☐

Bought at my local bookstore ☐ Bought at chain bookstore ☐

Bought at book exchange or used bookstore ☐

Borrowed from a friend ☐

Other (please indicate) _____

2 Did you enjoy reading it?

A lot ☐   A little ☐   Not at all ☐

3 What did you particularly like about this book?

Believable characters ☐   Easy to read ☐

Good value for money ☐   Enjoyable locations ☐

Interesting story ☐   Modern setting ☐

Other _____

4 What did you particularly dislike about this book?

_____

5 Would you buy another Scarlet book?

Yes ☐   No ☐

6 What other kinds of book do you enjoy reading?

Horror ☐   Puzzle books ☐   Historical fiction ☐

General fiction ☐ Crime/Detective ☐ Cookery ☐

Other (please indicate) _____

7 Which magazines do you enjoy reading?

1. _____

2. _____

3. _____

And now a little about you –

8 How old are you?

Under 25 ☐   25–34 ☐   35–44 ☐

45–54 ☐   55–64 ☐   over 65 ☐

cont.

9 What is your marital status?
Single ☐   Married/living with partner ☐
Widowed ☐   Separated/divorced ☐

10 What is your current occupation?
Employed full-time ☐   Employed part-time ☐
Student ☐   Housewife full-time ☐
Unemployed ☐   Retired ☐

11 Do you have children? If so, how many and how old are they?
_____
_____

12 What is your annual household income?

under $15,000	☐ or	£10,000	☐
$15–25,000	☐ or	£10–20,000	☐
$25–35,000	☐ or	£20–30,000	☐
$35–50,000	☐ or	£30–40,000	☐
over $50,000	☐ or	£40,000	☐

Miss/Mrs/Ms _____
Address _____
_____
_____

Thank you for completing this questionnaire. Now tear it out – put
it in an envelope and send it to:

Sally Cooper, Editor-in-Chief

USA/Can. address
SCARLET c/o London Bridge
85 River Rock Drive
Suite 202
Buffalo
NY 14207
USA

UK address/No stamp required
SCARLET
FREEPOST LON 3335
LONDON W8 4BR
*Please use block capitals for
address*

BLVEL/5/97

Scarlet titles coming next month:

REVENGE IS SWEET Jill Sheldon
Chloe Walker is a soft touch for anyone in trouble. Thomas
McGuirre is a man with no heart, set on revenge, no matter
who gets in his way. So something (or someone!) has to give!
But will it be Chloe . . . or Thomas?

GAME, SET AND MATCH Kathryn Bellamy
Melissa Farrell's career on the professional tennis circuit is
just taking off. One day, with a lot of hard work and
dedication, she may achieve her dream of winning Wim-
bledon. But Nick Lennox isn't prepared to wait for her.
Unlike the attractive bad boy of tennis, Ace Delaney . . .

MARRIED TO SINCLAIR Danielle Shaw
Jenny has been engaged to Cameron for several years, but
he calls it a day when he realizes that the family firm is far
more important to her than he could ever be. Then Jenny
meets Paul Hadley and realizes what love is all about. But
Paul is married to the glamorous Gina, who will never let
him go.

DARK CANVAS Julia Wild
Abbey has a steady, if dull, boyfriend and is at the height of
her career. But then someone begins to threaten her, and
Jake Westaway appoints himself her protector. But then he
starts to *want* her . . . even though she's his best friend's
woman!

Did You Know?

There are over 120 _NEW_ romance novels published each month in the US & Canada?

♥ *Romantic Times Magazine* is *THE ONLY SOURCE* that tells you what they are and where to find them–even if you live abroad!

♥ *Each issue* reviews *ALL* 120 titles, saving you time and money at the bookstores!

♥ *Lists mail-order* book stores who service international customers!

ROMANTIC TIMES MAGAZINE
〜 *Established 1981* 〜

Order a SAMPLE COPY Now!

FOR UNITED STATES & CANADA ORDERS:
$2.00 United States & Canada (U.S FUNDS ONLY)
CALL 1-800-989-8816*

* 800 NUMBER FOR US CREDIT CARD ORDERS ONLY

♥ **BY MAIL:** Send <u>US funds Only</u>. Make check payable to:
Romantic Times Magazine, 55 Bergen Street, Brooklyn, NY 11201 USA

♥ **TEL.: 718-237-1097** ♥ **FAX: 718-624-4231**

VISA • M/C • AMEX • DISCOVER ACCEPTED FOR US, CANADA & UK ORDERS!

FOR UNITED KINGDOM ORDERS: (Credit Card Orders Accepted!)
£2.00 Sterling–Check made payable to Robinson Publishing Ltd.

♥ **BY MAIL:** Check to above **DRAWN ON A UK BANK** to: Robinson Publishing Ltd., 7 Kensington Church Court, London W8 4SP England

♥ **E-MAIL CREDIT CARD ORDERS:** RTmag1@aol.com
♥ **VISIT OUR WEB SITE:** http://www.rt-online.com